THE MONSTER
OF FLORENCE

Magdalen Nabb was born in Lancashire in 1947 and trained as a potter. In 1975 she abandoned pottery, sold her home and her car, and moved to Florence with her son, knowing nobody and speaking no Italian. She has lived there ever since, and pursues a dual career as crime writer and children's author.

'Good plot, well-concealed clues and the whole put together with wit and elegance' *Daily Mail*

'With her latest book . . . [Nabb] has taken a quantum leap forward; this is a brilliant detective story.' T J Binyon in the *Evening Standard*

'She is magnificent on the medieval pageantry and sinister façades of her adopted Florence.' *Sunday Times*

'It takes a writer as good as Magdalen Nabb to remind us how subtle the art of the mystery can be. She does make it look easy, though . . . Nabb has Simenon's knack of unlocking the deeper mysteries of ordinary people's pedestrian lives' *New York Times*

THE MONSTER

OF

FLORENCE

MAGDALEN NABB

arrow books

Published in the United Kingdom in 2005 by Arrow Books

9 10

Copyright © 1996 Magdalen Nabb and 1999 Diogenes Verlag AG, Zurich

Magdalen Nabb has asserted her right under the Copyright, Designs
and Patents Act, 1988 to be identified as the author of this work

First published in the United Kingdom in 1996 by HarperCollins Publishers

Arrow Books
The Random House Group Limited
20 Vauxhall Bridge Road, London, SW1V 2SA

Random House Australia (Pty) Limited
20 Alfred Street, Milsons Point, Sydney
New South Wales 2061, Australia

Random House New Zealand Limited
18 Poland Road, Glenfield
Auckland 10, New Zealand

Random House (Pty) Limited
Endulini, 5a Jubilee Road, Parktown 2193, South Africa

The Random House Group Limited Reg. No. 954009

www.randomhouse.co.uk

A CIP catalogue record for this book is available from the British Library

ISBN 9780099489894

Typeset by SX Composing DTP, Rayleigh, Essex

Penguin Random House is committed to a sustainable future for
our business, our readers and our planet. This book is made from
Forest Stewardship Council® certified paper.

Printed and bound in Great Britain by Clays Ltd, St Ives plc

This book is a work of fiction. However, it was inspired by seven double homicides that took place between 1968 and 1985 in the area surrounding Florence. The factual details relating to these crimes are true, although the names of the victims have been changed. The depiction of the process and nature of the investigations is completely fictional. The names, characters and incidents portrayed in the story are the product of the author's imagination. Any resemblance to actual persons, living or dead, is entirely coincidental.

One

It was so dark in the cathedral square on that November Saturday evening that it seemed that it should certainly be cold. Instead of which, as the great bell in Giotto's marble tower struck six, the shoppers scurrying below it were overheated and out of temper. Somewhere among them a small child was crying and stamping in frustration. Marshal Guarnaccia pushed his way through the crowd wishing he hadn't been deceived into wearing an overcoat. Everything about the evening was wintry except the temperature and, having decided it was best not to go in uniform, he was now sweating profusely and regretting not only all that heavy wool on his back but his decision to walk through the centre of Florence instead of taking his car. He was always full of good intentions about getting rid of some of his excess weight and for all the good it ever did he might as well not bother.

People were climbing the marble steps towards the massive carved doors of the cathedral and Saturday evening Mass, summoned by the still tolling bell. The Marshal left the square by the narrow Via de' Servi, not wanting to face the worse crowds and roaring traffic of the broader and busier Via Martelli. Once in the quieter street he slowed down, hoping to sweat less and thinking through his excuse for the unofficial visit he was about to make. A funny business, nothing he could do anything about officially, of course. There were experts for that sort of thing. Still, he couldn't say no to an old friend. The lad must be thirty by now. The years went by so quickly.

Marco Landini had been about seventeen when the Marshal had first seen him at about ten-thirty on a hot Saturday night, slumped in the open doorway of a second-floor flat in Piazzo Santo Spirito, weeping. The ambulance had just left with the overdose victim. It left quietly, no sirens going. The boy was already dead. The Marshal stood there looking down at the one lying in the doorway. Rather than weeping it would be more accurate to say that he was howling, almost like a dog. He looked in good physical shape and he was well dressed. Not a hardened addict, obviously. But then those were the days when shooting up on a Saturday night was fashionable and playing hooky from school meant a day in bed with a Walkman blaring in the ears and a trickle of blood rolling down one dangling arm. Then the streets, discos and school lavatories were

2

strewn with hypodermics and the only parents who weren't afraid were those as innocent as they were ignorant.

'Come on, pull yourself together,' the Marshal had said gruffly, 'and get yourself home. Can you walk?'

The boy nodded and drew in his breath to block the howling.

'I'm all right. I didn't . . . I mean I haven't . . .'

'Get on your feet, then. Take yourself off.'

'Where are the others . . . ?' The boy had seemed only then to start realizing his situation. He rubbed a hand over his streaked red face like a child and stared in at the door of the flat. One small room was visible, bare except for two folding beds with stained mattresses on them and a filthy sink in one corner. Syringes, rubber tubes and squeezed halves of lemon were scattered about the filthy speckled tiles of the floor.

'What did you expect?' the Marshal asked. 'They ran when they saw the lad was dying.' It was odd enough, he added to himself, that they'd bothered to call for help.

'I called the ambulance,' the boy had said, as if in answer to his unspoken thought. 'I don't know who he was. He was their friend. Have they gone with him in the ambulance? They'll have to tell his mother, won't they? Oh God, just imagine . . . Sandro, where's Sandro?'

'Never mind Sandro, get on your feet.'

The boy stood up and tried to tidy himself, his gaze still drawn by the empty room.

'I should find Sandro, see if he's all right. He came here with me.'

'Well, he left without you. There are no friends in this game. I'll be the one who has to tell the dead boy's mother. Don't you realize I could arrest you? The others were sharper than you are. Do me a favour and go home. And remember, it might be *your* mother I have to tell next time.'

He hadn't arrested him, though he couldn't have said why for certain. Might have done him good, though the death he'd just witnessed was probably more than enough for him. In any case, there was something disarming about the boy. He'd even given him a coffee in the bar downstairs before sending him on his way and addressing himself to the problem of the den of vice above.

The death that night was more than enough. Marco's father, who turned out to be a well-known art historian and critic, sought out the Marshal, ostensibly to apologize and thank him. Marco himself had been the one who actually did the apologizing and thanking, after which his father sent him out of the room and tried to offer the Marshal money. The Marshal had refused and stared hard at Landini with bulging expressionless eyes. He didn't like him.

'I don't want anything,' he said. 'I'm paid to do my job.'

'Come now, surely . . .'

The Marshal had got to his feet then. 'Look after the boy,' he said by way of dismissal. A useless admonition as it turned out to be, because Landini no longer lived with Marco's mother but with another woman whom he was later to marry. He still maintained his first family and in consequence felt free to make the occasional *deus ex machina* appearance and lay down the law. Such was his visit to the Carabinieri Station at Palazzo Pitti, a source of deep embarrassment to his son. Poor Marco.

The Marshal came out into Piazza Santissima Annunziata and his glance was drawn to the right where the white swaddled babies on their blue medallions were illuminated along the front of the fifteenth-century orphanage. Blessed are the orphans, as people said, free from the plague of family problems. But Marco, and those like him, got the worst of both worlds. He crossed below the dark bulk of the equestrian statue and left the square to the right.

He hadn't been surprised at Marco's phone call the other day. Landini's death had been reported in all the papers and mentioned on the television news. He'd left a considerable collection of paintings.

'Have you heard?'

'Yes, I saw it in the *Nazione*.'

'He left me some money and the studio. I was a bit surprised, to tell you the truth, but I confess that it comes at a time when I really need it.'

'I'm glad for you.' He didn't add what he was thinking, that Landini had done little enough for his son when he was alive.

'Well, he was never much of a father to me when he was alive.'

As had always happened, ever since their first encounter, Marco seemed to be reading his thoughts.

5

'Now I can set up a studio with a friend who graduated in architecture with me. Well, I say a friend but – once we've got on our feet – we want to get married . . .'

'Good. So what's wrong?'

A moment's hesitation. 'Oh dear . . . I suppose it's true that I only get in touch with you when I've got a problem to dump on you.'

'No, no, it's not true at all. I only said that because I can tell by your voice that you're worried.'

'I am. Can I come and see you? You don't mind?'

What he'd been worried about was a painting, a seventeenth-century portrait in oils. It was not part of his father's collection or it wouldn't have been left in the studio. Landini had known for some time that his days were numbered and had put his affairs in order. He had gone so far as to remove the more worthy pieces of furniture from the studio his son was to inherit to his second wife's home. And yet there was this apparently valuable painting standing on an easel in the centre of the white marble floor unexplained, inexplicable.

Then came a letter from the Florence branch of a famous London auction house followed by a visit. All very discreet. Signor Landini had discussed with them the sale of an Antonio Franchi portrait of Anna Caterina Luisa dei Gherardini and had been kind enough to leave a photograph. Naturally, in the circumstances, should the countess no longer feel inclined to sell . . .

'The countess? They meant your mother?'

'Exactly. My mother has nothing, Marshal, other than

an old Florentine name. That's what he married her for. My father made money, new money, but the Gherardini name was useful to him, when he was starting out, in circles he intended to frequent. Anyway, that painting isn't hers and if it were he's the last person she'd allow to sell it . . .' He hesitated, then stopped.

The Marshal had watched and waited. The boy was hiding something but no doubt it would come out eventually. He made no comment on it and his large expressionless eyes gave no sign of being aware of it.

'My father did do quite a lot of dealing on his own account, apart from doing valuations and attributions for a fee, so there wouldn't have been anything so odd about an unidentified painting being in the studio if they hadn't brought my mother's name into it . . .'

'Are you afraid it's stolen?'

Marco looked down, his face starting to burn. 'Either that or it's a forgery.'

Again the Marshal watched and waited. That wasn't all or Marco would have relaxed. He didn't relax.

'Have you talked to your mother about this?'

'No. How can I? You realize that she'd be implicated? Besides, there's no question of its being her painting. She hated him, you know, and more than anything she hated being financially dependent on him because he thought that gave him the right to lay down the law about everything, and he did, too.'

'I can understand that, but what do you want to do? What do you want me to do?'

'I want to clear it up, without telling my mother, without the newspapers finding out. If it's stolen I want to get it to the real owner without a real scandal – surely I can do that? I didn't steal it and, after all, my father's dead so they can't prosecute him even if it does come out.'

'Well . . . I'm not sure what would happen, it's not my line of country. You're safe enough since it was presented to the auction house before you inherited. But your mother, I think you should tell her –'

'No! No . . . I can't do that.'

'In that case you need expert advice. I don't know anything about paintings, stolen or otherwise, and as for forgeries –'

'But you have a specialist group in Rome. I found that out for myself, and they are bound to know if it's listed as stolen.'

'And if it is? I can't control what happens next once I've given them the information.'

'Why should anything happen if I give it back?'

They can't even touch the thing, not even return it to its owner without opening an official enquiry.'

'But they can do it without letting it get in the papers.'

'Maybe . . .'

'I don't believe my father was a thief. I mean, I don't want to believe it; I suppose that's nearer the truth. Even though I hated him more than my mother did.'

The way he'd hated it when his father had sat there in that same chair that day twelve years before and offered the Marshal money. He hated the shame of it.

'I'll do what I can.'

'You will? Listen, if you could just find out whether there's a Franchi portrait listed as stolen. Just that, without mention of the title because it can't be correct. And I'll get on with my own researches on what Franchi paintings are in existence and where they are, in case it's a copy. I keep wondering – this might sound stupid – but I keep wondering if he left me with this problem on purpose. I think he always despised me.'

'No, no . . . I'm sure he didn't,' lied the Marshal.

'Oh yes. He thought me ingenuous, which for him meant I was a fool. You remember that drug business . . . he gave me such a hard time for that, not because I was experimenting with dangerous drugs but because I was the only one stupid enough – "cretinous enough" were his own words – to hang around and call an ambulance for that boy who died and so risk getting arrested. I know he only brought me round here to pay you off in case I should get into any more scrapes. He tried to, didn't he?'

'Yes. He tried.'

'I was sure, sitting out there in your waiting room. I knew. I don't think I've ever felt so ashamed in my life.'

'You needn't have. It wasn't your fault. But as far as this other business is concerned, you might well be right and it's all a joke at your expense, so we shouldn't do anything hasty. What we are going to do is have a coffee before we go any further.'

Thinking of which, the Marshal decided he could do with one now, and a glass of water as well. Sweating in this wretched woollen overcoat had brought on a thirst. He'd walked quite a way too, of course. He spotted a red neon sign on the other side of the dark narrow street not far ahead and crossed over in the hope that it was a bar. It wasn't, it was a trattoria, but he did find a bar right at the end on the corner.

'A coffee and a glass of mineral water.'

'Flat or fizzy?'

'Flat.' While he was waiting he fished a slip of paper out of his overcoat pocket and looked at the address Marco had written down for him.

'One coffee.'

'Thank you.'

'This glass do you?'

'A bigger one, I think. It's so hot for November . . .'

'Flu weather. My wife's gone down with it already.'

Via dei Della Robbia should be immediately to the right. The thick coffee scalded his tongue and he took a sip of water. Young Marco had certainly done his homework.

'You see, whether the painting is forged or stolen, my father could only have been some sort of middle man. He wouldn't have stolen it and couldn't have painted it. So I went through his diary and checked up every one of his contacts with the excuse of communicating my father's death to them. I think I've eliminated them all except this one. There was nothing in the diary about him except a surname and the time of an appointment. Since it's an unusual name, I looked it up in the phone book and there were only two. One's a woman, a veterinary surgeon, the other's this man, Ivo Benozzetti in Via dei Della Robbia. That's one of those nineteenth-century streets where the ground floors are studios.'

'You have been playing the detective!'

'I didn't mean . . . I mean I couldn't ask you to –'

'No, no, I was only joking. You've done a good job. So what next? Are you going to go and see him?'

'I was hoping you would.'

'Me?'

'Not officially, just as a friend of the family who's helping me out – well, that's true, isn't it?' Without giving the Marshal the chance to protest he went on, 'I had an idea, you see, that we could say – you could say – that my father had stipulated in his will that certain friends should be offered some little memento of him from the personal effects in his studio. You could ask him to meet me there and choose something.'

'Are there any personal effects in the studio?'

'Not many,' admitted Marco, 'but there are one or two framed photographs of him with famous people, you know the sort of thing – and there's a clock, an antique letter opener, enough to convince him, I hope. You needn't even mention the painting. After all, if he's involved he knows it's there. If it's his he might take it away, saying he'd left it to be valued.'

'And you'd let him take it?'

'Certainly I would. Then I'd be rid of the problem.'

'Mmph.'

11

The Marshal wasn't too sure about that but since it was clear that Marco would proceed alone if he refused and since, if he were absolutely honest, his own curiosity had been aroused, here he was. He paid for his coffee.

'I wonder . . . I'm looking for Via dei Della Robbia . . . ?'

'Just there to your right.'

'You don't know a man called Benozzetti, by any chance – I'm not sure that I've got the right door number – Ivo Benozzetti.'

'Never heard the name. I'd have remembered if I had, it's unusual, isn't it? Of course, I don't remember the name of everybody who comes in for a coffee. I might know him by sight.'

'He's an artist, I think.'

'Artist? It's a long time since this was an artists' quarter. Nothing but the street names left from those days.'

'Well, thanks anyway.'

As he peered at the tiny lights of the doorbells in the gloom he wondered whether, in the long run, it would be a better idea to present himself as a Marshal of the carabinieri rather than just a friend of the family. Both, he decided, pressing firmly on the bell with a large finger. He had enough experience of life to know that when you want to deceive somebody there's no better weapon than the truth.

'Yes?'

The Marshal leaned down to speak into the microphone.

'Guarnaccia, Marshal of carabinieri. I'm looking for Benozzetti, Ivo. The label on the ground-floor flat was marked only I, B.'

There was no response for a moment, then the voice said, 'Wait, please.'

He waited for almost five minutes but he would have stood there motionless for an hour if necessary. He didn't ring the bell again, either. He was quite used to this and it was all the same to him whether it was an old lag stuffing a pistol behind a brick in the chimney or a housewife straightening the cushions and whipping off her apron. Everybody has something to hide when The Law arrives, from the prime minister to the tramp.

The gate clicked open and the front door at the end of the path through thick laurel bushes was illuminated. The door opened just enough to admit him and without the man who opened it ever becoming visible to the outside world.

'Yes?' He was behind the now almost closed door and showing no inclination to allow the Marshal to intrude any further into the elegant high-ceilinged entrance hall. It was just as well, the Marshal thought, that he'd decided to introduce himself as a carabiniere. Of course, the man could refuse to admit him or not as he pleased just the same, but to refuse a carabiniere admittance would look bad, draw attention. Someone with only I. B. written on the doorbell wasn't too keen on drawing attention. Even so, the Marshal waited without a word, filling the doorway with his solid presence, no more likely to go away than one of the trees behind him. He maintained his silence until the man was forced to fill it.

'Has there been a robbery in the building? Some sort of accident? I've heard nothing.'

'Not an accident . . .' Leaving the other possibility open he added, 'I think we should talk inside. I won't disturb you long.'

The door opened then just long enough to admit him but Benozzetti, he noticed, stepped back out of sight of the street. Man must be paranoid . . . or . . .

The alternative explanation, half formed in the Marshal's mind, that he might be in some way scarred or deformed dissolved the minute the door closed. Benozzetti was a very fine man indeed, broad and muscular, his grey hair sleek and his face freshly shaven. He was wearing an impeccable and very expensive-looking suit. The Marshal took all of this in without appearing to look at the man. Ostensibly he was looking at a mass of tall plants standing in brass pots on the chequered marble floor and the fancy wrought-iron work of the lift. He reckoned he wouldn't be kept out here to talk. A man who couldn't tolerate being seen from the street would hardly let his neighbours in the building know his business. 'Come this way, please.' A small door set back in an alcove. Nothing at all this time on the bell.

Once inside it took all the Marshal's willpower not to stare about him. Of course, it was all one room with floor space equal to one of the large and elegant apartments above, but even so . . . And in the centre that massive

14

figure, whatever it was, swathed in polythene – and the safes! Who could need two safes that size, apart from a bank?

He wasn't staring about him. He took in what he could with his large, slightly bulging eyes without permitting himself to move his head one centimetre, and even then it was only his peripheral vision that was picking up the objects whilst his gaze was fixed on Benozzetti and he was explaining his errand with plodding meticulousness.

It wasn't much of an explanation since the Marshal was no fine talker. When it came to an end there was a short silence. There was something in the way Benozzetti was looking at him, nothing he could define, perhaps the eyes themselves which were as hard and cold as diamonds that caused the sweat on the Marshal's body to turn chilly. This man was surely dangerous.

'Are you all right?'

'Yes. Yes, I'm all right . . . I was overheated and then . . .'

'Sit down. I can't offer you anything other than this hard chair. The room is cold because I work with clay. It can't be allowed to dry out too rapidly. I rarely feel the cold myself.'

The Marshal could well believe it.

'If you'll excuse me, I'll bring another chair for myself. As you can see, comfort is not a priority.' He waved a hand vaguely. 'This is my life . . .'

He turned and strode towards the back of the studio, presumably in search of another chair. As he retreated it was just possible to see that the top of his left ear was missing. The Marshal didn't waste a second. Against the opposite wall was a large neatly made bed with a fur rug thrown over it and a screen partly obscuring it. A chest with a marble top and a lamp . . . those high cupboards along the rest of the wall might contain clothes but there was no other sign of domestic life in the room. The opposite wall was all shelving, tools, workbenches – but surely that was a cooker . . .

Benozzetti was back. The Marshal made no futile attempt to deceive him.

'Excuse me staring about a bit. I don't get to meet many artists in my walk of life.'

'You don't get to meet any' – Benozzetti adjusted the creases in his trousers and seated himself so that the damaged ear was out of sight – 'because there aren't any.'

'But surely you . . . I can see you're dedicated to your work.'

'I'm dedicated to art. I'm not an artist because the current commercialization of so-called art feeds on the self-publicist, dedicated not to art but to instant fame through glossy magazines, fashionable parties and prostitution to the critics, God help us, the critics.'

'Yes, well, I'm sure you're right but, of course, I don't know a lot about it – Landini, now . . .'

'Ha! You don't know a lot about it but you're a friend of the late lamented Landini! Isn't that what you said? A friend of the family?'

'Well, more a friend to the son, you know, to be exact. I'm afraid I must have embarrassed you.'

'Embarrassed me? Why is that?' Benozzetti seemed highly amused by the idea.

'Oh, you know, assuming you were a friend of his – he wasn't very specific in this business of the bequests so we're rather working in the dark, contacting all the likely people, but if you can't do with critics I suppose your relationship wasn't what I thought . . .'

'Ha! I like that. Yes. Well, Marshal, I don't know whether our relationship was what you thought since I don't know what you thought, now do I?'

Those cold glittering eyes were so hypnotic that the Marshal almost found himself saying that he thought that he had something to do with that mysterious painting, especially as he felt quite sure of it by this time. He was also sure that if he did come out and say it Benozzetti wouldn't care a bit. He was living on some other plane where it wouldn't matter and where the Marshal couldn't get at him. However, he didn't say it. Apart from anything else he had a feeling that Benozzetti was quite capable of saying it himself. So he contented himself with murmuring, 'Well, perhaps I've made a mistake and disturbed you for nothing . . .'

'Not in the least. I didn't mean to tease you. Landini was a friend and colleague and, yes, he was a critic but not so much of a fool as most of them. Ah, the experts, Marshal, the experts! Have you ever given them much thought?'

'I – no, no. Art experts, you mean? No.'

Benozzetti leaned forward and whispered fiercely, 'Naked!'

'What?' Was that why his eyes were so frightening? Was he a madman?

'Stark naked! The Emperor's new clothes! Naked as the day they were born. Naked in their ignorance and arrogance. Tell me, did you ever hear of a musicologist who couldn't play a note? A literary critic who couldn't even read or write? Even a football manager who'd never played a game in his life? Have you?'

'I don't suppose I have . . .'

'And I don't suppose you have, either. But the art expert, now, there's a really special man. He can't draw, he can't paint and he can't sculpt but he feels himself qualified to pronounce judgement on Leonardo, on Botticelli, on Michelangelo. A miracle of a man, wouldn't you say? He can't express the simplest concept with any visual or manual skill of his own but he can sit in judgement on genius. Ah, where would the world be without the expert – you know what he's there for, don't you? He's there at the service of the art dealer, not art or the artist. Now Landini, not being the worst of them, knew that was true. He wore the Emperor's new clothes with considerable panache and made himself a fine career out of doing it, but he had no illusions. And he had taste, he wasn't just a cataloguer. The rest of them might as well make laundry lists since lists are all they know how to make – you don't have a list of your own in your pocket, by any chance?'

'A list?'

'All right. I just wondered. If I'm not mistaken you

people have a specialist group that takes something of an interest in paintings.'

'Oh, I see . . . yes. No, no, I'm just —'

'A friend of the family.'

'That's right,' said the Marshal, his gaze becoming duller and blanker in retreat from those glittery cold eyes. Once, long ago in the early years of his marriage, his wife had screamed at him in exasperation, 'Can't you even quarrel? Answer me! Don't just roll over and play dead!' And he had been amazed. By this time he had seen his plump, peaceable son Giovanni do just that when attacked by his quick and nervous younger brother so now he knew it was true. He also knew it was effective. 'Though, as I said, more of a friend of young Marco's. Landini himself, now, I only met him once and that'd be over ten years ago. You're not a married man yourself?'

'No.'

'No, I thought not. That would be something you're working on, would it, under all that polythene? Clay, you said?'

'A nude figure. That's just one of the reasons why I never married. Everyone assumes that artists sleep with their models. A wife would have given me no peace.'

'Yes, well, you've certainly got it all worked out, this nice big space you can keep cool to suit your clay, nobody around to disturb you.' The Marshal shivered at the thought of such an existence. How odd a man he was. Such a fierce intelligence, incisive, aggressive even, and yet so easy to distract. Was that because so many things

19

made him angry so that he attacked anything that caught his attention like a tormented bull? Or was he just so unused to social intercourse that he had no experience of controlling conversation. If that were the case then the Marshal had the advantage over him. He was very used to controlling the conversation, chiefly by power of inertia. How very different from Benozzetti, who was on his feet again now, perhaps anxious for his visitor to leave. So be it. The Marshal stood up and waited in silence to be sent away. But Benozzetti strode to the back of the long room.

'Come here.'

The Marshal was only too pleased to obey the summons which took him past the two great safes. There was no sense risking a question about those at this stage . . .

He pulled himself up mentally. What was he thinking about? This wasn't a case he was on! He had to remind himself that the line about being a friend of the family and so on was actually the truth as well. There was no reason why he should ever set foot into this place again; once he'd convinced Benozzetti to go round to Marco's studio and see the painting, his part was finished.

'Over here!'

Well, there wasn't time to work out whether he'd convinced him or not . . . where the devil had the man got to?

'Here, Marshal.'

He was behind a huge easel and was carefully lifting a cloth that shrouded the painting standing on it. The

Marshal's heart sank. There was little doubt that he was about to be shown a painting and even less doubt that if he opened his mouth about it he'd make a fool of himself. Every time he was obliged to attend the opening of some exhibition in the Palatine Gallery at the Palazzo Pitti where his station was, his wife would remind him, 'Just keep quiet, Salva, and listen to what Dr Biondini says. You might learn something.' And he did his best, but though what Dr Biondini, the director of the gallery, said was very clear and sensible when he was saying it, the Marshal couldn't remember anything of it for more than a few minutes. Then when Biondini was kind enough, as he always was, to come and welcome him and ask him what he thought of the exhibition he always seemed to say the wrong thing. Sometimes he just looked puzzled and kind and quickly spotted someone he was obliged to go and speak to. The thing about Biondini was that, though he knew such a lot, he never gave himself airs or made you feel badly about not knowing, so it wasn't that much of an ordeal. The Marshal, rounding the easel, had a feeling that Benozzetti was a very different kettle of fish and that he'd do best to take his wife's advice and keep his mouth shut.

'Ah . . .' The Marshal's sigh of relief escaped him before he knew it.

'Yes, I'm glad you appreciate it. I'm showing it to you to demonstrate something. Of course it's a beautiful painting.'

'Beautiful,' said the Marshal contentedly. He could

manage this one all right. What was beautiful about the painting, as far as he was concerned, was that he was as familiar with it as he was with his own face in the mirror. It was the one that hung on the wall of the second room in the Palatine Gallery and next to it stood a commodious chair in which reposed, for a large part of the day, his good friend and fellow Sicilian Mario Di Luciano, a custodian. Mario came from the same little town in the province of Siracusa and he liked to chat about old times down home. The Marshal reckoned he'd probably spent as much time standing in front of that picture as Titian had. What a stroke of luck.

Benozzetti was roaring on, working himself into a lather about the quality of modern painting – no, modern paint.

'Acrylics! In five years they deteriorate, in ten they disintegrate! Look at the flesh tones on this portrait! Look here, and here! Flesh tones of this quality continue to develop and grow to their full beauty over a period of two hundred years. A painter who uses materials like that cares about painting, not about seeing himself in the next issue of some fashionable art magazine!'

And so on and on in the same vein. Of course, he was probably right, there was no denying that. You only had to look around the studio to see the man was a professional and must know what he was talking about. Only that didn't mean that anybody else knew what he was talking about and the Marshal soon gave up trying to follow him. Almost automatically, the way he did when

Mario the custodian was deep in some long-winded family saga, he took a step back. Then another. Then a step forward.

'That's funny . . .'

'I beg your pardon?'

The Marshal stepped back and then forward again, oblivious of his impolite interruption. 'Now isn't that a turn up . . . oh, it's nothing, just . . . you know the way these pictures just look like blobs and splashes when you're standing right up close to them and then you step back and all of a sudden they're as real as a photograph – I'm sorry, I interrupted you . . .' And he'd no idea either what the fellow had been saying except that it was something about making colours. He tried to pay attention but he couldn't help edging back and forward a bit, just to check that he hadn't been mistaken.

Determined to gain his attention, Benozzetti inserted himself between the Marshal and the easel and continued his angry discourse nose to nose. If the Marshal edged back he followed, beating the air with his right hand to mark the rhythm of his rhetoric and sending wafts of fine perfume into the Marshal's face.

'When I was twenty years of age and a student at the academy . . .'

Lord, were they going to have his entire life story? What time would it be? No chance of that ferocious stare losing its grip for a second to permit a glance down at his wristwatch. Snake's eyes . . .

'This is a man who calls himself a Professor of Fine

23

Arts! I didn't suffer it in silence, I can tell you. I stood up and interrupted him. I said, "Professor, you've made some comment about almost every painting in this end-of-year exhibition. Am I to understand that my own works are invisible to you, or is it that they are unworthy of your comments?" Do you know what he answered?'

'I . . . no . . .' The Marshal tried to back away from the man's hot breath and heavy perfume but Benozzetti closed in on him.

'"The only thing worthy of comment in your work," he said, without so much as a glance at it or me, "is its extraordinary antiquated style." The other students laughed. They laughed!' He broke off. He seemed to be staring straight through the Marshal rather than at him now. A few beads of sweat broke at his temples and then, quite suddenly, he began to laugh. A harsh and cheerless noise, it might easily have been a sort of strangulated sobbing, so that it wasn't until he spoke again that the Marshal could be sure.

'Well, I paid him back nicely for that one! It was so funny it kept me awake at night. I had to wait, of course, until October, but I didn't mind. It gave me the summer to think out the best way to pay him back. Then I remembered. You have to understand that, though it wasn't his subject, he often joined us in the life room if the model or the pose interested him – and more often it was the model, I can assure you. He kept an easel there and usually had a painting going. All I had to do was wait until everyone left for lunch, unscrew the supports holding his canvas and let the painting fall on the floor face down! Simple, you see? Then there was the pleasure of watching him find it and his mystified face as he checked the supports. He cleaned it up that first time as best he could and carried on and I waited until he'd put in plenty of work on it before it hit the dust again! That time I couldn't resist going over to him. I suggested that the easel was defective and offered him mine. The silly fool accepted it and *thanked* me. Doesn't that show how idiotic people are? He should have suspected at once. What reason had I to help him? And a half-witted fool like that sets himself up in judgement on me! You can't imagine how much I wanted to tell him the truth but I didn't. I left him looking ruefully at his painting which was ruined beyond hope and I went and sat down.'

The Marshal wished he could do the same. It must be late because he was beginning to feel not only tired but quite hungry. Above Benozzetti's finely tailored shoulder the eyes of the handsome young man in the portrait gazed down at him calmly. If he'd known his portrait was going to give rise to all this fury he would surely have been as baffled as the Marshal. What was the fellow going on about now?

'And *you* think I'm talking purely about content but you're wrong. You're wrong because the value, the *true* value of the content can be judged by the materials used. A cathedral is built of stone and marble and seasoned wood but you can knock up a garage or a tool shed from corrugated tin – well, you wouldn't use marble, would

25

you? And why? Because the idea, the content, as it were, has no intrinsic value *and it doesn't need to last*! Worthless materials for a worthless idea!'

The finger wagging in front of the Marshal's nose was suddenly whisked away. Benozzetti was reaching for a huge tome from a nearby bookshelf and searching through it for something. The Marshal looked at his familiar friend in the painting and murmured under his breath, 'It's a funny business even so . . .'

It was still bothering him. There was no getting away from the fact that the distance at which the painting stopped being all blobs and strokes and became clear as a photograph was one big stride more than it had always been before. Would there be any harm in asking? Why should there be? It might start another avalanche, of course, and he'd probably be unable to follow the answer but –

'Look. Here. And here.'

There were drawings he was being shown now, a whole page of them. Hands, all of them.

'Let me tell you something about this ink.'

'I – do you mind if I ask you something? I don't like interrupting what you were saying about the ink and so on, but it's about this painting . . .'

'What about it?'

'Well, there's something different about it and I thought you wouldn't object to explaining it to me since you know such a lot. It's something that's always fascinated me – in fact, I remember I once asked Dr Biondini about it and he did try to explain about it being something that happens in your brain, an illusion you create yourself, he said, only I can never understand why there isn't a distance where you can see it happen. Do you know what I mean? It's either the blobs or the perfect picture and you can never see it happen. I'm probably not explaining myself very well but, anyway, what I can't understand about this painting is why it happens at four strides away instead of three, like it always is with Titian – or like it always is with me . . . of course the light's different here, could that be the reason?'

He turned to Benozzetti and waited. What had he done? What was the matter with the man? His face was red but under the Marshal's gaze it drained itself of colour. The snake's eyes darted from the painting to the Marshal and back again. All he said was, 'Biondini?'

'That's right. He's the curator of the Palatine Gallery. He knows a lot about Titian.'

'Yes? And you. Marshal? What do you know a lot about?'

The voice was icy. He was reaching up for the cloth at the top of the easel.

'Me? Nothing. I mean I don't pretend . . .' Then it sank in. What in God's name had he been thinking about? How could he have made such a stupid mistake? What would the painting from the gallery be doing here? Just before the curtain dropped down and covered it he registered the difference. The same face, the same silk cloak but he was sitting differently and there was something missing in his hand –

27

It was gone.

'I'm afraid you're something of a fraud, Marshal. You know a great deal more than you like to admit.'

'No, no. That's not true.' But how could he explain about his friend Mario? He'd already made a fool of himself so he wasn't going to confess that as well.

'You can tell your friend Biondini' – Benozzetti's gesture invited the Marshal to leave – 'though I don't pretend to know how he found out about this painting, that it is not and won't be on the market and that the private collector who owns it doesn't want its existence bruited about and that if I receive a visit from him or anyone else from the Ministry I shall simply say that I painted this picture myself. Do you understand me? And if they doubt my ability to have painted it I can paint another in front of their eyes. I hope I've made myself clear. Now I'm sure that you have as busy an evening ahead of you as I have.'

He was trying to waft the Marshal out of the room, but if the Marshal had a talent it was for rooting himself to the spot when people wanted him out of the way.

'There was no offence meant,' he said, 'and Biondini's never heard of you or this painting as far as I know.' How had he got himself into this mess? He'd frightened this man badly without understanding how, and if he wanted him to make an appearance at Marco's studio after this he was going to have to offer him some sort of propitiatory confidence. He toyed with and rejected the story of Mario the custodian, not to save face now but because, like so many true and simple things, it wouldn't be believed. And that left only one possibility.

'Still,' he began, 'I owe you an apology. I have been hiding the real reason for my visit from you, but not for any sinister reason and nothing to do with Titian or with Dr Biondini. I was just chattering on, distracting you. I should have realized that a man of your intelligence would see through me but in my job I don't do much more than deal with snatched handbags, lost cameras and so on, so I'm a bit out of my depth. Anyway, I'd better tell you all. Young Marco wants you to go round to the studio, not to choose a memento of his father, though I know you'll be welcome to do that, but to look at a painting that's there. I'd rather not have mentioned it, just as I decided I'd rather not see it at all myself. The reason for that I don't need to tell you since you have the same problem yourself with the Titian there . . .'

'Not, strictly speaking, my problem. I'm restoring it, that's all.'

'Even so, you understand what I mean. It seems Marco's father intended to sell. The auctioneers have been to see him. But he can find no record of the painting in his father's collection and he's afraid of getting involved in something he can't deal with. Like me, he's out of his depth. He needs advice. I'd be grateful if you'd give him some and officially you and I have never met. It's up to you. Now I really will leave you in peace.'

Benozzetti showed him to the door in silence and in silence closed it behind him.

'Where on earth have you been?'

The table was laid for two in the tidy, brightly lit kitchen and Teresa was tasting something from a saucepan on the cooker.

'Have the boys eaten?'

'Half an hour ago. They were hungry. You didn't say you were going to be late.'

'No . . . well, I didn't think I would. There's a good smell; are we having pasta?'

'This sauce is for tomorrow's lunch. Supper's in the oven – oh, Captain Maestrangelo rang twice.'

'Twice?'

'He said ring him back. He wants you to go and see him tomorrow. That man never knows when it's Sunday, does he? I mean, he's very nice but you can tell he hasn't a family – Salva, don't stand there, you're in my way. And aren't you going to take your coat off?'

There were two things Teresa, in all the years of their marriage, refused to adapt to: one was her husband's incurable habit of homing straight in on her in the kitchen and planting his great uniformed bulk right in the middle of the room so that she had to push round him with her pans. The other was the army's incurable habit of expecting him to work on Sundays and sometimes even at night. She didn't actually complain about this or create problems for him. She was just surprised by it.

He went to take his coat off, calling, 'I wouldn't mind a shower. I've been too hot.'

'Be quick then. I'll switch the oven off.'

Dressing after his shower, he could hear the two boys in the living room squabbling over which channel to watch. He slipped a pair of old leather slippers on and went back into the kitchen. The good smell from the oven brought on a sharp pang of appetite along with a comfortable sense of its imminent satisfaction. That huge chilly studio . . . no warm kitchen there. But there'd been a cooker, he was sure he hadn't been mistaken about that. A cooker amongst all the paints and tools; funny people artists were and you couldn't judge them by normal standards.

'Ah . . . that looks good.' He reached for his napkin and the flask of red wine.

'Did you ring the Captain back?'

'Damn! Well, if it's only to fix a time for tomorrow it can wait till I've eaten this.'

Now that was a point. Captain Maestrangelo was an educated man. It might be a good idea to have a word with him about this business of Marco's, see what he thought. It was a point, but it was one the Marshal forgot along with Benozzetti and Titian and all the rest when he heard what Captain Maestrangelo had to say.

Two

On Sunday morning the city was still blanketed in warm, foggy dampness. The olive-green river slid smoothly between the high, ochre buildings and the soaked terra-cotta roofs seemed luminous.

When the Marshal crossed the river on his way to Headquarters he could see no further than the next bridge down with a few grey and ghostly trees beyond. Upriver to his right the Ponte Vecchio stood isolated, its usual backcloth of hills screened off by a curtain of fog. Because of this, and perhaps because it was Sunday and the lights in the jewellers' shops were off, the bridge looked like a deserted stage set seen in the dull light of morning. It was so quiet, too. Most of the brown and green shutters of the tall buildings along the embankment were still closed and the roads were empty of traffic.

It was the ideal time to walk about and look at the city and the Marshal and his wife were always saying they should make the effort to do it. They had got themselves organized two or three times and, armed with a guidebook, had taken the two boys with them. Somehow or other, though, it hadn't lasted. The boys were really a bit young to enjoy that sort of thing and once they had climbed to the top of Giotto's bell tower and seen the knights on armoured horses at the Stibbert Museum they got fed up and started to protest. Since they were also rather young to be left to their own devices all morning, the whole business had been dropped. A pity, though, really. They ought to have another try at it.

In the meantime, the Marshal savoured his walk, short though it was, and even stopped for a coffee in the bar almost opposite the barracks. He took his time with that too, looking at the long glass counter filled with decorated cakes and tarts which would soon be cleared by young families on their way to Sunday lunch at the grandparents'.

Inspired by this cheery colourful contrast to the dull day outside he decided to buy a cake himself and, since he could hardly appear before his Captain carrying the beribboned parcel, he would buy it now while there was still plenty of choice and collect it on his way home.

He chose a *torta della nonna,* a creamy tart sprinkled with almonds and icing sugar, and paid for it along with his coffee. As he crossed Via Borgo Ognissanti and entered the cloister of the ex-convent where Headquarters was housed, a squad car passed him driving out at high speed, piercing the Sunday morning quiet with its siren.

'Me?' The Marshal sat there stunned for a moment before remembering his position. 'I'm sorry . . . I didn't mean – I was just so surprised.' He was searching Captain Maestrangelo's face for some sort of clue, a hint at least of the explanation that wasn't forthcoming in words. All he could read there was embarrassment and something of anger. The Captain wasn't very communicative at the best of times, but the Marshal had known him for so many years that he was usually able to decipher something of what was happening behind the good-looking, deeply serious face. This time, though, the eyes were avoiding his and after a moment the smooth brown hands dropped the pen they had been turning over and over and the Captain stood up and walked over to the window. He stayed there looking out with his back to the Marshal, silent.

Why me? Why? The Marshal too remained silent but his troubled, slightly bulging eyes scanned the room as though the dark oil paintings, the soft leather furniture or the row of army calendars hanging from their red tassels might provide him with an answer to his question. All that came into his head was another, equally baffling question.

34

'And why now? I mean, nothing's happened that I've heard of. He hasn't killed for what . . . five years or so . . .'

'Five years, yes. In 1985.'

'Well, I don't know much about these things, of course, but I've heard it said by those who do know that likely as not he's dead.'

'It seems likely, yes. It could be, though,' the Captain was choosing his words carefully, 'that he's in prison for some other offence – that's just an example. What I'm trying to say is that there could be other reasons why he's no longer active.'

Not choosing his words, the Marshal corrected himself, but reciting them. 'Is that what this man Simonetti thinks?' he asked as blandly as possible.

The Captain hesitated and then turned to face him.

'I should have known better. You're a difficult man to deceive, Guarnaccia. I'm going to order some coffee to be brought up.' He came and sat down again and pressed the bell on his desk. But once more he took up his pen and didn't meet the Marshal's gaze.

'It's not often you try to deceive me. Don't tell me anything you shouldn't.' Then he frowned. 'Simonetti . . . isn't he the Prosecutor we had – ?'

A young carabiniere appeared at the door. The Captain ordered coffee and then waited until the door closed again.

'On the Becker case, yes. I thought you'd remember him.'

'Oh Lord . . .'

'Quite.'

Decent prosecutors who let you get on with your job and backed you up when necessary were few and far between and there was little love lost between the rest of them and the investigators who had to do their bidding. You don't learn the ins and outs of the criminal mind at university or in the drawing rooms of polite society. The best of them knew nothing and listened to those who did know. The worst of them knew nothing and listened to nobody. Simonetti belonged to the latter category and was always most elegantly dressed in court when taking credit for what you had achieved despite his arrogant misdirection of the case.

It wasn't that the Marshal blamed Simonetti for his own failure to resolve the Becker case, but he did blame him for ruining the life of an innocent man as an alternative to failing to arrest anybody. And that particular character trait left him puzzled now.

'I'm surprised he'd want to take this on,' he said. 'I mean . . . better men than him have had to give up on it when the trail was hot, as you might say, but now . . . and there was never a scrap of evidence as far as I've heard. He didn't strike me as a man who would care for such a public failure.'

'No, he wouldn't like that.'

Their coffee was brought and the Marshal stirred sugar into his thoughtfully before saying, 'In that case I suppose the Chief Public Prosecutor's dumped the thing on him and he's got no choice. That won't improve his temper.'

'The Chief Public Prosecutor and Simonetti,' replied the Captain, apparently addressing his pen, 'are old friends. They hunt together, I believe. Simonetti has ambitions. The Chief has a thorn in his side and that thorn is the Monster. This coming year will be the Chief's last year in office. Then he retires. He's made a name for himself; you know that he's had a lot of success in kidnapping cases which, as they often involved foreigners, made him something of a reputation abroad as well as here. He also had a lot of success against terrorism. It's been an energetic and, if you like, aggressive battle against crime and he's enjoyed every minute of it, no doubt.'

'But you don't like him.'

'Let's say he appears too often on television for my personal taste. Well, it's not my place to criticize the man and I'm sure he could hardly care less what I think. Even so, he's made enemies along the way, chiefly because his steamroller tactics leave a lot of walking wounded amongst his colleagues, as many as among the criminal fraternity, I would imagine. At any rate, when the Prosecutor General opened this Judicial Year his speech included some lengthy and unpleasant comments on the failure to apprehend the Florentine serial killer known as the Monster. All the Chief's years of success go for nothing if he retires as the man who failed to solve the case that's sold more newspapers than any other crime in his lifetime.'

'I see. Well, that's understandable, of course . . .'

'He set up a specialized squad for this case some time ago but its activities weren't much publicized in case nothing resulted.'

'And now something has?'

'Apparently. He wants a rather bigger team. Six men. Three from the civil police and three carabinieri.'

He was reciting again. He clearly wasn't going to explain why the Marshal had been chosen.

'Can I at least ask . . . even if you don't want to – who made the choice, of the three carabinieri, that is?'

'It was made here. We made it.'

'Thank you. I'd no right to ask, but thank you.'

'There's no reason why you should thank me. The business will be a nuisance to you, I'm afraid, but I wouldn't ask you to be so much absent from your station did you not have Lorenzini, who I know is extremely competent.'

'Yes. Yes, Lorenzini . . .'

'And however this business goes, I want you to know that I think a lot of you. You've done some good work in the past and I appreciate it. I'm sounding apologetic but it's certain that you won't enjoy being under the authority of the civil police and Simonetti's preference means that's how it will work even though you are three and three.'

Well, that perhaps explained the Captain's embarrassment and his anger also.

'I'll do my best not to let you down.'

'Do your best to cope and don't worry about letting me down. You won't be required to work any miracles, you can set your mind to rest about that.'

'I'm glad to hear it, given how little I know about such things. I wasn't even here when it began.'

'We all know very little, Marshal. The last time anything remotely resembling this happened in Italy was in 1927 and the police put up a poor show then.'

'So you're not very hopeful that anything will come of this, despite the new developments.'

'I don't know. I really don't know, and that's the truth.'

Again he got to his feet, clearly wanting the interview to be over. The Marshal got up and followed him to the door.

'They expect you at eight tomorrow morning.'

There was no doubt that the brief touch on the Marshal's shoulder as he said it was friendly, but there was no doubt either that his face as he watched the Marshal leave was dark with anger.

'Don't tell the boys.'

'For heaven's sake, Salva, as if I'd dream of talking about something like that to the boys.' Even so, Teresa, too, glanced anxiously at the door through which they'd charged the minute it stopped raining. The white Sunday tablecloth was still on and she had just cleared their plates and brought in coffee. 'Such a nasty affair . . .'

She didn't go on but the Marshal understood what she was feeling. She'd still been down in Sicily when most of the murders happened but the newspapers all over the country had made the most of such a ghoulish case of murder and sexual mutilation. What she was thinking, and he couldn't blame her, was that he'd brought it into the house. Wasn't that what he was feeling himself in not wanting the boys to know?

'Of course, the papers will be full of it,' she went on, 'and it'll be on television all the time. They're bound to be asking questions.'

'It doesn't matter as long as they don't know I'm involved. You needn't imagine my name'll ever be in the papers. Why me? That's what I still want to know. Why me? It makes no sense but there must be a reason. They didn't pick names out of a hat. Maestrangelo said they'd made the choice themselves but he looked angry.'

'And you can't imagine why?'

He stared at her. 'You mean you can?'

'I mean maybe he'd like it to be himself. So, if for some reason he was passed over . . .'

'No, no . . .'

'He's only human, you know.'

The Marshal sipped his coffee in silence, thinking. He was a great admirer of Captain Maestrangelo, seeing him as everything he himself was not: intelligent, well educated, a good speaker. He'd never thought a lot about the man's human qualities because they weren't what you noticed. Teresa would, of course, that was like her. She'd even said when they first met that Maestrangelo was a handsome man, and attractive to women, or that he would be if he smiled. That had certainly never crossed the Marshal's mind – but then, Maestrangelo never smiled. He was ambitious, that was true . . . but even so . . .

'No, no . . .' he said again. 'He has his ambitions, he'll end up a general, I'm sure of that, but however reliable he might be as an investigator it's not that way his ambitions lie. And then, a case like this, I can't see how it can come to anything with the best will in the world. All those years ago and there never was any evidence. No, no, he's not the man for anything risky or unusual.'

'Well, if you say so, but leaving that aside, I don't see why they shouldn't choose you.'

'He said, "We made the choice." He emphasized the "we". As though he were taking the responsibility but without liking it. It's the Colonel's responsibility, anything of that sort, but he hasn't been here much more than a month.'

'So the Captain must have recommended you – you know, you really shouldn't run yourself down the way you do. The Captain thinks a lot of you, you've solved some important cases.'

'I've never been on an important case. The only case I ever solved was when that poor creature Cipolla shot that Englishman. And he only did it by accident and after that he was just hanging around waiting for me to arrest him.'

'I'll grant you that – have a drop more coffee; I don't want any more.'

'It'll keep me awake.' He accepted it, even so.

'No, I'll grant you that but what about that jeweller who died years ago? You can't deny you found out who was responsible for that. I remember the whole story.'

'I didn't catch her. She was arrested somewhere up

near the Swiss border. She confessed. I never so much as signed my name to a report on that. And the same goes for that case in the potteries. I did sort that out, it's true, but the case was in the hands of the local force – it was out of my area.'

'Well, what about that foreigner in the fur coat? That was your case.'

'Yes, and I didn't solve it. The chap died in America and we never so much as got a glimpse of him – and what's more the Prosecutor on that job was the one who's in charge of this one so that rules out any danger of him thinking I'm some sort of Sherlock Holmes.'

'I still think you're running yourself down and that the Captain thinks very highly of you. He told me so when we first met, I remember it well.'

The time she'd said he was good-looking.

'He was just being polite.'

'No, he wasn't. I can tell the difference – and what about that poor crazy old woman near the butcher's. Now, I was here then – that's when I started to go to that butcher – you can't deny you found that dreadful man.'

'There was no arrest. I was too late. That's me all over, too slow.'

'He committed suicide! For goodness sake, Salva, you still found him!'

'Well . . . I suppose that's true enough, though if it hadn't been for that neighbour telling me . . . anyway, all right. I found him. So that's two. Him and Cipolla. Add that to a lot of stolen handbags, never recovered, and dozens of tourists with lost cameras and passports and it still doesn't make me Sherlock Holmes.'

But Teresa insisted and in the end she almost convinced him. Then she lectured him. People – apart from the Captain, who knew him well -- would think more of him if he thought more of himself and if he spoke up now and again and showed a bit of interest instead of just standing there staring into space. The Marshal was at once more comfortable. This was a line of reasoning more acceptable because more familiar. He'd been hearing it for years, from his mother and his teachers when he was small, and from his wife for the whole time they'd been married. As always, at the end of it he agreed with everything she'd said and resolved to make an effort to look alert and to speak up more, starting at eight tomorrow morning.

After all was said and done, this was an important case and, whatever the reason behind the choice might be, there was no getting away from the fact that he'd been chosen. He owed it to his Captain to keep his wits about him and he was going to do just that. Instead of sitting down with the paper after lunch he went straight to his office and plodded through all his outstanding paper-work. At five he called his young brigadier, Lorenzini, who was married and lived out of barracks, and together they prepared the daily orders for Monday.

By bedtime that night he felt that he had his world under control and his last thought as he dozed off was that, after all, it might prove a very interesting experience and he ought to consider himself both flattered and privileged.

At one-thirty in the morning his eyes opened and he was wide awake on the instant. He'd forgotten to telephone young Marco as he'd promised to do. Damn! He did hate to let someone down when he'd promised. Not only that, he'd forgotten that he'd reminded himself this morning, as he left that bar, to consult the Captain about the problem of the painting, but the new case had – and in that bar he'd bought a cake, an expensive cake, and left it there. So much for keeping his wits about him. A fine start. He'd have to do a lot better than that tomorrow morning. Whether it was his apprehension about tomorrow morning or his annoyance with himself for his forgetfulness, or just all those extra coffees he'd drunk, something kept him wakeful until the small hours. The next morning at eight o'clock he was rather more fuzzy headed and silent than usual.

It was nowhere near as bad as he'd expected. In the first place, he wasn't faced with a group of complete strangers. He knew both of the other carabinieri, that was the first thing he noted with relief. One of them, Ferrini, was a man of his own age with whom he'd once worked on a case, and though they were very different they got on well. The other, Bacci, he knew almost as well as his own children, having had him under his feet at Pitti whilst he waited for a place at the Officer School. Bacci must be about due for a promotion to captain by now, but his face was as boyish and ingenuous as ever and surely he was a bit young to be on a case like this? And that young policeman sitting opposite him didn't seem much more than a boy, either. That probably meant that the Marshal was getting old. Then, you had to remember that youngsters these days had special skills, computers and so on. The thought that they might be there because the job involved anything dynamic and dangerous crossed his mind briefly and vanished, and he returned comfortably to the idea of 'computers and so on', a phrase which covered and dismissed a whole area of investigative activity regarded by him with exaggerated respect and complete detachment.

Running his gaze over the other two policemen opposite he noticed, right facing himself, a face he knew but couldn't put a name to. The man was about his own age and when he caught the Marshal's eye he gave a faint nod of recognition before returning his gaze to the Prosecutor, Simonetti, who had launched into one of his speeches of the sort meant to sound friendly and improvised and which were carefully conceived and rehearsed. What *was* that chap's name? Di Maira, that was it. They'd come across each other years ago. The other he recognized as a tough and experienced detective. No need to wonder why he was there. Couldn't remember his name, though.

The room was overheated and quite a few of the men had lit cigarettes. The Marshal fished for his big white handkerchief and dabbed it unobtrusively at his sensitive eyes, which were suffering from both the increasing smoke and lack of sleep. Even so, he didn't feel as uncomfortable as he'd expected and he relaxed a little as he watched Simonetti hold forth. One thing was sure, he wasn't there against his will. His face, as he expounded, was pink with enthusiasm and it was clear that there were no doubts assailing his mind as to the future success of their efforts. Much as the Marshal disliked this sleek and arrogant man, he also envied him. Envied his talent for believing himself in the right – because the Marshal had no doubt at all that he did believe it. It wasn't a pose and that was why he was able to convince others. How does a man get that way? How does he account to himself for his mistakes, his wickedness, worst of all, his gaffes? Well, perhaps you had to be born that way and that was all there was to it. Not much fun for the people around you, of course. The way the man waved his arms about as if he were directing traffic – that must be a habit he'd developed in court, getting the full effect with the wide arms of his black silk gown which, the Marshal remembered, he always seemed to wear off the shoulder with a very fancy suit showing beneath. His plastron always used to be out of place as well – not crooked but carefully placed to look careless. Dislike for the man welled stronger in the Marshal's breast as he remembered Mario Querci, innocent witness to murder, who fell victim to this man's predatory instincts, was swooped on and borne away, then dropped when a meatier prey was offered. For Querci it had been too late because by then he'd been in prison, lost his job and his wife and child. Having no other resources, shocked and frightened beyond recovery, he killed himself. And Simonetti, assuming he'd even registered an event of so little importance so long after the fact, would never for a moment have doubted his right to do what he did. God help anyone who fell in his way in a case as important as this one. There'd be blood and fur everywhere once he started. Why was he thinking of him in that way? Simonetti wasn't thin, didn't have a beaky nose or anything . . . he was well set up and squarish . . . was it the Captain saying he and the Chief Public Prosecutor hunted together?

No. His eyes. It was his eyes, they were hooded and unnaturally bright. Hmph. Well, the trail was cold on this job, so if he thought he could solve it after all these years . . .

'Of the hundreds of anonymous communications received since 1981 – that is, after the point we knew we were dealing with a serial killer and the story broke in the papers – only three are of any real interest. Two of these are presumed to be from the killer himself and you'll find copies of them in the files you've been given. The third concerns the person we are presently investigating.

'This man had already come up on the computer because he had, as the letter suggests, been convicted of murder in his youth – a particularly vicious murder, the details of which are in your files – and because he was a known Peeping Tom. Some three years ago he was convicted of continued sexual abuse of his daughter. He is still serving his sentence in the prison of Sollicciano. Our enquiries have already shown that this man was living in the areas concerned at the time of the double homicides and must have known each specific area well since they are all places much frequented by courting couples and, as a consequence, by Peeping Toms. On receipt of this communication a search was made of his house and outbuildings but nothing of interest was discovered. Since that time we have been enquiring further into his activities and associates and he will shortly receive a judicial warning that he is under investigation for the double homicides of 1968, '74, '81 June, '81 October, '82, '83, '84 and '85. In the meantime you will study the case file provided. Then we shall act.'

He gathered his own files together and got to his feet, his smile bright with camaraderie and boyish charm.

'I've asked for coffee to be brought to you here and I hope that you will introduce yourselves. I look forward to working with you. Gentlemen, good morning.'

As Simonetti swept out, trailing imaginary silk behind him, the Marshal let out a long breath and congratulated himself for having stayed alert throughout the proceedings, which had gone on, he noted with a surreptitious glance at his watch, for a good two hours. It was fortunate that he wasn't required to demonstrate how alert he'd been because, in truth, apart from the bit about the anonymous letter and that last part about the judicial warning and the coffee, he couldn't have repeated a single word of what Simonetti had said.

Outside the Tribunal on the broad stone staircase a large group of journalists jostled and scribbled and gossiped. Though it was as warm as ever, their collars were turned up as fine specks of rain punctuated the grey mist.

'Don't worry, they're not waiting for us,' Ferrini said, sensing the Marshal's hesitation. 'The Chief Proc and Simonetti are giving a press conference any minute. They'll be on telly tonight and won't they be pleased.'

The Marshal made no comment and they started down the steps. Two carabinieri cars were waiting and Bacci was getting into the one in front.

Ferrini looked about for a third. 'You're not on foot?'

'I try to walk when I can. Besides, for short distances it's quicker.' The traffic was barely crawling past them and some drivers, irritated beyond the limits of their patience by endless queues and the grey, exhaust-laden atmosphere, were leaning on their horns.

'It's going to rain hard. We can drop you.'

The Marshal was easily convinced. He hated getting wet but mostly he wanted to talk to somebody about all this, somebody from his own force and of his own age and rank – only of course Ferrini wasn't any longer a marshal.

'I should congratulate you.' He offered a glance at the stars on Ferrini's epaulettes.

'Thanks.' They settled into the back of the car and the driver started signalling his hope of nosing his way into the mass of the cars crawling towards the river. 'To tell you the truth,' Ferrini added quietly, 'I've often regretted it. Oh, I suppose I could hardly have turned down the opportunity, but I was happier as an NCO. Ever since this' – he flicked a finger at an epaulette – 'I've been stuck in an office worrying about how to fight off the next transfer order. You know, when you refused I thought you were a fool. Now . . .'

The two or them had worked together successfully on a transsexual murder case and the Marshal would be eternally grateful to this man for acting as his guide to the underworld. Afterwards, when both of them were offered promotion to officer status, the Marshal had been horrified at the thought of Officer Training School, the exams, and posting to God knows where. He liked his job the way it was and he liked Florence and so did his family.

'At least you're still here,' he pointed out to Ferrini, 'and that's lucky.'

'It's not luck. It's the wife and kids – you know what it's like.'

'I know.'

'You did right. I've managed to stay here, at least for the moment, but the price is being stuck in an office moving paper about. I liked being out on a case, but there's no hope of me getting what I want in Florence. Anybody else my age is a lieutenant colonel and investigations are being run by lads half my age with the same rank. To get the sort of position I want – and I want to be an investigator, always did – I'd have to take a

transfer to some dump where nobody else wants to go.'
He stopped and leaned forward to the driver,
remembering: 'We're dropping the Marshal at the Pitti
Palace first.'

'Yes, sir.'

He leaned back again with a sigh. 'You did the right
thing. You've got your independence and you run your
own shop.'

'Well . . . not just at the moment.'

'How do you mean?'

'I mean, at the moment you're out of your office
investigating and I've certainly no independence on this
job.'

'You're right there. At the beck and call of the civil
police. I never thought I'd see the day. Well, none of it
means anything so it's as long as it's short. What d'you
think of Simonetti, anyway? Because I don't like him.'

'No.'

'Ever work with him?'

'Once.'

'Bit of a steamroller, is he?'

'Mm.'

'Well, I was glad to see you this morning, I can tell
you – is there no other road we can take?' This addition
was to the driver. They hadn't moved more than three
yards upriver.

'No, sir.'

'Well, wave your lolly and whip past up that bus route
or we'll be sitting here till tomorrow.'

The driver did as he was told and they made a heartening burst of speed as far as the next traffic lights. It was raining in earnest now, the big drops hissing and splashing into the churned-up muddy river. The miserable queues at the bus stops huddled down into collars and under umbrellas that blocked the narrow pavements so that passers-by had to step into the road and almost under the wheels of the honking cars.

The queue of traffic on the left bank making for the Ponte Vecchio moved steadily for a while and then snarled up. A municipal policeman, his white helmet streaming with rain, was waving at some invisible transgressor and blowing his whistle angrily.

'I was glad to see you, too,' the Marshal said when the noise level had subsided a bit, 'though I don't know why I should have been there at all, and that's the truth.'

'No?' Ferrini gave him a sidelong look but if he knew the reason he wasn't saying. 'You're right about its being quicker to walk. You'd get wet, though. Thing is not to get flu, at least not until the strategic moment.'

'Is there a strategic moment for getting flu?'

'There will be on this case. You can't afford to waste flu when you don't need it. Listen, I'm thinking, we've about a month's reading to do here in three days.' He patted the file on the seat beside him. 'When you've had a glance through what do you say we get together on it?'

'That's a good idea.' Far from getting through a month's reading in three days the Marshal felt he was likely to need three months.

'Good. You're here. Give me a ring – wait' – he fished out a card – 'use my direct number – and I wouldn't say too much about our getting together. You understand me.'

'Of course.' The Marshal, who had never said too much about anything in his life, nevertheless realized that the situation was anomalous. As he watched his friend being driven away under the stone archway he wondered if other secret alliances were being formed among the six men and what it would all lead to. He didn't feel comfortable about it himself. He didn't feel comfortable at all.

Three

'I'm behind a tree so he can't see me but I can see him. So: he's standing right there looking into the car – it's pitch-black, right, and he's near the car watching them screwing, as close as I am to you now, and he's got a gun in one hand and a knife in the other. I can see the knife glinting. So, I'm standing there, right, and I see them start getting dressed and I can see everything she's got, every detail, and he's standing there, like a statue, he is, and they pull their jeans on but nothing on top and then he shoots. Eight, nine, ten times, he shoots, easy, and then he goes round to the passenger side and starts dragging her out . . .'

His voice trailed off, waiting perhaps for the Marshal to contradict or prompt him, or at least to interrupt with a question, but the Marshal remained silent, bulging eyes expressionless, his big hands planted on the desk before him.

'Anyway . . . so . . . he drags her out and away from the car and he rips her jeans off and opens her legs –'

'Get out,' said the Marshal quietly.

'Wait! He's got the knife –'

'Get out,' repeated the Marshal, and stood up.

The old man on the other side of the desk was small and fat and the buttons of his check shirt barely met over his stomach. His eyes were rheumy and glittering with the pleasure he'd got out of telling even this much of his story.

'There's no call for taking it out on me,' he said, pulling his green overcoat round him and putting his hat on. 'I'm doing my duty telling you, that's all. You ought to thank me.'

'Take yourself off home and don't let me see you in here again or you'll be sorry.'

'I've done no harm . . .'

When the door closed behind him the Marshal went to the window and opened it for a moment, feeling the need for clean air. If this was a foretaste of what life was going to be like once the names of all the investigators were known . . . Not that it was Bertelli's first visit. He was forever coming round with his invented stories, but in the first place he habitually buttonholed one of the younger carabinieri – an eighteen-year-old National Service lad – and would get through quite a long tale before the unsuspecting boy would cotton on. In the second place, his stories were undoubtedly lifted more or less straight from the pornographic magazines his tiny restoration workshop was crammed with, but with the sexes reversed. He would be sitting in the bath, having forgotten to lock the front door and the woman from the next flat would just walk straight in and start touching him, etc., etc.

Now the newspapers were splashing the Monster again he had no need of his magazine stories. The Marshal tried to remember whether he'd been round during the eighties when 'Monster fever' was at its height but he was pretty sure not. He'd probably presented himself at Headquarters across at Borgo Ognissanti to whoever was on the case then.

The door opened behind him. Surely the wretched man wasn't still –

'Marshal?' It was Brigadier Lorenzini. 'There's that young man still waiting to see you. Had you forgotten?'

'Marco. Of course. It had gone out of my head for a minute. Listen, don't let that character in here again, all right?'

He reached for his greatcoat from the coat stand behind the door.

'Give me Signora Dini's handbag and I'll go down to Porta Romana with it.'

'You want me to deal with the young man?'

'He'll come with me. Where is he? Marco?'

Landini stood up as he saw the Marshal come out, buttoning his coat.

'If you haven't got time to see me I'll . . .'

'No, no. If you don't mind a short walk we can talk on the way.' He adjusted his hat and Lorenzini held out the old lady's handbag.

'No, no! For heaven's sake find a polythene bag for it, I can't carry it like that. Well, Marco, I should have called you before now and I'm sorry. It's a bad time.'

'I can imagine. I heard – well, it's in the papers, so . . .'

'Hmph. Let's go.' He took the polythene bag and the two of them went off down the narrow stairs together.

It had been raining on and off for days and the gravel walk they took through the Boboli Gardens behind the palace was soaked. It was both pleasanter and more practical to walk that way rather than down the Via Romana, narrow and busy as it was. The pavement was only wide enough for one person, so it would have been impossible to carry on a conversation, even supposing you could make yourself heard over the echoing din of traffic roaring between the high buildings.

The gardens, on the other hand, were even quieter than usual since the dampness and fog discouraged the tourists visiting the galleries in the palace from venturing out there. Not a single person was sitting on the damp stone tiers of the amphitheatre as they passed below it, and the cats, whose diet was supplemented by what they could cadge in the way of picnic-lunch leavings, wandered about wet and disconsolate and very much disposed to be quarrelsome.

'It's not going to be as easy as I thought.' Marco was searching for a lighter in the pocket of his tweed jacket.

'I imagined at the start that it would be quite straight-forward because Franchi kept very careful records of every one of his paintings, who commissioned them and how much he was paid. It looked as if all I had to do – since this painting doesn't belong to my family – was to prove that no such painting existed, as Franchi had kept no record of it. I'm assuming now it's a forgery. If it isn't, and it does show up in Franchi's records then I'll have to face the fact that it might be stolen. Only it seems it's not that simple. First of all, there are more paintings than he lists, quite a lot more, especially portraits like this one, because during the time when he was court painter here at the Pitti Palace the Grand Duchess, Princess Violante, had him paint all her ladies in waiting for her. Those are all listed by him as commissioned by her but – and it's a big but – he made further copies of those same portraits and I can't count on his having listed all of those.'

'Why should he copy his own pictures?'

'Money. It wasn't always easy to get your money out of people as rich as they were.' He waved a hand to his right where hundreds of orange and lemon trees sheltered from the rigours of winter in the long conservatory. 'They were always keen on commissioning work but less keen on paying for it. Franchi made ends meet by copying those portraits for the young ladies themselves. They, not being rich and powerful, paid up. They got theirs cheaper, of course, since they were copies and took less time and effort to produce, but you can imagine that the Grand Duchess wouldn't have approved of this commercial initiative and, what's worse, in some cases he gave the Princess herself copies because he'd already made portraits of these ladies and been paid by the sitters. I doubt he gave her a discount.'

'No. Well, I see your point. It's a bit difficult . . .'

'You haven't heard the worst. On top of that, Franchi being the most famous painter in town, a lot less famous painters made some pretty efficient copies of his works, sometimes real size, sometimes reduced to cut production costs – and Franchi himself made copies of pictures by painters he admired!'

'In that case it's a real mess.'

'It's a mess all right as far as attribution is concerned and as for my problem . . . wait, I'll show you where I found all this. . .'

They paused a moment beneath the white marble statue of Pegasus, and Marco searched his pockets for a small notebook.

'I found all this out only this morning and I just had to come straight to you. Here: "Ordered on February 10th, 1692 by the Prior of San Marco for the Grand Prince who wished to remove Fra Bartolommeo's beautiful and celebrated painting of San Marco to his own palace, replacing it by a careful copy made by our Antonio Franchi, the most choice of all Florentine painters, who executed same with such exquisite perfection in the imitation that it truly seems to be the original." So there you are.'

'Mmph.'

'So you can imagine. It's a lot more complicated than I bargained for.'

'Can't somebody help you? Somebody expert, I mean.'

'Somebody will have to – at least to read the *Thieme/Becker* for me. I don't know a word of German.'

'Read what?'

'It's the standard dictionary of artists. I thought of getting some German history of art student to help me with that so I wouldn't have to explain anything.'

'No, no, Marco, you can't deal with this on your own –'

'I can't tell anyone. If this picture is a fake, think how many others there might have been. If I'm honest with myself I have to admit that I always knew, or felt, that my father had more money than could be explained but I could hardly say so. Of course, there's no saying how much he made out of authentications and so on, and he was quite capable, anyway, of appearing to be richer than he was. He was a great showman, you know.'

'I can imagine.'

Marco pushed his hands deep into his pockets and looked down at the wet gravel as they walked.

'At times I don't blame him for despising me.'

'And you're going to such lengths to protect him.'

'To protect my mother.'

'But surely, if she wasn't in any way involved . . . And they were divorced.'

'She suffered enough from him when he was alive. Another story of this sort would kill her.'

The Marshal walked on in silence and only a brief sidelong glance betrayed his having registered that 'another'. Marco, his head still lowered, his face dark, seemed unaware of his mistake. They went on their way for a while with only their crunching footsteps and the chinking of birds in the sad wintry laurels for company. The Marshal was willing to bide his time. A forced confidence was never more than half a confidence and he knew Marco well enough to be sure that he was held back by shame, not guilt. A gleam of sunlight was just beginning to penetrate the fog and in its faint warmth the wet bay leaves released their perfume, which mingled with the sharper scent of their pruned and burning branches. The gardeners tidying the laurel maze rising on their left were silent and invisible. Only the thin plumes of smoke told where they were.

'There's one thing I think you should do,' the Marshal said at last, 'and that's go to one of the bigger antique dealers in the city – do you know any of them personally?'

'I know two. One was at school with me and works for his father now in the business.'

'Go to him, then. All of them have a list of stolen paintings to look out for. You must look through it. You know I can't help you, otherwise, with the best will in the world . . .'

'No. Of course you can't. I'm sorry, I shouldn't have –'

'Don't worry about it, just check. I should have thought on and suggested it before. It's just that I've got a lot on my plate at the moment.'

'Without my inventing work for you. I've no business to expect you to talk to Benozzetti – though perhaps if I checked on that list first –'

'Oh, I've seen Benozzetti.'

'You have?'

'And for what it's worth, I think he might well be a forger. Restorer, that's what he says, but there's something there that doesn't smell right. He was defensive and, I thought, a bit crazy.'

'I've heard say that all forgers are a bit crazy. But did he bite? Will he come to the studio?'

'I don't know, Marco. I don't think I made much of a job of it, to be honest.' Again he could only repeat, 'You need an expert.' He did his best to explain about Benozzetti showing him the painting but it was hardly possible since he didn't altogether understand it himself.

'Do you mean it was a copy of one of the paintings in the gallery here?'

'No. A copy, no. It was like it, but there was something different and there was something to do with where I was standing . . . But in any case, the arm or the hand was different and perhaps the way he was sitting . . . No, it wasn't a copy.'

'Then it was just the sort of thing I've been talking about! "In the style of", the way they copied Franchi – or even the way he copied himself, because he'd make little changes like that, especially if the sitter had no say in the matter the first time round because the work was commissioned by the Princess Violante.'

'This wasn't your man, though. This was Titian. I'm sure of that.'

'It was? What was the title?'

'It's a portrait of a man. I don't recall any particular title. I could show it to you. Anyway, he said he was restoring it for the owner but that if anyone from the Ministry of Arts came round he'd say he'd painted it himself and that if they didn't believe it he'd paint another.'

Marco stared at him. 'He sounds crazy all right, but even so, it's quite possible that he's only restoring it and that the owner hasn't declared it to the Ministry. I wish I'd seen it, though, now I've read a bit about these things.'

'Go there.'

'Me?'

'Why not? I've prepared the ground.'

'Well, I was hoping he'd come to me. I want to see him looking at the Franchi painting, if Franchi it is. What's he like, anyway? What does he look like? Act like?'

'Pretty impressive to look at. Well built and very well dressed. Sharp, even if he is a bit crazy . . . Maybe I should say fanatical. Go there and see for yourself if he doesn't get in touch with you.'

'You don't think . . . I wouldn't be a danger to him, would I?'

'No, no. I shouldn't think so.'

'Even though this painting I've got . . . well, it's evidence, isn't it?'

'It isn't evidence of anything, but if it worries you just

wait for him to get in touch and, if you like, I'll try and be there if he comes to see you.'

'And if he doesn't get in touch?'

'You just carry on with your researches and see what you come up with. Something's bound to become clearer if you insist. We'll go out by this gate.'

They left the gardens and came out into Via Romana.

'I don't know if you want to wait for me.' The Marshal indicated the plastic carrier bag. 'I'll have to stay a few minutes with the old lady, check that all her documents are here and so on.'

'I won't, I think. I can get a bus from Porta Romana that will take me right to the studio and I want to get on straightaway with my research. I'll check that list first, I promise you.' He held out his hand. 'Thanks for everything.'

'I haven't been much help, but keep in touch – don't give up on it.'

'I won't. I'll phone you.'

The Marshal pressed the doorbell, watching him walk away. There was something about him . . . He always looked defenceless. A twinge of doubt assailed him for having said Benozzetti wouldn't regard him as dangerous.

'Who is it?'

'Marshal Guarnaccia, signora. I've brought your bag.'

'Ooh, how kind . . .'

Not that he or his men had found it. As usual it was the rubbish collectors. They often found stolen bags emptied of their cash and dumped in wastebins, and people were only too glad to have their cheque books and identity cards returned. That was especially true of someone as elderly and frail as this poor soul who was in no condition to be queuing for hours to get the documents replaced. He had a reason, though, for bringing it back to her rather than sending one of his carabinieri. Teresa had slipped a fifty thousand note into it, knowing that the old lady couldn't possibly survive until next pension day having lost her little all to a drug addict. Knowing, too, that she was too proud to ask for help.

'Another time, signora,' the Marshal suggested, 'you slip your money into your pocket with your keys. Don't carry a handbag in these narrow streets where it's so easy for some lad on a moped to snatch it!'

'Eeh, Marshal, at my age it's difficult to change your habits. It wouldn't feel right to be out without a nice handbag and gloves. I will think about it, though.' She offered him a sweet from the glass dish on the dark polished sideboard. 'I still can't understand this fifty thousand note.'

She smoothed it out and placed it carefully next to the dish on a strip of lace-edged embroidery. The pendulum of a wall clock ticked loudly in the dark room as she sat down opposite him with a little sigh that was the only indication of the terrible pain caused by her arthritic limbs.

'It's not so much a question of your pension being stolen,' insisted the Marshal, 'or even the time and trouble getting new documents would cause you. What I'm worried about is that you might by instinct keep hold of your bag and be dragged into the road. You'd get very badly hurt. I've seen it happen many a time, so think on.'

'I will. I'll remember. Though I don't think there's any chance of my keeping hold of anything with these hands.'

She regarded the shiny twisted joints compassionately as though they were beings apart from her. 'Ah, things have changed since I was young. I'm still trying to think . . . I could swear I only had twenty thousand and a little bit of change – and it was in my purse and that's gone. Of course, my memory's not what it was . . .'

'You probably slipped it in there in an absent moment. Now I must be on my way. You'll remember about not carrying a bag?'

'Oh yes, I'll remember . . .' It was clear to the Marshal that she had already forgotten. 'I'm trying to think if my daughter might have put it in there when she came to see me last month. She lives in Rome now, you know.'

'Yes.' He adjusted his hat at the door and escaped, leaving her with this pleasing if improbable train of thought.

The Marshal walked back up Via Romana, steering carefully so as to allow a shopper to squeeze by him every so often without his having to step into the road in the path of the hurtling orange buses roaring at his back. When he reached the junction at Piazza San Felice he was more than tempted to stop at the brightly lit chemist's where for once there was no queue and the chemist himself was holding court, seated with a couple of local people at the table on the right. The Marshal hesitated as the white-coated man raised a hand in greeting but then, with an inward sigh, he returned the greeting and went on to Piazza Pitti where the huge file on the 'Monster' case awaited his attention. As it happened, quite a number of other things and people were awaiting his attention and at half past eight in the evening the file still lay closed on his desk. He would have preferred not to take it with him but the alternative, coming into his office after supper, was too miserable a thought to contemplate and so he tucked the thing under his arm as he turned out the lights and locked up.

'What have you got there?' Teresa asked, without really looking, as she tried to get to the fridge to open it.

'Nothing.'

'Don't stand there. Aren't you going to have a shower?'

He left the file in the bedroom where there was no chance of the boys seeing it and then got showered and changed. Teresa, with the same idea in mind, waited until the boys had gone to do their homework before asking, as she stacked the plates in the dishwasher, 'How did you get on?'

'It wasn't as bad as I expected.'

'Things never are.'

He told her about young Bacci, whom she'd never met as she'd still been down at home in Sicily in those days.

'But he must be a bit young and inexperienced, surely, for a big case like that?'

'He'll get some experience now, then,' he answered crossly, unwilling to admit that the same thought had crossed his own mind. 'Anyway, he'll be as pleased as punch. He always fancied himself as a detective.' He got up. 'I need a coffee.'

'But you never have coffee after supper.'

'I've got to stay awake, go through some paperwork. I'll make it.'

'I'll go and get the boys moving, then.'

As he waited for the coffee to bubble up he opened the file on the kitchen table. He felt a bit depressed, but it wasn't because of the case. He realized what it was as he poured his coffee out and sat down. It was that this sitting alone in the kitchen with paperwork in front of him was a strong reminder of the bad old days before Teresa and the boys had come up to Florence, released to him by the death of his mother whom Teresa had cared for after her stroke. That was the only time in his life that he'd lived alone and he'd hated every minute of it. And – that was it – talking about the days when Bacci had been with him had been an even stronger reminder. How glad he was now to think of Teresa there, having a moment's peace while the boys were in their room playing and quarrelling instead of doing their homework. He spooned sugar into the thick scalding coffee and drank it in two sips. So stimulated and comforted, he opened the file and faced its terrible contents.

FACTS RELATING TO THE SEVEN DOUBLE HOMICIDES COMMITTED IN THE AREA SURROUNDING FLORENCE BETWEEN 1974 AND 1985 BY PERSON OR PERSONS KNOWN AS THE 'MONSTER'.

1985   On the 9th September 1985 in the early hours of the afternoon the carabinieri on duty in the Station of San Casciano Val di Pesa were informed that in a wooded area adjacent to Via degli Scopeti, a stretch of road linking San Casciano with the Via Cassia which runs between Siena and Florence, a body had just been found. The marshal commanding the station repaired immediately to the zone indicated with his men and established that the body was that of a young man who had received a number of gunshot wounds and knife wounds in various parts of his body. The body itself was partly hidden by scrub and a pile of empty paint tins which had been tossed on to it. In the clearing immediately above it and very close by stood a Volkswagen Golf. The car was white and had French numberplates: beside it a Canadian-style tent had been pitched. The tent showed a large rent in the cloth at the back. Inside lay the naked body of a young woman who likewise had received numerous gunshot and stab wounds. The woman's body also showed evidence of mutilation, the pudenda and left breast having been removed.

It was evident before the autopsy confirmed it, given the mutilation suffered by the female victim and the weapons used to perpetrate the crime, that this was the latest in a series of murders committed by the mysterious criminal which popular fancy had denominated 'The Monster of Florence'. It was also immediately evident that the firearm used was yet again the Beretta 22 Long Rifle, now responsible for 16 deaths.

1968   This weapon, an automatic pistol, of the type frequently used on firing ranges, was first identified after the murder in August 1968 of Belinda Muscas née Lubino and Amadeo Lo Russo to which Belinda Muscas's husband Sergio Muscas confessed. Since Muscas was still serving his sentence when the present series of killings began, it may be assumed that the weapon changed hands after the '68 murder. Muscas later retracted his confession though he was nevertheless condemned to life imprisonment.

1974   Six years after the 1968 murder, on Saturday 14th September 1974 in the Borgo San Lorenzo area to the north of Florence, Piero Galli and Sandra Palladini were murdered in their parked car.

Notified by passers-by, the carabinieri arrived on the scene to find the half-naked body of the young man supine in the driver's seat of a Fiat 127, later established as belonging to his father, whilst that of the girl, completely naked, lay outside and to the rear of the car. The contents of the girl's handbag were scattered around. The bag was later discovered in a nearby field. The girl was supine with the upper and lower limbs spreadeagled and a vine branch inserted in the vagina. At first sight both victims appeared to have been stabbed to death with something in the nature of a screwdriver or an awl but an autopsy later revealed that they had first been shot and then attacked with a knife. The man had received at least five bullet wounds from which he had died immediately. His stab wounds had been inflicted postmortem. The girl had received three bullet wounds in her right arm which had not killed her. She had then been killed with a knife. The autopsy revealed 96 clearly identifiable stab wounds, a few of them mortal but the rest inflicted postmortem, over the entire trunk but concentrated in the abdominal region in the pubic area.

Ballistics reports identified the firearm as a Beretta 22 LR model 73 or 74 and the ammunition as Winchester H series with copper-coated lead bullets. The knife was estimated to be 10/12 cm long and 1.5 cm wide with a single-edged blade.

No connection was made at this stage with the 1968 murder of so long before, particularly as the mutilation of the girl's body indicated that the murderer or murderers in this case must clearly be maniacal and sexually deviant.

Seven years had gone by and the unsolved murder of 1974 was virtually forgotten when on Saturday 6th June 1981 at approximately 23.45 in Via dell'Arrigo, Scandicci, another young courting couple was murdered. The bodies of Gino Fani and Caterina Di Paola were discovered accidentally by a police sergeant taking a country walk near his home at 9 o'clock on the morning after the crime, together with his small son. The sergeant first noticed a Fiat Ritmo, dark red in colour, parked in the lane. Its doors were closed but on the ground near the driver's side lay a woman's handbag with its contents scattered around it. Closer inspection revealed the driver's window to be smashed. Sitting at the wheel of the car, the head turned inwards, was the body of a bearded young man with wounds in the throat.

The sergeant gave the alarm and was joined by a squad car bringing his colleagues. Only after this did they discover, at the bottom of a steep bank falling away from the road, the body of a girl lying supine with legs apart. Her T-shirt and jeans were ripped and slashed revealing that the pubic area had been crudely excised. The body lay approximately 20 yards from the car but there were no signs of its having been dragged.

The victims were transported to the Medico-Legal Institute where an autopsy revealed that both had died from gunshot wounds whilst still inside the car. Successively, the man had received three stab wounds, two of them near the neck and superficial, the third a deeper wound in the chest. The excision of the girl's pudenda had been done with an extremely sharp knife. The clothing, particularly the belt, jeans and pants, had been slashed with great precision and decisiveness, denuding in one stroke the area to be excised without the slightest damage to the underlying skin. According to the pathologist, Professor Mario Forli, this implied some skill and experience on the part of the murderer. Further, the cleanness of the cuts excising the pudenda and the evenness indicated an ability in the use of cutting instruments and that in his opinion this constituted a point of *considerable, even decisive importance.* A witness saw a car, a red Taurus, parked a few metres from the scene of the crime that night.

The ballistics reports indicated that the two people were killed by a minimum of seven wounds from a firearm and that the said firearm was a Beretta 22-calibre automatic pistol used in the Galli/Palladini murder of 1974. The ammunition was also of the same type, Winchester H, but in this case the bullets were not copper coated.

Only a very few months were to pass before the next murder of a young courting couple. Silvio Benci and Sara Contini went out on the evening of Thursday 22nd October because there was to be a general strike the next day so they needn't get up for work. At the end of their evening out they parked their car in a country lane between the vineyards near Calenzano to the north of Florence. Their bodies were discovered lying on each side of their VW Golf, the man half naked and riddled with bullet and stab wounds; the girl lying supine near the edge of a ditch with similar wounds and the pubis excised. Dr Forli concluded in his autopsy report that both had been shot through the front window on the passenger side of the car and that they were still alive when the first stab wounds were inflicted. The knife was single edged, approximately 3 cm wide and not less than 5–7 cm long. The bodies showed signs of having been dragged.

The excision appeared to have been done with the same knife as the stabbing but differed from the preceding murder in that it was done with considerably less precision and took in a much larger area so that the abdominal wall had been cut through all its layers, leaving a large area of the abdominal cavity exposed and part of the intestine punctured.

Ballistics reports identified the same Beretta 22 used in the two preceding murders. A red Alfa GT was seen leaving the scene by two couples approaching it in search of somewhere to park. An Identikit was prepared from their description of the lone male driver.

1982   The murderer struck again on 19th June 1982 at approximately 23.45 in the countryside near Montespertoli to the south west of Florence. This time the victims of the Beretta 22 Long Rifle were Piero Merlini and Anna Montini, both residents of Montespertoli. They had parked in a little clearing off the country road where a stream ran parallel to the road on the opposite side. For the first time the killer made a mistake. He failed to shoot the young man to death in seconds as he had always done before. Merlini, badly wounded but still capable of movement, managed to start his car and tried to drive away. In his panic-stricken attempt to back out of the clearing he overshot the road and backed his car into the stream where it stuck. The killer calmly following him, shot out the front lights with one bullet each. After emptying his pistol into the two victims he smashed the rear lights with some pointed object and removed the car keys which he tossed away. The killer was sufficiently disturbed by the episode as to leave without further damage to the bodies. In fact, Merlini was not dead. He died in hospital at 8 a.m. the following day without regaining consciousness.

Nine cartridge cases were found at the scene, one inside the car, the rest in three groups, the first group of three in the clearing and mixed with fragments of glass from the left front car window, the second two, at the edge of the road just out of the clearing, and the third near the opposite side of the road. It was through this grouping of the cartridge cases that the dynamics of the killing were established.

1983   Little more than a year later, on the night of 9th September 1983, in a grassy clearing near Galluzzo to the south of Florence, two German boys, Herman Mainz and Ulrich Richter, were shot to death in their Volkswagen camper. Although the murder was committed with the same Beretta 22, no-further damage was done to the bodies, possibly because the killer realized on entering the camper that he had made a mistake. Ulrich Richter had very long wavy blond hair and he may well have mistaken him for a girl.

It should be mentioned here that at the time of the Mainz/Richter murder the Beretta had already been identified as that used in the Muscas/Lo Russo murder of 1968.

Late in the evening of Sunday 29th July 1984, in Vicchio di Mugello to the north of Florence, a young couple, Carlo Salvini and Patrizia Renzetti, were murdered in their parked car. The murder showed all the characteristics of the previous ones: the new moon, the car parked in a country lane, a course of water nearby. The dead boy was found on the back seat of the car wearing only a vest and underpants. Not far from the car, behind a bush, lay the completely naked body of the girl, supine with legs apart. The pudenda and left breast had been cut away. The autopsy established that both victims had been shot through the car window and then attacked with the knife. The body of the girl, who had already taken off her jeans, was dragged by the ankles to a distance of about 10 yards. The killer had then removed her T-shirt and brassiere and ripped and cut away her pants. For the first time he cut away the left breast as well as the pudenda. The instrument was a single-edged knife with the same characteristics as that used in the previous mutilations.

Ballistics reports established that the firearm used was the Beretta 22 Long Rifle series 70 of the previous killings.

1985 The last in this series of killings was the above-mentioned murder of the French couple, Nathalie Monde and Maurice Clément, camping in the San

Casciano area in 1985. The autopsy carried out by Professor Forli on the woman's body, which was closed inside the tent, showed that the victim had been hit by four bullets, three of which penetrated the skull, and one the thorax. The man had been hit by four bullets, one in the mouth, two in the upper left arm and one in the right elbow. All the shots were fired at close quarters, estimated at not more than 15–20 inches, some from outside the tent, some from inside, but all from the front opening. It is probable that the man was lying supine with the woman on top of him. The woman died from the gunshot wounds whilst still inside the tent but the man, who was only superficially wounded, attempted to escape. He succeeded in getting out of the tent and ran for approximately 30 yards in the direction of the woods before the killer overtook him and stabbed him to death. He was then lifted and thrown down the bank into the scrub where the body was discovered.

According to the pathologist, the woman's naked body was then dragged partially out of the tent by the feet and the pudenda removed with ample and decisive strokes. The left breast was then cut away with a technique similar to that used on Patrizia Renzetti. Finally, the body of the woman was put back into the tent. The whole operation is estimated to have been completed within 9 minutes.

On the day following the crime an envelope was delivered to the Public Prosecutor's office, addressed to the only woman prosecutor to have worked on the case. The address was formed from letters cut from a magazine and contained a spelling mistake. Inside was a sheet of paper folded and glued at its edges. Inside the paper container was a small polythene bag. The bag contained a cube of flesh from Nathalie Monde's left breast.

Four

A thread of gilding glittered through the clean green and white marble of San Miniato for a moment and then the façade was swallowed in evergreen as the car neared the top of the avenue. The city spread itself below them to the right. It must have rained yet again during the night and the pattern of red roofs glowed this morning in the mild November sunshine.

'River's swollen,' remarked Ferrini. 'You can always tell by that yellowy colour and the thick shine on it. I saw some film once of the flood. Did you ever see it?'

'Yes. I saw it.'

'Buses being tossed along through the streets like they were matchwood. The place looks better from up here.'

More than anything it looked so quiet and sleepy, its

towers and domes rising out of the terracotta tapestry in the tepid misty light. The truth was that they were obliged to drive this way because they would otherwise have been trapped in the snarling filth of the traffic down there for hours. Ferrini turned away to look at Guarnaccia, silent behind his dark glasses.

'You don't look too suited. Disapprove of his Nibs's speech this morning, did you?'

'I can't say I understood it.'

'You were here in the eighties, surely?'

'Well,' admitted the Marshal, 'I was, but I had better things to do than follow all the ins and outs of some Instructing Judge's squabble with the Public Prosecutor's office.'

'In that case, take my advice. Get the ins and outs of it sorted now or you'll put your foot in it and that wouldn't do at all, not with our friend Simonetti at the helm. Where do we go first? Scandicci, I suppose, if they're turning here.'

There were four cars in the procession, all of them unmarked. All of the passengers were in plain clothes. They didn't want to attract too much attention as they visited the scenes of the Monster's crimes. Simonetti had actually called him the Monster, which had surprised the Marshal, though, of course, he did so himself, as everyone did. He had no other name. Simonetti's explanation had been plausible enough. The rest of his speech, too, had been plausible enough but the Marshal, whilst admitting he didn't understand it, hadn't believed it either.

'I feel bound to make a purely lexical observation before going any further. If I have used, and continue to use, the term "Monster" during the investigation to indicate the author of the crimes, this is for merely practical, time-saving purposes and is absolutely devoid of any moral weight, much less of critical weight. No value judgement is implied.

'I would also remind you that the official clearing of the names of all the Angius family by the Instructing Judge formerly involved in this investigation means that the line of enquiry involving the Sardinian group connected with the 1968 murder of Belinda Muscas and Amadeo Lo Russo is now closed. The Instructing Judge's report was punctilious, comprehensive and highly detailed and it was from him that we were given to understand that the confusing, contradictory and, I might say, evanescent elements of that story never had and can never have any value in a court of law.

'Nevertheless, the conviction for this murder in 1970 of Belinda Muscas's husband, Sergio Muscas, should not necessarily be regarded as definitive despite his confession, later retracted. The convicted man, even whilst insisting on his own guilt, clearly demonstrated that the crime could not have been perpetrated in the manner he described and that one or more persons other than himself must have been involved. This is clearly not the moment to try to get to the bottom of what might or might not have been a crime of passion, just as it might or might not have been some sort of settling of accounts between rival Sardinian clans.

Sufficient to say that for the purpose of our present investigation the Sardinian line is irrelevant, given that the Beretta 22, the only solid fact which connects that crime to those of the Monster could only too easily have changed hands between 1968 and 1974.'

And that was that. The 'Instructing Judge formerly involved' and his years of fruitless struggle were consigned to the archives. The Marshal knew too little about it all to have any real opinion on the matter. He did, however, have a real opinion about Simonetti who was making signs at their driver now from the larger car slowing down in front.

'Surely we're not here . . . ?' The Marshal peered out. They were still on an asphalted road.

'He's pointing out the disco, here to the right.'

A strange pagoda-shaped building set in a garden at a fork in the road.

'They left there about eleven and drove on up the hill here to park.' The cars picked up speed again between an olive grove high on their left and orchards and vineyards sloping down to their right.

'Here we are.' The cars were slowing again and turning into a narrow country lane.

'Have you been here before?' The Marshal felt around for his hat, remembered he wasn't in uniform and opened the car door.

'In the good old days when I was a marshal I worked on this case for a bit, '81 and again in '83. This one was '81.'

They left the cars and walked a little further along the gravelly ochre lane, breathing in the sweet damp air that still smelled faintly of wine lees. To one side of them tiny black and green beads ripened among silvery olive branches and on the other, red and yellow leaves fell from the vines as tiny birds searched for the treasure of some forgotten bunch of grapes, withered and sweet with a bloom of mildew on them.

'The boy's body was in the car, as you know . . .' Simonetti consulted his clipboard, loaded with maps and photographs. 'And the girl's body lay here. Now, there are two possible versions: one is that, since the body wasn't dragged, he carried her this distance before working on her with the knife. The other is that she was trying to escape and he caught up with her here.'

'Excuse me . . . ?' It was young Lieutenant Bacci who had travelled in the last car and was now standing behind the Marshal. 'I understand she'd been hit by five bullets so does that mean the first hypothesis is the more likely – ?'

'I'll make one thing clear,' Simonetti said with a smile hardly consonant with his words. 'I'm not interested in hypotheses. There have been enough hypotheses in the past about these crimes to last us all a lifetime. If we don't know something for sure we don't know it. Full stop. And while we're about it, I'll say a word on another, to some extent related, subject. If you look around you you'll see that the scene of the crime consists of a country lane, some trees and bushes, a nearby stream. The crime was committed between ten and twelve on a night of the new moon. You will find that these conditions will be the same at every one of the seven scenes we visit and we've heard enough hypotheses about that to last us a lifetime, too. I am not interested in occult explanations of any of these conditions and I'm telling you this because the idiotic explanations of these things didn't come from the newspapers as one might reasonably expect, but from people calling themselves serious investigators. As far as this enquiry is concerned, the new moon is the darkest time of the month when a lurking murderer can reasonably expect not to be seen lurking. Likewise he needs bushes or vines to hide behind just as he needs water to wash off the blood after his butchering activities. And since couples who park their cars to make love do so in a quiet country lane and not, as a rule, on the motorway, I think that deals with the matter.'

Simonetti began to move towards his car. Ferrini made a wry face at the Marshal and murmured, 'A perfectly sane explanation. Pity we're dealing with a maniac . . .'

But the Marshal was watching the unfortunate Bacci who had provoked the tirade and had to resist giving the lad a comforting pat on the shoulder. Bacci was his superior officer. His poor young face was white.

They drove on across the hills, taking in all the sites to the south of Florence, Montespertoli, Gli Scopeti, Galluzzo. As they drove, the mist on the hills thickened and the smudge of the city visible in the valley far below became fainter and fainter until, just after eleven, it began to rain. At the last scene to the south, near Galluzzo, their feet were sinking into the already well-moistened ground and fat raindrops dislodged the last of the glowing leaves from the vines. In the distance, the bruised sky was punctuated by black cypresses and umbrella pines. Beneath their wet boots plastic carrier bags were trodden in with cigarette packets, syringes, bits of used condoms and scraps of pages torn from pornographic magazines.

They used the motorway to bypass the city and reach the hills to the north. The Marshal continued to stick close to Ferrini who, every so often, was able to pass him some titbit of remembered information that hadn't figured in the written synopsis they had been given.

'That was when they arrested Sassetti, a Peeping Tom. Remember?'

'Vaguely.'

'He was chatting in the bar early on Sunday morning about the Monster having struck again when nobody had found the bodies. Well, he'd found them, of course. He made no bones about his Saturday night activities but he never said a word about what he'd seen or found. They say he was terrified of something. Can you imagine what he could have been frightened of that was worse than being in prison accused of being the Monster?'

'Not really . . .'

'Me neither. They had to let him out, of course, in October when the Monster did for these two here.'

They were now standing around a stone cross marking the spot where Silvio Benci and Sara Contini had been found. It stood between rows of vines and carried their names and the legend: ' "They died for love", October 22, 1981.'

The six men were standing with their backs to the lane where their cars were parked whilst Simonetti consulted his clipboard. To their right loomed the great bulk of the Calvana, the mountain plateau which divided this area from Prato to the north. It was a cold and inhospitable-looking mass at the best of times. Banks of dirty cloud rolled along its flat top and its slopes looked so dark a blue as to be almost black. The Marshal glanced back at the cross and then up at the menacing wet mass.

'The Sardinian line of enquiry . . .' murmured Ferrini, reading his thoughts.

Up there, as they both knew, Sardinian bandits and shepherds inhabited lightless, long-abandoned cottages. There they made their cheeses, hid machine guns, pistols, chloroform, kidnap victims. The police couldn't get anywhere near them without being spotted half an hour before their arrival and the ground was too rough and stony to land a helicopter. It was a sinister place, as sinister as the place marked by the stone cross. Prosecutor Simonetti kept his back turned to it and continued his perfectly sane account of how a man attacked two complete strangers and took away with him parts of the woman's body.

'In this case the mutilation was more vicious and more extensive, exposing as it did a large part of the intestine and even perforating it. A large lump of subcutaneous fat was found stuck to the inside of the girl's thigh.

Gentlemen, at this point I think we should break for lunch.'

In the restaurant, the Marshal noted that the young policeman who, up to now, had never opened his mouth, was sticking as close to Bacci as he himself was to Ferrini. He was evidently attempting to get some sort of conversation going with Bacci without attracting any attention, but Bacci, no doubt still stinging from Simonetti's tirade earlier, was pretty unresponsive. The two police investigators were equally silent but for different reasons. From what the Marshal knew of them they weren't the type to waste breath on hypotheses, much less polite chatter. They saved their breath for the moment when they could use it to say, 'I arrest you . . .' and in the meantime used it to cool their pasta. One of them had an angry-looking scar on the back of the hand turning his fork, which was almost certainly the result of a stray bullet. The Marshal reached for the grated cheese and wondered with an inward sigh what Teresa and the boys were having for lunch.

The light was dying when they reached the last scene, which, in fact, was that of the first of the maniac's crimes in 1974. The rain was coming down more heavily now so that shoulders and feet were soaked and tempers short.

'Marshal . . . ?'

'Lieutenant.'

Bacci had been eyeing the Marshal for some time, as the latter well knew, before deciding to speak.

'I just wondered . . .' He glanced to his right where

Simonetti was talking intensely with one of the investigators who every now and then nodded and looked about him as he listened. 'You don't mind if I ask your advice?'

'Not at all.'

'It's just that . . . You've worked with him before, haven't you?'

'Once.' There was no need to name him. 'Just forget it. Don't worry about it.'

'I can't really help worrying. This is such a very important case and, apart from that, the fact that we're working together with the police means we really ought to try to put up a good show. Don't you agree?'

The Marshal began moving towards the car.

'The last thing I want to do,' insisted Bacci, following, 'is to make a bad impression.'

'Don't worry about it. He was just using you to make that speech to us all. It wasn't anything personal.'

'But even so . . .' Bacci glanced over his shoulder to where Simonetti was now deep in intimate conversation with both investigators, one of whom was listening, the other smoking and looking in another direction. Simonetti's driver had got out of the car and was holding an umbrella over him but the other two seemed indifferent to the rain falling steadily on their heads.

'Those two, for instance, Esposito and Di Maira . . . They solved that big drug case, do you remember? The one where they were exporting heroin in shoe boxes. And Esposito – he got that bullet wound in a shoot out in

Piazza Santa Maria Novella. I heard him telling Noferini at one point when we were up at Galluzzo.'

'Noferini? Is he the young policeman?'

'The lieutenant, yes.'

'Well, take my advice. Stick close to him. Talk to him. He'll always know more about it than you do. Take your lead from him. It's their show, this, don't forget it.'

'I won't. The last thing I want to do is to blot my copybook at this stage.'

'You're due for promotion, you mean.'

'It's not only that – I shouldn't be bothering you with my business . . .'

'No, no . . . Leaving aside all else, I've known you a long time – since you were what? Eighteen or so, I suppose.'

'Eighteen, yes. Anyway, you know my situation, my mother being widowed, and so on, and my sister still at university . . . It's been a bit difficult.'

'You've been a good son.'

'I hope so, but . . . In short, I want to get married and once I've got this promotion, on a captain's pay I think I can manage it all . . .'

'Good. Good.' The Marshal put an approving hand on Bacci's shoulder. 'I hope she deserves you.'

'Oh yes.' The young man's face was pink. 'She's . . .'

'Good, good.'

'But you see, Marshal, I don't want her to have to work – oh, she can as long as she wants to, I don't mean it in that way, in an old-fashioned way. She enjoys her job, she teaches Italian in a school for foreign students.

But we do want children and with the best will in the world I'll be no help to her – you know what it's like in this job.'

'I know.' Nobody knew better after those long years of lonely separation. But how much worse it must have been for his wife with two small children and his sick mother on her hands. 'You're right there.'

'Well, all I mean is that at least I should provide enough money for her not to be forced to work when she shouldn't need to. And now, being chosen for this case might mean that I'll get to be a captain a bit sooner than otherwise . . . You know what I mean.'

The Marshal didn't. 'Has that been said?'

'Well, hinted at. As long as I do a good job.'

'I see. Lieutenant, we're getting wet.'

'Of course. I'm sorry, I didn't mean to –'

'I suggest you get into your car.' The Marshal himself looked about along the roadside for a flat stone to scrape the mud and wet grass from his boots and, failing to find one, scraped and rubbed them clean as best he could on a small grassy hillock.

Ferrini was already in the car. The windscreen wipers were on fast and the heater was quickly steaming up the windows. They had to wait a moment until they cleared.

'Christ, I'm soaked,' grumbled Ferrini. 'Is that heater on full? A friend of yours, is he, that youngster?'

'Bacci? I've known him since he was eighteen. He was with me at Pitti before he went to the Military Academy.'

'You'd better keep an eye on him, then. He looks a bit

ingenuous to me to be coming up against Simonetti. Put his foot right in it this morning.'

'Yes. Well, I've warned him to take his cue from that police lieutenant, Noferini, I think he was called.'

'You did right. That one knows which side his bread's buttered on. A bit of a whizz kid with computers, too, I've heard. Did all the preliminary work on this job. Legend has it they started with about a hundred thousand names which, if you think about it, must cover every able-bodied male in Florence. Then they reduced it to those with previous convictions for violence and so forth.'

'And now?'

'And now we wait and see. Last I heard it was down to ten but it beats me what happens after that. You knock on ten doors asking, "Excuse me, sir, are you by any chance the Monster?" "No," he says, "I'm not." Thank you very much and goodbye. This rain's coming down even harder. Turn that heating down a bit, now, will you? Sweating on the inside and soaked on the outside. What a day!'

The rain was indeed coming down even harder, rattling against the windscreen so that the wipers at their fastest could barely keep it clear, and spraying up under their wheels. Once they hit the road into the northern periphery of the city they were obliged to sit in long queues with the rain beating steadily on the roof and angry horns hooting before and behind them. Ferrini talked on, as steady as the rain, explaining the quarrel, the rift between the Public Prosecutor's office and the examining magistrate.

'Of course, you could understand the PP's impatience to a certain extent. It had been going on for years, the newspapers wrote about nothing else. There had been four different monsters arrested and each time the real one struck again. If you ask me, nobody concerned knew what they were doing or even what they ought to be doing. They were all running round like scalded hens.'

'I'm not surprised. I don't know what I'd have done in their place. It's all so bizarre.'

'All right, it's bizarre. But I know what I'd have done. I'd have run it like a routine murder enquiry, run all the usual checks and looked for an informer because there'd have been one. You can't tell me that all those Peeping Toms trailing around the countryside on a Saturday night didn't come across him. To hell with bizarre, it was the way they were running the enquiry that was bizarre! They were so busy with their psychological profiles and weird explanations that half the routine work went for a burton. Did you ever hear of a murder case where nobody checks the victim's blood group? Anyway, the PP's office was fed up to the back teeth and this new enquiry was started up whilst the Sardinian one was still running. A compromise, they called it. That was in '84. "A different approach" was what Simonetti called it when the new investigation was set up with the present Chief Proc in charge and Simonetti as his sidekick. Worked out very nicely for them both, all things considered. "A fresh, unprejudiced approach," they said. "No Sardinians need apply." Then, when the Instructing Judge protested

Simonetti said to him, "If your theories are correct then our respective results must converge." Never crossed his mind, naturally, that if they didn't he might have got it wrong.'

That was exactly the way the Marshal's thoughts had been running that first morning as he'd listened to Simonetti holding forth. Always so sure of being right, even in the face of incontrovertible evidence of being wrong.

'It's true, of course,' he pointed out now in an excess of fair-mindedness, 'that's what would happen if they were both right.'

'In a perfect world,' Ferrini laughed, 'they'd both be right and they'd both be able to prove they were right and they'd each be holding half the physical evidence and the Monster could be photographed between them confessing all. It's not a scene I can easily imagine, I don't know about you. And if any physical evidence does turn up I can tell you now that, whoever finds it, it'll be ours. Past experience. In any case, by this time we're on our own so no converging need be looked for. All we're looking for is a likely suspect who can be put behind bars and, unlike the last four, stay there. Open that window just a crack, there's steam coming off us – No, no! Forget I said that. We don't want a shower.' The driver pressed the button and the window slid back up. 'No signs of it letting up . . . If there's one thing I can't stand it's people who lean on their horns in traffic jams – look at that stupid sod trying to get past us on the pavement . . .

Imbecile! What was I saying? Oh, yes. Now, our pal the Monster – or Cicci, the Monster of Scandicci, as he's popularly known, packed in years ago, in 1985, for reasons unknown. Could be dead, could have left the country, could be inside. Anyway, it's been long enough for safety. I mean, if we get it wrong again we won't get found out, shouldn't do, anyway. The odds are against it and luck tends to follow people like Simonetti, don't you find?'

'I suppose so . . .' There was no getting away from the fact that all these ideas had passed, however briefly, through his mind as they'd tramped from murder scene to murder scene throughout the long wet day. Even so, when his own thoughts were put into words by Ferrini they seemed somehow heavier, cruder.

'You're a bit cynical. . .' was his only comment.

'Come on, Guarnaccia, what else can you be in this job?'

The Marshal stared out at the rain and exhaust fumes, the huddled shoppers trying to protect their legs from splashing cars, the polythene sheets over the greengrocer's wares. Ferrini was right about that, at least: there was no sign of it letting up. He'd always had a sharp tongue in his head, the Marshal remembered that from when they'd worked on the transsexual murder together. Still, he had been cynical then but now he was bitter with it. Of course, it could have been that, working alone on a case they'd had a good handle on, they'd been too absorbed in the job for this sort of chitchat. They'd been left strictly alone to get on with it, too, which was a rare pleasure. So, maybe it wasn't Ferrini who'd changed but the situation. Or it was since he'd been promoted to officer. Thank God, the Marshal thought, that he'd refused. Not that he'd imagined what the problems might be. He just didn't want to go back to school and make a fool of himself. Nor did he want to start moving about the country again, uprooting his wife and children every few years. He was very happy where he was, Monster or no Monster. One way or another, this would eventually be over and he'd be back to stolen cameras and lost bicycles and worrying about having enough men to guard the openings of exhibitions in the galleries . . . Here they were, thank heavens . . .

The huge stones darkened with rain and the black iron bars at the ground-floor windows gave the long façade a prison-like air, but for the Marshal the Pitti Palace was home and he had to suppress a sigh of relief as the car splashed to a stop in the wet gravel at the entrance.

'I expect I'll see you tomorrow.' He opened the car door.

'What you want to do' – Ferrini prodded him sharply in the upper arm – 'is to read the Instructing Judge's report.'

'I expect you're right . . .'

What he wanted to do, the Marshal thought, getting himself up the stairs as fast as he could and feeling in his pocket for keys, was have a long hot shower. And what's more, nothing, he said to himself, is going to stop me.

To make sure that nothing did he went straight to his

quarters without checking in with young Brigadier Lorenzini.

'Salva? Is that you? Good heavens, you're wet through.'

'I know.'

'If you're getting back into uniform, have a good hot shower first.'

'I will.'

'And then a hot drink. Do you want coffee or do you fancy hot chocolate?'

'Anything. Coffee.'

And within minutes the hot water was pouring over him, bringing comfort to every damp and aching bone and sluicing away monsters and murders and public prosecutors all. He lingered as long as he decently could with the water as hot as he could bear, gradually relaxing with the thought that the rest of the evening was his own, or at least could be spent in his own familiar world, in his own familiar uniform doing his own job.

He lingered in the kitchen, too, standing there, coffee cup in hand, trying to make the tiny espresso last.

'Oh, do sit down, Salva!'

'I haven't time.' And he stood there, at peace with the world, as Teresa squeezed past him.

'I'm trying to get out to the shops if you'll let me unload the dishwasher.'

'Am I in your way . . . ? You can't go out in this!'

'I'll have to. I've nothing for the boys' school snack tomorrow. I suppose I could wait half an hour or so and see if it stops . . .'

She paused and looked out of the window at the steady drumming rain. He put down his cup and went over to stand behind her. 'Wait till it stops,' he advised her. 'There's no great hurry, is there? Don't get wet.'

He enveloped her small form in a big hug.

'I must get back to the office.'

Not for the first time, as he entered the waiting room, he thanked God for Brigadier Lorenzini in whose hands he could safely leave his station. Two people sat waiting, pretending to read back issues of *The Carabinieri*. Both looked up at him hopefully as he entered and greeted them politely, then went back to leafing through their magazines as he popped his head round the corner of the duty room. Di Nuccio sat there typing furiously with two fingers and his colleague was talking quietly to the two men out on patrol through the radio switchboard. The Marshal opened the door of his own office where Lorenzini was at the desk, apparently concluding a piece of business. The heavy young man in front of him was getting to his feet and putting away the log book of a car. The Marshal nodded to him as he let him out.

'Stolen car?'

Lorenzini got up and gathered a stack of papers together. 'A found car, if you can believe it. We'd found it before he'd even noticed it was stolen. Whoever stole it couldn't find anywhere to park it so he left it in the middle of the road. What sort of a day did you have?'

'Wet. We did seven crime scenes, four of them in heavy rain.'

'Cheery. Why seven and not eight?'

'Simonetti's not interested in the '68 murder. I suppose he's right. It was a normal murder, not a serial killer job, and weapons do change hands,' he said.

'A *murder* weapon?'

'I know. It's not true. Of course, though, it could have been stolen.'

'Hm. Funnily enough . . . it's the only one I've seen – scene of the crime, I mean. I used to live near Signa as a kid.'

'You? But you can hardly have been born in '68.'

'I was four. I don't mean I was round there the day after the murder, budding investigator! No, it was just a kids' game later when I was at school. We used to call it the haunted lane and see if we could frighten ourselves to death going down there alone on dark winter afternoons, pretending to search for the gun in the stream.'

'Pity you didn't find it.'

'I bet we would have done if it had been there. Whoever owned the land must have got fed up with us in the end and he put a chain and padlock on the entrance to the lane. Oh, well, I've got two more people to see out there.'

'I'll deal with them.'

'You don't mind? I could get the paperwork on this car seen to.'

'Show them in.' The Marshal eased himself into his familiar chair with a sigh of pleasure. 'Are they together?'

''Fraid not. And one of them's foreign. Are you sure . . . ?'

'Show him in, show him in.'

The undersigned complainant, Raymond Poigne, born in Sheffield, Great Britain, 1947, who thought his camera might have been stolen, though it was true, as his wife Marilyn had said to him, that he could have left it in that last bar and who was sorry he couldn't speak Italian but knew a bit of French if that could help, must have been as surprised as he was pleased to find himself greeted like a long-lost friend.

ANOTHER MONSTER!
5th time lucky?

At a press conference held yesterday evening at Police Headquarters, Prosecutor Simonetti announced that he would shortly make a formal accusation against the man he believes to be the Monster of Florence. The Prosecutor was not prepared to reveal the name at this stage, but the Anti-Monster Squad has been increased to double its former size and is working round the clock. The Prosecutor described a visit today to all the scenes of the Monster's crimes, a visit undertaken in absolute secrecy and in plain clothes. Despite pressure from journalists he made no revelations about what he had discovered, or even what precisely he was looking for. 'It was vital that we checked every scene,' he said, 'though I can't say anything further at this stage. The reason for secrecy must be obvious:

we could hardly have got on with our business surrounded by journalists.'

Asked if he was confident about the new accusation given past form the Prosecutor was emphatic: 'I am absolutely confident that the Monster will not strike again. I know over the past few years public opinion has tended towards the idea that the Monster enquiry was suspended or even consigned to the archives, but this is not the case. It was precisely when everything appeared static that we were working our hardest on every possible hypothesis. No stone has been left unturned.'

The Prosecutor pointed out that his office had been dealing all the while with its normal workload and that it was a measure of the commitment of his men that they had nevertheless achieved so much, considering the complexity of the case.

So what is really new about this enquiry to bring it to the headlines?

'First and most importantly, we're using new methods, much more sophisticated methods. The serial killer is a totally new and unknown phenomenon in the criminality of this country. This means we're starting from scratch. To understand the type of murderer we are dealing with we have had the series of killings analysed by a team of psychiatrists and psychologists, ballistics experts and police pathologists. We knew with their help what we were looking for.'

Did this mean that past errors would not be repeated?

'Certainly. But that is in no sense a criticism of the work done on this case in the past, all of which was necessary and carried out with great scrupulousness.'

And the rumour about a hundred thousand men being checked? Was there any truth in it?

'Yes, more or less. On the list of names we imposed a catalogue of sex-related offences and on that again a catalogue of convictions for violence. We also checked out hundreds of licence plates of people coming into the city from motorway exits on certain dates.'

Adding all that to the number of people already kept under observation over the past ten years, how many people must have been checked all together?

'Thousands. There was a period when we were literally submerged under anonymous letters. Wherever there was a shadow of genuine doubt or suspicion we did a house search. This was always done with the greatest delicacy and care so as not to damage the reputation of an innocent man. In very, very few cases did the news leak out despite all our precautions. Our net was spread very wide in a way that only the use of a computer could render possible.'

The famous, or infamous, Beretta 22 is still missing.

'For the moment it's still missing. We did a census of all 22-calibre pistols sold before 1968 in Florence, Tuscany and elsewhere. We began with the Beretta factory and the thousands of pistols supplied to the retailers. Then we checked the customers but, of course, that only took us so far because, as you can imagine, after that anything can happen. Guns change hands, they're stolen, and so on. A dozen people could have owned that Beretta for all we know, and still we had to check the obvious which in itself took months.'

And still the Beretta 22 is missing?

'And we're still looking.'

THE OTHER VICTIMS

The Monster may have slain innocent young couples but the list of his victims doesn't end there. Many more lives have been destroyed by his hand, though he has always 'intervened' in the end and secured their release from prison where they were held, accused of his crimes.

FLAVIO VARGIUS. Sardinian, builder, married with 3 children. In the '60s he was the lover of the murdered Belinda Muscas, first victim of the Beretta 22. It was Belinda's husband, Sergio Muscas, who accused Flavio of the murder of his wife and her new lover, but Flavio had an alibi and Sergio was arrested and convicted of the murder. Throughout his trial he continued to accuse Vargius but he was given 14 years and also convicted of calumny. When the enquiry was reopened in 1982 because of the Beretta connection with the Monster's crimes, Sergio Muscas again accused Flavio, who was arrested for the '68 murder and suspected of the Monster's killings to date. He proved a tough nut to crack when interrogated in prison and had to be released after the killing of the two German boys in their camper in Galluzzo. Flavio was later arrested in France for traffic in drugs.

SILVANO VARGIUS. Builder, brother to Flavio, married, one child, the last in the line of suspects. Brought into the limelight in 1985 when he was accused of murdering his wife Margherita in Sardinia in 1960 and passing her death off as suicide. In 1986 he was suspected of the '68 murder at Signa since he, even before his brother, had been the lover of Belinda Muscas; following on this he was suspected of being the Monster, though the accusation was never formalized. He was acquitted in 1988 of the murder of his wife and vanished on his release from prison. In 1989 Instructing Judge Romola acquitted him of the informal charges relating to the double homicides.

SERGIO MUSCAS. Widower, one child, at the centre of the 1968 Muscas/Lo Russo murder enquiry.

Never actually accused of being the Monster since he was in prison when the crimes started, but returned to centre stage when the Beretta 22 connection reopened the '68 case in 1982. He continued to accuse his wife's lovers, particularly the Vargius brothers, and then made the same allegations against his own brother, Fabio. At the time of his conviction for the murder of his wife, Belinda, and her lover he was also convicted of calumny.

FABIO MUSCAS. Became involved in the Monster enquiry through his brother Sergio who, after having accused his wife's lovers, particularly Flavio Vargius, changed his story and accused his brother Fabio. Fabio was arrested in January 1984 on a warrant issued by Instructing Judge Romola. The proof against Fabio? A note written in his hand to his brother Sergio: 'Keep accusing Vargius to protect the family.' Then a scalpel which he claimed he used for cutting cork, and certain sexual habits. The nightmare ended for him in 1984 when, on July 29th, Patrizia Renzetti and Carlo Salvini were murdered in Vicchio. Fabio Muscas was freed on October 2nd, 1984.

ELIO SASSETTI. Married, three children, chauffeur. A confessed Peeping Tom. It was this habit which got him into trouble. On the night between the 6th and

7th June, 1981, when Gino Fani and Caterina Di Paola were murdered near Scandicci, Sassetti was out spying on couples with a friend and his car, a Ford Taurus, was seen parked near the scene of the crime. He must have seen something because the next day he was spreading the news of the murder by the Monster long before the bodies had been found. He was arrested for false witness and then accused of the murders. He remained in prison throughout the summer. He was released on October 22nd when the Monster struck again, killing Silvio Benci and Sara Contini.

The Marshal finished reading and sat with the newspaper on his chest for a while, musing. Then he glanced again at Simonetti's account of their doings of yesterday.

He must be used to it, reading about himself all the time. Odd how the article didn't really relate to the experience, but then, that was journalism. They had to make a bit of a story. Anyway, the Marshal wasn't used to it at all and it was an odd sensation, though not, if he had to be perfectly honest with himself, an altogether unpleasant one.

Five

'Good morning, Marshal. How are you?' Dr Biondini looked up from his checklist as the Marshal came out of his station and appeared at the back of the truck.

'Oh, I can't complain . . . I couldn't have a quick word with you, could I?'

'Of course, just give me a minute. This is the last.'

The painting, padded and wrapped, was loaded into the back and closed in.

'These are the Florentine landscapes going up to the Fort – you're going to come to the opening, I hope?'

'I'll be there – at least, I should be . . . Things are a bit difficult at the moment.'

'Ah! The Monster hunt! How's it going? All right, you

107

can leave and I'll follow you! Thank you.' The van's engine started up. 'Are you on your way somewhere?'

'To Police Headquarters.' The carabiniere at the wheel of the Marshal's car started his engine, too, but the Marshal signalled to him that he wasn't ready to leave yet and he turned it off again. The exhaust fumes sat low in the still muggy air and the Marshal, reaching automatically for his dark glasses, pushed them back in his pocket with a glance at the uniformly grey sky. Unpleasant though this weather was it gave some relief to his eyes which wept copiously in strong sunlight. He explained as best he could about the circumstances in which his young friend Marco had inherited the Franchi painting. Biondini looked a bit surprised.

'Who did the attribution?'

'I don't know; wouldn't Landini himself have done it, being such an expert?'

'Not his period. I suppose the auctioneers could have had someone out from London – it has been authenticated?'

'I couldn't say. All Marco told me was that it was supposed to be by Antonio Franchi – wait . . . I'm sure he said that the letter he received from the auction house actually named the painter. I'm afraid I can't remember now whether the painting's signed or not. He might have told me, but . . .'

'Well, that's neither here nor there. But the provenance? If this young man inherited it from Landini, where did Landini get it? That at least must be on record. Landini was no fool.'

'No, he wasn't. But the painting, you see, was in the family. A portrait supposedly of one of the dei Gherardini ancestors. You don't look convinced.'

'Well, to be honest, Marshal, I'm not – you don't mind if we walk towards my car? I must be there for the unloading.'

'Yes, of course. I shouldn't be delaying you . . .'

They walked together under the stone archway beneath the great iron lantern. Coming out the other side, Biondini took the beige raincoat that had been thrown over one shoulder and put it on.

'It seems to be getting colder. One doesn't know what on earth to wear in this wretched weather, but I'm determined not to get soaked to the skin again as I did yesterday – or was it the day before?'

'The day before . . . I did, too. Can you tell me why you're not too convinced about this painting? You don't think, even without seeing it, that it's an Antonio Franchi?'

Biondini laughed. 'I'm no genius, and no clairvoyant, either! You have such a high opinion of my talents that it's always cheering to talk to you!'

Had he made a fool of himself again? 'I only meant, well, that you are an expert – it's your job, isn't it – so you could have some reason . . .'

'Yes, I do, and as a matter of fact I know Franchi's work particularly well. I've written one or two papers on him, but that doesn't mean I can identify a painting of his without so much as seeing a photograph of it – is there a photograph available?'

'I don't know, I could ask.'

'I'd like to see it if there is. The thing is that I was responsible for almost all the Franchi attributions where attributions were necessary – leaving aside, obviously, the larger works done for various churches and convents where the paintings had never been removed and there were clear records. That's why I'm a bit sceptical of a dei Gherardini portrait that nobody knows about. Franchi himself, you see, kept such careful records.'

'Marco said that – but he also said Franchi copied his own stuff.'

'Indeed he did, but he kept careful records of those, too. There are one or two paintings missing – missing in the sense of nobody knows who owns them now or whether they've been destroyed – but not a Gherardini portrait. It's a bureaucratic question, you see, rather than a question of attribution. My best advice to your young friend is to enjoy the painting if he likes it, and if it really has been in the family for generations then it has a special value for him whether it's by Franchi or not, wouldn't you say?'

'I suppose so . . .'

'Here's my car, such as it is. I ought to have been a Landini myself then I'd be driving a huge fancy car instead of this little Fiat. We'll never get rich working for the state, Marshal.'

The Marshal could only sigh in agreement, his own little car being of the same model, though perhaps not so old as this one. Biondini was searching for his keys.

'Why is he worried, anyway? Ah, here they are . . .'

'Worried?'

'Landini's son. Why should he have been worried enough to come to you in the first place?'

Hadn't the Marshal asked himself that, known that there was something Marco wasn't telling him?

'He . . . He'd never heard of such a painting being in the family and thought, well . . . If it turned out to be a forgery, his mother's name . . .'

'A forgery? Why should he think that? It could just be a mistaken attribution. What brought forgery to mind?'

But the more Biondini put his own doubts into words, the more the Marshal tried to deny them. 'He was checking through his father's diaries, wondering about the painting. There was a phone number of a man who claims he's a restorer . . .'

'I should think Landini knew a number of restorers, must have done. Who was it? I should know him, if only by name.'

'Benozzetti.'

'Benozzetti? No. A strange name, isn't it? No, there's no restorer in Florence by that name – not one on Landini's level. Can I give you a lift somewhere? Where did you say you were going? Ah, Police Headquarters. Then I can't, can I? I've no permit to go through the centre . . . There, it is starting to rain and just look at my windscreen . . . I'm sure I had a wash leather but there are so many books and papers in this car and I never get a minute . . .'

'It's there, there on the floor to your left. The thing is that Marco really could do with selling this picture. He needs the money to set up an architect's studio and to get married.'

'Money? Didn't he inherit a fortune from his father?'

'No. No, he didn't. A small studio and this picture, that's all.'

'Well, I'm afraid if he does sell, it won't bring him much. The state can't afford to buy anything these days and to find a private buyer here won't be easy. It would be illegal to export it so he'd better not try anything of that sort.'

'I'm sure he doesn't intend to – and what you might not consider much, in terms of big art sales, might be an amount that makes all the difference to him.'

'No doubt. Well, let him try. If the painting's his to sell, and you say you've checked on that, then let him sell. The attribution isn't his problem, he's just selling a painting. The auctioneers know how to look after themselves and their important clients. Any doubts they might have will be evident to the initiated from the way it's presented in their catalogue. Let him sell and good luck to him. Remember, I'd be interested to see a photograph.'

'I will. I'll ask about it. I'm sorry to have taken up your time.'

'Don't worry – and tell young Landini not to worry. He'll find that there's no such thing as a forgery in this world!'

'Now what the devil did he mean by that?' muttered

the Marshal to himself as he made his way back under the arch to his waiting car.

'Now, what exactly do we mean by that? The word "Monster" itself would seem to suggest something exceptional, but we must remember that whilst here in Italy such cases are extremely rare, the phenomenon of the serial killer is today a widespread one, and in America alone a great many criminals of this type have been captured and studied whilst a great many more are still at large and active. We are talking here about men who kill, not for money or revenge but for "recreational" or sexual motives which are personal to the killer and unconnected to the victim.

'By this time we are quite sure that our "Monster" falls into the category of the sexually perverted – not all of whom become killers, or are even violent, but who may have that tendency.'

The Marshal was trying to force himself to concentrate, and, as usual, was more fascinated by Simonetti himself than by anything he was saying.

'I wouldn't say he was good-looking,' he protested to himself. This was because Simonetti's picture had been in the paper alongside that article about the investigation and Teresa had said how good-looking he was.

'Good-looking?'

'Of course he is. Look at those fine dark eyes. He's a very handsome man. Trust you not to notice. And so elegant, too – of course, it's a very flattering outfit, that white lace cravat thing against the black silk, don't you think?'

113

'*Boh.*'

He had fingered the plain little black tie of his uniform and gone back to his office in a bad temper.

'He will tend, if captured, to collaborate, one might say excessively, with the authorities, often undergoing religious conversion whilst in prison – but beware – if released into the community he will, immediately on being left to his own devices, fall into his former behaviour pattern and start to kill again. A great scandal was caused in Spain when a serial killer, released for good conduct, killed again immediately. The father of his young victim collected two million signatures to convince judges to give more severe penalties for this type of crime. We find the same thing happening in Switzerland where a life sentence can mean a maximum of fifteen years. The prisoner can then be released. And even before that, good behaviour can mean that the prisoner is allowed out every so often. Now, your sexual pervert is in most cases a model prisoner who gives his gaolers no problems at all so he is the first to obtain permits and early release; apparently all efforts of psychiatrists to warn of the dangers involved have fallen on deaf ears and had no effect whatever on the traditional system obtaining within prisons.'

Besides which, it's all very well having fine eyes but what about the way he looked at people, which was really intolerable. That sneering expression, sneering now at the psychiatrists who'd spent God knows how long preparing that pile of stuff on the table in front of him.

'I'm not going to ask you to read the whole of this profile prepared for us by the FBI in Quantico, Virginia. It would take up too much of your time – time which I have every intention of taking up for more practical purposes than ploughing your way through psycho jargon!'

'Cue for laughter,' whispered Ferrini beside him as the men facing them across the table dutifully chuckled, and the Marshal's eyes bulged even more than usual. He was aware of Bacci's attempt at joining in the responses to his left and felt, without turning to look at him, that the young man was still very tense. It might be as well to say a word to him when he got the chance because if he didn't ease up he might start to really get on Simonetti's nerves, causing him to ask for a replacement. Bacci would never get over that. Really, Bacci never got over anything. Too much responsibility too young, that was probably why . . . Now he'd lost track, but really, with the best will in the world . . . It wasn't the way he was used to working and you can't teach an old dog new tricks. All this theoretical stuff instead of getting out there and looking the people concerned in the face, looking at their houses, their clothes, smelling their world, watching their expressions as they lied to you . . . Fine dark eyes, indeed . . .

'So, apart from what will by now be obvious to you, that we're looking for a man who will have previous convictions for violent and sexually perverted behaviour, we are also seeking someone reasonably expert in the use of firearms and of a single-edged knife. Please bear in

115

mind that whilst we couldn't in the early stages necessarily exclude a surgeon, nor were we necessarily looking for one. In a city full of artisans like Florence a great many people work with knives of this sort: people dealing with animal skins, or, further along the line, the hundreds of people in Florence producing belts, bags, shoes, fur coats and so on. In the early stages we left no stone unturned in this respect, which cost us an enormous amount of time and trouble. Our psychiatric profile also offers us some clues or suggestions which we've tried to bear in mind throughout our investigation where relevant. It is probable, though not certain, that our suspect is someone likely to be cruel to any creature younger, weaker, more vulnerable than himself. This behaviour might take the form of cruelty to animals or ill treatment of women and/or children. He may also be the victim of uncontrollable rages and fits of jealousy and obsessed by violent, probably sexually oriented, fantasies. His behaviour may be menacing to others and it may be very difficult for him to calm down after a fit of violent rage. Sometimes this dysfunctional rage is camouflaged by a mask of normalcy, but it is nonetheless there. We should also be looking at neurological symptoms such as migraine headaches, extra-powerful sensitivity to sound or light, a chronic inability to remember numbers or letters or to confuse them, headaches that seem to move along one side of the head, impaired speech after severe headaches or disturbing bright lights that seem to originate from behind the eyelids. These are all the problems which might be the result or symptoms of cardiovascular problems that affect the neurological system and could, over the long term, affect the person's behaviour.

'Now, we must be a bit careful here – I'm looking at all your faces and I can see the sort of reactions we all get on reading anything medical.' Simonetti looked about him with a brilliant smile. 'Don't any of you try to tell me that as I was reading all that you weren't starting to wonder about yourselves. "I suffer from migraine headaches"; "I'm jealous of my wife or girlfriend"; "I can't spell". Am I right? Well, keep calm. The insidious nature of these behaviour patterns, as our expert is fortunately kind enough to point out in this report, means that, by themselves, the patterns are usually benign. However, in combination with one another, such patterns become progressively more dangerous and can compromise a person's ability to function in society. And – this is a very important factor – once the boundary between violent fantasy and actual violence has been crossed, the next act of violence is going to be very easy to commit. I won't bore you any further with theories. I think at this point we should take a preliminary look at our suspect so that you'll have his background filled in when you meet him later today – by the way, the press have got hold of something, I don't know how, but just in case, I've taken every possible precaution and I'm sure you'll appreciate my motives for reconvening here this afternoon at two-thirty before moving on to a destination where I shall have our suspect brought. I'm relying on your good sense here in assuming that you understand the reasons for this. I don't think for a minute that any of you would leak any information to the press, but it's to your advantage to know that if there is a leak, you can't be suspected of it. I wonder if, before we go any further, a coffee might be in order – keep you all awake during my dull perorations . . .'

Another brilliant smile denied any such real necessity but the young policeman, Noferini, was already on his feet, bright-eyed and bushy-tailed as ever.

'I'll see to it.'

The Marshal, at least, was glad enough of a chance to stretch his legs after sitting still so long, whilst the others felt in their pockets for cigarettes.

He stood a moment looking down at the traffic splashing through the rain in Via Zara until he became conscious of a drift of smoke at his shoulder and turned, expecting to find Ferrini beside him. He couldn't have been more surprised when he saw the scarred hand lifting the cigarette which was parked between the thin lips as the hand was offered.

'Guarnaccia, I've just realized who you are.'

What did that mean? The Marshal searched his mind for the name of this detective. The formal introductions had been made at the first meeting but they hadn't resulted in much and the Marshal's mind was a blank.

'Esposito,' the other man offered. 'I must confess your name rang no bells with me at first, though I remembered

Ferrini. You worked on that transsexual murder together, am I right?'

'Yes. Yes, we did.'

'I thought so. My compliments. A real textbook investigation. I followed it.'

'You did?'

'I certainly did. Impressive. Very impressive.'

The Marshal could only stare at him in astonishment.

'When I cottoned on to who you were I was a bit surprised that you were here at all, you know what I mean? Just goes to show it doesn't always pay to listen to gossip.'

At which point their coffee arrived and the Marshal had to keep his amazement to himself for the next hour or so as Simonetti introduced the character and previous convictions of the Suspect.

'A violent man, a morbidly jealous man, a man of whom his family and even his friends are afraid. He was born in the Mugello area, north of Florence, in 1925 to a peasant family and he himself has worked as a peasant farmer for most of his life. His first conviction came in 1951 at the age of twenty-six when he quarrelled with a girl he was engaged to and she started a relationship with another man. Refusing to accept this situation he followed the two of them one night into the woods near the village and hid himself to watch. The couple began to make love and at a certain moment, at the moment when the man uncovered the woman's left breast, he leapt from his hiding place and attacked! His attack was furious, swift and deadly and in a matter of seconds his rival lay bleeding to death from stab wounds. But that wasn't enough, his rage still wasn't spent. He then began kicking at the head of the prostrate and dying man, kicking and kicking until the brains were spilling out of the shattered skull and one eye was loosed from its socket. His rival was dead but still he wasn't satisfied, and what happens next is what separates this man's crime from so many other banal crimes of passion. What he did next was to turn to his ex-fiancée and say to her, "Now it's your turn." And right there, on the ground, beside the bleeding corpse of her lover, he raped her.

'Hours later, he returned to the scene of the crime. Evidently unmoved even by the results of his viciousness, he went through the dead man's pockets and stole his wallet which contained twenty thousand lire. He then dragged the body deeper into the woods and hid it.

'By the time this case came to court, enquiries had revealed that he had made numerous threats against his victim prior to the murder and the prosecution claimed premeditation with intent to rob. The accused insisted on his story of a surprise discovery of the couple and a moment of blind rage and jealousy. The court accepted his plea. He was condemned to twenty-two years' imprisonment of which he served thirteen.

'On coming out of prison in 1964 he returned to live with his mother and worked for some time as a cobbler, a job which gave him considerable expertise with blades and awl. He had, of course, done his National Service at the usual age and so was quite capable of handling a firearm.

'He soon married his present wife and rumour has it, though there's no proof of this, that he actually bought her from a band of tinkers passing through the area. Be that as it may, she and her father moved in with our Suspect and his mother and before long, discovering an incestuous relationship between his wife and her father, he threw the father out.

'In 1969 he left his mother's house and moved to a village in the countryside to the south of Florence, then to the nearby village of Pontino where he is still resident. A daughter was born to the couple in the meantime and she was the innocent cause of the sentence he is at present serving in prison.

'This young woman, now twenty-six years old, confided one day in her employer – she's in domestic service – that her father had abused her from the time she was nine years old. For years and years he had forced her into every possible variation of sexual intercourse. The little girl had been obliged to sleep in her father's bed whilst her mother was sent to sleep in the child's bedroom. The employer – whose identity will be protected because of the excessive press interest in this case – convinced the young woman to report the abuse officially.

'The mother confirmed her daughter's denunciation, made with the encouragement and protection of the girl's employer, explaining that neither of them had dared

121

speak out against him because he beat them frequently and savagely.

'Apparently, these sessions with his daughter were not limited to the bedroom. She and her mother described being taken out in the car at night by the father and being made to perform sexual acts, some of them perverted, in the car or even outside on the ground in the woods. There seems to have been no limit to what he required of them.'

Simonetti paused and looked at them all, one by one, before announcing, 'In a little over a month's time this man will be released from prison. We know that as long as he has been inside there have been no more of these murders. We know we are dealing with a killer in our Suspect because he has been convicted of murder, and an extremely vicious murder at that. We know we are dealing with a man who is sexually perverted to an extent which all of us find difficult to imagine, almost impossible to contemplate, to accept. Nevertheless, he is about to be returned to his family and loosed on our society. We can't prevent this because we have no proof against him. Your job, our job, is to find that proof. Gentlemen, I have every intention that we should find it, no holds barred.'

He paused again and then opened a thin file which lay next to the psychiatric profile on the table in front of him. Inside it was a transparent plastic envelope containing a single sheet of paper.

'Given his previous conviction for a crime of violence, we already had this man's name listed as a possible suspect. We also received, some years ago, an anonymous communication which, like all such communications, was checked out at once. A search was made of his home without results and the matter dropped, particularly as, at that stage, we had no reason to suspect him of any sexual perversions. Following on the accusation by his daughter we remembered this letter and examined it again.'

He slid the sheet from its transparent cover.

'It is addressed to the Marshal of Pontino and was passed on to the examining magistrate by him.'

Will you please investigate the murderer of Pontino because he's the one who killed all those couples in cars.

    He is vicious and violent.
    He's a Peeping Tom.
    He's a dirty pervert and you should arrest him.

'As you know, an anonymous letter has no value in a court of law. Nevertheless, given a situation in which all the people surrounding this man, including, for obvious reasons, his family, go in fear of him, it is hardly surprising that any information which could damage him is likely to reach us anonymously. This is particularly so now that he is about to be released from prison. Consequently, any such communications must be regarded in a serious light.'

He glanced at his watch. 'I think, if I want you back here by two-thirty, I'd better let you go to lunch. Please be punctual. We have a lot to get through this afternoon.'

But first they had to get through the cold rainy streets and find somewhere to eat, since, apart from Bacci who lived on that side of the city, they had no hope of getting home and back in the time given.

The police contingent disappeared on their own account and Ferrini and the Marshal stood hesitating inside the main entrance, buttoning their raincoats and adjusting their hats. The marble floor was patterned with dirty wet footprints and on the steps outside a group of journalists huddled under umbrellas.

'Oh! Marshal!' It was Nesti from *Nazione* who broke away from the group and stopped them as they came out.

'Nesti. How are things?'

'Fine. Glad to see you. Just the man to tell us where the meeting this afternoon's going to be.'

'I can't do that.'

'Of course you can. You know Simonetti – whips up all this mystery to keep us interested and then makes sure there's a leak. You know he'll be furious if we don't turn up.'

The Marshal stared at him. 'Well . . . I suppose you might be right but if you are we're not the people you're looking for. He hasn't told us where we're going.'

'Typical! He's never been on the best of terms with the carabinieri. He'll leak everything through the police so as to attract press sympathy to them. You have to admit he's sharp – there they go! Excuse me . . .'

Nesti ran off in the wake of his fellow journalists who

had spotted the two detectives across the street. The Marshal couldn't help noticing that, whatever the result might be, the conversation was going on a lot longer than a simple denial would necessitate.

'Do you think Nesti was right?'

Ferrini only shrugged. 'Who gives a stuff? Let's get something to eat.' And he continued down the steps, the Marshal in his wake.

'Are we heading for somewhere in particular? I don't know this part of town.'

'There's a good place down here on the left. Friend of mine. He'll give us a good meal and a good price. Just stick with me.'

The Marshal did as he was told, wondering as they dodged in out of the rain and were met by a roaring log fire and a wonderful smell of cooking, why some men always did know a chap who would give you a discount, find you a good used car, a seat in a booked-up train, a room in a full hotel, a ticket for the match. Also why he himself had always been excluded from this brotherhood. It was a closed world to him but he was grateful enough to Ferrini for his membership when he saw a table prepared for them on the instant and a bottle of good wine set on the white cloth. And just as the troops were lining up for the daily battle between conscience and appetite, Ferrini waved away waiter and menu and started pouring. 'Piero knows what to give us. Leave it all to him.'

A truce was instantly declared.

'Ah . . .' An even deeper sigh as a generous bowl of

spaghetti was set before him. 'That looks perfect.' And all his troubles vanished as he plunged his fork into the glistening tomato sauce.

'The intestines are spilling out here, as you can see, and you can probably make out the perforation here. Now, compare this for a moment to the slide before . . . there we are. Practically three clean cuts and the pudenda is excised. There's a big difference which you must interpret as best you can. Are you looking at a different weapon, a different hand, a different level of anger, even? Let's go back now to the first victim, 1974, Sandra Palladini. Ninety-six stab wounds, deep stab wounds all in the thorax and abdomen. So what's your level of anger here? Nobody in a normal condition could inflict ninety-six stab wounds as deep as that. You'd have to be in a frenzy, induced perhaps by drugs, by madness, by alcohol, who knows? Caterina Di Paola again: one stab wound. One. Then the three clean cuts. Let's switch this thing off for a minute and you can look at the photographs you have in your files. Can we have the lights on?'

Only the lights on the platform came on. The rest of the bunker courtroom with the empty cages along its length and empty tables and chairs for the public remained in shadow.

They were seated where judge and jury would normally be seated, facing the public and with a view of a screen on their right which was placed where the jury but not the public could see relevant slides. Professor Forli stayed where he was in front of the screen and paced about, as was his wont, whilst he talked.

There had been no time to express their surprise when the professor appeared from the wings instead of the suspect and Simonetti's brief introduction had merely mentioned in passing that they were taking advantage of Forli's availability and the equipment which the courtroom provided. After that the professor had launched into his explanations and the professor, once launched, was unstoppable. He was a good pathologist, the best there was, but he was also a born teacher and he was teaching them now, having quite forgotten that they were not his students.

'Entry wound in upper left arm, no exit wound because the bullet's lodged in the heart. The second bullet – fired from inside the window – victim already dead, enters centre back of neck here and –'

'So the body slumped forward on death.'

Silence. It wasn't Bacci this time but Simonetti, settled back in his chair, arms folded, smiling.

'I beg your pardon?' Forli obviously wasn't used to having his students interrupt him.

'I was just pointing out that if the first bullet entered the left arm and the second entered the back of the neck then the body must have slumped forward.'

'Oh.' Forli considered this for a moment and then asked politely, 'Were you there?'

'Was I . . .? No, I was simply –'

'I wasn't there either so I can't say whether the body slumped forward in death or spun sideways away from the driver's door on the impact of the first bullet or whether the assassin pushed or pulled the victim forward. We'll continue.'

Forli continued for another hour or so without apparently drawing breath. When he had said all he had to say and had shown the rest of the slides, he was about to switch off the projector but Simonetti stopped him.

'Just in case, while we're waiting, we want to go through our notes and look at something again.'

'These slides must go back to the Medico-Legal Institute.'

'You'll have them back within two or three hours.'

For a moment Forli looked puzzled, then he looked amused.

'I understand. Good morning to you.' He picked up his battered briefcase and shambled off down the long darkened room.

What had he understood? The Marshal was asking himself this and Ferrini was prodding him and whispering, 'That was a good one, "Were you there?" I liked that. Thank God somebody has the guts to tell him where to get off . . . This must be it . . .'

Simonetti was on his feet, his hands clasped behind him as though pushing his gown back, looking towards the door next to the cages. The Marshal followed his glance in time to see the door open and two carabinieri appear in the doorway.

What had he been expecting? Perhaps he couldn't have explained exactly what, had anybody asked him. He must have constructed some sort of image in his head over the last couple of weeks. How could he have failed to? But he'd never tried to clarify it, much less put it into words and now he couldn't remember what it had been at all. Only that it wasn't anything like this. Nothing odd about that. He was no expert so nothing he could have imagined had any value. Even so . . .

He strained sideways a bit in the hope of seeing better. The others were doing the same but the Suspect was so small that he was almost entirely obliterated by his escort of four men, all of them tall and robust.

They couldn't see much of him but they could hear him. He was crying, and crying very loudly, the way children do when they want to gain their parents' attention. In the moment when they did get a better view of his face, blood-red, swollen, wet with saliva, snot and tears, he also saw them and at once began to scream:

'It's not me you want! I'm not the one! It's not me!'

Six

'Do you understand the accusations made against you?'

'I don't understand anything. What do you expect me to understand? I'm just a peasant farmer. I've spent my life digging in the fields, sweating for every penny. I don't know what's happening. I don't know what you want from me.'

'You are accused of the murder of Herman Mainz and Ulrich Richter and of Nathalie Monde and Maurice Clément. By implication, since we intend to demonstrate by ballistic and medico-legal evidence that all the double homicides in this series were committed by the same hand, you will be accused of all the murders attributed to the so-called Monster of Florence. Do you intend to answer our questions?'

'How can I answer your questions? I don't know what you're talking about. I'm just a poor farmer. What questions? You can't ask me questions. I'm not the man you want!'

With an exaggerated sigh of forced patience, Simonetti turned to the lawyer sitting by the Suspect's side.

'Would you care to elucidate?'

'We'll answer your questions.' He put a hand on the Suspect's arm. 'It's all right, now. Keep calm.'

'It's not all right! Why is he accusing me? Why me? What did I ever do to him? He wants to crucify me and he *knows* it's not me, so why? Why?'

He rubbed a thick hand over his face, still wet and dark red, and began sobbing loudly again. Simonetti pursed his lips in amusement.

'You're wasting your performance on us, you know. You'd do well to wait at least until there are a few journalists present – and I'm not allowing them to see you today so you might as well save your energy.'

The Suspect put his head down in his hands and the lawyer bent close to his ear and whispered something. The Suspect whimpered in protest but nevertheless became quieter.

'May we proceed?'

The Marshal observed the Suspect, who now raised his head and watched each of them in turn, seeking perhaps for a sign of sympathy. He didn't look at anyone directly but sideways on out of one shiny eye, which seemed not to belong to the weeping red face but to be looking

131

through it like an eye peering from behind a mask. Are we, the Marshal wondered, looking at the face of the man who did that? 'That' was right behind the Suspect's head on the screen. A torso, punctured, bruised and bleeding, one breast cut away and the pudenda gouged into a red and black cavity that appeared and disappeared as the Suspect's brush of thick white hair moved before it in agitation.

'It's because I'm poor and ignorant, because I didn't even finish primary school. I've spent a lifetime sweating for every penny, trying to put a bit aside the way I was taught –'

'Would you mind . . . ?' Simonetti appealed to the lawyer to stop him. It took some time. In the Marshal's opinion, this was a futile exercise, anyway. He'd been expecting he didn't know quite what by way of the Suspect, but in any case, something out of the ordinary – a monster, a novelty, something at least unfamiliar. But this character was only too familiar and he was the worst kind of all to deal with. Logic had no meaning for him. He was of the stout-denial brigade and nothing would ever shift him, no matter how much proof you waved before his eyes. And the worst thing was that his was the best defence in the world. The Marshal had seen so many like him and knew that unless you could trick them into a confession, nothing shifted them. A clever man, caught out in a lie or discrepancy, gives in. A stupid man goes on denying and denying, making up a different set of lies day after day, admitting they're lies and still denying. Perhaps after all, you shouldn't really call it stupidity because after the eighth or ninth version of the story you couldn't possibly know what to believe, so unless you had physical proof . . .

No holds barred, Simonetti had said, but where would that get him with a character like this unless he did find physical proof – the gun . . . or the pieces missing from that mutilated body there behind the white head . . .

The lawyer was on his feet, trying to restrain the Suspect's violent reactions to every question. The Marshal didn't envy him his job because he would be getting the same garbled lies as they were now hearing in public. That was another fixed rule. Never tell your lawyer the truth. He looked like somebody . . . somebody the Marshal had arrested years ago but the name wouldn't come. That same pig's eye, violent, he'd killed an old woman but his name . . . same clothes, too, the patterned shirt, its collar creased and open, the big coloured lozenges on the jumper, the too-tight checked jacket, it was almost a uniform. The bulging stomach never quite contained by the outgrown clothing.

'Poisonous little bitch!' Sweat was pouring from his temples and rolling down under the creased collar. His eyes were so swollen with crying they were almost shut. 'Poisonous sodding little bitch!'

'Come, come now, you're not trying to blame your daughter for what you did to her, surely?' The angrier the

Suspect became the more Simonetti enjoyed his own super-calmness.

'Filthy little creep trying to ruin me, ruin me! She'll burn in hell for this . . . She'll burn . . . that's the thanks I get for bringing her up, for working and sweating all my life, for making sacrifices to give her a roof over her head. She didn't refuse the house I bought her, the little bitch, she didn't refuse that, did she? What harm did I ever do her to make her ruin me like this? Jesus fucking –'

'Please advise your client to refrain from swearing and blaspheming.'

'I'll curse as much as I want and blaspheme as much as I want and if there's a God in heaven you'll burn in hell for what you're doing, along with that miserable bitch whose throat I should have slit when she was born so's she couldn't bring me to this.'

He only stopped shouting to cry again. Then his voice was lowered to a pitiful whine:

'I feel ill. I'm sick, you're murdering a sick man . . . Oh God help me, my heart . . . you're killing me . . .'

'My client is ill. The prison medical report will demonstrate . . .'

'Yes, yes, we know all about the prison medical report. Your client has, if I'm not mistaken, some cardiovascular problems.'

At this Simonetti gave his squad a significant glance and then addressed the lawyer again. 'Yes? Is that the case?'

'He suffers from angina. He's not at all strong and he's getting on in years. He can't be subjected to –'

'He's going to be subjected to an enquiry followed by a trial and no medical report is going to stop that happening. Now, if you'd care to remove him' – he looked at his watch – 'for ten minutes and no longer. Give him a glass of water and then bring him back.'

'He's going to need more than a glass of water. His medication –'

'You will give him whatever he requires and be back here in ten minutes precisely with your client in a calmer frame of mind. I'm sure you, at least, realize that his behaviour is as damaging to him as it is time wasting for us.'

Which was true, the Marshal thought as the four carabinieri led their charge away, followed by his fussing little lawyer. But it was also true that the man really did look ill. His blood pressure must be desperately high and his face was purple by now. And what, in any case, were they achieving? In real terms this was simply Simonetti's way of introducing them to the Suspect. The episode had no other meaning that he could think of so, surely, if the man was feeling ill they could leave it at that?

Nobody seemed inclined to chat during the interval. It might have been because the grotesqueness of the Suspect's behaviour had disconcerted them, or it might have been the slide still projected on the screen – the Marshal looked at Bacci and could tell that he was trying not to see it. Simonetti was sitting at the back with his legs crossed and his arms folded, his face serene and confident, quite prepared to let the ten minutes pass in silence if necessary.

Not too surprisingly it was Ferrini who spoke up.

'I suppose smoking's not allowed . . .'

Simonetti raised an eyebrow and then in silence indicated that they should leave the courtroom by the opposite exit to that used by the Suspect. He looked at his watch as the smokers rose. 'Be punctual.'

For the first time in his life the Marshal wished he smoked. It wasn't because he felt in need of any stimulant or even a distraction, but because he didn't want to be left there with Simonetti, and somehow the size of the bunker courtroom, its vast unlit stretches, inhibited him from walking about to stretch his legs as he did in the small room where they usually convened. Not that he was quite alone with Simonetti since Bacci was a non-smoker too, but that was no help. The lad looked sick to the stomach, perhaps because of the slide still projected on the screen. What good reason was there for leaving it there all this time? Surely Simonetti's intention couldn't be to distress them the way the thing was distressing Bacci? All of them had seen worse in their time and even Bacci himself oughtn't to be so susceptible. Whatever was the matter with him?

He found the opportunity to ask when Simonetti suddenly left them, striding down the length of the dark room and engaging someone in conversation just outside the public entrance, presumably the man on guard there.

'It's not squeamishness,' Bacci explained, 'even though

it's . . .' He glanced again at the large screen but didn't find the words to say what it was. 'It's just that I can't look at it without thinking of the risks I ran . . . You know how at first, before anyone realized it was a maniac – I mean nobody took precautions until . . .'

'I see.' It was true that the Monster had overturned the sex lives of Bacci's whole generation. With the housing problem as bad as it was, youngsters had to go on living with their parents until they got married and usually even after that. Their only chance of privacy was when they were alone in their car. There they could exchange love and secrets, make their plans, giggle at their private jokes. There they had been screened by thick vines and guarded by tall black cypresses on peaceful moonlit nights. Until that first bullet came out of nowhere . . .

'It could have been her . . . Us. That's why I – she has long dark curls just like that.'

Which must have been why he couldn't drag his eyes from the photo he didn't want to see. The poor body was so punctured and torn that there was little to recognize about it except its youth, and the head was out of frame. The long curls had undoubtedly been drawn back so as not to obscure the knife cuts on the slim neck, but one dark strand had escaped and curled forward over the smooth unmarked shoulder.

'The risks I took . . .' repeated Bacci. 'I mean, I keep seeing it happen, like watching a film . . .'

'Pull yourself together,' the Marshal said. Then he remembered that the youngster was his superior officer but there seemed little point in adding 'sir' to such a remark. 'It's as well not to get too involved, just get on with the job.'

'I intend to. I really intend to.' Bacci fixed his earnest gaze on the Marshal. 'I've got a number of books, English and American. I'm going to read up all the case histories available, for a start. After all, none of us knows anything about this sort of thing.' Bacci the perfect student. He hadn't changed much since he was eighteen.

The Marshal was saved from having to comment on the idea of looking for the Monster in a bookshop by the return of Simonetti and the other men.

The Suspect, when they brought him back, was quieter, though his face was still red and his forehead creased in a deep frown. He kept looking about him as though hoping to see a way out. He kept his voice lowered this time round, presumably on the strict instructions of his lawyer, maintaining an injured whine.

'It's not true that I'm a Peeping Tom, I've never been a Peeping Tom. What time have I got for stuff like that? I have to work for a living, I've worked like a slave all my life. Anything I've got I've sweated for, putting a bit aside each week the way I was taught. D'you think I've got time to be trailing around the countryside at night when I've been breaking my back all day? I'm a sick man, the doctors can tell you that, a sick man not a Peeping Tom. I'm being made a victim of and anybody who says I'm a Peeping Tom's out to get me with their lies.'

The tears were rolling fast again, though he didn't sob aloud the way he'd done before. His head lolled sideways and his big fists clenched and unclenched themselves on his fat knees.

'What sort of man would want to be watching other people? You'd have to be sick to get any excitement out of that. I'm a normal married man.'

'A normal married man?' repeated Simonetti. 'Who raped his own child? You said before you were a sick man which sounds more like the truth.'

'He's twisting my words!' wailed the Suspect, waving an accusing hand at his tormentor and appealing to the others. 'He's taking advantage of me because I'm a poor ignorant peasant and he's clever!' He began crying again.

'No, no, no,' counselled his lawyer, getting hold of his shoulders in the hope of restraining another violent outburst. He didn't look as though he was going to be successful, but before the outburst could happen there was a commotion at the public entrance.

'What is it?' shouted Simonetti angrily, peering through the gloom.

The guard showed his face. 'I'm sorry, sir.' He vanished again.

'I'll deal with this.' Simonetti stamped down the steps of the stage and strode down the room.

'Well, well,' murmured Ferrini in the Marshal's ear. 'Journalists. What a surprise.'

The Marshal said nothing, feeling, like the unfortunate Suspect, that Simonetti was too clever for him and that if he wanted to manipulate the press that was his business.

A photographer wandered into the room alone and made his way towards the stage. So, he must be letting them in. No one else appeared and voices were still raised outside the room. It wasn't like Simonetti to waste so much time and surely his decision on this had already been made one way or the other?

The Marshal was staring down the room, wondering at the delay, half listening to the row out there, half to the urgent murmurs of the lawyer to his sniffing client when the first flash went off.

'You bastard!' screamed the Suspect, jumping up from his chair and overturning it. 'You've got no right to do that! You've got no right!'

He raised his fist and started towards the photographer, his face crazed and purple, his menacing figure outlined against the mutilated corpse. The flash went again and the photographer leapt off the stage and ran.

This portrait pleased the Grand Duke and Duchess very much and the Prince Corsini was given the job of summoning the painter to court. He seemed reluctant at first, not believing himself to be up to the level required by such a task; but in the end, convinced and reassured by Corsini, he accepted, and 'at nine in the evening (it was in August) I went to the Pitti Palace and was introduced to the Grand Duchess who received me with great courtesy and when the Princess was brought in I began the portrait. Within an hour and a half by God's grace I was able to sketch in such a good likeness that the Grand Duchess, getting up and putting on her glasses, said in that bellowing voice she has: "Good, good! If you finish it as well as you have begun it I shall declare myself well satisfied!" A good many ladies in waiting came to see it and were all amazed by the likeness and said: "That is our Princess exactly!" At last I finished it and succeeded not only with the likeness but with everything else, such as the clothing and the background scenery.' This was Antonio's entrance into the Grand Ducal Court according to his own account, but it should not be forgotten that already, some years previously, he had executed some copies for the Grand Duke. As regards the number of portraits of Princess Anna Maria Luisa, Franchi confirms that there were seven, differing from Baldinucci who has destroyed this certainty. It is probable that among the seven there were the two portraits mentioned by Bartolozzi (1754), one to send to Madrid when it seemed likely that the Princess would marry Charles II, recently widowed, the other sent to Düsseldorf for the marriage with the Palatine Elector Johann Wilhelm. Another was certainly the one ordered by her brother, the Grand Prince Ferdinando. It seems probable that the beautiful oval portrait attributed to an unknown artist is also by Franchi. Franchi himself says he did only two portraits of the Grand Prince; according to Bartolozzi, as well as the portrait of the Prince in full armour, there are another two. The notebooks in which Franchi kept his accounts show that the number is far greater, but, as in other cases, we are faced with the problem of distinguishing variations and repetitions from the originals. We do have an order for a portrait of the Prince dated 18th January 1687. Another order, dated June 1688, is for two more portraits, together with a copy of one of them 'which copy he sent to the bride'. The fifteen scudi shown in Franchi's accounts as the first instalment paid in August is confirmed in the palace accounts and dated 4th August 1688. Two more large portraits are registered as having been commissioned in 1688, but in a separate file we find a note of 'two original head-and-shoulder portraits, a full-length portrait in fashionable clothes, another full-length in armour, another three-quarter-length in armour, plus three copies'.

'You see?' interrupted Marco, impatient of the Marshal's slow reading.

'I haven't finished . . .'

'There's no need to read all of it, it just goes on like that. You do see what it means? The records are not clear at all. I think the picture is really genuine.'

In the Marshal's opinion he was believing what he

wanted to believe, but since we are all of us guilty of that he only said, 'Is it mentioned at all?'

'You mean by name? There's no specific mention of a portrait of Anna Caterina Luisa dei Gherardini, no, but there are all these portraits listed as Portrait of an Unknown Lady as this or that mythical character. Add to that we know he painted the ladies in waiting and I know from my mother that Anna Caterina was a lady in waiting . . .'

He followed the Marshal's gaze to the painting propped on an easel. 'What do you think of her?'

'Well, I don't know . . . She's very pretty but that frock's a bit funny.'

'Oh, she's not dressed as a lady of fashion of her time – she's meant to be Flora.'

'Ah. With all the flowers. Well, it's very nice.'

The face was smooth and round, the lips a deep red cupid bow. Pink and white and yellow flowers were twined through her hair and her head was tilted a little down to the left to let one shining ringlet curl over her bare shoulder. Her breast was as plump and white as a dove's and only just touched by the coloured draperies held in place by a pale hand from which more flowers spilled.

'There's another almost exactly like it of Lucrezia Corsini. I went to see it yesterday. He did two of her, one almost full-length and the other to the waist like this one. Only the position of the hands changes. Anyway, now you've seen her – oh dear, I wish there was somewhere you could sit. I'm sorry – wait a minute . . .'

Marco began pushing piles of drawing paper off a crate

of some sort. The studio was full to bursting point with paper and equipment but apart from the father's antique desk there was no furniture.

'There, can you manage with that? I can't tell you how grateful I am that you found time to come. I'd almost given up hope. I must have called four or five times and I'm afraid your brigadier – what's his name again?'

'Lorenzini.'

'Lorenzini, that's it. He must be sick of me calling, but you're out all the time.'

'I know. I meant to try and get here last week but it's not easy at the moment with one thing and another.' The Marshal lowered himself cautiously on to the crate but it seemed solid enough.

'Is it really him?' Marco perched on the edge of the cluttered desk.

'What?'

'That photo that was in all the papers . . .'

'Oh.' The Marshal sighed. 'I really don't know . . .'

'He looked violent enough, I must say. And it's true, isn't it, that there hasn't been another murder since he's been inside?'

'Almost true. He was still free in the summer of '86 and '87 and there were no murders then so that's far from being proof. The papers can invent anything they feel like but we need proof.'

'But you must have some or you wouldn't have accused him. You know, to be honest, I find it impossible to imagine *anybody* doing what he did. But then, imagine somebody raping their own child. When I read that article I decided I should stop complaining about my father. Anyway, let me tell you where I got this.' He patted the book which he'd been showing the Marshal and which still lay open beside him on the desk. 'I got it from Benozzetti!'

'He's been and gone? I thought –'

'No, no, he'll be here shortly. But what I didn't want to tell you on the phone was that I went to see him first. I waited and waited and it looked to me as if he'd decided not to bother so I took my courage in both hands and followed your advice and went there. You won't think it needed much courage, I know, when you're spending your time with your Monster, who looks as though he'd slit your throat as soon as look at you, but even so, I was pretty nervous about it. So much depends on her.' He nodded toward the portrait of his ancestor. I've got to get this place properly set up. Look at that – I'm working on the computer on the floor! Luckily I've got a bit of work in from a firm of architects in Modena. It's well paid enough but it's only draughtsman's work really, and until I can get the money to finish setting up here I can't receive a client, even if I'm lucky enough to get one. So, I went there with bated breath and, do you know, he was really nice to me.'

'Why shouldn't he be?' The Marshal shifted a little on the hard crate, trying not to cause a landslide amongst the stack of large folders that was leaning against it.

'Don't worry about that stuff, it won't break. I'm sorry about the cold in here, but I suppose my father never used the place except for storing stuff. I'll have to buy a heater of some sort.' He was wearing three sweaters but his hands were bluish, even so. 'Anyway, I don't know why I didn't expect him to be pleasant but I didn't. Perhaps because you didn't like him.'

'He probably didn't like me,' pointed out the Marshal, 'though it struck me that although he didn't take to me he seemed glad enough to have somebody to talk to. You were a better audience, I should imagine.'

'Because I'm my father's son, you mean?'

'I didn't mean that but you might be right.'

'He's an interesting character, you know.'

'I never doubted it.'

'Anyway, he showed me some of his own work which, to be honest, was pretty old-fashioned stuff, though well crafted. And he was restoring something that looked to me like Mantegna.'

'And you're sure he was restoring it?'

'Oh yes, he said so, and he told me about his early years in Rome when he was learning restoration from some old chap there. He kept saying things like, "If I'd only had a son like you," and stuff of that sort. A lot of artisans are that way, don't you find? And even if they do have a son the son usually couldn't care less about learning a craft. No money in it these days. I felt sorry for him in a way, shut in that weird studio, seeing nobody. He seems to have no friends, no family.'

'But it's his own doing,' pointed out the Marshal.

'I'm not so sure – well, in a way it is. It's just that from one or two things he let drop I've an idea he's not altogether to blame. He was put in an institution when he was nine, that's one thing that came out – oh, he wasn't complaining about it. On the contrary, he said he was happier there and that he'd been able to learn to draw.'

'He was an orphan?'

'No. Definitely not because he said he went back home to his parents – a father and stepmother, his own mother died when he was a tiny kid – when he was fourteen. I was the one who brought the subject of parents up. I still find it difficult to talk about my father without my hackles rising. What surprised me was that, even though they were friends, Benozzetti didn't defend him.

"Get away from them as soon as you can!

That's the thing to do. Get away."

'As if he'd quite forgotten my father was dead. Did you notice, when you met him, a weird scar round his ear?'

'And a piece of the left ear missing.'

'Of course, it's your job to notice things . . . Anyway, he was ranting on about parents – he does rant, doesn't he?'

'Yes.'

'It would drive you nuts if you had to listen to him for any length of time. So, he went on and on until he was purple in the face and at the end he said, "Your father left you his studio. My father left me this!" And he pointed at that scar. Then he went dead silent. I was pretty sure he wished he hadn't let that out. He practically pushed me out the door after that. If you think about it, the scar,

147

being taken away from his parents – a head injury like that might have made him – you know, odd. And it did cross my mind that maybe all those years he was in some sort of clinic. If he blamed his father maybe it was a road accident, something of that sort, and his father was responsible.'

'Maybe.'

'I can see by your face that you don't feel any sympathy for him.'

'No, no . . . It's not – to tell you the truth, not long ago, I had a word with Dr Biondini at the Palatine Gallery. I thought he might be able to throw a bit of light on your problem.'

'And could he?'

'He told me there's no restorer in Florence by that name.'

'By that . . . Benozzetti?'

'Exactly.'

'But surely he can't prove that? I mean, my father knew him.'

'I know. But that's the point. To be specific, he said there was no restorer of that name at your father's level. Those were more or less his words.'

'But we know there is. We've both just talked to him. You've met him.'

'We've talked to him. We don't know that he's a restorer.'

'You mean you think he's a forger!' Marco's face reddened and he jumped away from the desk and began

148

moving about the room, picking things up and putting them down in almost the same place. Then he stopped and looked the Marshal in the face, pushing a hand angrily through the hair that fell on his forehead.

'I was the one to say it, wasn't I? If it's not stolen I'll have to face up to the fact that it might be a forgery. I said it. D'you remember?'

'I remember.'

'And it's true, only I didn't want to face it. I still don't want to face it because if this is a forgery it means . . .'

'What does it mean, Marco? Is there something else you should have told me?'

'What? No, of course not. It's just that . . . There could have been others, couldn't there? I mean, there wouldn't be just this one . . .'

'That's not necessarily true.'

'No, but . . . No. Oh God, I thought, I really thought I could go through with it and sell the wretched thing.' He looked at the picture now with hatred.

'So, sell it.'

'What?'

'I told you I talked to Dr Biondini. He said if you want to sell it, sell it. There's nothing illegal about that.'

'But you've practically said it's a forgery.'

'I don't know whether it is or not but, apparently, provided you make no claims as to what it is no harm can come of it.'

'But the auctioneers will make claims.'

'Biondini says they can protect themselves. I don't

know how but I never heard of them ending up inside so you can assume it's true. Is there a photograph?'

'Of the painting? Yes. No . . . there will be. They kept it for their catalogue.'

The Marshal said nothing, realizing that this implied a decision already taken, and Marco's face darkened still more.

'I don't know. Once I'd seen Benozzetti and he seemed all right – besides, you've just said yourself I might as well sell it.'

'That's right,' the Marshal said blandly. 'If you could let me have a copy of the photograph for Biondini he'd be grateful. He's something of an expert on this painter so he'd like to see it. Just out of interest, you understand.'

'All right. I'll send it to you when I get it back. Don't you think I should get him to look at the painting?'

'That's up to you. The auctioneers must have had it looked at already to have made their decision – though Biondini did say he'd also be interested to know who'd seen it. Someone from London, he thought it probably was.'

He shifted his weight on the hard crate and spoke without looking the young man in the face, not wanting to embarrass him. 'While our friend was letting things drop . . . he didn't mention what might be in those two big safes he has there?'

'The safes . . .' Marco's mind seemed to be elsewhere. 'Yes, I know what's in them. He opened one of them while I was there.'

'He did?'

'Yes. It's just stuff he works with, ground minerals – that sort of thing – for making colours.'

'Colours . . . ? In a safe hefty enough for a bank?'

'Oh yes, it's very valuable stuff. He showed me some lapis lazuli, that's what was always used for the Virgin's cloak, the most expensive blue in the world.'

'Ah. And did he open the other safe, too?'

'No, but that's where he keeps his paintings – not his own, the ones he buys; he's spent everything he earned in a lifetime on paintings. Well, you can see he has nothing else. He said – this sounds weird but I suppose it might be true – that he had an Etruscan bronze packed in a metal crate and buried behind the studio. There's a bit of a garden there.'

'Mmph.'

'You don't believe it? But remember the floor. He's on the ground floor and in 1966 he lost a fortune. What wasn't damaged in the studio was destroyed in the vaults of a bank in safe deposit boxes. He hadn't declared or insured the contents – that's him!'

The Marshal got up stiffly from his crate and waited hat in hand for Benozzetti's entrance. He didn't intend to stay long. There was no doubt in his mind that Benozzetti would tell Marco more than he would tell him. Even so, he was curious to see the man outside of his lair, in a more mundane setting. Not to mention watching his face as he looked at the portrait. Whether Benozzetti would be equally eager to see the Marshal again was another matter. Oddly enough, it seemed as if he were delighted.

'Well, well! The knowledgeable Marshal! So we're to have your opinion, too. Perfect!'

And there wasn't a trace of irony in his voice. They shook hands without the Marshal opening his mouth. Benozzetti seemed bigger and more impressive than ever – perhaps because the room was small – and more elegant than ever, perhaps in contrast to Marco in his layers of shabby sweaters. Remembering the deathly cold in that great studio, the Marshal decided there was no danger of his suffering from the cellar-like chill in this windowless room.

As imperceptibly as he could manage, the Marshal stepped back from the waft of perfume the man carried with him, a vain attempt in such a small space. He never took his gaze from Benozzetti's face and was fascinated to see that though he was directly in front of the painting he didn't once look at it. There might have been a blank space where the easel stood and the glittering eyes slid around it in search of something else to fix on. They fixed on a photograph in a silver frame on the wall beyond the easel and he walked past the painting to look.

'Ha! Do you know who the man on your father's left is?'

Marco went closer. 'No. I know the senator but not that man.'

'He's a famous London dealer. Very famous. I've done a great deal of business with him myself.'

'I never met him. I didn't live with my father, so – I'm sorry there's nowhere to sit.'

But Benozzetti was clearly in no mood for sitting. He shifted jerkily about the room, looking at drawings, boxes of inks, the computer.

'You need money. You must set up this studio properly. In a suitable style for receiving clients. This won't do.'

He waved a manicured hand at the general mess.

In his left hand he was carrying a hat, the old-fashioned sort that men had worn in the forties and fifties but which nobody wore now. It looked new and expensive and exactly matched his heavy dark-blue overcoat. He was, of course, old fashioned in everything, as much in his ideas as in his clothes.

Marco pushed a hand into the pocket of his jeans and reddened a little.

'It's what I intend to do. That is, if I can sell this painting.'

'Sell it.'

'You think it's genuine?'

'Of course it's genuine. Your father was slightly less of a fool than others of his kind. It's a good painting. Sell. Sell. What does the Marshal here think you should do?'

'He says sell.'

'There you are then! It's an excellent painting. The Marchese Anna Caterina Luisa dei Gherardini as Flora. It's perfect. Sell. You need the money.'

He looked feverish, the Marshal thought, and too agitated to be confined in one room. There was nothing left for him to fix his snake's eyes on except the Marshal or the painting.

'I have to leave. I have a great deal to do.'

'Of course.' Marco moved to open the door for him. 'The auction —'

'I'll be there.'

He left without saying goodbye to the Marshal, agitation having overcome his manners. The Marshal stood quietly where he was, watching. He noticed that Benozzetti put on his hat well before he was out the door and that he pulled it slightly to the left, covering part of the scar tissue and casting a shadow over the damaged ear. Perhaps not just old fashioned, then.

He also noticed, though he made no comment on it to Marco as he in his turn took leave, that Benozzetti had not once mentioned the name of Antonio Franchi, and not once had he looked at the painting.

'Oh, Salva, no!'

'I can't help it.'

'But at Christmas!'

'It's not my fault and I don't see the use in talking about it.'

'You don't see the use in talking about it? The first time since the day we met that we've been separated at Christmas? Even when I was still down home and you were here? And you don't see the use in talking about it?'

Teresa had every intention of talking about it, and at length. The boys were out doing a little secret Christmas shopping in the square. That was a strategic mistake on his part. He should have made his announcement when they were in, because she disapproved of quarrelling in front of the children. But then, he hadn't been expecting a quarrel. He'd been expecting sympathy and couldn't for the life of him understand what he'd done to deserve all this anger.

'Why can't somebody else take your place? Somebody who has their family here and won't be alone?'

'Oh, Teresa, you know this is a particular case . . .'

'It's particular, all right, if it means us going down without you and you spending your Christmas without a soul near you. I'll say it's particular! It's nothing but a trumped-up story, anyway!'

'What!'

'Arresting this man, whatever he's called. They'd have arrested him years ago if it had been him.'

'Teresa . . .'

'He's just an old man. There's no proof.'

'It's our job to find it. Aren't you being a bit unreasonable?'

'Of course I'm being unreasonable! And what are you being? Arresting an old man just for show and splashing that terrible picture all over the newspapers where children can see it!'

As always happened, the more agitated she got, the more quiet he became. Now he only murmured, 'You surely aren't blaming me for that . . .'

155

'No! I'm blaming you for ruining our Christmas!'

'What do you want us to do? Decide he's not guilty so as not to spoil Christmas?'

'I don't care what you do but I'll tell you this: If you're going to insist on persecuting that dreadful old man I'm stopping here and the boys with me.'

'But you've booked your tickets.'

'And you've booked yours. We're not going.'

Later, in bed, she had a little cry.

'I'm not crying for that. I'm crying because I'm ashamed of myself, making a scene when you've got so much worry on your hands. It was no way to behave.'

'It doesn't matter.'

'Of course it matters. What's the use of us being together if we don't help each other?'

'You do help.' He stroked her head tentatively in the dark.

'I haven't seen you in a state like this since Toto was a baby. There isn't something else wrong, is there?'

'No.'

'You're not ill?'

'No, give me your hanky.'

She felt for it and blew her nose. 'It's just . . .'

'What? As long as you're not ill, there's nothing that can't be sorted out.'

'It's just . . . Thinking of the long journey down without you. It brought it all back. When we had to do it, we did it. We just gritted our teeth and got on with it. The interminable journeys and then telephoning you once a week and sometimes I couldn't hear you.'

'What do you mean, you couldn't hear me? No, keep it, you're still crying. What do you mean?'

'I could never hear you so well, sometimes because of the line and sometimes because you mumble and grumble.'

'I could always hear you.'

'I used to shout.'

'That's true.'

'I never realized how miserable I was. Do you know, except when your mother died I don't think I shed a tear in all those years. I couldn't afford to let myself go.'

'But why are you crying now?'

'Because now I can afford to, I suppose. The minute I thought of that train journey it all came out. Years of it. I don't want to go, Salva.'

'Stay here, then.' He pulled her head on to his shoulder. He went on stroking her head for some time until her breathing settled back to normal.

After a while he said, 'I wonder what I was saying.'

'When?'

'When you couldn't hear me.'

'Goodness knows. You never said much.'

'No.'

'Even so, it used to upset me when I couldn't catch your words. I've just thought . . . The children are going to be upset if we don't go down, aren't they?'

'I suppose so. But your family even more so.'

'And what about your sister?'

'What about her?'

'She was supposed to spend Christmas with us, with my family. She was counting on it. You know how lonely she is now your mother's gone and we've left.'

'She can still go.'

'Of course she can but she won't, not without us. It's my family, after all. Do you think she'll come up here?'

'You could ask her, but you know how she is about travelling alone.'

'I'll have to phone her. And my sister – and see if I can get the money back on the tickets, and talk to the boys, and if we're not going we should have posted the presents weeks ago . . .'

Sensing which way the wind was blowing, even half asleep as he was, he managed to murmur, 'Don't worry . . . and if you think you should go I'm sure I can get at least a couple of days off and fly to Catania . . .'

She left with the boys on Christmas Eve, not without shedding a tear at the station.

'Did we make the right decision?'

'I think so. I'll be working round the clock. At least I'll feel better for knowing you've got your family around you and the boys are having a good time with their cousins.'

'Give me that parcel – now: the fridge is full and there are still two jars of that meat sauce. Don't forget to use it up. It'll not keep more than a few days. Salva, are you listening? Giovanni, keep hold of that bag, never let go of your bag on the station like that.'

'It's heavy!'

'Do as you're told. Salva?'

'Get on the train and stop worrying. I'll phone you.'

'And you'll shout?'

'And I'll shout. Get on the train, it's leaving.'

He watched it go, his heart a dead weight inside him.

On Christmas morning at eight o'clock when the journalists were sleeping off their midnight suppers, the Suspect was released from prison. There wasn't a soul in sight at the prison gates, but as an extra precaution he was driven home in a bread van.

Seven

'Holy Mother of God, can't we just get to sleep? If I'm dead on my feet tomorrow it'll be worse. What am I supposed to tell them? It's you they're after so what am I supposed to say?'

'You'll keep your mouth shut! You say what I've told you to say and then you keep your mouth shut! Stupid bitch that you are, they'll run rings round you. You say you and me have worked hard all our lives and never done any harm to anybody. And you don't start gabbling on, do you hear me?

'We've worked hard all our lives and never –'

'I don't know anything . . .'

'We've worked hard all our lives.'

'All our lives . . .'

'And we've never done any harm to anybody.'

'Any harm to anybody. But what if – ?'

'Are you listening? What if, what if! Of course they'll keep on at you but you know nothing, right? You know nothing so you say nothing. You say, "I don't know anything except we've worked hard all our lives and never done any harm to anybody." Because if you say one word more they'll make something of it, mark my words, and they'll write it down. They write everything down and then you're done for. Then they'll say, "His wife said this," and, "his wife said that." In court they'll say it, stupid buggers that they are. They'll do for you if you open your mouth, so watch it. They twist every word you say and if you forget something and make a mistake and then remember, they say you're lying. So keep it short, d'you understand! "We've worked hard all our lives and never done any harm to anybody, neither me nor my husband. So leave us in peace!"'

'Oh, Holy Mother of God, how will I manage . . . Damn, blast and set fire to them all, what am I supposed to . . . ? Me and my husband have always . . . We've never . . . Mother of God . . .'

'I'm not getting anything . . . I've lost her . . .'

Young Noferini was sitting at the controls but all his efforts produced nothing more than shuffling sounds and static.

The Marshal understood nothing of the technical problems but said, 'She's crying. She's probably buried her head in the pillow.' He got up from the edge of the

161

stone-hard single bed where he'd been sitting and walked about a bit, out of sight of the small low window. His shoes were noisy on the uneven red tiles. It was almost two-thirty in the morning and the room was as cold as death. He'd been sitting in his greatcoat and now he fished in his pockets and put his leather gloves back on. Just their luck that the house opposite the Suspect's had no heating. So many of these old country cottages had been abandoned by the peasant farmers for whom they'd been built and taken over by young couples escaping from the city or, as often as not, by foreigners. But not this one. Except for the television and the washing machine this one was the same as it had been for centuries and the only fireplace, huge and stacked with oak and olive wood, was in the kitchen.

'Are you still getting nothing?'

'Not a sausage. I think he must have got up . . . That's him . . . I can't make out a word, probably gone for a pee. You're right, though, she's crying.'

'No wonder. I'm going downstairs for two minutes.'

He took a shaded torch with him. The kitchen was much warmer and the remains of a small log still glowed under the ash when he blew on it. A tiny mouse, pink eared and long nosed, popped up from behind the wood pile and fixed him with a beady-eyed stare that was more annoyed than frightened. It vanished again, waiting for this out-of-hours intruder to take himself off.

He remembered his mother and her unrelenting war against these cheeky field mice who came in each night for shelter and whatever they could find to eat. Their strict timetable had only ever been disturbed by births, deaths and marriages, never by The Law.

He found a poker and turned the glowing log over to warm his hands. Goodness only knew the extent to which their presence was disturbing the family, never mind the mice. There was a man in his fifties, still working for the countess who owned all this land but for a wage, now, not as a peasant. He hadn't left his cottage for a flat in the village because, though his wife was all for it, he refused to leave his vegetable garden and his rabbits. His wife, Marilena, her name was, had not forgiven him for this and clearly never would. The Marshal didn't blame her. A spanking new little flat, central heating, smooth new floors, no smoke and ash, no stairs for her tired legs to haul buckets and laundry up and down . . .

It would have been paradise for the exhausted woman and would surely have guaranteed her a more cheerful and probably longer old age. There was a grown-up daughter in the house, too, a lumpish-looking girl who worked in the sausage factory near the village. She rarely opened her mouth, even when young Noferini attempted to kid her along in the hope of keeping the atmosphere relaxed. The husband's old mother had died recently, which was why there was an empty bedroom to watch from.

The family never complained. They couldn't. Before the Suspect was released, they and all their neighbours had complained bitterly and publicly that the man was known to be dangerous and that it was outrageous they should be exposed to his presence. Their fear seemed genuine, though the Marshal privately considered it exaggerated. They could hear him shouting and raging at his wife every evening, but that wasn't the reason so much as their knowing, now it had been in the papers, that he had murdered a man in another village forty years before. As for his being accused of being the Monster, that seemed to leave most of the villagers unmoved, except that some of them got angry because of the number of journalists and sightseers hanging about day after day. Well, that would get worse before it got better.

The pink ears appeared from behind the log again and the mouse eyed him severely. The Marshal sighed and turned away from the feeble source of heat to face the icy bedroom again.

'How's it going?'

'He's back in bed.'

'Lucky him.'

'I think he took some aspirin or something. In any case, he's gone to sleep. She's still moaning to herself but you can't make half of it out.'

'Mother of God . . . What will I . . . ? We work, we've always – and we haven't done any harm, haven't done any harm . . . I can't . . . How can I – ? What will they ask me? I'll just say we work hard, I don't know anything and we work . . . Mother of God. No . . . I'll say no. They can't make me. I'll say . . . I'll say no, I'll walk. No, thank you very much, I'll walk and I can walk back . . . I can get a bus and then walk. I don't want them to make me get in a car. What will they do to me? I don't want . . . I don't . . . Police Station, oh God . . .'

'Good morning, signora.'

'Good morning. Can I offer you – ?'

'No, signora, nothing. We'll be going now.'

She always insisted on offering, though they'd explained over and over that they wouldn't take anything. The husband had already left for work. They'd seen him go from the upstairs window at the same time as his neighbour, the Suspect. They had nodded to one another. Then the police car had come for the Suspect's wife. She had let herself be put into the car without a murmur. She had been awake all night and had risen just after six. She was probably too exhausted to react. The Marshal had come down after seeing her driven away.

'Good morning, signorina.'

''Morning.' She answered without looking up as she always did, then sat down in front of the breakfast her mother had set out. In silence she broke up a brioche and dropped pieces into a bowl of *caffellatte*, fishing them out again with her spoon. She kept her head low over the bowl and her eyes almost closed. Her mother stood near the smoking fire, polishing her shoes for her.

'Here. You've a ladder in that stocking.'

'It doesn't matter.'

'Will you be out tonight?'

'Moh.'

'I don't want you coming home by yourself, even if . . .'

She didn't finish the sentence though she clearly meant 'even if we have got two carabinieri in the house.'

'Mind what I say. Are you listening?'

'Stefano'll bring me home.'

'Well, don't let him leave you at the villa. The road's not that bad. A fine thing, thinking more of his car springs than of you, especially after what it said in the paper. Am I right?'

The appeal was to the Marshal who was standing silently near the door wishing Noferini would hurry up in the bathroom so they could get to the bar for their breakfast.

'It's always as well to be careful,' he conceded without committing himself to any comment on 'what it said in the paper'. He knew well enough what she was referring to. An article warning couples that every time the wrong man had been arrested and accused of being the Monster, the real Monster had struck again immediately. It seemed highly unlikely that it would happen this time, even if they did turn out to have made another mistake. The Monster, be he the Suspect or anyone else, had been out of action for too many years. But far be it from the Marshal to hazard any such opinion to these people. He was aware, nevertheless, that extra patrols were out on Saturday nights, especially at new moon, despite the fact that it was midwinter and all the murders had been committed in the heat of summer. Simonetti was hedging his bets. When Noferini did appear and they left, Marilena was still reading the riot act to her daughter and her voice followed them along the stony track that met the country road at the gates of a villa and then curved left towards the village. During the day a man from the local carabinieri station kept an eye on the Suspect as he worked on the land. No attempt was made to hide from him the fact that he was being watched. All that mattered was to make sure that he removed nothing from his house before the search was about to take place. They were pretty sure he knew that his telephone was tapped, or guessed it might be, judging from some of his calls. He was unlikely to have guessed that the house was bugged.

Knowing that every crime reporter in Tuscany was camping out in the bar in the main square, they stopped at a smaller place near the road down to Florence.

'Two coffees, one brioche, one toasted sandwich, right? Or was it one coffee, one *caffellatte*? I've got you muddled up.'

'Two coffees.' The *caffellatte* was Bacci, the Marshal imagined. Ferrini would be more likely to add grappa to his coffee than milk.

'How's it going?' enquired the barman, slapping two cups under the coffee machine. 'Any news?' He always asked, though he never got an answer. 'You know what I say?' he proceeded cheerfully – he never took offence – 'It's that girl I feel sorry for.'

'You mean his daughter?'

'That's right. A young woman she is, by this time, though she's not right in the head. They say they'll have to take her away.'

'Who says?'

'Oh, people . . . Father Damiani, for one. He's had it up to here. Here you are. The toast'll take another minute. I mean to say, that little flat's right on the square. She can't put her head out of the door because of the journalists. Of course, there's those as are glad enough of all the money this business has brought in.'

'Yes,' observed the Marshal, getting his drift. 'I suppose you're a bit out of it, being the furthest away from his house.'

'I can do without making money out of other people's misfortunes. They've been in here, you know, all these journalists. Somebody or other from the telly as well. I say the same to all of them. Leave that girl out of it. It's not right. She's not responsible for what her father has or hasn't done. She's had enough trouble. Anyway, profit or no profit, everybody's going to be fed up of this lot before it's over.'

'That's true,' said the Marshal.

'It's like some sort of lottery. Everybody you meet it's the same question: "Are you for the Guilties or the Not Guilties?" There are people keeping a book on it – did you know that?'

'No, I didn't.'

'One toast.'

'Thanks.' Noferini sank his teeth into it hungrily, ignoring the barman as he always did. For a young policeman like him, an enquiry meant sitting at a computer or at that contraption he'd been fiddling with this morning, not listening to gossip in the bar. The Marshal listened.

'What you can't get into their heads, these journalists, is that nobody round here knows him. What he's like, who are his friends, does he come in here, does he fight with his neighbours, does he drink, is he nasty, is he a pervert, is he a Peeping Tom . . . ? And you should hear the answers they get! From people who've never said two words to the man, who didn't even know he existed until they saw his picture in the paper! There was a fellow last night – on the eight o'clock news, this is, if you can believe me, spouting on for ten minutes with he's this and he's that, he's terrorizing the whole village! Fat-headed twit. Anything to be on the telly, that's what it comes down to, or to get your name in the papers.'

'Well' – the Marshal blotted his mouth with a paper napkin – 'I suppose some of them must know him.'

'You suppose wrong. Pardon me, but he only moved here just before they arrested him for messing with that poor girl. All the time he's been theoretically living here he's been in prison. They know him as well as I knew him. Good morning, Good afternoon, Goodbye.'

'He did come in here, then?'

'A time or two, like anybody else.'

'But you weren't frightened of him?'

169

'Frightened of him? That's all rubbish to get attention. I've nothing against him and I couldn't give a toss whether he's guilty or not. If he's guilty he goes back inside, but if they do him for it and he's not guilty, then that's all right by me. After what he did to his daughter he can stay inside for the rest of his life. Best place for him. It was bad enough what he did to her but can you imagine having to tell it all in court? She didn't want to testify, you know, she told them. She never wanted to.'

'Surely she wouldn't have made the accusation if –'

'That's what she told my wife. She was in tears. She said, "I didn't want to sign it but they made me. I didn't want to go to prison, that's why I signed it." Of course, as I say, she's not right in the head.'

'No.'

'And no wonder with a father like that. What she must have gone through. They ought to take her away.'

'Are we going?' Noferini asked, impatient of the barman's diatribe.

'Just a minute. There's something I want to buy. You get in the car and I'll be right with you.' He'd spotted a glass counter behind which were little stockings full of presents for the Epiphany, chocolates and whistles and plastic cars and coal made of sugar for when they'd been naughty. But would they arrive in time? And wouldn't anything so flimsy get crushed in the post? Would Teresa already have bought them? Did it matter if she had since he was far away? Were they getting too old? If they were

170

they might be offended – in any case, he suddenly remembered, they'll be back on the sixth of January because school would be starting.

'Have you decided?' the barman asked, poised.

'Nothing . . .' the Marshal muttered. 'Nothing . . .'

A quarter to twelve. What was the use? He'd lain there for hours trying to get to sleep, or even pretending he was asleep, but it was hopeless. He was too old for this sort of thing. Only young people can fall asleep at the drop of a hat or stay in bed after a late night. Once you get past a certain age you're awake at your usual time no matter what. And as for trying to go to bed at nine in the morning . . .

The light . . . that might be the problem. He got wearily out of bed and closed the shutters behind the white curtain.

'That should be better . . .'

He got back under the blankets and tried again, reaching out across the empty space beside him. He felt unbalanced on his own in the wide bed and unconsciously pulled at Teresa's pillow until it turned and occupied her place. He was so tired that his body ached and his eyes hurt. And he was hungry. He only noticed it now that he was settled there in the dark. He shouldn't be hungry, not at twelve, because he never had lunch before about two. Nevertheless, his stomach rumbled and a sharp pain stabbed him in the middle. Would he sleep if he ate something? Got something down

171

him with a big glass of warming red wine? The thought of moving put him off, not to mention the thought of cooking. There was no bread, of course, so he couldn't make a quick sandwich. What was there? The last bit of sauce for pasta. He'd never stay on his feet until the water boiled. He could fancy something tasty, though . . . If he'd thought on he could have bought a couple of those toasted sandwiches Noferini always ate from that bar this morning. They'd have been ready in two ticks and with that cheese and salty ham inside them they'd have gone down very nicely with a glass of red.

The more he thought about it the more acute his hunger became and the more his tiredness tried to fight it down. Mentally, he went through the motions of getting up, getting dressed and going out to buy either sandwiches from a bar or bread from a baker's, but even the thought exhausted him. He sighed and burrowed deeper into his pillow in the hope that the oblivion of sleep would bring escape from the mouth-watering menus he couldn't drive out of his head.

'I'm on a diet!' he suddenly said aloud, and the machinations of his stomach lurched to a stop. Infuriated with himself he hauled over on to his left side and slammed his head down on the pillow. That settled that.

'Blast!' was the last thing he said aloud before falling asleep without prior notice. He'd barely had time to try and explain to a puzzled Teresa why he hadn't just told her if he wanted something to eat when the phone rang and woke him up again. It was ten past twelve.

'Mario!' It was the voice of a very old and fractious woman.

'This is not –'

'Mario! Why didn't you ring home last night?' A very old, very fractious woman from Calabria.

'Signora, you've got the wrong number.'

'Who are you?'

'Signora, you've –'

'What are you doing in my Mario's house?'

After a while he gave up on her and replaced the receiver. He was now wide awake and as fractious as his caller. He turned the bell off on the private phone, leaving only the army phone on. Then he stumped into the kitchen and put on a pan of water to boil. While he was waiting for that he got dressed and remade the bed with military precision. He would just have to have an early night.

'The dog's food . . .'

'What about the dog's food?'

'He . . .'

With almost every question it was the same. She'd manage half an answer perhaps and then stop. It didn't help to prompt her. They waited in silence, a silence as loud as a scream. She resembled her father, short and stocky. Her legs dangled like a child's from the chair and she seemed sometimes to stretch her foot, trying to reach firm ground but barely touching the floor with the toe of her dusty shoe. She clutched the edges of the plastic chair as tightly as she could, her knuckles white with the strain.

'He made us eat it.'

'The dog food? Dog food out of a tin?'

'No. It was lungs and stuff, boiled up. And old bread . . . He said . . .'

'What did he say?'

Another silence. Then: 'He said it was good enough for me and my mum. He said we were stupider than the dog.'

'He was fond of the dog?' The unaccustomed effort of keeping his voice down and his tone unaggressive was beginning to tell on Simonetti. They had heard more silences than words from this poor creature in the last hour but he had clearly no intention of letting up. The others, including the Marshal, would be almost as glad as the girl herself when this interview came to an end.

'What sort of dog was it?'

'It was brown. Not so big.'

It was lucky for Simonetti that he had the transcripts from the trial at the end of which the Suspect had been condemned for abusing his daughter. It meant he knew the answers. All he was doing was rehearsing the girl in his selection of the questions he thought relevant. How long must this have taken the first time round, the first time she'd had to tell these things?

'Was it a hunting dog?'

'Yes, he used to hit it with a stick and make it scream.'

'And did he hit you with a stick, too?'

'Sometimes.'

'Not often?'

Silence.

'Did he hit you with a stick every day?'

'Once he did when I didn't do my homework.'

'And the other times?'

'The other times he used his fists.'

'Why did he do that; can you remember?'

'When I wanted to go out.'

'And the other reasons?'

Nothing. They could hear their own breathing as they waited and waited. Her face, behind thick glasses, showed no sign of her inner struggle but her dangling feet made jerky little movements and sometimes she accidentally kicked herself in the ankle. Her wrinkled stockings showed the dirty mark this left each time. She was twenty-six but it was impossible not to think of her as anything other than an ageing child. Of course, in real terms, that was exactly what she was. When she spoke after these lengthy pauses it was, quite normally, as though there had been no gap in the conversation at all.

'Sometimes he hit me because I didn't want to go in his bed.'

'Was that at night?'

'Not always at night. He used to wake me up some-times when I was asleep in the night or else in the morning.'

'And what happened when he did that?'

Silence. Her hands tightened even more on the chair.

'You have nothing to be frightened of here. We're all your friends. If there are things you don't like saying you

175

can just answer yes or no. When he made you get in his bed did he force you to have oral sex?'

'No.'

'He didn't? What did he do? Did he do something else?'

'Yes.' Another long silence and the twisting, kicking feet. 'He . . .'

The room had grown far too hot. There was no reason why they shouldn't take their jackets off, the Marshal thought, but he didn't move. It was impossible to break the tension her silences and sudden brief bursts of speech had caused to accumulate.

'He made me put his . . . thing . . . in my mouth.'

'I see. Can you remember how old you were the first time that happened?'

'Nine. Once my mum told him to give over but he said shut up.'

'She was very frightened of him, wasn't she? Did he hit her a lot, too?'

'He always hit her when he got mad at her and once he said he'd slit her throat.'

'Was that because she tried to stop him touching you?'

'No. It was because she spilt his pasta on the floor. There was some wet on the floor and she slipped and it spilt out of the dish and he ate her dinner and she had to eat the stuff that had spilt.'

'Did he once throw an axe at your mother?'

'Yes, but he missed her and it stuck in the door. It was because of the eggs.'

'What eggs? Did she break some and he was angry?'

'No. It was the countess brought them. She said I didn't eat enough and she told my mum off because we had all those chickens and she never gave me any eggs or chicken to eat.'

'And why didn't she?'

'They were for selling, they weren't for us, so the countess brought us a dozen eggs and my mum made some tagliatelle. He thought they were his eggs and she'd pinched them so he threw an axe.'

'And did the countess ever bring you anything again?'

'Yes. A lot of things, but my mum never took them.'

'Because she was too frightened?'

'Yes.'

'How long did your father go on making you go to bed with him?'

'Until I was about nineteen. Then I left home and lived in the flat.'

'Signorina, you'll have to forgive me for asking you this because I know how upsetting it is for you but it's very important that these people here today understand how your father treated you when you were small. Do you understand that?'

'I think so . . .'

'To make it less embarrassing for you, you can just answer yes or no if you want to.'

Remembering the failure of his last attempt at this he kept it simple.

'Did your father, when he forced you to go to bed with him, put any objects inside you?'

'He put . . . He . . .' Her face burned and she pressed her thighs together, trying to stop it happening even now. 'Cucumber.'

'Thank you. Do you know what a vibrator is?'

'Yes. A rubber "thing" as well. He made me use a rubber "thing". He said if he let me go out I'd be doing it with anybody and I'd get pregnant. He said I was safer with him.'

'Tell me about the vibrator.'

'He made me use it.'

'On yourself?'

'Sometimes. Sometimes on him. You can't get pregnant that way.'

'You've never been pregnant?'

'No. When I was late that time it was only because I wasn't so well.'

'But you had to have a little check-up at the hospital, is that right?'

'Yes.'

'And you knew they would ask you if you might be pregnant?'

'He said they'd ask me. He said I hadn't to tell them about him touching me. He said to tell them I'd been with boys.'

'But you hadn't?'

'No. I'd never do that because of Father Damiani. Father Damiani –'

'Of course you wouldn't. I know you're a good Catholic and you go to church every Sunday.'

'I used to go every morning before I went in hospital.'

'Now I want to go on to something else. You can go on answering yes or no if you prefer. Did these things with your father sometimes happen outside your home, in the car, for instance?'

She opened her mouth but only a faint moan came out. The feet began jerking rapidly.

'Just take your time.'

Another little moan. Her breathing became audible. Even then, the eyes behind the thick glasses might have been blind they were so devoid of expression.

'Signorina?' Why didn't he leave her be? Couldn't he see by now that any break he made in the silence doubled its length?

After a further long wait she made another attempt that ended in a whimper. The next effort produced, 'The car.'

'He took you out with him in the car? And your mother?'

'Both of us.'

'Did he take you to the woods?'

'Yes.'

'At night?'

Some sort of assent. A faint noise, a nod.

'Can you tell us what happened when he took you both to the woods?'

But her whimpers now were meaningless, there was no way of telling whether she was agreeing or protesting. Then even these noises ceased. She fell totally silent. Only her feet moved and some small beads of moisture formed in the down on her upper lip. Her fear was the biggest presence in the room. The Marshal recognized it, the smell of it. A very particular odour of sweat which he associated with prison and with certain moments just before an arrest. And the asylum. He'd been trying to think where else he'd smelled it. It was in the asylum.

'She's not right in the head, and no wonder . . .'

The barman at Pontino had said it.

'One of you would be in the parked car with him and the other would get out? Or sometimes he would get out? Was that because somebody had to keep watch? Did he make you take all your clothes off?'

There was no point in going on with this. Why didn't he give up? She was paralysed with fear. How had she done it? Families like hers, though not criminal, regard the police as a threat rather than as protection. What could have got into this terrified, incoherent creature that made her get up one morning, years after it was all over, and present herself to the police to tell from scratch this story that was choking her now? The Marshal couldn't see her doing it. And yet she'd done it, and not to the Marshal of carabinieri in her own village which would have been more comprehensible. He, at least, was a familiar figure, seen every day of her life, seen in the bar, in the grocer's, chatting at the market in the square. That's where you'd expect her to go – of course, she might have done that first and then the thing had snowballed.

'He used to take pornographic magazines along, didn't he?'

'Can you tell us about that?'

'Can you answer yes or no?'

'He showed you the pictures and told you to do the things being done in them?'

If she were that frightened of her father why did she even bother? Unless . . . unless something else frightened her more and that was what pushed her. Had she seen something? She wasn't living with her parents but in the little flat in the village square.

She was breathing too hard. There was a limit to how long you could stay as rigid as that. The hands clutching the seat of the chair hadn't relaxed their grip for a second since the interview began.

'You acted out the scenes, as it were, from these magazines.'

'Only in the car or on the ground or in the woods, as well?'

Still nothing. He'd have to give up.

If you murdered two people, pulled their bodies about . . . There wouldn't be all that much blood since most of the stab wounds were inflicted postmortem and he would wash in the stream which was always nearby. Even so . . .

No matter how you looked at it there was no sense in it unless she were frightened of something more immediate. He thought of the Suspect, imagining him coming home with a pistol, bloodstained clothing, and a bag containing . . .

'*My mum once told him to give over but he said shut up.*' If that was the total sum of his wife's reaction to the raping of her nine-year-old daughter it was unlikely that she'd have given him much trouble. He pictured the same scene at the girl's flat. It was possible but somehow less probable, right on the village square and not all that late on a Saturday night. Of course, there was no knowing what plans he had for the trophies he brought with him. It was impossible to make sensible deductions about somebody whose most important action was beyond understanding.

'*I didn't want to go to prison, that's why* . . .' So, she was frightened of being considered an accomplice if she didn't give him away . . . Only she didn't, did she? She went and told the police he'd abused her. That would serve to put him inside, of course, remove the problem for a bit. Looking at her now he didn't believe it. He didn't believe it because she didn't look capable of anything so calculated. And supposing she'd done it by instinct, what took her so long? The last murder happened just two years before she turned up at the police station.

He also didn't believe it because, no matter how sorry he felt for her years of helpless suffering and for her present pitiful condition, he knew beyond a doubt as he watched her that her silence was a lie.

*

Noferini was asleep. The Marshal sat near the switch-board he didn't understand and never touched, looking out of the small uncurtained window at the white shape of the Suspect's house. At a certain hour, when the white house was in darkness and the squabbling voices ceased, Noferini would turn the volume on full so that the slightest word or movement would be magnified. Then they would take turns to get a little sleep. Noferini had just stretched himself out on the hard bed, covered himself with an army blanket and within seconds had rolled on to his side and begun snoring very faintly. The Marshal envied him. He couldn't remember when he'd last had a decent sleep. Having failed to make up his lost hours in the mornings, he was now finding himself wakeful at nights as well, whether he had to be here or not. Despite this, he had no intention of waking Noferini up after a couple of hours as he'd asked. Undisturbed, he would sleep on throughout the night. The search warrant for the Suspect's house was now signed and the search would start tomorrow morning. The warrant hadn't been easy to get since the judge had looked askance both at the original anonymous letter of accusation and another, more recently arrived, suggesting that if the house and garden were searched with a metal detector something of interest would be found. Anonymous letters are out of order in court and can't be used, but Simonetti fought for the right to check this one out and in the end the judge, reluctant to protect someone whom the newspapers had now defined as a monster in his own right, whether he was the Monster or not, had signed the warrant. The search would begin early next morning. Neither the Marshal nor Noferini was expected to appear before lunch, but the Marshal was quite certain that whatever he might decide himself, Noferini would be over there first thing bobbing about like a squirrel whether he'd had any sleep or not.

With a snort and a rustle of eiderdown the Suspect shifted in his sleep. The Marshal turned to the dark shape against the just visible paler darkness of the whitewashed wall but the boy slept soundly. Once you'd forgiven him his overdone enthusiasm, which owed more to youth and inexperience than to calculation or ambition, you couldn't help liking the lad.

It had been Ferrini who'd first christened him 'the squirrel', though whether that was because of the feathery light eyebrows that met over a turned-up nose or because of the intentness with which he collected information to store in his beloved computer wasn't clear. The boy slept as hard as he worked . . .

The Marshal turned back to the window. It wasn't, thank God, as cold as it had been. The air was more humid and no stars were visible. It would probably rain tomorrow.

He settled in his chair and his thoughts turned to the problem of the frightened, daughter. There was something in the back of his mind . . . something quite apart from her concealing silences and it wasn't about her father, either, though he was sure, even so, that it was to do with sex. The

Marshal was the first to admit that he was no great brain and that logical thought was pretty much beyond him. He either knew things or he didn't. But there was something going on here that he'd never come across before and that he found difficult to define, even to himself – goodness knows, he didn't ask much of himself in the way of clear explanations. It was somehow the case that every path you took led you back to the same place. All arguments were circular. If you started thinking that the Suspect wouldn't have done so and so because he would have been crazy to risk it, you then remembered that if he slaughtered sixteen people he didn't know from Adam then, of course, he *was* crazy, so then what? And if it made no sense that the daughter should have gone to the police about her father so long after it was all over, well, she didn't have any sense, did she? Round and round and on to the next baffling episode. That was a problem, too. A backlog of twenty years of case notes which, though he'd never admitted it to anybody, he'd never quite finished reading because of the present workload, plus at least some of his usual duties – Lorenzini had to have some free time – had made it impossible. He didn't blame anybody for that. He blamed his own slowness, since everybody else had presumably managed. But this became yet another circular argument because even though he knew he was slow, and even though he felt like someone trying to understand a film that's being run past him on fast forward, he was also convinced that there wasn't enough information there. This was a conviction based on nothing at all. It had been there all the time but hadn't come to the surface until he'd watched Simonetti questioning the daughter. He'd had the transcript of the trial there and he was selecting parts of it which would help in showing the Suspect as the probable Monster. It wasn't unreasonable to wonder whether all the rest of the information they'd been given had been edited in the same fashion. If it had, was that out of order or just sensible? The Marshal wasn't sure, but he was sure that he could hardly be the one to bring the question up since he was the only member of the squad who had failed to get through the information he had been given. It was one of the things he wouldn't mind having a word with Ferrini about but it was becoming increasingly difficult to find the opportunity to talk now that they'd been split up and were working different shifts. He had managed, when they'd just taken the daughter away, to ask him quietly:

'*Do you think that was necessary? I mean, in front of so many men?*'

'*She's going to have to do it in front of a full courtroom.*'

'*But she could be heard in camera, surely?*'

'*She could but she won't be. At least, not unless we find that Beretta 22 under his pillow. She's the best, and might be the only, weapon the prosecution's got.*'

'*He can't be tried for the same crime again.*'

'*No. But he will be, mark my words. And for that murder of forty years ago, too. Use your head, Guarnaccia. Otherwise the trial'd last two minutes. "You are the Monster of Florence." "No I'm not." Jury retires.*'

'Then it won't go to trial.'

'Won't it?'

What a business. He stared across at the faint shape of the Suspect's house. They might find something but he hadn't much hope. The Suspect did know his phone was tapped, they knew that by now. That was the latest from the barman who was highly amused by the story because apparently the only reason it bothered him was not that the police might catch him giving himself away but that it might somehow double his phone bill. He still didn't seem to know the house was bugged, though. Probably thought that sort of thing only happened in spy films. What was he supposed to be thinking about? The daughter. He'd been trying to remember something she'd said and it was the barman . . . where did he come into it? The barman's eyebrows met in the middle. That wasn't right, it was Noferini who shouldn't have been behind that bar, anyway. He was supposed to be getting some sleep. Round and round in circles. The alarm! His hand shot out to switch it off so it wouldn't wake Teresa but instead of a clock on the bedside table he hit something bristling with knobs and switches and someone else turned off the alarm.

'Blast!' He came to himself, realizing that he had accidentally hit the control board and switched off half a dozen things, including the volume.

Noferini was off the bed and beside him in half a second, crouching in front of the board to bring back the sound.

'Shift yourself. Get off your backside!'

'There he is. What's he doing up at five? Was that his alarm going off?'

'I suppose it must have been.' Five? He'd fallen asleep, then. He must have been asleep for a good three hours. 'Made me jump. I hope I haven't done any damage.'

'No. What d'you think he's doing? Listen . . .'

Whatever it was, he was doing it a long way from a microphone. He was swearing at his wife as usual and they could just about hear her fainter lament along with the noise of something being dragged. Possibly a piece of furniture. Every now and then they picked up the odd word or phrase.

'In here . . .'

'. . . bitch . . .'

'Mouth shut. Get hold . . .'

They looked at each other in the dark.

'The skips!' whispered Noferini, as though the voice coming from the switchboard could pick up his words. 'They're round the back of his house!'

They started down the stairs. These country houses had only one door. If he was pulling that gun and ammunition from its hiding place to dump it into the municipal skip so that it would be removed the next day they needed to catch him at it. They opened the door.

'Whatever he's doing, he's doing it in the dark; he knows we're here, doesn't he?'

'He doesn't know about the bugs.'

It was true that without the listening devices they'd

have had a hard time knowing what he was doing. The night was dark as only night in the country can be. That was what he'd been waiting for. Not so much as a star. They'd had to grope their way in a wide arc round to the back of his house where the skips were, and more than once they bumped into invisible trees. The positive side of this was that he wouldn't see them either. They settled near a cypress tree at a distance and waited.

'What's taking him so long?' whispered Noferini after a while.

The Marshal didn't know and didn't answer. Speculation was pointless and they might be heard. After all, he could have the gun cemented into the wall for all they knew, or under a sealed-down flagstone in the floor. All they could do was wait.

Noferini's ears were sharper than his and the Marshal sensed his having picked up something before he heard it himself.

A shape moved near the skip and the lid creaked open. A thud. Then it creaked shut. He hadn't let it slam. They moved forward but before they could reach the skip they heard it open again and saw the vague outline of someone reaching in. They ran the last few steps but the arm must have been withdrawn because the skip slammed shut. Noferini grabbed at a sleeve, but the invisible figure wriggled out of his grasp with a little cry of fear and shot away.

'Torch!'

The Marshal had already wrenched it from his pocket

and now its beam made a cone of light in the blackness. It picked up the figure of a tall thin man disappearing behind the house they had come out of. When they got there he'd gone. They stood still a moment and listened for footsteps to tell them which direction he'd taken. They heard nothing. It was as if they'd imagined him. He might have been a ghost, except for the fact that Noferini was still holding a jacket by the sleeve.

Eight

'How long exactly between his putting it in there and the other man removing it?' Simonetti was furious with them but what was to be done about it?

It was Noferini, always quicker than the Marshal, and driven by nervousness now, who answered:

'Only seconds, sir. We hadn't taken more than three steps before we heard the lid open again.'

'Then they'd arranged it. How did they arrange it? He's been under observation, his phone's tapped. How did they communicate? Has he sent any letters? That would account for the delay.'

The Marshal coughed.

'Well? Are you disagreeing with me?'

'No, no . . .' Who would dare? 'I don't know if he's sent

any letters. We're only here at night. Besides, his wife could have posted something. She's sure to have been to the post office to pay her household bills and so on . . .'

'So?'

'I just thought that perhaps the delay was because of the weather.'

'The *weather*?'

'That's right. That and the new moon. It was totally dark last night. If it hadn't been, we'd have seen him.'

'The new moon. Yes, I see . . .' He looked at the Marshal with a different expression, then gave him a pat on the arm. 'Good . . .'

The Marshal was annoyed for the rest of the day, not with Simonetti so much as with himself. He had fed Simonetti a line that would result in a full-page article in tomorrow's *Nazione*. He had also, just for a moment, felt rewarded by that pat on the arm. Like the schoolboy with a star on his composition or the good dog who has fetched the newspaper.

He had been right about one thing: the weather had changed. It was raining hard. The search had begun indoors, in a sort of storeroom off the kitchen. The kitchen itself was encumbered with cables taking lights for the film cameras to the dark storeroom. The Marshal, coming out of the sitting room behind Simonetti, stepped over the cables and went outside to where three men were pulling the wheeled rubbish skip into the yard. Once it was there they stood a while looking at it. There wasn't a lot they could do with it at this point. They couldn't open it because of the rain. It would have to be removed to Florence to the police laboratories. Of course they had all, including Simonetti, glimpsed inside, but without much hope. It seemed inevitable that whatever the Suspect had wanted to get rid of had been put there only so it could be removed by his friend or accomplice. The Marshal was put out by this because he wouldn't have thought him far thinking enough for such a plan. He had seen him as the usual deny-everything type with a well-developed sense of danger on an animal level, but not a cool planner. Not that. It wasn't often he misjudged his man. And yet, there it was. He'd seen the other man for himself, in as much as you could say you'd seen anything in that solid darkness. They would check through the rubbish anyway in the faint hope that if the gun had lain there, however briefly, there might be a trace of grease on one of the plastic rubbish bags.

He stood there, motionless, the rain beating down on him, observing in silence the men messing around the skip. They were arguing now about the best way to transport it. They had thick, rainproof jackets on and amphibian boots. He ought to go home. Even if he had no hope of sleeping he could at least put more suitable clothing on. He hadn't had so much as a coffee either but he was too tired to come to any decision, even about breakfast, so he stayed where he was. Behind him in the kitchen someone had begun hammering. Were they demolishing the place or what? The Suspect, who had the right to be present during the search, had not gone to work. He was raising his voice now in tearful protest at whatever they were damaging.

Just a little way down the lane was another cottage. There were a number of journalists in there. The Marshal had spotted them when they appeared briefly on the roof to take photographs, but it was both wet and dangerous on the loose red tiles and there was very little to see so they had spent most of the morning inside out of sight. No doubt they'd paid a small fortune to the householder for this privilege.

It was stupid to stand there getting wet.

'What are you standing there getting wet for?' Ferrini appeared beside him. He'd arrived this morning and so was suitably dressed.

'I was thinking . . .' lied the Marshal, whose mind was a blank.

'Come inside and think.'

The Marshal followed him docilely.

'This is a business,' Ferrini muttered. 'I mean about last night.'

'Yes.' Seeing Ferrini was pulling off his wet rainproof, the Marshal unbuttoned his soaked greatcoat. 'It bothers me, to tell you the truth.'

'Did he give you hell?'

'Not exactly . . . it's bothering me because I wouldn't have thought it of him.'

'Simonetti?'

'No, no . . . I mean –' He inclined his head towards the door of the storeroom where the Suspect was weeping and his wife was trying to push past him to get in there. Somebody had smashed some bottles of tomato preserve and she was more infuriated by that than by any accusations levelled against her husband.

'Damn and blast it, all that work and trouble – and who's going to pay for it all? Who's going to pay?'

'They're trying to ruin me! What have I ever done that they want to crucify me?'

'I think we'll withdraw.' Ferrini indicated the next room and they left the kitchen, closing the door on the noise.

'We'll stay off the film set for a bit, I think. I wanted a quiet word with you. What did you mean, anyway, about our friend in there?'

'I'm just surprised, that's all. I mean, it was a well-thought-out plan and it worked . . .'

'Ah. Yes, well. You know, Simonetti likes to make out that our Suspect's as clever as Houdini. The cold-blooded killer winging through the night and homing in on his victims, sleeping in his coffin all day. Our very own local Dracula. So, he won't be put out by last night's tricks, will he?'

'No. No, he's not. He's pleased, I think, as far as that goes. Though, if we've lost the gun as a result . . .'

'If he thought he'd lost the gun as a result you'd be out of a job by now.'

'It would be the natural thing to think, though, wouldn't it?'

'Humph. Anyway, I'm inclined to agree with you. I

wouldn't have thought him capable of it, either. Not his style. Still, from Simonetti's point of view, a story like that and a spot of gun grease on one of the bags of rubbish in that skip is a lot better than finding nothing at all. And believe me, if somebody wants to hide something as small as a gun in the countryside there's no way anybody could ever find it.'

'That's true.'

'I don't know why you don't go and get some sleep.'

'I can't manage to sleep at all during the day. There were one or two things I wanted to ask you.' But he was so tired that he couldn't remember for the life of him what they were.

The search continued, slow and laborious, moving from the storeroom to the kitchen. Every inch of the building had to be filmed and any object removed required a written report with a detailed description. They were looking, without much hope, for the gun, but they were also looking for any object belonging to any of the victims. Something from the handbags he'd gone through and emptied. There had never been any clear idea of any particular object missing from the victims, which was one reason why everything had to be filmed. After a certain period of time they would return to the house and take note of anything that had been removed by the Suspect.

When the Marshal and Ferrini left at lunch time, the lights and cameras had just been switched off. A niche in the kitchen wall containing a statue of the Madonna had been dismantled and the brickwork behind it destroyed with an electric drill. Plaster dust was settling on the white hair of the Suspect, who lay with his head down in his arms at the kitchen table, sobbing. Outside his wife screamed abuse at an intruding journalist, managing to crack him over the head with a sweeping brush as he ran for his life.

'Later!' the Marshal mouthed at the face looking in at the window. It was the man from the house across the way, probably just back from work in the fields, as it was sixish. 'You shouldn't be here.' He waved him away. The man looked disgruntled but he went.

They were still searching the kitchen, looking now at a huge scratched sideboard, the drawers and cupboards of which were crammed with the stuff that always accumulates in the most-used room of a house. Simonetti himself and Di Maira were doing the actual searching. The Marshal's part was simpler. It was his job to make a written description of anything they might decide to remove and to put everything exactly back in place when they moved on. As yet they hadn't decided to take anything. They had filmed the area before starting and were now filming the open drawers as they were emptied.

'Excuse me,' the Marshal ventured to interrupt. 'This postcard . . .'

'What about it?' Simonetti, crouched in front of the cupboard, didn't look up.

'It's a nuisance, but I think we'll have to do the first

part of the filming here again. It must have fallen on the floor or somebody knocked it off by accident.'

'Leave it there. It probably fell out of this cupboard.'

'No, no . . . it was propped up here at the back. I happened to notice it this morning.'

'All right, all right. Just leave it there. I'll see that it gets filmed if it's of any interest.'

The Marshal replaced the card carefully where he remembered seeing it earlier and the cameraman moved forward to do a close-up of a biscuit tin that Simonetti was trying to open. Di Maira stood back and as he did so the postcard caught his eye. He gave the Marshal a sharp glance and quickly turned away.

Behind them, the Suspect came in carrying a bucket full of new-laid eggs.

'I'm just trying to get on with my work,' he wailed, his meaty face as tear-stained as ever. 'I've worked all my life, I've made myself ill. My heart's done for, and this is what I get.'

He put down the bucket of eggs and, spotting what Simonetti had just succeeded in opening, his wail increased in volume:

'This is what it's got me! Strangers going through all my belongings, strangers poking about in my private things, making a joke of the pathetic few lire I've scraped together over years and years of back-breaking work. I did my best to do as my father taught me and put that little bit by each week – thank God he's not alive today to see what it's all come to. But God'll pay you back for this!

He's going to see to it that you burn in hell for persecuting an innocent man. A scapegoat! That's what I am, a scapegoat, because I'm too old and sick and worn out to defend myself.'

'Oh God,' sighed Simonetti, sick of this diatribe, as indeed they all were. 'That's it. Tidy up here. We'll move on next door . . .'

'My rabbits! You're not touching my rabbits! The shock'd kill them like it's killing me! Not my rabbits . . .'

He trailed after them, sobbing as they went out the kitchen door and in at the next door on the yard to where fat brown rabbits crouched in overcrowded cages in the smelly darkness.

The Marshal remained behind to put everything back in place. When he'd finished, he shut the cupboards and then tried to shut the drawer at the top, but it stuck. It was far too full and he tried to rearrange the stuff, thinking something must be sticking up. There were stacks of household bills, light bulbs in boxes, spare plugs and bits of wire, a hammer, tubes of glue, a holy picture, a screwtop jam jar with mixed nails in it, broken pencils and half-used ballpoints with no tops and a big roll of brown plastic sticky tape for parcels. The roll of tape looked the most likely culprit. The Marshal made a deeper space for it and laid it flat. The drawer still wouldn't shut. Then he remembered a trick. It wasn't something he'd discovered for himself. A colleague had told him about it after finding a hidden pistol and the sticky tape had reminded him of it now.

'Dead simple, really. They make a parcel of it, put it right at the back of a drawer and tape it to the inside back of the chest so that when you pull the drawer out it stays at the back. What happened was, I pulled the drawer out too far altogether. It fell down behind it, still taped to the back of the chest and the drawer wouldn't shut. Not bad really. If I hadn't yanked at the drawer because I'd lost my patience I'd probably never have found the thing.'

The Marshal didn't lose his patience. He slid the drawer out carefully and put it on the table. Then he bent to look. The parcel was flat and oblong, wrapped in something black, probably a rubbish bag, and stuck to the inside back of the sideboard with the plastic sticky tape.

There was a sudden commotion followed by a piercing scream out in the yard. The Marshal straightened up and went to the door.

'He'll kill me! He'll blame me and he'll kill me! He's bound to blame me! Oh, Holy Mother of God!'

'Stay where you are, we'll get them back.'

But the rabbits, a whole cage full of them, had no intention of being got back in without giving everybody a good run for their money. It was the first time in their lives they'd had the possibility of moving more than a few centimetres and they intended to make the most of it, scattering in a dozen directions at once in the pouring rain, ears down and bobtails up.

The Marshal assumed that Simonetti would not be joining in the chase and went next door to tell him what he'd found.

The parcel was filmed in its hiding place, before being removed and opened.

'Money . . .'

Wads of used notes, each with an elastic band round it. They filmed it spread out on the black rubbish bag.

'Our friend obviously doesn't believe in banks,' was Simonetti's only comment. 'Thank you. You may as well stick it back where you found it.' He left with the cameraman.

Outside, the rabbit hunt continued, with the Suspect's wails and imprecations now added to his wife's screams.

The Marshal counted the hundred thousand notes in one of the wads. Then he counted the wads and put them back in the bag. A hundred and thirty million lire. He closed the parcel with fresh tape and reached to the back of the drawer cavity to stick it back in place.

That was as much as he earned himself in four years. In the biscuit tin that Simonetti had opened there had been a savings book with another eighty million or so, and a pile of share certificates made out to the bearer. He hadn't been able to see how much they were worth.

When he finished tidying he went to the window and stood a moment watching the chaotic scene outside.

'Hmph,' he said to himself aloud. He didn't add anything else, conscious of the bugs concealed in the room. Still, that didn't prevent his thinking that, despite all his years of sweating on the land, his own father's hens and rabbits had never resulted in wads of shares and bank notes.

As he walked out the kitchen door he encountered Noferini. The boy was wet and red in the face and clutching a soaked and trembling rabbit. Apparently he hadn't been too tired to join in the chase.

'We've got them all!'

'Good. Because they must be worth their weight in gold.'

Noferini stared after him.

At the gate someone was waiting, hidden by a vast green cotton umbrella of the sort country people use.

'Marshal?' It was the man from the house across the road again.

'I'm on my way over to you. My gloves are upstairs.'

'It's about my coat.'

'What coat?' The Marshal kept walking. He'd had enough for today.

'*My* coat! I'm not asking for it. I'll tell you the truth, he scares me. I'm keeping away from him.' He held the huge umbrella over them both as the Marshal crossed the dirt road. 'I said to my wife, I said they're bound to come across it while they're searching his house. Am I right? I said I'm not asking him for it. You never know. Only it's what I go to work in, so I could do with it. But I'm not one for taking risks and he frightened the life out of me going for me like that. Curiosity killed the cat, the wife said, but I'd just got up for a piss and I heard you going down. Anyway, it's a green windjammer, if you take a quick look round you'll find it. What was it he threw in the skip, anyway? It was something hard, I can tell you that much, but I hadn't the chance for more than a quick prod at it before he grabbed me.'

The Marshal stopped, closed his eyes for a second and then turned back.

'Come with me.'

'You're kidding!' On the other end of the line, the head of police laboratories couldn't suppress a laugh.

'No. It's true, I'm afraid.'

'Better keep that out of the papers.'

'Yes.'

'Wouldn't look good.'

'No.'

'You're taking it badly.'

'No, no . . . I'm exhausted, that's all. I've just got back to my station after being on duty for over thirty hours.'

'Not much fun.'

'No.'

'And it's not as though I've got anything interesting for you, though I must say it never ceases to amaze me what people throw away, even after all these years. I mean, a dead dog, for instance. I could understand it in the city but in the country why not bury it? Pretty high it is, too. Now then . . . We've got a whole lot of Walt Disney films on tape and, in contrast to that, a rubbish bag filled with porn – that's probably his stuff, wouldn't you think?'

'Could be. Is it anything special?'

'Not really. Straight-up-and-down hard core. Sort you can buy at any newspaper kiosk. Then we've got half a sofa. Half of it! Is somebody still sitting on the other half, d'you think?'

'There was another skip. Perhaps . . .'

'All right. I was just trying to cheer you up.'

He was a new man and the Marshal had never met him, but he certainly was cheerful. Of course, he hadn't been on his feet for thirty-six hours, most of it on an empty stomach. The Marshal had shown sufficient foresight to put some water on to boil in the kitchen before embarking on this call. The list went on and on . . .

'And . . . Let me see – right: I knew there was something that would amuse you. There's a smashed video camera!'

Why should that be funny? The Marshal was nonplussed.

'You didn't see the news last night?'

'I – no, no, I didn't.'

'Ah, well. His wife has got it in for the journalists – not that you can blame her – and there was this bit of film of her on the eight o'clock news last night. All she's doing is sweeping the yard, but all of a sudden she spots the camera and she's coming towards it, brush raised ready to kill. You get just a few seconds of spinning image and then it goes black. Everybody thought the cameraman was running for his life but it looks like she got bull's-eye.'

'Yes.'

'After that we've got three chicken-feed bags, ripped, a rabbit's head – probably the property of the dead dog – and five black sacks of everyday rubbish, all of which we've gone through carefully just in case. Usual stuff:

coffee grounds, tomato tins, vegetable peelings. That's about it. You would have preferred a Beretta 22 Long Rifle, or even a spot of grease from one, I know, but no luck.'

'Well, I wasn't hoping for it.'

'I suppose not. It would have been too good to be true, wouldn't it? As for what we did find . . . was he just up early spring cleaning, do you think?'

'It's winter.'

'Oh well, I've done what I can for you. Make of it what you will.'

The Marshal, who could make nothing of it and was pretty well past caring, ate a huge bowl of spaghetti in front of the television and then went to bed.

The next morning was beautiful. The marble towers in the city washed by the heavy rain, glittered in the strong winter sunshine. In the country the sky was deep blue against the tall black cypresses in a way that never happens in the muggy heat of summer. The air was so cold and clean it was intoxicating and the Marshal felt more cheerful than he had for weeks. When they drove round the village square at Pontino he saw it was market day and the stall holders were setting out their wares, plastic flowers, buckets and brushes, cheeses, eggs and chickens, long johns and frilly knickers, bunches of tiny stored tomatoes, sacks of potatoes and barrels of salt cod under running water. The men of the village stood gossiping near the bars, the women near the stalls.

It took some time for the jeep to nose its way through it all and take the yellow stony road that led past a deserted villa to the little group of houses where the Suspect lived.

The road ran straight over the hilltops to the glistening horizon and so gave the impression of being very long. It ran between vineyards and olive groves and past the cypress avenue leading to a huge and crumbling villa on their right. Along the balustraded roof of the villa terracotta Roman ladies were silhouetted against the blue sky. The gate to the avenue lay rusting by the roadside. Just after the villa the road swung away to their left and they embarked very slowly on the stony track to the right. Within a few minutes they were back to the captured rabbits in their stinking darkness and the scowling red-faced Suspect sitting at the kitchen table, his trousers held up with string. He was furiously denying ever having set eyes on the pile of pornographic magazines that the smiling Simonetti had brought back with him this fine morning.

The Marshal listened for a moment, his eyes scanning the room. Something that ought to be there was missing but he wasn't concentrating enough to remember what it was because he was also looking about him for Ferrini. That morning they were to search the vegetable garden, orchard and vineyard, so perhaps he was out there. He went out to see. He found Bacci and Noferini laying some old vine supports across the passageway which led between a barn wall and the house to the garden. The passage was almost knee deep in water and the supports would at least allow them to cross from one patch of thick mud to another.

'Ferrini arrived?'

Bacci straightened up. 'He called in sick. Flu, I think.'

That was bad news. Well, there you are. The Marshal himself had got soaked to the skin yesterday and his wet clothes had dried on him during the long day's work, and yet it was Ferrini, all correctly kitted out for the weather, who was now sick. He was really quite put out because Ferrini was the only person he felt at ease with and a word exchanged here and there helped to lighten things up a bit.

As it was, he passed his morning more or less in silence, replacing the thousand bits and pieces that had been moved from the potting shed, trying to remember to stand out of the way of the cameraman, taking notes to order. The one positive element of the morning, apart from the bright winter sun, was that during a short break for reloading the camera, he noted out of the corner of his eye Simonetti having a word with Bacci. It appeared to be a friendly word, given that he had a hand on the young man's shoulder, and the Marshal was glad of it. However little he desired the man's approval for himself, he recognized that it was a good thing for Bacci.

Because of this he was a bit surprised to see Bacci looking far from happy when they found themselves working side by side after the lunch break. They had been told to dig up a little pear tree which someone on the local force said he'd seen the Suspect change the position of for no apparent reason. The Suspect explained tearfully that it hadn't been getting enough light and that if they moved it now it would die. Simonetti thought he might have buried something under cover of moving the tree, which was now lying on its side near the big hole they'd made.

'Nothing here,' the Marshal said.

'No.'

'We'll replant the tree but I'm afraid he's right. It'll probably die.'

Bacci picked up the delicate little tree and stared at it without answering.

'Is something the matter?'

Bacci went on staring at the tree. He looked dazed. Then, with a sidelong glance at where the others were working, he said, 'Yes. There is. Can I talk to you?'

'Go on. Nobody can hear us from over there.'

'They could see us . . . They'll notice. Do you mind if I come to see you this evening?'

'If that's what you want.'

Still Bacci stood looking dazed. And if the Marshal wasn't mistaken he was also a little frightened. When he made no move after a few more minutes, he suggested, 'Shall we get on with replanting this tree, then, Lieutenant?' And they got on.

They had almost finished when the Suspect came panting up to them, purple and gasping in his distress.

'My little pear tree! My little pear tree! You've killed it!'

'I'm sorry,' the Marshal offered, 'we've done our best . . .'

The Suspect raised his tear-stained face and his thick, cracked hands to the heavens.

'God help me! God help me! I'm an innocent man! Why is this happening to me? You'll burn in hell for this!'

The last remark was addressed not to God or to the Marshal but to Simonetti who was crouched near the flooded passageway, too intent on something he was looking at there to listen. Only the cameraman behind him turned to look their way. His video camera was in one hand and not on his shoulder so it must have been switched off. He wasn't interested in filming the Suspect's rages but other people were. When the Marshal looked up in the direction of the nearby roof there were two or three newsmen filming. This was just the stuff for them. Then a shout went up:

'Camera!' It was Simonetti and something in the urgency of his voice stopped the Suspect in mid curse.

'What's he doing?' He started to run back. 'That bag of shit! What's he doing?'

'He must have found something,' the Marshal said, throwing down the spade. 'Let's take a look.'

'Don't!' Bacci's voice was even more urgent than Simonetti's. 'Stay away.' His fingers clutched the Marshal's arm. 'Stay here.'

'How did you know?'

Ferrini grinned. 'Sit down and make yourself comfortable. I'm going to bring us a bottle of very special grappa. Blows the top off your head but good, really good. I imagine you need it.'

The Marshal sat down in a big armchair and stared

across the highly polished floor to a glass-fronted cabinet against the opposite wall. It contained lead models of carabinieri in historic uniforms. Ferrini's wife and children were in the kitchen nearby. He could hear the television and their chatter.

'Here you are.' Instead of being colourless, the grappa in its tall very thin bottle was faintly tinged with green because of the bunch of basil leaves that appeared to grow inside it. Ferrini filled two tiny glasses.

'Tell me all.' He settled in a chair opposite the Marshal.

'How did you know?' he insisted.

'You're exaggerating. I didn't know what they'd find.'

'But you knew it would be planted.'

'Guarnaccia! That anonymous letter.'

'But you didn't even see it.'

'No. Did you?'

'No . . . I see what you mean . . .'

'So it was a bullet?'

'A twenty-two. It has been loaded and unloaded and it's the right brand, of course.'

'Even so, you need hardly worry that it's been loaded in *that* twenty-two. We've got – what? Something like fifty-three recovered bullets. Anyway, however many there are, if this was one of them the defence would suss it out. They wouldn't dare go that far. Too easily checked. No, this is purely for the benefit of Joe Public. The newspapers and telly will have a good time of it without overdoing the details of the ballistics report. You'll see that on the day *that* becomes available to the press they'll be given something better to distract them. I suppose there'll be a break in the film somewhere before it, but that won't sell any papers, will it? I'm sorry to have missed the show really, but there are times when it's wiser not to be among those present. Let's hear the details then.'

'I wasn't nearby when they actually found it –'

'Surprise, surprise.'

'I suppose you're right. And that's why Bacci would have been with me. Anyway, they'd laid those wooden supports down across this puddle and it was jammed quite deeply into the surface inside one of those holes where the support wires pass through.'

'The obvious place to store your bullets. So how did he explain finding it if it was so embedded?'

'It had rained a lot. He said he saw the exposed surface glinting.'

'Do me a favour! I thought he was brighter than that. Anyway, that proves to you that it's only for Joe Public. Nobody else would swallow that. It's young Bacci I feel sorry for. It was a rotten trick to choose him instead of one of his own cronies.'

'He knows how urgently Bacci needs his promotion.'

'Still, it was a squalid trick. Everybody's pulled tricks on suspects in their time. I know I have. But if it had gone wrong and the suspect had turned out to be innocent rather than confessing then I'd have been the only one to pay for my mistake. What did he want him to do, anyway? Be the one to spot it glinting?'

'No, no . . . It was a quite different set-up. He started

chatting to Bacci this morning when the camera was being reloaded. They were walking about near the vegetable garden. I remember seeing them and thinking . . . Anyway, it seems Simonetti was making small talk about the weather and the amount of mud around and how difficult it was making the job.'

'*My feet got soaked yesterday. All in a day's work, of course, but I can't afford to be ill just now.*'

'*No, sir, I suppose not.*'

'*We're not issued with those wonderful amphibians they give to you carabinieri so I bought myself these. What do you think?*'

'*They look pretty robust.*'

'*They're quite similar to yours, though I don't know whether the tread's quite as deep. I forget what make they are, now . . . It's written underneath but with all this mud . . .*'

Ferrini roared with laughter: 'Don't tell me! He washed off the mud and there was the twenty-two bullet glinting!'

'Wedged between the treads.'

'He's a bigger imbecile than I thought. And what was poor Bacci's role in all this?'

'Simonetti pointed out it was unfortunate that the camera was switched off and that he expected Bacci to repeat their conversation for a written report and then later at a press conference.'

'And he had the courage to refuse?'

'He didn't actually refuse, thank God. As far as I can gather he didn't say anything much at all.'

'Too gob-smacked to speak?'

'I suppose so. Luckily, our Suspect decided to interrupt them with a fit of hysterics just at that point. Then the camera was on again and the moment had passed. Even so, Simonetti must have worked it out for himself, if not that Bacci was unwilling, that he was too nervous for the job. However good his innocent young face might look in front of the telecameras it wouldn't do to have him stammering and blushing and giving the game away. At any rate, he slipped the bullet into his pocket and presumably stuck it in the vine support later in the day.'

'Let's hope for the best, then – for Bacci, that is.'

'He'd been intending to talk to me about it this evening. He looked as sick as a dog and I even wondered if he was going down with something, like you. That's when I remembered you telling me never waste the flu because there was always a strategic moment for having it.'

'That's right. I've worked my balls off with forty degrees of fever in my time so as not to miss the right moment for being ill. Incidentally, I called you last night to warn you but you didn't answer.'

'I went to bed very early.'

'You're lucky you can sleep through the phone. I never can.'

'Oh, I can't, that's why I –'

'What?'

'I turned the bell off the other morning. I must have forgotten.'

'It doesn't matter. Will you have another drop?'

'No, no . . .' Teresa! She would have rung him, too. The phone had been turned off for two days and a night and here he was at Borgo Ognissanti in Ferrini's quarters when she'd surely be trying again.

'I must get home.'

'Suit yourself. Listen, you're not going to make a tragedy out of this, I hope? It means nothing in the long run and he's not worth risking your job for. He's a killer, anyway, and as for what he did to his daughter . . .'

'I know . . .' He'd wanted to talk to Ferrini about that but he really must get back. Poor Teresa would be in a state of panic.

'Wait. There's something I'd better give you. I've been having a look through this myself while having my flu.'

'What is it?' The Marshal's heart sank as a thick sheaf of papers was put into his hand.

'You'll see for yourself. Better forewarned than surprised. When you've read it, make up your mind that's the way it went and there's nobody involved worth taking any risks for. Take my advice on that.'

The Marshal was willing to take any amount of advice but he wished, as he plodded the long dark corridors of the barracks, that people wouldn't give him so much to read. Patrol cars were starting up noisily in the echoing cloister below him to the right. On his left the doors of all the offices which had once been monks' cells were closed and locked. It was late and Teresa would be worried.

She *was* worried. She was also furious. He'd have done

better just to say he'd been working all hours and leave out the bit about having turned the phone off. He never did think on before letting himself in for this sort of thing. He waited for her to wind down so they could have a bit of a chat. He was in no hurry to get back to the stuff he was supposed to be reading. He'd read only the premise – it was a judge's report on the release of some earlier Monster suspects – and the thought of a hundred and sixty pages of legal jargon was not encouraging.

'You're not ill or anything, are you?'

'No, no . . . I'm all right.'

'You're not. You're overtired. It's the sort of thing you do all the time when you're overtired, forgetting things like that. Have you been eating properly?'

She'd forgiven him. They had a nice long chat which meant Teresa did all the chatting and he – as she often said – intoned the responses. He said good night to her reluctantly and then made a decision. He'd take the wretched thing to bed, and if he fell asleep over it that was too bad. Legal jargon was as effective as any sleeping pill and at least his conscience would be clear. He'd have done his best.

He was quite wrong. First of all, it wasn't written in legal jargon but in forceful and impassioned prose. Secondly, far from sending him to sleep it kept him awake the entire night. And when he did fall asleep at dawn with the papers scattered all ways on the floor beside his bed, it was to dream the same images that his reading had conjured up. That was something which often happened

215

to him when he was distressed by some case he was working on. This story happened over twenty years ago but the distress it had caused the author of the report vibrated in every line. His frustration and anger were alive because they had found no release.

Nine

THE INSTRUCTING JUDGE, TRIBUNAL OF FLORENCE

<u>PART 1</u>
-1968-

1.1. DISCOVERY OF A DOUBLE HOMICIDE

At two in the morning of 22 August 1968, Renzo Rossini hears his doorbell ringing repeatedly in Via Torrente 154A at San Felice, a stretch of the trunk road between Florence and Pistoia, part of the municipality of Campi Bisenzio. He goes downstairs and, leaning out of the ground-floor window, sees a little boy of about six or seven who says: *'Let me in because I'm tired out and my dad's poorly in bed. And will you take me home? Because my mum and uncle are dead in the car.'*

Having got over his surprise, Rossini brings the boy inside and asks his name. He says he's called Nicolino and that he lives in Lastra a Signa. Then he repeats his first statement and adds that the car is down the lane across the road from Rossini's house and that there's a light winking on and off. Nicolino is dressed in shorts and T-shirt. He has socks on but no shoes. Rossini drives to the nearest carabinieri station and brings back the carabiniere on duty. Together the three of them set out in the car down the lane that crosses the fields facing Rossini's house and leads towards Signa.

They don't get very far because they soon find the road blocked by boulders and before too long they have to give up and turn back.

They take the main road into Signa (the Pistoia road) and then, following the child's directions, try to get into the lane from the other end. *'We went to the pictures and it was in the war and a house went on fire and then we went up there past the cemetery.'*

Not far beyond the cemetery, the road forks and a few yards further on, a stony track leads off the main road to the right and follows the Vingone torrent which itself is to the right of the lane and screened from it at this season by giant reeds. Later investigation will demonstrate that this lane does, in fact, after one or two deviations, come out on the Pistoia road exactly opposite Rossini's house.

About fifty yards along the lane they see the back of a white car with its right indicator flashing.

On shining the torch into the vehicle they see the dead bodies of a man and a woman.

There is no light at the scene, not even moonlight.

1.2. SCENE OF CRIME AND PRELIMINARY EXAMINATION OF VICTIMS

On arrival at the scene, the carabinieri of Signa establish that the right rear door of the car is ajar, the front left window open a few inches and the right one halfway down.

When they open the driver's (left) door, a man's shoe falls out. On the right, between the door frame and the passenger seat where the man lies, they find a woman's handbag and a handkerchief.

The man's corpse is supine because the seat has been let down to the level of the back seat. His hands are holding his trousers together. They are unbuttoned and his belt is undone. There is blood on his left shoulder and knee.

The woman is leaning back in the driver's seat with her head drooping towards the left and her arms dangling at her sides. Her body is bared up to the groin. Her shoes are under the other seat. On her partly bared breast, bullet wounds can be clearly seen. There is blood around the area of the navel. The gold chain round her neck is broken in two places and the intermediate fragment is stuck to her skin with sweat.

Behind the right front seat they find a calibre-22 L.R. bullet. Three cartridges with an H on the base, of the same calibre, are found in the left side of the car. Later on they will find two more cartridges wedged down the back of the rear seat and another among the woman's clothing. Three bullets are in her body and one in the man's.

On the floor between the front and back seats there is a pair of children's shoes, assumed to belong to Nicolino.

A local doctor is called in and certifies that the couple both died from haemorrhage caused by gunshot wounds. The autopsy will reveal some months later that each victim was hit four times and that the entry wounds on both are very close together, with the exception of one shot fired into the woman's arm. This, and the different trajectory suggest either that the woman moved after the bullet hit her arm first or that the shots were fired from two different positions, which could also imply two attackers. The question is open to discussion.

The position of the woman's body is explained in an account of the murder given two days later by her husband, Sergio Muscas, who also described how the man lost his shoe and why the indicator was on. He offered no explanation, however, of the man's attempt to pull up his trousers at the moment of his death. He does say that, before the shots were fired, his wife was lying on top of the man. Consequently, it may be that he could have spotted someone approaching and instinctively tried to cover himself.

The woman's handbag was found to contain 27 thousand lire, which does not seem to have interested the killer. Both bodies are found to have been moved after death. Muscas, in confessing to the murder of his wife and her lover, says he was the one to pull his wife's body off the man's. With reference to what happened immediately after the murder it is Nicolino who tells the carabinieri: *'My mum had put her money under the seat in the car and Uncle Fabio looked in my mum's bag and then he felt round in the glove compartment and then he went away.'* There was no way of knowing at this date whether the child's story was credible, but it is apparently accepted at face value at the time.

1.3. ANALYSIS OF NICOLINO'S BEHAVIOUR

A further observation is necessary in this generic description of the crime. First of all, we can assume with certainty that Nicolino was in the car when the crime took place, not only because he appeared about an hour later, knowing all about his mother's death, in a house an hour's walk away, and because his shoes were still in the car, but also because he was capable of indicating two possible routes for reaching the scene of the crime.

He must have seen the murder take place since, even if he was asleep, the first shots must have awakened him. (Experts established that no silencer was used.) But this does not mean that he must have seen and recognized the person or persons who fired the shots. He would have seen the bodies being moved, i.e. unless he was removed from the car himself before this occurred. This brings us to the manner of his arrival at the Rossini house at two in the morning.

It cannot be absolutely excluded that Nicolino reached the Pistoia road by himself but it does seem highly unlikely. The distance from the murder vehicle to the Rossini house is about a mile and can be covered on foot in a minimum of thirty and a maximum of sixty minutes. The lane runs in a more or less straight line, except near the end where it turns to the right and a little bridge over the Vingone torrent (little more than a dry ditch in summer) connects it to another lane. There, turning left and continuing in the original direction, one gets a head-on view of the Pistoia road and the Rossini house. The house is very noticeable, even at night. It is large and white and has a floodlight attached to it just below the roof (as have a number of houses along this road, which is otherwise unlit). To reach the house, Nicolino had then to cross the main road. It was, at the time of the murder, impossible to make this journey even on a moped or bicycle, and it was difficult even on foot with stout shoes. (The local Marshal tried it out with the child the following day.)

But Nicolino made the journey in total darkness and stockinged feet, and his socks were neither torn nor dirty. Finally, along the lane there are a number of cottages and a number of forks in the road, not to mention the fact that it would have been easier for the child to leave the lane by the same way he'd entered it in the car. He would have reached the road to Signa in about one minute and there was a house right there on the corner where he could have asked for help.

Unless the child was accompanied by an adult who knew the way perfectly in the dark and had good reason for choosing it, his journey makes no sense.

Nicolino's overall behaviour makes no sense, unless, likewise, directed by an adult. His first words on being admitted by Rossini seem rehearsed and carefully chosen. He must know his own surname but admits only to Nicolino. He refuses to give a more specific address than Lastra a Signa. He tells of his father being ill in bed before mentioning that his mother has just been murdered. Being ill in bed is Sergio Muscas's alibi until he confesses. In all this he expresses no emotion. He doesn't cry. He is sufficiently calm and in possession of himself to offer them not one but two ways of reaching the scene of the crime. It is almost impossible not to believe that Nicolino was accompanied to the Rossini house and told to ring there and recite only the information he has been given. As a consequence, there is considerable delay in the identification of the victims and, inevitably, in the arrival of the carabinieri at the home of Sergio Muscas.

Nicolino's request to be let in and allowed to sleep and then to be taken home does not seem a natural reaction to what he has just experienced. His behaviour is altogether unnatural. The intention of whoever instructed him was evidently that of having the carabinieri go first with Nicolino to his home and discover his father, Sergio Muscas, ill in bed as described. They would not have expected a very young, very sleepy and frightened child to have been capable of taking them instead back to the scene of the crime, given the dark and devious route by which he had been removed from it. This, nevertheless, is what he does, tranquilly indicating the bloody scene inside the car from which he has escaped unharmed.

1.4. DISTANCES

The next thing the investigators look at is the problem of distances. It is about three miles from Lastra a Signa, where Nicolino went to the last showing at the cinema that night with his mother and 'uncle', to the lane where they parked to make love. The road is steep and winding. Whoever followed them would have needed a vehicle. An ambush prepared in the lane is ruled out since they don't use this spot particularly often. In any case, the killer needed to get away from the scene at speed. Sergio Muscas, who will shortly confess to the crime, has no vehicle.

1.5. THE VICTIMS AND THE FIRST SUSPECTS

The dead woman is identified by the local Marshal of the carabinieri as Belinda Muscas, née Lubino, Sardinian, married to Sergio Muscas, also Sardinian, who is about twenty years older than his wife. The woman was much talked about in the village because of her many lovers and her husband's tolerance.

One of these lovers, another Sardinian by the name of Flavio Vargius, was discovered in bed with her by his wife, Valeria, who made a great public scene of the matter, which resulted in Flavio's imprisonment for concubinage. Muscas, it seems, didn't so much as bat an eyelid. On the contrary, he looked after a few small matters for Flavio whilst the latter was in prison. When Flavio came out he continued his relationship with Belinda to the extent of moving in with her when Sergio had to go to hospital for an operation. Flavio was jealous of Belinda, unlike her husband, and threatened violence if she went with other men. The threats evidently didn't bother Belinda who continued to take on a variety of lovers, including the unfortunate Amadeo Lo Russo, the 'uncle' who was murdered with her, an immigrant builder from Sicily.

The local Marshal knows all these characters well. He questions everybody concerned, including Belinda's family and that of Lo Russo, but his real targets are the husband, Sergio Muscas, and Flavio Vargius, the ex-lover. He has the two of them brought in for interrogation. He knows Sergio to be weak and cowardly but can imagine him conniving at the murder. The carabinieri come for him at six in the morning. He is awake and dressed and shows no sign of being ill. He says, '*I knew you'd be coming.*'

He is rubbing a thick layer of grease into his hands.

'Hmph . . .' Having read on to the end of the next chapter the Marshal got out of bed and into his slippers and dressing gown. 'Paraffin tests . . .' Sergio's had been positive, despite the grease, but they weren't a hundred

225

per cent reliable. In this case, of course, the husband was bound to be suspect number one, anyway, whether the test was positive or not.

He went into the kitchen and then stopped. What had he got up for? He had no idea. The fridge motor buzzed into life and attracted his attention but there wasn't much inside to hold it. He wasn't really hungry, anyway. He was tired and ought to be asleep but some need or other was nagging at him. For want of a better idea he put some water on to boil for camomile tea. While he waited for it he pulled a chair away from the table and sat down, hands planted on his knees, frowning.

Sergio Muscas had confessed and denied, confessed and denied, or rather, the other way round. He'd denied it at first, saying he was ill in bed, as the little boy had told them. Then, when they were doing the paraffin test on him he saw Flavio Vargius, one of his wife's lovers, being tested, too, and instantly accused him. Nothing was more likely, but Flavio's test came out negative and after that everything fell apart because they let Sergio go home with the child that night and cook up a series of lies and contradictory versions that would be polluted even more by the rest of the family and never really understood.

'Why did they let that happen?' The Marshal addressed his question to the teabag as he poured boiling water on it. Funny how camomile tea always brought back his childhood. He couldn't remember being given it very often. Just that smell, maybe, like soaked grass on a muggy wet day.

He thought of that six-year-old child trailing home in the summer dusk with his half-witted father to a silent mother-less house, perhaps knowing his father, with or without help, had shot her. Did they both lie awake all night with their separate fears? He thought of one of his own little boys in Nicolino's place and the thought was more than he could stand. He got to his feet, realizing what it was that he'd needed when he got up, and it certainly wasn't camomile tea. It was the need to be there, to look into the child's eyes and know when he was lying, know when he was afraid and when he was just trying to please by saying what people wanted to hear. The Marshal's way of going about finding the truth had very little to do with what people told him or with written statements taken by someone else. It was to do with people's expressions, their fidgeting hands, the smell of their sweat. And the house, too, the house, broken down and flood damaged, that Sergio and the boy went back to that night. He needed to see it and smell it, not read about it. With a sigh he ambled back to the bedroom with his drink, trying to get a grip on Sergio's weird behaviour, despite the difficulty of looking at him through the distorting glass of someone else's eyes. Why had he suddenly shifted his accusation to Flavio's brother, Silvano? Silvano was another of his wife's countless boyfriends.

'*Silvano Vargius had a gun and he didn't like my wife going with other men. I was ill in bed. It was him that did it!*'

Nobody had taken much notice of this accusation. Silvano wasn't known to the police at all and he had an alibi. Who would have given up Sergio, the husband, with no alibi and a positive paraffin test, not to mention a confession, for this unknown quantity? Sergio's accusation was worthless. How could he know who did it unless he was there himself to see it happen? Seeing that nobody believed him, Sergio, however imbecilic he was supposed to be, understood exactly why.

'All right, I was there, but it was his idea. He said I'd be better off without her. I didn't want to but he made me. We followed them in Silvano's car after the cinema. They'd put Nicolino in the back and I watched all the way but his head never showed above the back seat so I knew he was asleep. When we got out of the car he gave me the gun and said there were eight shots.'

That was one of the things that rang true, to the judge then and to the Marshal now. There had been eight shots but the autopsy hadn't been done yet, so Sergio had no way of knowing unless he'd been there. That and his story of separating the bodies.

'I pulled her off him, holding on to the steering wheel for leverage – that's why the indicator went on. Then I dragged him back into his seat and the gearstick pulled his shoe off. That was when the kiddie woke up.'

'And the gun?'

'I chucked it in the ditch.'

'We've searched the ditch. You didn't chuck it in the ditch.'

'All right, that bit's not true. I gave it back to him, but all the rest is true. I gave it back to him and I told him I'd done

as he'd said and that I'd spared the kid. When he killed his wife back in Sardinia the kid was spared that time, as well.'

'Killed his wife? What do you mean by that?'

'I'm just saying, that's all.'

I'd have looked into that, at least, the Marshal thought, sipping the last drops of tea. But would he? He'd have noted it but, after the confrontation, wouldn't it have seemed a waste of time? Hindsight was all very well but this whole story had collapsed in a matter of hours when Silvano Vargius had been brought face to face with Sergio and his accusations.

'I don't want to see him.'

'You've accused him. You have to see him. Sit down there.'

'I want a glass of water.'

'Later. Sit down.'

And he sat down. The door facing him opened and Silvano Vargius came in with a carabiniere behind him. On the instant, Sergio leapt from his chair and fell on his knees in front of Silvano, sobbing. They tried to pull him to his feet but he clung to Silvano's legs with tears running down his cheeks, screaming.

'Don't blame me! Don't! I didn't meant it, it was them, they hit me and confused me. Please don't blame me. It was Flavio, I told them right from the start it was Flavio but they wouldn't believe me!'

They got him back to his chair in the end, still sobbing, then they looked at Silvano who just stood there as cool as a cucumber and didn't even comment on the accusation against himself, except to repeat his alibi, that he was playing billiards at a bar where he and Angius, the friend he was playing with, were well known.

'*I don't know about my brother. I couldn't say where he was.*'

Then he was allowed to leave. It was true that nobody could possibly have understood what motive he could have had for helping Sergio to kill his wife, not to mention the even odder business of Sergio's tearful pleas for forgiveness. The truth was that Sergio went to trial and was convicted without anybody concerned having understood anything, and it was no wonder. Sergio, after that confrontation, had accused just about every one of his wife's lovers, a list of them as long as your arm, before going back to accusing Flavio and sticking there. He didn't have much to offer by way of a motive, even for himself.

'*I was worn out, I just couldn't cope any more. And I was sick to death of him screwing my wife in front of my eyes.*'

'Hm.' The accomplice was Flavio, then, or so he said, but what Flavio's motive was supposed to be remained a mystery.

'Some of it's true, though, that's what's wrong.' The Marshal made this illogical remark aloud, as he gave his pillows a thump and tried to find his place among the jumbled sheets of the report. What was wrong was that it ought to be the false bits of the story that didn't fit but here it was the true bits.

'There's something or somebody missing. If I could have been there . . .'

Once he managed to find his place he was pleased, at least, to find that the Marshal who had been there was a man after his own heart and did something he would have done himself.

PART THREE
-1968: NICOLINO-

3.1. ACCOMPANIMENT

The day after the murder, Nicolino returns to the scene of the crime in daylight with the local Marshal and they walk together from the scene to the Pistoia road and the Rossini house, taking about 50 minutes. On the way, the Marshal points out how difficult the road is, with the boulders they have to climb over. He insists that Nicolino could not have made such a journey without his shoes.

'Listen, Nicolino, you can see as well as me that it's impossible to walk along here in your socks. Perhaps you came another way.'

'It was this way and I walked it.'

'Now then, Nicolino, I'll tell you what: either you tell me the truth, or tonight we walk this road again in the dark without any shoes.'

'No! My dad took me! My dad took me and he gave me a donkey ride!'

At this point in their walk, the two of them reach the little bridge where the road deviates to the right and then left again to run straight to the Pistoia road and the Rossini house, 50 yards or so away and in full view. There, the child stops and says that was where his dad left him and turned back, telling him to ring at the white house with the light and tell them his dad was ill in bed.

3.2. CORROBORATION

At this point, Sergio, his father, is questioned again about who accompanied Nicolino. According to his last version it was Flavio, but when he hears what his son has told the Marshal he immediately changes his story to coincide with the child's, admitting that he himself accompanied the boy. The matter seems clear, but when they take Sergio to the Rossini house and ask him to show them the way he took back after leaving the child, the mystery deepens. In the first place, Sergio talks of the house as a peasant's grey stone cottage when in fact, unlike the other buildings on the road, it is conspicuously not a cottage, being newish, large and painted white. When they get there it is evening and the floodlight on the front of the house is lit, as it was on the night of the murder, but he doesn't even seem to recognize that. They set out along the lane across the field opposite but, despite the landmark of the little bridge, he fails to recognize the deviation and continues along the left fork to come out near the centre of Signa, a good two miles from the murder scene. His mistake is pointed out to him but he remains confused and when they try the journey in reverse he takes three wrong turnings before hitting on the lane where Belinda and Lo Russo turned in that night.

In the car on the return journey to prison he remarks: *'There's no use in me contradicting the child. Everybody's*

*going to believe him rather than me just because he's an
innocent kid. But that doesn't mean he's telling the truth.'*

Asked why he thought the child should be lying, he
claims that Flavio threatened to kill the child if he talked.
He adds that he was afraid of this himself which was why,
for a time, he accused Silvano instead.

3.3. CREDIBILITY

None of the versions of who accompanied Nicolino
appears credible: Whilst it is understandable that such
accomplices as have not been seen and identified by the
child would not want to take him away in the car with
them, the risk of taking the child all that way and then
walking back to the scene of the crime would be enormous
for any of them. And are we to believe that whoever stayed
behind hung about for two hours beside the newly
murdered corpses, waiting to take the child's escort home?
The mystery of who accompanied Nicolino will remain
unsolved throughout the investigation, trial and appeal.

3.4. THE UNCLES

After his father's arrest, Nicolino is placed in an
orphanage where carabinieri and magistrates question
him further. The first thing to be cleared up was the
child's initial description of the murder which had
included the words: *'Uncle Fabio looked in my mum's bag
and then he felt around in the glove compartment and
then he went away.'*

When he is asked to repeat this at the orphanage

'Uncle Fabio' becomes 'Uncle Flavio'. The child calls his mother's lovers uncle but he really does have an Uncle Fabio. He is Sergio's brother and Fabio and Tina Muscas, his wife, have looked after Nicolino until his placement in the orphanage. He goes to them at weekends and, though reluctantly, they will eventually adopt him. The child has no one else in the world except his grandfather, Sergio and Fabio's very aged and infirm father. Was Nicolino's changing the name a mistake or was he simply confusing the two men? He is asked then to describe Fabio.

'He's got curly hair and a moustache and he works in a big place making bread and he's got a little girl called Dina. She's my cousin and she's six.'

'That's right. We've seen her. And does she have a clockwork train like yours?'

'It's not mine. The lady said I could play with it. I don't want to stay here. I don't want to sleep here.'

'You don't like sleeping here?'

'No. There are noises and I can hear them and when I wake up the bed's all wet.'

'Perhaps you'll be able to go and stay with your cousin Dina again and Uncle Fabio and Aunty Tina. Can you remember now who it was who looked in your mum's handbag?'

'Uncle Flavio.'

'Flavio Vargius?'

'Yes.'

'And what did he look like? Could you see him in the dark?'

'The little light was going on and off.'

'So you saw him? Tell us what he looked like.'

'He had a white shirt and curly hair and a moustache.'

'But Nicolino that's your Uncle Fabio. Was it Fabio who looked in your mum's bag?'

'No.'

'Did you not want to tell us about your Uncle Fabio being there?'

'I haven't to. My aunty said and my dad.'

The child continues to play with the train in silence for some time without being asked anything. His questioners state in their report that they wish to avoid contradicting the instructions of such family as Nicolino has left to him. His mother is dead, his father in prison. Fabio and Tina Muscas are his only hope of a home. Should the police use their authority to try and transfer his trust to them the only result will be that he tells them, not the truth, but whatever he thinks they want to hear. When asked, after a pause, if he likes his uncles – without specifying any name – he says:

'Some uncles are nice and some are horrible.'

'What sort of uncle is Flavio?'

'A horrible one because once when my dad was in hospital and my mum wasn't there he hit me hard.'

3.5. SILVANO BEHIND THE REEDS
It is decided to leave the child in peace for a few days, after which he is questioned again about who was present at the scene of the crime. The transcription is direct:

'Who did you see that night?'

'I didn't see anybody.'

'But remember you told us you saw Flavio?'

'Yes.'

'Do you know what Flavio looks like?'

'Yes.'

This time he gives an accurate description of Flavio, adding:

'My dad went in hospital and Flavio came to live at my house.'

'And was he there that night?'

'Every night, he slept in my mum's bed.'

'But the night you were in the car and somebody fired a gun?'

'My dad was there, and he gave me a donkey ride.'

'And did Flavio go with you and your dad?'

'No. I think there was a man, only I don't know who he was. But it wasn't Flavio. No.'

'And can you remember when you said he was? Why did you say that?'

'Because my dad told me to and my aunty.'

'But Flavio wasn't really there?'

'No. Silvano was standing in the reeds.'

'Silvano? What does Silvano look like?'

His description is vaguer. He knows Silvano less well than Flavio.

'You didn't tell us before that you saw Silvano. Why was that?'

'I can't remember.'

236

'You can't remember if you saw him or you can't remember why you didn't tell us?'

'I don't know. There was a noise and he was in the reeds.'

The child at this point becomes fractious and refuses to answer any more questions, saying he is tired. While this seems perfectly comprehensible, it is the first time it has ever happened. He is usually exceptionally co-operative and, if anything, too anxious to please.

At Sergio's trial, Nicolino says he only saw his dad that night. Sergio Muscas is condemned for murder and for calumny against Flavio and Silvano Vargius.

'Well, I wouldn't have been satisfied with that,' growled the Marshal, letting the chapter fall on to the floor beside the bed.

Ten

By a quarter to three in the morning the Marshal really was hungry and thirsty, and he went back to the fridge to conduct a more serious investigation of the contents.

'And if anybody had done the same in '68 . . .'

But nobody had. When they did it was 1982 after the Montespertoli murder when an anonymous letter had told the judge to check the documents of the '68 trial of Sergio Muscas. It must have seemed like an incredible piece of luck that, taped inside the file, was a transparent package of cartridges and bullets recovered at the scene of the crime. There was no question about it, it was the Monster's gun. This lifeline had come just in time when they'd had to release Elio Sassetti who'd been arrested after talking about the Scandicci murder when nobody had found the bodies yet. His car had been there, too, somebody had seen it.

'And that,' said the Marshal aloud, extracting a pan from the cupboard under the sink, since the fridge had still produced nothing, 'is another thing I wouldn't have been satisfied with. All right, so there was another murder while he was inside so it wasn't him – but that doesn't alter the fact that his car was there that night in Scandicci and that he knew. He could have seen the whole thing. Oh well . . .' If he wouldn't talk he wouldn't. Hindsight again. Even so, there must have been some way of finding out *why* he wouldn't talk, damn it . . .

The Marshal ran some hot water into the pan, a thing his wife disapproved of but he could never see why. He lit the gas, quite oblivious by now of the fact that it wasn't supper time but three in the morning. He set himself a place at the kitchen table and then rummaged in a cupboard for a jar of his wife's tomato preserve . . .

'*And* he was a Peeping Tom. I'd have kept on to him . . .'

But nobody had. Too fired up by this new development of the '68 gun. Everybody running after Sergio Muscas again, but you can't do that. You can't just abandon solid facts like Sassetti's car and his knowing about the murder just because some new, more interesting theory presents itself. You have to connect them. That's what was wrong in '68, the true facts didn't connect so they were abandoned. And then in 1982 the same thing. Everybody insisted that Sergio had been telling the truth, that he'd had an accomplice. Well, of course he had. He'd no car, no gun. But then you had to connect that accomplice with Elio Sassetti, you couldn't just forget him.

'Damn!' He managed to splash himself as the tomatoes hit the oil and garlic in the little pan. The chapter he'd just read hadn't even pointed out that Elio Sassetti and Flavio Vargius, the one Sergio continued to accuse as his accomplice, lived in the same village and were both Peeping Toms, maybe in the same gang. There was something there, there had to be. Sergio was out of prison by then and living in an ex-prisoners' home in the far north. Nobody suspected him of the Florentine murders, they'd even given him that in writing. But still he wouldn't talk, still he wouldn't produce that one key that would open up the '68 murder.

Sergio, thought the Marshal, stirring the glistening sauce slowly about, hadn't changed a bit, even though he'd served his sentence and for him it was all over.

'It was Flavio Vargius. I was ill in bed.'

'If you were ill in bed how could you know it was Flavio?'

'It was him, he'd have killed the boy if I'd accused him.'

'But you did accuse him. You're accusing him now. Who's to prevent him killing your son now? Why accuse him now?'

'I'm accusing him because he did it.'

'Do you realize the implications? Do you understand that the same gun has killed another eight people?'

'You can't accuse me. You said.'

'Nobody is accusing you! Eight people have been murdered. We want to know who's got that gun.'

'I threw it in the ditch.'

And how they'd refrained from throttling the man was a mystery. The Marshal sat down to his pasta and gave it a liberal showering of cheese. They had not told the papers at that stage, which was sensible, but something else had leaked to the journalists, a story that Piero Merlini was still alive when they found him after the Montespertoli murder and had given a description of the killer. It wasn't true. The poor boy had been alive all right but had died in hospital without regaining consciousness. Still, the story was published and the day after, before the judge could get back from his talks with Sergio, Flavio Vargius had upped and disappeared, drawing the full force of the investigation after him.

They'd gone to see his wife first, of course. The Marshal, munching hard, suddenly stopped. There was something about that visit to Vargius's wife that he'd made a mental note about. What was it? He ate on, trying to remember but not remembering. He could swear it was something to do with the Suspect, but how could that possibly be? The Suspect, as such, hadn't even existed in 1982. What the devil could it have been? They'd gone to Flavio's house to question his wife . . . it was there somewhere . . . she must have been a right character, set into the husband right away, saying he'd beaten her up so badly that she was deaf in one ear, which when it all came out wasn't true. Was that it? The Suspect was said to beat

241

his wife. Try as he would he couldn't remember the connection. Anyway, Vargius's wife had made an official complaint and with that warrant and not too much effort they'd managed to find him and arrest him and suspect number two was in prison. But they weren't out of the woods yet by a long chalk. To prove he was the Monster they needed to prove that he had that gun and so did the '68 job. For that they needed the testimony of Sergio Muscas, the world's most unreliable witness. And Sergio had now decided to exonerate himself completely. If he wasn't admitting to being at the scene, his accusation of Flavio was useless. The investigators decided to do a bit of listening in.

Perhaps he'd been mistaken. The Marshal got up and rinsed his dish. Perhaps it hadn't been Flavio and his wife he'd made a mental note about, but Sergio's brother Fabio and his wife. Muddling the names up like that poor child after the murder. He went back to the bedroom and found the page with the transcript of their intercepted calls. They called each other every evening because Tina was in hospital, dying of cancer. Any hopes the investigators might have started out with that on her death bed the woman would have told the truth were soon dashed. How could it be otherwise? She was about to leave her daughter Dina orphaned of her mother. If her husband were to be arrested for involvement in the '68 murder the girl would be fatherless, too. The Marshal took the relevant sheets into the sitting room and sat down in his usual armchair in front of the television.

F: 'How are you feeling?'

T: 'Much the same. I'd feel better at home.'

F: 'They know best.'

T: 'Do they? I don't want to die in this place.'

F: 'You're not going to die. Nobody said you're going to die.'

T: That's as may be. Have you talked to Sergio?'

F: 'I've tried. It's not easy on the telephone. Maybe I should go up there.'

T: 'Well, if you do, don't start giving him any ideas about coming back here. He can stay where he is.'

F: 'He's my brother, after all.'

T: 'And don't I know it. He's brought us all nothing but trouble. It was a black day's work when your father arranged that marriage of his.'

F: 'He did it for the best. Nobody could have known how she'd turn out. You'd have thought she'd have been grateful for any husband, dirt poor like they were. Besides, who else would have had him? You know he's not right in the head.'

T: 'I know that bitch couldn't keep her knickers on for two minutes together. Don't think I don't know all the men in the village called her the Queen Bee. Your father ruined himself paying off Sergio's debts, and why? Because she was giving money away to all her fancy men. That money would have come to us! If she'd kept her hands on that insurance money –'

F: 'Keep your tone down.'

T: 'Did your father have to sell the house or didn't he?

243

With Sergio in prison that would have been ours. What about your daughter, what about her? She'd have had a home of her own! That's men all over. Never think about anybody but themselves. And get Nicolino to ring his father. If him and Sergio don't stick to the same story –'

F: 'They will stick to it. He'll keep accusing Flavio Vargius. As long as they do that I'm all right.'

T: 'That's what you think. They've neither of them the sense they were born with. Has Nicolino been going to work?'

F: 'On and off.'

T: 'I suppose that means no.'

F: 'I'm doing my best.'

T: 'Just don't give him any money.'

F: 'That's all very well but . . .'

T: 'Just don't give him any. And when he's questioned he's to say he was asleep in the back of the car and he can't remember anything. He didn't see anybody. Is that clear?'

F: 'I've told him that. It's this thieving I'm worried about. If I don't give him money he's going to get it somewhere as long as he's on drugs. If he gets arrested –'

T: 'You'll be the one arrested if you're not careful. It's nothing short of a miracle that Sergio hasn't talked now he's out.'

F: 'He won't, though, he's determined on that.'

T: 'Well, I hope you're right. We don't want that coming

244

out on top of everything else. He's brought enough shame on us as it is.'

F: 'You know what he is. And Nicolino's no better. I'm doing my best but they've both got a screw loose and I can't change that.'

A screw loose . . . well, there was no doubt about that. Even so, why protect his brother who'd left him to take the rap and now left him to live out his life in a hospice? There was Nicolino, of course, Sergio must have known he needed his brother and sister-in-law to look after the child. But now? He was no longer a child. And what about whoever else Sergio was protecting?

'He'll keep accusing Flavio Vargius.'

What was he hiding?

'We don't want that coming out on top of everything else.'

But what? You could follow the scenario up to a point. This wretched Belinda was the moral and economic ruin of the family so little wonder Fabio helped Sergio to get rid of her.

'Uncle Flavio looked in my mum's bag and then he felt round in the glove compartment . . .'

The insurance money. Just before the murder, Sergio and Belinda had cashed an insurance claim for injuries Sergio had received in an accident on his moped. It was a considerable sum and evidently Belinda had got her hands on it. That's what Fabio was after. But Fabio had no gun and no car, like Sergio. Somebody provided those things. *'We don't want that coming out. We don't want . . .'*

'Salva? Is that you?'

'Of course it's me. What's happened? Why are you calling me in the middle of the night?'

'It's not the middle of the night, it's your usual time for getting up.'

The Marshal, having stumbled into the hall in the dark, dropped a sheet of paper he was holding and felt around for the light switch. What was the matter was that he wasn't in bed and he couldn't work out why. For some reason his fuddled brain was convinced this call was from the hospital. What hospital? Why?

'I thought I'd better tell you, Nunziata's not too good.'

So it was a premonition. 'She's in hospital.'

'Good heavens, no. She's off colour, so I thought . . .'

Slowly, as she talked, he gathered his wits and remembered the document he'd been reading. He must have fallen asleep over it in the sitting room. He remembered papers scattering to the floor as he'd shot out of his armchair at the first ring.

He couldn't be sure that he'd read all the things he was beginning to remember because he'd probably dreamt some of it, must have, because Ferrini had featured among the characters he'd been reading about and that couldn't be right. There'd been something else, as well, near the end. Something that he remembered as

246

being dramatic and that he'd tried and tried to understand but the words had slid sideways in front of his tired eyes and no matter how hard he'd tried to concentrate it had been impossible to force them to stay still long enough to read.

'I just thought, to be on the safe side, she should do some tests and since I'm here . . .'

'But I thought you were coming home tomorrow.'

'She is your sister, Salva. It'll only mean a couple of days more. The doctor said . . .'

And yet he was almost convinced that it had been real, that he had read it, or tried to read it . . . now it would take hours to get all this stuff back in order. He leaned down and, with the receiver blocked under his chin, gathered up such pages as he could reach.

'Of course, it's her liver,' he said. 'You know how fond she is of her food and you can imagine at Christmas . . .'

'I know. She'll have to go on a diet, for what good it does, like somebody else I won't name. Are you all right?'

'What?'

'Are you all right? You sound a bit distracted.'

'I've just woken up. When *will* you be coming home, then?'

The arrest of Flavio. He remembered that. He'd been more or less awake when he'd read that. He dropped it on the rug and spread some more papers to separate them and find the chapter heading he'd read last. He was sure it had been a chapter heading that had stuck in his mind and that he'd been unable to decipher the text below it. That was it . . . then Ferrini had appeared so he must have fallen asleep. He hadn't actually appeared but he was there, behind the tall reeds, and the child had lifted a pale hand in the dark and pointed.

'*There was a noise . . .*'

'*It's all right. I'll take you home.*'

'*And will you give me a piggy back?*'

'*Get moving!*'

There had been another voice, and he felt the small hand, cold with fear, slide itself into his own. He had started walking, not wanting to alarm the child, but he realized that in this total darkness he'd never manage. He didn't even know where the child lived.

'*Will my mum come?*'

'*No, she's dead.*'

'*But tomorrow will she come?*'

He'd been carrying the child then but he was so tiny and cold he weighed nothing at all. And why didn't he cry? They had plodded along in the darkness and Ferrini's voice had come from behind the reeds.

'*You'll never find the right road. There's a page missing.*'

A page missing. It was just a dream, then, caused by his letting the papers fall as he fell asleep.

'*I'd better go.*'

'*Are you sure you're all right, Salva?*'

'*Of course I am. But if I don't get moving I'll be late. Besides, I haven't had coffee yet.*'

'*Ah, that's what's wrong with you.*'

'Ring me tonight. Say hello to the boys. Are they enjoying themselves?'

'They're all right, but they stay up late every night, so they're still fast asleep.'

He could feel the tiny hand in his, as cold as death.

'Tell them . . .'

'What shall I tell them?'

'Tell them . . . nothing, tell them to have a good time.'

He stood for a moment after hanging up, staring about him with his huge eyes, his forehead creased in a slight frown. Then he made for the bedroom.

'Ouffa!'

He wasn't cut out for reading. A good night's sleep would have been more to the point. Even so, he gathered up the piles of papers from there and the sitting room and took them through to the kitchen with him.

There he got the coffee on and sat down at the table to begin sorting through the muddle he'd made. He didn't even think of glancing out of the window to check on the weather which was what he always did in the mornings. The first part of the document was in order since he'd been wide awake when he'd read it. Some of the chapter leading up to Flavio's arrest had got muddled, but it was all more or less together and he put it back in order and set all the chapters, up to and including that one, aside.

'Right . . .'

Coffee first. It was bubbling up. He turned it off and poured himself a tiny cupful.

The muddle wasn't nearly as bad as he'd thought, it was just the bit he'd read last that was in confusion, the pages as muddled as his memory of them. He scanned them as he put them in order, separating dream and fact as he went.

Amelio Vargius, Flavio's nephew and his accomplice in some recent crimes, including an arms theft for which Flavio was wanted at the time of his arrest, said Flavio was unfairly arrested for the '68 murder, that he was always being accused unjustly when other people got away with things they'd really done. It transpired that Amelio's relationship with his real father, Silvano Vargius, was so negative that he had been to all intents and purposes adopted by his uncle, so it was understandable that he should go out of his way to defend him. This same transferral of affection likewise explained why Silvano was so very bitter against his brother Flavio, confirming that he was Belinda Muscas's lover at the time of the murder. He admitted that he, too, had had an affair with Belinda but that it had ended long before Flavio took up with her. He confirmed stories of Flavio's violent jealousy, whilst failing to confirm Flavio's alibi.

A young man by the name of Salvatore Angius, a friend of both Silvano and Flavio, recounted that he had been in prison with Sergio Muscas twice in 1969 and 1970 and that Sergio had told him he was innocent and Flavio had murdered Belinda and Lo Russo. Other witnesses claimed that Flavio Vargius had a Beretta 22 and was often seen practising shooting with his nephew in the woods near his home. He could produce no alibi for the times when the couples had been murdered.

During 1981 extensive checks had been made on the registration numbers of cars being driven by men alone in the countryside at night in the hope of tracking down solitary Peeping Toms. These numbers were looked at again now and though none could be traced to Flavio, one did turn out to belong to the nephew Amelio who might well have lent it to him.

Enquiries revealed that Flavio was a habitual Peeping Tom from the same band as Elio Sassetti. Bullets and cartridges were then recovered from the woods where he had been seen shooting. They were Winchester 22-calibre with an H impressed on the base, the ammunition used by the serial killer.

The warrant for Flavio Vargius's arrest was signed on 6th November, 1982.

The Marshal put aside this chapter and the next, imagining the frustration of the investigators when that little house of cards had been blown down. Not only had Flavio been checked by psychiatrists and found to be perfectly normal, but the bullets found in the woods turned out to have been fired from a quite different gun, the one he used, as he had quite truthfully told them, for playing target shooting with his nephew. And if that weren't enough, while they still had him in prison in September 1983, Herman Mainz and Ulrich Richter were shot and killed in their camper with the Beretta 22 L.R.

So much for Flavio. At which point, after a visit from

his brother which must have gone badly, Sergio suddenly accused *him*, producing as evidence a note in his brother's hand which said:

'*Keep accusing Vargius. You have to protect the family.*'

There should have followed a report on the investigation leading to Fabio's arrest but the Marshal couldn't find it. If he remembered rightly, Fabio had some pretty weird sexual habits and an alarming collection of knives which he claimed were for his hobby of carving cork. None of it had come to anything because they'd had to release him after the next murder in Vicchio. Where was the thing? That must have been the missing page he'd dreamt about, perhaps aware of having dropped it as he fell asleep. He ran it to earth at last under the television and put it back in the pile.

'Even so,' muttered the Marshal as he went off to the shower, 'he was in up to his neck in that '68 job with Sergio, though nobody will ever prove it now.'

He wasn't feeling as tired as he had a right to. Whatever the reason, it was encouraging. And even more encouraging was the thought that all being well, this would be the last day of their much-publicized search of the Suspect's house. He'd had enough of that.

'I've had enough,' the Marshal said.

'What about you, Bacci?'

'No, thanks.'

'Then I'll finish it.' Ferrini forked the last slice of salami on to his plate.

They were in the back of the little bar where they regularly ate breakfast and where four tiny tables were set each day for cheap lunches cooked by the barman's wife and her mother. He kept one table for them by arrangement and they went there in relays. The other three tables were occupied by workmen from the sausage factory. The salami presumably came from there. There was no menu. If you didn't want the meat they'd prepared you could ask for an omelette instead. There was always pasta with either meat or tomato sauce. Today it was meat sauce. The barman's wife set their three bowls down.

'Everything all right?'

'Fine . . . you can take it.' Ferrini popped the last scrap of salami on to a piece of bread and let her remove his plate.

'In a perfect world,' he went on, continuing the discourse that the last slice had interrupted, 'everybody'd be in uniform – well, not exactly in uniform but identifiable. The Monsters of this world ought to go about with knives hanging from their belts and have green faces and little horns so when you caught one you could say, "Ah! A Monster!" I remember a chap I arrested once. Burglar. He went about Florence wearing a striped T-shirt, driving a little truck with ropes and ladders on the back and a blonde gangster's-moll-type girl beside him. And when he was on the job he'd wear a black mask.'

'But he'd surely have got caught,' protested Bacci, looking at the Marshal to see if Ferrini was just having them on.

'He did.' Ferrini wound a generous forkful of spaghetti. 'All the time. Spent more of his life inside than out but he didn't mind that. Part of the job. He just wanted to be a burglar. The trouble with this case is that even if you pick the right man you'd have a job proving it without the gun.'

'They always confess,' Bacci offered. 'That's what I've read. They enjoy dodging and teasing and playing the investigators but once the game's over and reality steps in they confess.'

'Well, that's as may be, but I don't think we're in any danger of reality stepping in here, eh, Guarnaccia? Did you read that stuff?'

'A lot of it. I've still some to go. Did you read it when it was first published?'

'I haven't read it – not all of it; I've skimmed through it. I knew already what was in it. Being at Headquarters I couldn't help but know what was going on from the men on the job. Have you got to the missing page yet?'

The Marshal stared at him.

'Second to the last chapter?'

'You mean . . . there really is a page missing? I don't think –'

'No, no. Second to the last chapter. It's headed: "The Missing Page". That's when things got interesting, you'll see. Now then' – he picked up the jug of red wine – 'Bacci? Give me your glass.'

He poured the wine and pushed it back. 'Get this down you and don't take life so seriously. It's never worth it.

Tell you what, though, I'll be glad if we really do finish the job today. I should have thought, in the circumstances, they could have done without emptying the poor bastard's wine vat. I think even I'd have cried. Right, what's it to be? The breaded veal cutlet or an omelette?'

'I thought an omelette because –'

'Your diet. But you're about to remember how bad eggs are for your liver. You're all liverish in your family, you told me so yourself this morning. So: three veal cutlets and a nice green salad. Signora? We're ready for you!'

It seemed as though they really would finish today. The Marshal and Ferrini were in the tiny bedroom of the daughter's flat. From the window they could see the piazza and its little church. The young woman was not present. Her name was still on the doorbell but she no longer appeared to be living there.

'Where is she, do we know?' the Marshal asked as he moved a few clothes about in the nearly empty drawers.

'There's a question,' said Ferrini, grinning. 'We do but we don't. She's being "protected" from the journalists.'

'I was wondering . . .' The Marshal closed the bottom drawer of the dressing table and walked over to the window. 'It struck me as funny and I've been meaning to mention it to you.'

'Eh? What's funny?'

'I don't know . . . this business of this young woman suddenly deciding to bring an action against her father. It doesn't sound right to me.'

'Does anything in this whole business sound right to you?'

'No . . . no, it doesn't but, after all, this was before and – Well, it sounds all right on the surface but I never heard of such a thing. I mean, she's grown up and she no longer lives at home. Can you imagine her getting up one morning and saying, "Well, it's a nice day: I think I'll go and report my father for raping me from when I was nine." She can hardly get two words out about it now, three years later. She's desperately embarrassed, she doesn't want to talk. She's frightened.'

'That's true. She's certainly frightened.'

'Well, it doesn't ring true to me. I've been meaning to mention it to you for a while but what with one thing and another . . . Then, last night, reading about Flavio Vargius, it struck me.'

'What's he got to do with it?'

'Nothing. But when they thought he was the Monster and he disappeared they needed a warrant so as to get hold of him fast and investigate him.'

'And?'

'And they didn't have any real evidence to warrant arresting him as the Monster. The judge's report said something like, "A visit to his wife Valeria resulted in her reporting him for domestic violence. They arrested him for that and were able to keep him inside. Then another murder happened . . ."'

Ferrini stopped dragging the mattress off the bed and turned to look at the Marshal. 'I see . . . Right. You mean they'd already chosen him as the Suspect. He went to prison and another murder, for one reason or other, didn't happen, so they felt safe.'

'Not just that. They'd made him into a monster. You've heard the people in the village, read the articles in the paper – and if we're honest, we've said it ourselves: what does it matter if he's not guilty? The murders have stopped and given what he did to that girl . . .'

'It's true. You're right. But that's a pretty clever move for an imbecile like Simonetti, I'd have thought.'

'He's not pulling the strings, though, is he? He'll go down if this show doesn't come off, but I doubt if he'll get the credit if it does.'

'That's true, too, only – I'm being the devil's advocate here – they couldn't actually force the girl to sign, could they? Or force her to give evidence. You've seen what she's like.'

'I've seen that she's frightened. I just don't know why. The barman – where we have lunch – he said something one day . . . something like she'd told his wife she'd *had* to sign, that otherwise she would have gone to prison.'

Ferrini shrugged. 'But she's completely off her head. I suppose they could have got the story out of her and then, once she realized what it meant she tried to back out. It's one thing confiding in a friendly employer, another having to testify in court. They might have come on a bit strong with her in terms of, "You told us this story and if you don't sign it looks as if you were lying to us." Something of that sort might have happened, but I can't see anything more than that in it. Local Marshal's probably known her all her life, knew how to handle her.'

'No . . .'

'No? He's been here for years, hasn't he?'

'Police Headquarters is where all this happened. I found a tiny reference to it in his file. She didn't go to the Marshal of carabinieri here in the village at all, I asked him. He told me Police Headquarters and he was no more convinced by the story than I am. Of course, this employer she's supposed to have confided in would know whether the story's true or not but she, if I remember rightly –'

'Must remain anonymous because of the press interest, etcetera. So, we can't check.'

'No. But it's not credible, is it?'

'No,' Ferrini admitted, looking at his colleague, now with a bit more respect. 'No, I'm afraid you're right. It's not credible at all.'

As expected, the search came to an end towards seven that evening. All they had taken away at the end of it was the bullet from the garden and, from the farmhouse kitchen, a plastic soapdish containing a few worthless trinkets which the Suspect said belonged to his daughter but which might have been among the contents of the murdered girls' handbags. The Chief Public Prosecutor, interviewed on the eight o'clock news, said he wasn't by any means disappointed, that the enquiry was proceeding as planned and that he wasn't able to reveal anything further at present.

'And if that's supposed to sound like there's a lot you could reveal if you wanted to . . .' mumbled the Marshal, with one eye on the screen as he struggled with the can opener.

'Ouch! Blasted thing . . .' He sniffed at the soup warily and then tipped it into a pan big enough to boil a couple of hens. He could have gone over to the mess but he was too tired and, besides, he wanted to get back to the Missing Page. While the soup was warming, he remembered that he ought to get the washing out of the washing machine. He opened the door and pulled at the damp bundle of mixed shirts and socks and underwear which was entangled in a tracksuit belonging to one of the boys. His own stuff hadn't been enough to make a full load and it seemed wasteful to run it half empty. It all smelled a bit odd. Perhaps it shouldn't have been left in there so long . . . was it two days or three?

'Mmph . . .' His white shirts didn't look quite right but he decided that was because they were still wet.

A sudden hissing noise sent him back to the cooker in time to prevent the brightly coloured soup from boiling over. This was ridiculous. He'd looked after himself for years and was a perfectly adequate cook when it came to the two or three dishes he knew how to prepare. But in the old days he hadn't had this Monster business to contend with and there'd been time to do his bit of shopping every day.

'It doesn't taste like any minestrone I ever ate.' He broke off a chunk of rather stale bread and dipped it unhappily into the offensive mixture. Not that he wanted to be unreasonable, but if his sister hadn't overstuffed herself at Christmas while he'd been left here alone to work all hours and have no Christmas dinner at all . . .

He soon forgot his troubles when he took up the judge's document again. His only interruption was when he realized something was annoying him and got up to switch off the small black and white television. After that he didn't pause until he reached the end and even then he went back and read over some of it again, hoping that what it said couldn't be true and that on a second reading it might end differently. But it didn't.

Eleven

PART SIX
-1984–5-

6.1. THE MISSING PAGE

This page concerns Silvano Vargius.

As has already been observed, Sergio Muscas, on the few occasions when he withdrew his accusations against Flavio Vargius, transferred them to Flavio's brother Silvano. The last time this happened was in 1984 when Flavio was under arrest and Sergio was being questioned yet again about his accomplice in the '68 murder. The transferral, as always, was of short duration and the one-page report of it separated from the main file as being irrelevant. Only after the murder of the two German boys seemed to demonstrate Flavio's innocence did the investigators find and re-examine it. Its contents ran as follows:

> Quite suddenly, for no apparent reason, Muscas began to talk about Silvano Vargius: *'Still it's true that Silvano was no better than he should be. He killed his wife before he left Sardinia and the kid was saved that time as well – no, I'm not saying anything against Silvano. I'm not suggesting anything. Silvano Vargius had a car.'*

6.2. SERGIO'S AMBIGUITY

Muscas had made this reference to the death of Silvano's wife the first time he accused him in '68 but immediately after that he confessed and the seemingly irrelevant remark, though recorded, was ignored as being an invention. As regards the car, Sergio by now knew that his other accusations were against people who did not possess a car and so were unconvincing.

As regards Muscas's original accusation against Silvano it should be remembered that when the latter was brought to Sergio's cell for a confrontation Sergio fell to his knees sobbing and begging for forgiveness. When the case went to trial in 1970, Silvano was present and was wearing the dead woman's engagement ring.

6.3. CAUSE OF AMBIGUITY

A re-examination of the documents of Sergio's trial revealed an alarming piece of information. Sergio's sister-in-law Tina declared in the witness box that Belinda Muscas had frequently declared that Nicolino was not Sergio's son but the son of one of the Vargius brothers. Tina said she didn't know which brother was referred to but that Sergio himself admitted the story was true. In fact, the brother referred to could only have been Silvano. At the time of Nicolino's conception, Flavio was still living in Sardinia. Silvano had just arrived in Tuscany and was living with the Muscas couple. This puts Sergio's twice-repeated statement, *'He killed his wife . . . and the kid was saved that time as well,'* in an even more alarming light. What remained unclear was a credible motive for Silvano's having killed Belinda and any reason why Sergio, instead of accusing him openly, continued to accuse his brother.

In 1985 Sergio was questioned again about Flavio, once it was clear that he was not guilty of the six double homicides committed since 1974.

'It's true that I was lying about Flavio when I accused him. It's true as well that Silvano wanted me to accuse Flavio because they'd quarrelled. They didn't quarrel about Belinda, though. It was to do with Amelio, Silvano's kid. He always said Flavio had ruined him, teaching him to steal and to hate his own father. Silvano took the kid to live with him when he married again but it went badly. He ran away from home and went to work for a shepherd for a bit – a bad sort – I forget his name but he was always in and out of prison and in my book it was him got the kid

involved in thieving, not Flavio. Anyway, then he did go and live with Flavio for a bit and that was when him and Silvano started fighting. It's not true that it was because Silvano had picked up with Belinda again – I know he said he didn't but he did. It wasn't her, it was that he was pissed off about his kid running away and he even went to the carabinieri to try and get him brought back, claimed the kid had stolen a truck and a moped from him and set fire to his workshop. Silvano reckoned it was all Flavio's fault. I don't know whether it was or not. It's true the lad got caught trying to steal an Alfa Romeo when he was fifteen or so but it was only a kid's trick so it came to nothing. He just had a passion for red sports cars. I think he pinched a few of them – or he tried to – until he bought himself one when he came home – he took off from Flavio's after only a few months and went somewhere up north to his mother's sister. Stayed away for years. Anyway, that's all there was to it. Silvano called that corrupting him and he never forgave Flavio and that's why he wanted me to accuse him. You can believe me or not as you want but I swear it wasn't because of Belinda. Now I've told you the truth, but Flavio did it, anyway, and if you bring him here I'll accuse him to his face.'

Checking began on every contradictory element of his latest statement.

6.4. SILVANO VARGIUS IN 1968
Silvano's alibi for the night of 22 August 1968 had

presumably been checked verbally but there was no written record of this. Silvano claimed to have been playing billiards that night with a young man called Salvatore Angius. Angius, a homeless Sardinian labourer, was indebted to Silvano for a number of reasons. He had employed him on building jobs and found him places to live. Most of the people questioned seemed to regard the younger man as having been treated as an adopted son. Angius was still living in Tuscany and working as a builder. On being questioned in 1984 he said he had often played billiards with Silvano but had never been sure about the exact day they'd played that week, but nobody had brought the matter up again and then Sergio was convicted. He was still in touch with Silvano but he wasn't working for him now. Silvano, he said, had an emergency house call firm now, the sort you call if you lock yourself out or your pipes burst.

The employees of Silvano's firm 'Domestic Emergencies' were questioned in the spring of 1984. Two disturbing facts emerged about Silvano's 1968 alibi: the first was that the relationship between him and the much younger Angius was a homosexual one. The second was that the address given by Angius when asked to confirm Silvano's alibi in '68 was that of his brother. Salvatore Angius had used his brother's address for years as his official place of residence but had never lived there. In August 1968 he was actually living on the Pistoia road at number 156 on the stretch known as Via Torrente. That is, he was living next door to the Rossini house where

Nicolino had been left that night, in the peasant's cottage which Sergio had mistakenly described as the Rossini house.

6.5. SILVANO VARGIUS IN 1984–5

Two new lines of enquiry were now opened. In Florence an extensive and detailed report was made by the carabinieri of Silvano Vargius's way of life, medical and social history and, in particular, sexual habits. In Sardinia, magistrates reopened the enquiry into the death of Silvano's wife in 1960, which had been treated as suicide at the time.

Silvano's second wife had left him in 1981. She was traced and questioned as to his sexual habits, as was his present partner. Both women testified that they had been forced into group sex, organized by Silvano, in which he sometimes participated, sometimes not. His wife also described homo-heterosexual encounters which Silvano organized with certain couples of their acquaintance and stated that she had left Silvano because of his unacceptable sexual habits. This was confirmed on examination of documents relating to their separation. Silvano denounced his wife for abandoning the conjugal roof (Civil Code para. 146 absolves the husband of supporting his separated or divorced wife if she abandons her home and refuses to return). Although this was patently the case here, judgement was in favour of the wife because of his violence and sexual practices. His wife also revealed that Silvano had been in a psychiatric hospital during 1981.

At this point the ambiguity of Sergio Muscas as regards Silvano becomes explicable. Confronted with the above information, Sergio admitted that Silvano had sexual relations not only with Belinda but with Sergio himself. He confessed that while Belinda enjoyed her relationship with Silvano and all that it entailed, she also enjoyed herself with her other lovers, including Flavio, but Sergio himself was totally dominated by Silvano. It was true that at his request Sergio brought home other men for his wife, to satisfy Silvano's taste for group sex and voyeurism, and that his remark about Flavio's *screwing my wife in front of my eyes* was to be taken literally and in truth referred to Silvano more than Flavio. He recounted now that Silvano would organize group sex with other men for Belinda in the Cascine park and that on these occasions it was his habit to take along both Sergio and the child Nicolino.

Two things were now clear: Sergio was so dominated by Silvano that, even to save himself, he hadn't had the courage to accuse him to his face but fell to his knees crying and begging for forgiveness, and that the other principal reason for his reticence was shame. In the culture he belonged to, homosexuality was something so shameful and disgusting that its existence was not even acknowledged. It is notable, also, that though Sergio was too weak to react against his wife's behaviour, he was the one to separate the lovers' bodies after the murder so that they were not discovered in the lovemaking position.

Unfortunately, at this stage Sergio's subservience to Silvano, and his overpowering shame, meant that he would still not make a clear unequivocal statement regarding the '68 murder so as to facilitate the investigation of the later crimes.

6.6. 1960

In 1960 Silvano was still living in his native village in Sardinia. He was married with a one-year-old son, Amelio. When his wife was found dead with an unlit gas canister turned on in the room, she was presumed to have committed suicide. The little boy, in his cot nearby, was saved. The case exhibited such strong analogies with the '68 murder – especially given the new information that Nicolino was also Silvano's son – that the case was reopened and the wife's body exhumed.

However, the results of an autopsy had only a negative value. A body exhumed after twenty-five years was obviously not in a condition to provide accurate positive information.

Enquiries as to the likelihood of the woman's wishing to commit suicide revealed that she had decided to leave Silvano because of his violence and had obtained a position as a residential housekeeper at an orphanage in another village. She was to leave and take up this position on the morning after she was found dead. It was likely, according to the information received, that Silvano, with the help of his wife's brother, smothered her with a pillow to prevent her leaving and damaging Silvano's pride and her own family's respectability. Again, this could in judicial terms have only a negative value, i.e. there was evidence against the likelihood of the woman's having wanted to commit suicide, but no real proof of Silvano's guilt.

6.7. THE BERETTA 22 L.R.

Ever since it was established that the Beretta 22 used in the double homicides was the same one used in '68, efforts to trace its provenance were intensified. Of the guns of this type, regularly licensed but reported missing by their legitimate owners, was one belonging to a Sardinian emigrant worker, returned home after many years working in Belgium. He had died some years before in his native village and the gun had never been found. It was the same village where Silvano Vargius was born and which he left after his wife's 'suicide' in 1960. The gun disappeared at the same time as he did. The owner of the gun was the uncle of Silvano's wife.

6.8. 1985 SILVANO'S MOVEMENTS

From this point on, all of Silvano's movements, habits and activities were checked on. The following points were established:

1. Given the type of job he did, Silvano had no fixed hours. He was frequently absent during the night responding to emergency calls, and such absences were not notable.

2. For obvious reasons he kept, and was expert in using, both knives and awls such as were used on the female victims.

3. He also owned a miner's lamp to be attached to the head and which must have been necessary to a killer working on the bodies in total darkness.

4. Silvano was unable to furnish alibis for any of the double homicides when required to do so, except for the '83 murder of the German boys. He claimed that he had been called out to an emergency in the centre of Florence at the house of a known prostitute. A singular but not necessarily helpful circumstance was that a receipt from Silvano's firm was indeed found in the prostitute's house, but it was dated 1982 not 1983 and it was discovered because the house was being searched after she had been murdered in 1984.

An attempt was made to follow Silvano, particularly on the darkest night of the month, but this was extremely difficult to achieve in the country without being seen by him and on most occasions he eluded his followers. This was the case on the 29th July 1984. On that night Carlo Salvini and Patrizia Renzetti were murdered in their car at Vicchio.

The following morning a search of Silvano's house revealed the presence of a bloodstained rag. The blood on the rag was of two distinct groups and further analyses revealed the presence of gunpowder.

'But why didn't they arrest him?' The Marshal had resisted ringing Ferrini in the middle of the night, the minute he finished reading about the missing page, but even though almost twenty-four hours had passed and they were seated together in his office, he still felt stunned.

'I mean, the Prosecutor working with Romola, to have taken the enquiry that far, must have been on his side?'

'Does he name him? Remember, I haven't read the thing.'

'No. No, he doesn't . . .'

'Mm. A small point but an important one. The Prosecutor running the enquiry was suddenly, when it came to the crunch, put on another case and someone else took his place. Ask me who.'

'Who?'

'Simonetti.'

'Dear God.'

'All he had to do was lie doggo. It's not the Instructing Judge's job to prosecute. He signs the warrants but the Prosecutor has to request him to do it. He didn't. And now he's got his reward. Fame and fortune will be his.'

'If he carries it off. He did try and prosecute, Romola, whether it was his job or not. This . . .' The document lay on the Marshal's desk between them. 'It's supposed to be an acquittal but it isn't. You say you didn't read it . . .'

'I had no reason to. I knew all along what was going on. Anybody who didn't know wouldn't be interested. An abandoned enquiry is hardly news.'

'I know . . . I'm not so good at explaining myself but it's not just what's in it . . . it's the way it's written. I've not read much of this sort of thing. Our job's over long before a case gets to this stage so I admit I'm no expert . . .'

The Marshal had been staring sightlessly at the map of his quarter on the wall, as he so often did when musing, but now he turned his big troubled eyes on Ferrini. 'Whatever this document pretends to be it's really an accusation. In a funny sort of way it reminded me, the way he accused Silvano, of the way Sergio Muscas accused him. "Silvano's wife died in Sardinia and the kid was saved that time, too. I'm not making any allusions. Silvano Vargius had a car . . ." It's like that, you see. What the judge really means is what Sergio meant: I'm not accusing him but he did it. And then there's so much anger in it. He's very bitter.'

'Wouldn't you be?'

'I don't know because I don't understand why. Why should they have done that?'

Ferrini shrugged. 'I only know the gossip that was going around at the time. That they didn't want Romola's Monster just because he was Romola's. Some ambitious soul I won't name didn't want him taking the credit, so he opened a completely new line of enquiry. That was when Flavio was in prison and – oops! Wrong again – the two Germans were killed. Then the fight for the evidence started. They had that camper removed with the bodies inside it before you could say Jack

Robinson. And before any external measurements had been taken, presumably to get it out of the clutches of Romola and the carabinieri and into the custody of Simonetti and the police.'

'I just can't believe it . . .'

'You can't? Well, I was there. It was before I came to work in the city. I was out there in charge of the local station and I found the bodies.'

'You were?'

'You bet I was. I saw them drive the camper away and I knew the measurements hadn't been taken. So, what do you expect to happen if you drive a van along a country lane and it's got bullet holes through the windows?'

'The glass shattered, I suppose.'

'You suppose right. There were bullet holes through the metal body, too, of course, but since they hadn't been measured from the ground . . . The whole thing was a shambles.'

'But it's not . . . When I said I couldn't believe it I didn't mean anything so specific, I just meant I couldn't believe that even the most ambitious person . . . a case as serious as this . . .'

'For a really ambitious person nothing's more serious than his own career. Listen, I've managed without a smoke for an hour so as not to fog up your office but I can't hold out any longer, d'you mind?'

The Marshal didn't answer. He was staring at the map again.

'I'll take your silence for consent. Where's Bacci got to? I thought he was bringing us some stuff?'

'He'll be here. He had to go home and get it. I told him after that bullet episode that he shouldn't go about openly with those books. I've noticed what's-his-name giving him odd looks . . . What is he called?'

'Esposito?'

'No, no, the other one. Esposito's the one with the scar.'

'You're right. You mean Di Maira, then.'

'Di Maira, yes. I always get the impression he's watching us more than he's watching the Suspect – this'll be Bacci now.'

The Marshal got up when the bell rang and went through the darkened waiting room to look through the spy hole and open the door.

Ferrini grinned when he saw Bacci hesitate before the cloud of cigarette smoke that was rapidly filling the tiny office.

'Oh, come on in, Bacci. I won't say "It won't kill you" because along with all the car fumes in this town it probably will. Come and give us a few subtitles on this FBI stuff of yours.'

If anyone had asked the Marshal for an explanation of why he was going where he was going he'd have been hard put to find one. As it was, nobody asked him because nobody knew. They'd been given half a day's freedom after all the fuss of the search, and if the Marshal had been himself he'd have done a trip to the supermarket and given his quarters a good sweep out. But he wasn't himself, and it was difficult enough to keep his mind on his driving. He hadn't been on this road for years, not since being involved in that case out in the potteries. The landscape had changed. There were factories, service stations, new blocks of flats, an ugly, raw-looking sprawl. The traffic was heavy, but then it always had been . . . He should be coming up to where he had to make a right turn. There. Lastra a Signa. He couldn't have said why he hadn't told anybody, at least, not precisely why. There were some things he didn't tell Ferrini when he might have done, perhaps because Ferrini sometimes seemed to be laughing at him. He was so cynical. Not telling Bacci anything – well, they'd been agreed on that without really having to say it. There was really no point in burdening him with more doubts than he had already.

They had let him talk on without ever mentioning the document still lying on the desk.

'You see, I've been through all the available statistics on this type of crime and, even without taking anything else into consideration, he's just too old. Serial killers, lust killers, they really get into their stride in their twenties, so whoever did these murders should only be in his thirties now. I did find one exception, but even he started in his thirties and that was because his mother kept him practically chained up in the house until she died. He'd have started earlier if he'd been free. Apart from him the only exceptions to the rule are those who started unusually early. This boy here killed his first victim at twelve years old, this one at fourteen and this one at fifteen had already killed four. Accusing a man in his sixties makes no sense.'

But that wasn't all that made no sense. There was that FBI profile Simonetti had read to them in abbreviated form so as not to 'bore them with a jot of jargon'. He'd taken care not to bore them with a lot of facts, either. Cruelty to the weak, such as children and animals, he'd said, and the Suspect hit his dog with a stick. It was a far cry from the children in the FBI case notes, those who did such things as cutting off a cat's paws and tail and then burying it alive, or dousing a horse's tail in petrol and setting light to it. They set fire to buildings, too. Schools, for instance, when they thought they'd been ill-treated or unfairly punished, their own homes before running away, cars in the street. They robbed and burned and tortured, and when they were big enough and strong enough and had the means, they killed. The Suspect was just a foul-tempered, dirty old man like hundreds of others. He bore no relation at all to those young men in the photographs Bacci had shown them. Some were crazed and pitiful creatures, others terrifying, cold-blooded young men shown laughing as they were led into court, totally isolated from the rest of humanity which they had loathed and derided. But all of them were young, all of them came from poor backgrounds, all of them were cut off from human affection. They had, for the most part, been beaten senseless until their brains were irreparably damaged, starved, raped. Some had been tortured by their mothers, forced to watch them perform as prostitutes. Others had been orphaned as tiny children and left in the hands of people who despised and ill-treated them.

The catalogue of their crimes, the torn and mutilated bodies, the dead raw flesh eaten or 'raped' or used to decorate the room, was terrifying. Yet there was something even more terrifying in the catalogue of their own sufferings, something so dark and relentlessly evil that in the end it seemed preferable to be the victim than the killer.

And their Suspect was a dirty old man. He'd killed his rival in love, killed him brutally, too. But how could you connect that with slaughtering strangers and stealing body parts? The Marshal decided that he, at least, couldn't and that he had no intention of trying. As for the business of the daughter, that was far from being clear. But how much information might have been withheld there, too?

Disturbed and distracted as he was, he overshot the little town of Signa, where he'd meant to make his first stop, and so had to turn back. There was a small car park in front of a bar in the square, and he stopped there and got out to look at the cinema opposite.

THE GARDE CIN A

The façade was small and low and the tops of the trees

in the garden beyond could be seen. They'd have grown a lot in over twenty years. A plank had been nailed across the peeling doors and the G of Garden was hanging crookedly, about to fall as the N had done. It was so dismal, so forlorn, that it gave the impression of having been closed up on the night of that murder, avoided as a haunted place.

'*We went to the pictures and it was in the war and a house went on fire and then we went up there past the cemetery.*'

The rest of the little square was cheerful and busy, which made the crumbling grey cinema look like a bad tooth in a healthy smiling mouth.

The Marshal stepped into the bar and ordered a coffee. It was a clean bright place with shelves full of boxes of chocolates and fancy liqueurs. There were two small tables with pink linen cloths on them and a man in a green loden overcoat was sitting at one of them reading the local paper.

'One coffee coming up.'

'Thanks. You don't happen to know when that cinema across the road closed down, do you?'

'I really couldn't say. Before my time, anyway, and I took over here five or six years ago. Ask Franco there. Franco? You'll know when the Garden Cinema shut down, you've been here longer than me.'

'Born here. I couldn't tell you the exact year, not to swear to, but it'll be a good ten years or so. Didn't get all that much custom since they built that bigger open-air place down near the supermarket, and there was already the one at the Communist Club. I know the owner of the premises, if that's what you're after, but she's in her eighties and I don't think she's interested in selling.'

'No, no . . . Just curiosity.' Not that he'd expected anyone to believe him but it didn't matter. It mattered that he wasn't in uniform. He'd no intention of calling to pay his respects to the local force. It seemed to him that anybody who knew anything at all about this business was bound to have taken sides at some point, and while it seemed clear that the carabinieri had lined up on the side of Romola, that didn't mean someone would want to get involved in crossing the Public Prosecutor's office.

Why he should want to do it himself was a moot point. It hadn't been by any choice of his that he was chasing a Suspect he didn't suspect, but then that was probably what was irritating him into trying to get past the smoke screen and deal with something concrete. Like that bloodstained rag. The carabinieri had found it inside a flat straw bag hidden beneath blankets in a wardrobe. Two pieces of clean cotton printed with yellow flowers and between them the third piece, with its red and grey stains. Silvano had been there watching and he hadn't turned a hair. When they asked him afterwards to explain the blood and gunpowder he had only shrugged.

'*I know nothing about it. Never seen the bag before, though I suppose some woman might have left it here –*

*perhaps the woman I used to live with. If you say it's blood,
it's blood – but there can't be gunpowder on it.'*

And what sort of sense did that make? Either he knew
or he didn't know. And so Romola wanted to arrest him
and the Public Prosecutor's office refused. Romola asked
for the rag to be sent to England where DNA testing was
now possible. The Public Prosecutor's office refused. The
rag was sent instead for further testing in Rome and a
report was finally produced in December 1987, three
years and five months after the rag was found. The report
said the sample was too old for significant conclusions to
be drawn.

In desperation Romola managed to get Silvano
arrested for the murder of his first wife and he was
removed to prison to stand trial in Sardinia. And the
material evidence was too old there, too. Silvano was
acquitted. He was at once ordered to present himself
before the magistrate in Florence to answer questions
about a certain Beretta 22 L.R. Instead of which he left the
country. Then the murders stopped.

The Marshal paid for his coffee and got back in the car,
feeling better, at least, for having seen with his own eyes
that broken-down cinema where this whole story had
begun on the hot and very dark night of 22nd August 1968.

Not that it was easy, just now, to imagine the heat.
There was an icy wind blowing fit to freeze your ears off.
He switched on the engine and let it warm up as he fished
his notes and the rough map Lorenzini had drawn up for
him out of his pocket. He decided to proceed in the same

order as the original investigators. He would go back a little by the way he'd come and take the Pistoia road as far as the Rossini house.

It was a long, straight road and the traffic was moving fast. It was similar to the road he'd taken out of Florence, with the same symptoms of sleepy countryside pimpled with rashes of new building here and there. It really wasn't possible to go slowly enough to read the house numbers. When he tried there was an angry chorus of hooting and, once again, he overshot his mark and had to turn back. Well and good. The road he then had to take was, in any case, on the other side. He made an inspired guess, stopped his car as he turned in, and then got out to look at the white house on the other side of the road. Then he waited for a gap in the traffic and crossed. There was really no need to do that. The house was clearly numbered and recognizable, anyway, by the floodlight attached to it. But he couldn't help himself. He needed the house, not its number. He needed the real, the concrete. He had no idea whether the Rossini family still lived there but he didn't care. He just wanted to speak to someone, anyone, establish human contact with this twenty-year-old story.

The green shutters of 154 were closed. At 154A a woman was peering out from between tight lace curtains. 152, the other half of the building, housed a trattoria. An elderly woman there was sweeping the steps and the last late luncheon customers were getting into their cars in the cindered space beside the whitewashed building.

'Good afternoon.'

She carried on sweeping and looked up at him.

'We're closed. It's almost half past three.'

'That's all right. It was just some information I wanted. That lane across the road . . . If I'm not mistaken it's a short cut to Signa. Only I haven't been around these parts for years and I'm sure it sometimes used to be impassable. I thought, living here, you might know . . .'

She'd barely paid him any attention once she'd established that it was too late to eat, but now her lips tightened and she stopped her sweeping to stare at him.

'You can get through.'

'Thank you.'

'Don't mention it.' She gave him a black look and turned her back on him, starting to sweep again. When he was getting into his car he caught her watching him, peeping round from the side entrance, thinking, no doubt, that she was invisible. He sensed those lace curtains twitch slightly, too, and he felt the glittering eyes of the old woman trained on him as he started the engine. They were old enough to remember the story. Perhaps they thought he was a nosy journalist. Or perhaps he was becoming paranoid. For all he knew, they thought he was a tax inspector and they hadn't even lived there long enough to know anything about the '68 murder. Next to the big white house was a stone farmhouse building with three doors. In one of those, Salvatore Angius had been living, and nobody had ever found out. Why hadn't they? Why hadn't they knocked at every door in the block that night and asked, 'Did you see a small child cross the road alone? Did you see a man watching him?' It was easy enough to criticize, of course, from this distance. Nevertheless, he was quite sure he'd have done it, and in doing it he'd have seen this Angius and broken Silvano's alibi then instead of sixteen years later.

The woman with the sweeping brush came round to the front of the white building and stared across at him defiantly. He turned into the lane and drove down it, staying in second gear. He was being foolish. He wouldn't have broken Silvano's alibi because Silvano would never have given such an alibi if he hadn't felt safe to do it. Angius had given his official address as being his brother's house and before anybody could give the matter any thought Sergio Muscas had changed his story and the hue and cry was all for Flavio.

This stony lane was clear enough, all right, probably because a couple of small factories, little more than long sheds, had been built in the fields. There was no sign of the boulders which had demonstrated that the child couldn't have arrived by car and that he'd have torn and dirtied his socks if he'd walked.

Even so, something was wrong. There was no sign of the Vingone which would have been running beside the road behind a screen of tall reeds. He slowed down more, looking about him. There was a line of reeds in the distance to his right but that was neither here nor there since they should have been to his left. The road was curving and rising now. It met another, wider country road that petered out to his right and became a tarred road to his left where there were a number of houses. This was all wrong. He stopped, wondering what to do. An old man with a stick appeared from the direction of the tarmac road and sat down on a low wall to get his breath, despite the cold which had reddened his hands and face.

'Excuse me! I'm looking for the road that comes out near the cemetery!'

The old man sat motionless and gave no sign of having heard, perhaps because of the wind. The Marshal got out of the car and approached him.

'Excuse me? I'm looking for the cemetery. I thought this was a short cut. An old friend of mine's buried there . . .' He really was getting paranoid, but he couldn't help imagining Di Maira, who always seemed to be watching him, following in his tracks.

'He was looking for the lane where that couple were killed . . .'

'He had a Sicilian accent . . .'

'The cemetery?'

'Yes, I thought this road led there.'

'You're miles away.'

'But can't I cut across these fields?'

'You're miles off. This is Signa from here on. You'll have to go up that road there into the centre. Then go back a mile or so till you get to the town hall and take the road to Castelletti. It's about two miles, maybe a bit more, further on than that. You can't miss it.'

'But . . . The Vingone – doesn't the Vingone pass by here?'

'No, no. It's beyond the town centre. If you turn left you'll cross it. The traffic goes over the bridge.'

'But it's only a stream, the one I'm talking about. I understand it crossed these fields.'

'I don't know about that. The river's all I know. You'll see when you cross it.'

The Marshal got back in his car. How could he possibly have got so lost? The lane started right opposite the Rossini house and came straight here. Then he remembered: somewhere in the judge's report there had been that episode where Sergio, having confessed to the murder, said he had accompanied his son. They'd asked him to show them the way, starting from the Rossini house, and he'd ended up near Signa over a mile away from the scene of the crime. So he hadn't known the road either. They had both made the same mistake.

From the other end, then. He fished out Lorenzini's sketch again. The cinema, the town hall, the road to Castelletti, the cemetery . . .

He set off again with the sketch propped against the windscreen.

Lorenzini had done a good job. After a couple of miles, just as the old man had said, he passed the marble pillars and wrought-iron gates of the cemetery, with its rows of black cypresses. Next there should be a fork . . . there . . .

then the first lane off to the right. He signalled but couldn't turn. The chain Lorenzini had mentioned as having been put up all those years ago was still closing the lane. He pulled in and got out of the car to check it. There was nothing to be done. The chain was thick and heavy and rusty and the padlock held firm. He locked his car, climbed over, and set off down the lane on foot. This was all right. A high bank topped by tall reeds hid the stream on the right from his view. About twenty, twenty-five yards . . . A curve that would have hidden the car from anyone passing on the road. And the car that followed? That too would have had to be hidden from the road. Had it slid down here with the engine cut and the lights out? It was probable.

To his left were open fields. The grass was long and thick because the weather had been so mild and wet until Christmas. But now the freezing wind coming from the mountains, faintly visible on the purplish horizon, was howling across the fields so that the grass was billowing in green and silver waves. The Marshal stood still, his ears and face burning and his fingers, even in thick leather gloves, beginning to ache.

The fierce iciness of the wind, whipping his cheeks and taking his breath away, was so cleansing, so exhilarating an antidote to his accumulated tiredness and stress, that he stood there for some time without thinking of anything.

It was that small voice from long ago that brought him back.

'*Silvano was standing in the reeds.*'

He turned to look. The reeds were dead now, their canes dry and broken. They wouldn't hide anyone. But in August they would have been thick and rustling with leaves.

'*There was a noise and he was in the reeds.*'

The black night had been windless and hot. Seven shots and one shot. That was the only safe way. Silvano had to make sure they were dead before he could risk letting the incompetent Sergio fire at them so as to inculpate himself. Seven shots entering the bodies close together, centre target. One shot, thought to have come from another direction, only just hitting her arm and grazing her side. And by then Silvano was hidden in the reeds as the child awoke and his dad pulled him out of the car. He'd seen his uncle, too, going through his mum's handbag.

'*Get moving!*'

That had to be Silvano's voice. There was no other way. He would never have been fool enough to risk being seen driving Sergio and the child back to Signa. Sergio had to take the child away himself and perhaps be picked up on the Pistoia road. But how had Sergio found his way in the darkness if he wasn't familiar with the road? Who was familiar with the road? Angius. Salvatore Angius, young and penniless friend and lover of Silvano, who lived at the other end of that road and maybe used it as a short cut to Signa because he had no vehicle.

'*Was anyone else with your dad?*'

'*I think there was a man only I don't know who he was.*'

That was probably true. He didn't know – and what interest could it have for a child whose mother has just been murdered?

It was as clear as it would ever get unless Sergio one day told the truth. An unlikely event.

The immediate problem was to get his car on to this lane so as to try and come out on the Pistoia road. He wasn't intending to try it on foot. It took an hour or so each way and the cold winter afternoon was already darkening. He walked on a little and saw a decently maintained track coming from the direction of a cluster of houses beyond the fields further forward to his left. Beyond that he saw a car going by and felt pretty certain that the track was simply the next turning along the road to the one he'd come in by. He walked back to his car. It was true, thank goodness for that. A half-mile or so further along the main road he found the cluster of houses and the beginning of the lane, and within a few minutes he was joining the lane of the murder scene and proceeding in the direction of the Rossini house.

'Ah . . .' There ahead was the explanation of his mistake. The lane curved right, and there in front of him was the tiny bridge over the stream where Nicolino said he'd been set down. You had to cross the bridge to pick up another little road coming from Signa, the one he'd driven down without noticing the bridge and the deviation at all. There was, in fact, nothing odd or contradictory about Sergio's mistakes at all. He'd been driven to the scene of the crime in Silvano's car and taken no notice in the thick darkness of where the lane began. He'd probably then been accompanied to this end where you couldn't go wrong anyway, there was no way forward other than the right one.

There was no way forward now, though, at all, because across the front of the bridge hung yet another heavy rusting chain and padlock.

'Blast . . .' The Marshal was about to give up and go back when he thought he might take a bit of his own advice. '*Check everything. Don't take anything for granted.*' He said it often enough to the young carabinieri in his care. Without any real hope he climbed out of the car and approached the bridge.

'Which just goes to show . . .'

The padlock was hanging open. All he had to do was to drop the chain to the ground. At a quickened pace the Marshal returned to his car and drove across, careful to stop again and replace the chain behind him, always feeling Di Maira's steely gaze on his back.

There! Ahead, the last little stretch of the lane hit the Pistoia road. And right facing him was the big white house with its floodlight. Number 154.

With a little grunt of satisfaction he signalled and turned on to the main road back in the direction of Florence. This was his world, the real world, where you checked things and they were true or not. His satisfaction was out of all proportion to what he had obtained. It had

289

to do with his putting an end to any attempt at believing the unbelievable, and with a deep conviction that if he checked out a few more confused routes from both ends he might find the right road at last.

Twelve

PART SEVEN
-THE BLOODSTAINED RAG-

7.1. THE RAG

On 30 July '84, the day after the Vicchio murder which was, if possible, even more horrifying than the previous ones, house searches were made of anyone who had for any reason been suspected up to now. Among these was Silvano Vargius.

The search of his house brought to light a flat, round, straw bag lying underneath heavy blankets in a cupboard. The bag contained three pieces of cloth, assumed to be cotton. Two of these pieces were printed with yellow flowers and sandwiched between them was the third piece which was plain white and stained with grey and blood-red marks. Suspecting that the red stains might indeed be blood, the carabinieri removed the bag and its contents. Silvano was present and showed no concern whatsoever. A report was made and consigned to the Public Prosecutor's office, along with the bag, and Silvano was asked to produce an alibi for the previous night.

Some months then passed but the consignment of the rag and the accompanying report produced no response from the Public Prosecutor's office. Eventually, *in April 1985,* the rag was sent to be tested. The results of these tests showed that the red stains were blood and that the rag also had traces of gunpowder.

Silvano Vargius was unable to furnish a convincing alibi and this office suggested that the Prosecutor should ask that the accusation against him be formalized. The suggestion was rejected.

The reason given was that the bloodstained rag could not be the basis of a specific formal accusation since it was evidence in a preliminary, generic enquiry into the whole series of murders and the said enquiry was not under instruction.

This office then requested the relative documentation. The Chief Prosecutor delivered this, together with a letter expressing doubts as to the value of the material evidence concerned and on the basis of these doubts requested the acquittal here presented.

Such a request, whilst preventing the enquiry here documented from proceeding, does not alter the fact that until further tests prove evidence to the contrary, the bloodstained rag remains a piece of evidence which is, in however limited a way, of value.

The rag was discovered in the home of a suspect against whom other significant evidence had already been gathered with regard to the '68 murder. It was found the morning after a double homicide had been committed with the same gun used in '68. The suspect could produce no alibi.

However little was known about the origins and reasons for the presence of the rag in the suspect's home, it seems evident that the proper enquiries and tests should have been made, even considering these as being of positive value to the accused in defending himself from suspicion.

The Public Prosecutor's refusal to proceed with the tests even at an informal level was defended in his accompanying letter as follows: '. . . *it seems to me incredible that Vargius, who had already been searched (after the previous murder) should, while still under suspicion in this same enquiry, keep a bloodstained rag, which could connect him with the murder, in his bedroom.*'

A fact is a fact. A piece of material evidence remains such regardless of whether we are capable at this stage of understanding the whys and wherefores of it. In the absence of scientific proof any suppositions about its positive or negative value remain just that: suppositions.

7.2. PROVENANCE

Silvano maintained, not unreasonably, given the nature of the object, that the straw bag belonged to one of the women who had frequented the house. He attributed it, rather uncertainly, to his ex-partner. This woman, however, had ceased to cohabit with him a year previously. Shown the bag, she denied its being hers.

Vargius's second wife had left him even earlier (in 1981) and she denied ever having seen the bag.

His present partner, likewise, had never seen the bag before. The only person who claimed to recognize the bag was the cleaner who said she'd seen it around the house during the previous winter and spring but had no idea what it might contain.

Obviously, ownership of the straw bag is of relative unimportance compared to what it contained. The bag was in the house at Silvano's disposition no matter who first owned it, which is all that counts.

To the Public Prosecutor's comment that it is incredible that Silvano, under suspicion, should keep such damaging evidence in the house, one could well respond that it is equally incredible that such a piece of cloth should be kept between two other clean pieces, carefully placed in a bag and hidden under blankets in a cupboard, if it were nothing more than a dirty rag. It is not improbable that suitable tests carried out immediately would have solved the mystery.

7.3. THE BLOODSTAINS

Preliminary tests carried out in Florence showed the rag to be stained with human blood group O. Further tests carried out in Rome in May 1986, *a year and ten months after the evidence was delivered by the carabinieri to the Prosecutor's office,* revealed that there were stains of two different blood groups, B and O Rh pos. The identification of the B group was less certain than the O because of the rag being polluted by other substances previously (such as washing powder).

The final report, deposited in December 1987, *three years and five months after the evidence was delivered* stated that the bloodstains were rather old and that such conclusions as had been drawn were insignificant because of this.

At this point in history, scientific progress had made DNA matching possible. Whilst such tests were not yet being used in this country, they could have been carried out in Great Britain where the inventor of the tests himself assured us that he could work on a sample as small as that available. Whilst the victims of all the homicides had been buried without the conservation of samples, it would at least have been possible to match the DNA to samples taken from Vargius and his current partner.

The DNA tests were not carried out.

There remained only the evidence of the blood groups. The Prosecutor's statement that the rag carried only one blood group, and that it was the group to which

Silvano's partner belonged, is unacceptable. Two groups were identified when the evidence was fresh. It was Silvano's ex-partner who was blood group B and she had been gone a year. Carlo Salvini, victim of the Vicchio murder, was blood group O, which was first identified on the rag, but so was Silvano himself. Since half the population of Italy is blood group O and a large part is group B there seemed little point in proceeding with blood tests on other members of Silvano's family, who might have had some connection with the rag.

In the absence of scientific evidence, the bloodstained rag cannot be used against Silvano Vargius *but its existence remains a cause of suspicion against him,* because if it cannot be accepted, at a merely hypothetical level, as proof against him, by the same token it cannot be used as hypothetical evidence in his defence as suggested by the Public Prosecutor ('It is incredible that Vargius who had already been searched', etc . . .).

7.4. THE GUNPOWDER

About the presence of gunpowder on the rag there are no scientific doubts. We can only agree with the Public Prosecutor's comment, 'Who could reasonably assert that the traces are residue from the Beretta 22 pistol used to commit the crimes?'

Nobody could, of course. The ballistics report states: *'Currently available scientific tests do not allow us to identify the ammunition from which this gunpowder came.'*

The fact remains that the gunpowder, from whatever

ammunition, is present, and no explanation has been offered for it. Silvano Vargius stated clearly under questioning that the blood on the rag might well be human blood but it was impossible that there was also gunpowder on it. A statement which must leave us perplexed, since he also states that the bag and its contents are not his and he knows nothing about them.

The fact remains that the experts' reports provided on the bloodstained rag offer no judicially valid proof that the rag is in any way connected to the crimes in question.

7.5. ALIBI AND SEARCH

Checks on the alibi offered by Silvano Vargius for the night of the Vicchio murder are remarkable chiefly for their resemblance to the same checks carried out after the '68 murder. According to Vargius, he left the house at about nine-thirty and returned an hour later. The purpose of the outing was to take his current partner and her little girl for an ice cream in the centre of Florence. The woman, when questioned, stated that such an outing occurred so rarely that it would be memorable and that she had no recollection of it as regards that date. They had, she said, gone out once for an ice cream. She remembered it well and it was on another evening. The mechanics of this alibi are easily recognized from '68 when Vargius claimed he had been playing billiards with a friend who later realized that, though they had played billiards one evening that week, it was not on that date.

297

Silvano Vargius went out a second time on the night of the Vicchio murder, in order to find his dog, between ten and half past ten. He then left the house a third time between three and three-thirty in the morning 'to go jogging'.

As in '68, Vargius's companion at first confirmed the part of the alibi which involved her, but she later recounted that he had insisted that she do so and that, on attempting to reconstruct that evening for herself, she found that no such outing occurred on that date. The result of the checks made indicates that there was nothing to prove that Silvano could not have driven to Vicchio to commit the murders that night.

When Silvano was subsequently asked to provide an alibi for the 1985 murder, the same situation repeated itself in that Silvano had the time and opportunity to commit the murder. However, no conclusions could be drawn since there was some argument as to when the murder was committed (during the night of Saturday/Sunday or Sunday/Monday). The bodies were not discovered until Monday afternoon.

7.6. CONCLUSION

The information collected about Silvano Vargius was extremely suggestive: the death of his young wife in 1960, his strange sexual relationships with men and women, couples and groups, his manic depressive states which resulted in hospitalization in 1981, his probable part in the '68 murder and the ambiguity of his relationship with his brother Flavio, all serve to build up an image of an altogether remarkable personality.

However, none of the evidence listed above can be translated into proof such as would be acceptable in court. The evidence, such as it is, was considered sufficient to warrant Silvano's being ordered to present himself before the carabinieri to answer accusations by Sergio Muscas of his responsibility for the '68 murder and by his ex-partner, who claimed he'd always kept a pistol in the bedroom during the time she was living with him.

However, when Silvano was released from prison on being acquitted of murdering his first wife, he not only failed to present himself before the authorities in Florence as ordered but he left the country.

THEREFORE:

At the request of the Public Prosecutor's office –

IT IS HEREBY DECLARED:

That no further proceedings will be taken against –
1) VARGIUS FLAVIO
2) VARGIUS SILVANO
3) MUSCAS FABIO
Florence, 13 December 1989   The Instructing Judge
                                                           Michele Romola

'Well, *I'd* have arrested him,' mumbled the Marshal, dropping the last of the report on to the floor by the bed and rubbing at his tired eyes. 'Whole thing's a disgrace. If we had even half that amount of evidence against our wretched Suspect . . .'

He felt himself drifting into unconsciousness even as he decided to switch his lamp off and go to sleep. It was dark, though, anyway. The Marshal's most urgent wish was that the man beside him would keep quiet. He didn't want to be distracted. He couldn't understand quite why the scene passing before his eyes should be lit by a red glow when he'd just turned the lights off. Perhaps it was because otherwise, in the thick warm darkness, you wouldn't be able to see anything.

His heart was beating very loudly and he knew the reason was fear, without his feeling the fear itself very clearly. In any case, he had to watch. He'd never been a Peeping Tom and he'd never even been able to imagine what it would feel like. Of course, he was here for work, so that was different.

The man beside him uttered a little panic-stricken whine.

'Hush . . .'

Concentrate. He had to concentrate. He was being given the chance to see everything and he must take in every detail. The thin figure dressed in black was pulling the girl's body down the little slope below him, now. She was naked and her skin glowed pink because of the red light. Infrared, that's what it was . . .

He was laying the pink body down and spreading the limbs. His movements were fast and jerky like in a silent film. Before beginning work in earnest he seemed to rear up and stare straight at the Marshal, his red-tinged eyes glittering. But only one of the eyes, its pupil dilated with drugs, made contact with the Marshal's own gaze. The other was fixed and dead.

Then he plunged down again, grunting.

'No . . .' But the scene rolled on inexorably, and beside the Marshal the Suspect began crying loudly. 'Don't . . . Be quiet.' To the Marshal's relief he wasn't shown the mutilation. The man appeared to be making frenzied love to the acquiescent body and it was left to him to work out for himself that each rapid kiss and bite at the neck was really a small knife cut, and that when he grasped her left breast and pushed himself into her with his other hand it was really the knife at work, cutting deeper.

The howling at his side grew louder. How could he cope with both problems at once? It was too much. Fortunately the Suspect was so tiny a version of his normal self that the easiest answer was to pick him up and take him away.

He tucked the tearful creature under his left arm and turned to go along the dark road.

'Come away. It's nothing to do with you.'

He must have spoken aloud. He opened his eyes and could still sense the sound of his own voice in the room as his eyes gradually focused on the white wall, the muslin curtain, his dressing gown on the chair. He was sweating and his breath was shallow. His head seemed to have a great weight dragging it down behind. There was still that residue of fear that nightmares always leave in their wake and he was shamefacedly glad that he'd dropped off leaving the light on. He'd have been even more glad to find Teresa beside him. She'd have got out of bed, saying crossly as she always did, 'If you can't eat at a proper time at least eat something light. You might well have nightmares . . .' Then she'd make him a camomile tea. He could make himself one, then he'd feel as though she were with him. He struggled into a sitting position, trying to breathe normally, trying to shake the effects of the nightmare off. But although most of it had developed in that illogical way which seemed so real at the time and dissolved the instant you opened your eyes, the image of the killer remained clear and detailed. It showed no signs at all of dissolving on impact with the waking world. He'd been thin, thin faced and sharp featured, and his hair had been clipped very close to his head.

'Camomile . . .' He got out of bed to go and make it. He didn't think he had indigestion at all – he was more likely just overtired – but the tea would be soothing, anyway.

Sometimes, when you dream about somebody you know they have another person's appearance. Could it be something of that sort?

'Better sleep on it . . .'

But the truth was that he wasn't too comfortable about falling asleep again just yet. Besides, he was really very wide awake now. He carried the tea into his bedroom and set it down near the bedside lamp. Now there's where the answer might be. He'd just finished the Romola report

302

when he dropped off and before that he'd been looking at the book lying next to the lamp. It was one of Bacci's books of case histories. Typewritten sheets were slotted in at intervals where Bacci had chosen a case he thought might be useful and given them a translation. In some cases Bacci had translated himself, making a precis, leaving out anything he thought irrelevant and writing very much in the style of an official report. The others, done by his girlfriend, who'd offered to give him a hand so as to speed things up, were complete, since she couldn't know what was relevant and what wasn't. It was something of hers he'd been reading. That glass eye was something she'd written about.

He soon found it.

'I went to school but I don't remember nothing about no lessons. I remember my ma put me in a dress. She made me go to school in this dress and she said that'll learn you to behave like a boy and not be screamin' and hollerin' every time you get a beatin'. She give some terrible beatin's.

There was a teacher once give me some shoes because I didn't have none and she beat me for that, for acceptin' them shoes. And she beat me when I didn't want to watch her with men. She liked me to watch her with her johns. I grew up watching her like that till I was fourteen, then I left home. I hated all my life. I hated everybody. You ask me if I ever loved somebody, I don't think so. There was the

mule and I loved him, I think. We was like friends
and I'd talk to him. In the summer he'd have these
sores on his legs and I'd tell him I know them sores
hurt you, boy, I know that. I knew they hurt him
because I had them the same as him. We was both
hungry all the time as well and I'd get somethin' for
me and somethin' for him. He'd eat most anythin'
and then he'd lick my hand for a long time and I
liked that. I liked sleeping near him some of the
time, 'specially after a real bad beatin'. He was soft
and quiet and he'd breathe on me, warm like and
I'd feel good. Only then my ma caught me doing
that and she said you love that mule, don't you? You
love him? And I said I guessed maybe I loved him
and she came out right away with a shotgun and she
shot him right there in the yard. Then she beat the
hell out of me because she had to pay for the truck
that came and took him. They tied his four feet
together and drug him off and his head was bent
back, trailin' behind like he was still lookin' at me,
and it was my fault he was killed. I never loved
nothin' after that. I'm bad all through like she said.
That was one hell of a beatin', but that wasn't when
my eye got took out, that was another time and I
don't remember much of that because I didn't wake
up for days. It was one of my "uncles" took me to
the hospital and they took my eye out. He said I fell
downstairs and I didn't say nothin', not then. He
wasn't really my uncle, he was one of her johns but

he talked to me once in a while and he was the one first showed me about sex and stuff. He used to do it to animals. He killed 'em first and then he did it and showed me how. He said you should get yourself some girl as well, you're fourteen. So I went after this girl but she wouldn't let me do it to her. She was scared of my eye, of the hole. Lots of people was scared of that because stuff come out of it all the time. She said I smelled bad too and she wouldn't let me touch her. I had to kill her to get sex. Most of the time I had to do that, wasn't no other way to get it. Killin's the only thing I was ever good at and now I've been caught I'm not scared of dying. That's the best thing for somebody like me. I know that.'

That's who it was, then. He'd got the glass eye later. Even so, it wasn't his face, battered and crazy, that he'd seen in his dream. It was a younger man.

The Marshal flicked through the photos at the centre of the book, but this man wasn't there. The only other book was a series of essays. No photographs in that, only tables and graphs and maps. Bacci had taken one or two notes and transferred them in Italian on to one folded sheet of typing paper slotted in at the back. It looked drier, less disturbing reading and it might be better to stick to that until he could get off to sleep again.

Background dimensions
Social class

It was dry stuff, all right, and should send him off to sleep in no time at all.

Each of Bacci's underlinings was numbered so that you could easily find the corresponding translation on the loose sheet. It was all done in pencil.

'Ouff!' The Marshal began flicking through the book faster, his eyelids drooping. An underlining in red ink stopped him. Oddly enough it wasn't numbered. In the margin where the number should have been was written in Italian *Is this us?* Next to that a large exclamation mark. So why hadn't he translated it, if it was so important? The Marshal stared at the original text, vainly trying to make something of it. It was about Special Investigation Forces, he could manage that much, but what they were saying about them he had no hope of deciphering. He closed his eyes and rested his head back on the pillow. Sleep. He needed to go to sleep.

*

'No! That's a lie!'

'Refrain from making comments. Answer the question.'

'What question? You're not asking me a question, you're telling me a lie.'

Simonetti glanced at the Suspect's lawyer, who laid a restraining hand on his client's shoulder and whispered urgently to him.

'No, I can't. I can't listen to him. He just wants to crucify me. How can I keep calm?'

'The couple on this occasion lived near your village and already knew what you looked like before we showed them your photograph. You were lying on the bonnet of their car and when the young man looked up at the conclusion of their activities he found your face staring straight into his. Two more witnesses who had parked in the San Casciano area on a Saturday night in July of that same year saw you standing near their car holding a metallic object which they are sure was a gun. They started their car and drove away at once. The third couple saw you in broad daylight when they were out walking. You were standing near a hedge peering through it into a field, a clearing which was frequently used by couples at night. Your scooter, described as grey with a broken saddle and a spoke twisted and hanging from the wheel, was leaning against the gate into the field.'

'That's a lie! I haven't got a grey scooter, I've *never* had a grey scooter!'

'You have a scooter with a damaged saddle.'

'But it's red!'

'Please don't raise your voice. We have examined your scooter and removed a small sample of paint. There were traces of other colours underneath, including grey.'

'I bought it used. It was red when I bought it. You can ask the mechanic in the village. I bought it from him.'

'We checked with the mechanic. He's not sure what colour it was when he sold it to you. He thinks that you might have painted it red.'

'The bastard – he's lying. He's got it in for me because of a deal I made with some spare parts that he –'

'Please answer my questions without making comments. Also bear in mind that we have questioned all the other members of the band of Peeping Toms –'

'I'm not a Peeping Tom and they won't tell you any different.'

And that was true, thought the Marshal, who, together with Ferrini and the two police detectives, was watching this scene in silence. They hadn't really questioned all the band, only two of them, but they admitted to nothing. The first of them, shaking with fear, hadn't even got in the door before he burst out, 'I used to have a snack with him now and then. That's all. I hardly know him. He's not even a friend. We'd have a coffee and a sandwich in the bar, like you do. Just if we happened to be there at the same time –'

'Please sit down and give us your full name and address.'

'What?'

'Sit down and be quiet. We haven't asked you anything yet.'

But the man, who must have been about sixty, was so terrified that though he allowed them to push him into a chair he couldn't listen to or understand anything they said to him. He just stared sightlessly at each of them in turn, repeating, 'Just a snack, that's all. I never went anywhere with him. I hardly know him. We used to have coffee and a sandwich . . .'

The other one was more in possession of his wits and told exactly the same story.

But why? That's what the Marshal couldn't understand as he watched the Suspect's red face crumple and the tears begin to flow. To deny everything and anything was, of course, standard practice for men like the Suspect and his friends, and it all sounded logical enough on the surface. The Monster was a Peeping Tom so deny being a Peeping Tom. The Suspect was accused so deny knowing the Suspect. It was natural enough for them to be frightened. But something was wrong. After all, given the stage things had reached, the Suspect would surely be wiser to admit his voyeuristic vice which would explain his presence in certain places at night. There were hundreds of these men about. It didn't make them murderers. Were they frightened of something else? It all slid out of your grasp. The Marshal had no doubt that the Suspect really was a Peeping Tom, even allowing for half this stuff Simonetti was coming up with being invented.

It was the same feeling he'd had about the business of

the daughter. He didn't disbelieve that the Suspect had abused her. And she was still lying.

Simonetti never tired of tormenting the Suspect.

'Why don't you tell the truth?'

That was it exactly. Why didn't he? If you considered the fact that Simonetti's accusations were false then that meant the last thing he wanted to hear was the truth. The truth, in this case, was what would help the Suspect. But he was lying. This whole drama which should have been a battle for the truth was really a battle of lies, a fight to get one set of lies believed rather than another. The truth, evidently, would serve the purpose of neither side.

'This note in your sketch book here: it's a car licence number after which you've written "couple". Would you like to explain that, as a non-Peeping Tom?'

'I didn't write it, it's not my writing.'

'It's not your writing? Whose writing is it, then? It's your book. It was in your house. Whose writing is it, come on!'

'I don't know. Maybe it *is* mine. I can't remember every little thing I scribble down.'

'In that case, let's assume you scribbled down this car number with the word "couple" next to it. What does it mean?'

'I can't remember.'

'But you did write it.'

'You're trying to trick me! You're persecuting an innocent lamb!'

Under cover of a lot of howling, sniffing and handkerchief flourishing, the Suspect had a brief whispered consultation with his lawyer, who patted him on the arm and then looked at Simonetti.

'He thinks he might have remembered.'

'We await the story with bated breath.'

The Suspect blew his nose loudly and messily and then wiped his eyes.

'I remember seeing a couple one night parked in the lane right under my bedroom window. I think I took their number. I was intending to warn them off. There's no cause for that right under people's noses. I had a daughter to think of. It's not right.'

'Moral indignation. You amaze me.'

'It was for their own good. It was when there were couples being murdered. It was for their own safety and look where it's got me!'

'Where indeed. Let's come now to these little trinkets here.' He held out his hand without looking behind him and Esposito, the detective with the scarred hand, passed him the soapdish full of cheap necklaces and bracelets.

'What about these?'

'What about them?'

'What story can you tell me about these? You needn't tell us that they're not yours. We'll take it as read that you don't wear girls' jewellery. Well?'

The Suspect was silent. He seemed not to know what to make of this at all. He fixed the soapdish with one pig-like eye, his face turned a little away from it.

'I told you . . .' he began uncertainly. 'I told you when

311

you took them that they were my daughter's – If it's the stuff you took . . .'

This time at least the Marshal understood. When they'd removed this stuff from the Suspect's house, he'd told them that. Now he was quite clearly worried that these trinkets weren't the same trinkets and that he had no way of proving it. They must have been listed on the search report but how detailed would the description be? If it came to that, all girls wore this pretty, worthless stuff, on sale in every department store. Nothing easier than for the mother of one of the victims to claim one of these pieces as her daughter's.

'We're waiting.'

'I . . . the stuff you took away was my daughter's, I suppose.'

'You suppose? Do you still say the same?'

'It all looks alike to me, it's just plastic stuff. Why don't you ask her?'

'I shall. I want your answer now. These trinkets were found on your property. What explanation do you give for their presence there?'

The lawyer, too, looked worried now. He excused himself and gave a lengthy sotto voce piece of advice to his sniffing client, deciding, in the end, to speak for him.

'My client stated in good faith that the trinkets removed from his house belonged to his daughter. He can't be sure of recognizing those things now since they are not his personal property and he has never had occasion to examine them closely.'

At which Simonetti shrugged his shoulders and passed the soapdish back to Esposito.

'Tell me about your gun.'

'I have no gun! I've only ever had a blank pistol, the sort you use for keeping dogs away from your chickens.'

'The bullet found in your garden wasn't a blank.'

'No! Because you put that bullet there! *You* did it!'

He was on his feet, raging, his face purple. The Marshal was sure that if this went on he'd have some sort of attack. In fact, almost at once, he fell back into the chair, breathing with difficulty. His colour drained away and his skin became clammy and greyish with a tinge of blue around his lips.

The lawyer got up. 'You have to stop. He needs to take his medicine. He needs a doctor.'

'We'll stop for an hour.'

In the end it was almost two hours before the doctor would consider letting them continue. In the meantime they went out for a coffee and Simonetti received the journalists who were hanging about on the steps when they returned.

'He certainly doesn't waste a minute,' muttered Ferrini. 'By the way, what became of your young friend Bacci?'

'I was going to ask you the same thing.'

Ferrini shrugged. 'Could have been his day off, I suppose.'

'No, no . . . I talked to him last night and asked him to bring me a list I need. He said nothing about not being here today. Can we go in if you've finished your cigarette? I wanted to ask you a couple of things before everybody gets back.'

They sat down at the table facing the Suspect's chair. The smell of his sweaty fear was still in the room, a physical presence.

'Poor bugger,' Ferrini remarked. 'I doubt he could get more than he deserves, but poor bugger, even so.'

'I was thinking,' the Marshal said, struggling to organize the disjointed images in his head into some sort of comprehensible verbal form, 'this is the second interrogation since the search ended . . .'

'And?'

'If I'd been asking the questions, I think I'd have wanted to know where all that money came from.'

'An interesting point, but I've a feeling nobody will ask.'

'But why?'

Ferrini shrugged. 'Why? It's all the same. You don't earn money from killing strangers. You could steal it, I suppose, but I don't think there's any reason to suppose any of those kids had money, and what bit they did have was left intact.'

'Yes . . . But . . . What I'm trying to say is, he's not the killer, is he? So –'

'So he might be a bank robber. I think I understand what you mean but the point is, nobody needs a bank robber, do they? They need a Monster, so nobody's got time to waste on anything that doesn't help with that.'

'You're right, of course. It was a lot of money, though.'

'You don't give up, do you? I'll tell you something. If I were on the wrong side of the law I wouldn't care to have you after me. You're like a bulldog that won't let go of a bone. Don't waste your energy! You won't get paid for it and in this particular case you won't get thanked for it, either.'

'You're right, of course . . .'

'So you keep saying, but you don't let go of the bone, anyway.'

'It was a lot of money.'

'Oh God.'

'And that's a decent little house he's got. Nice bit of land with it. Then there's the flat near the square he bought for the girl. I don't own a house or a flat. It's a worry how we'll manage when I retire.'

Ferrini sat and looked at him. Then he resigned himself. 'All right. Let's hear it all.'

'It's a worry,' repeated the Marshal, oblivious of Ferrini's irony. 'I often think of it . . . He keeps chickens.'

'Eh? How did chickens get into the conversation?'

'The Suspect. He keeps chickens and a few rabbits. He grows vegetables. He makes his own wine and oil. He's been an agricultural labourer practically all his life –'

'As he tells us every time we see him.'

'Yes. Yes, he does. It's important to listen to what people tell you. Sometimes when you least expect it, they're telling you the truth. The other thing he keeps telling us is that he's always been careful, always put

315

something away for a rainy day, like his father taught him. His father was a peasant.'

'Well, so he'll have ripped off the landowner all his life and stuffed the proceeds in the mattress.'

'Yes . . .'

'All right, all right . . . We add it up and we don't get two houses, a drawer full of millions and a sizeable block of shares. Add to that we don't think he's the Monster, but what do you want to do about it? What's the use of answering questions nobody's asking?'

The Marshal didn't even answer. His face was dark and set.

'Oh Christ Almighty, I remember that face. You got like this on that transsexual case and there was no getting a sensible word out of you until it was over.'

'And' – the Marshal prodded the table – 'she said she was threatened with prison.'

'And if that doesn't prove my point . . . *Who* was threatened with prison?'

But before he could get an answer, assuming there would have been an answer forthcoming, the door to the conference room burst open and a flustered young man appeared.

'Prosecutor Simonetti?'

'I think he's talking to the press. Is something wrong?'

The young man came in. He was carrying a thick packet which he placed on the table.

'He's going to have my guts for garters, that's all . . .'

He sat down and looked at them both. 'Listen, you

must know him better than I do. I'll throw myself on your mercy. What I did was stupid, I know that, but what I don't know is how badly I've screwed up. I mean, how much will the delay matter and can we keep it from the press – that's all he cares about, everybody says.'

'They're probably right.' Ferrini was as amused as he was baffled. 'How about telling us what you're talking about, starting with who you are.'

'Police lab,' the Marshal said. 'You were there that day in the rain when they took the rubbish skips away.'

'And made a complete fool of myself.'

'That,' the Marshal said, 'makes two of us.'

'You mean you know?'

'I don't know anything, except that I was there and I was too slow. I should have caught him with whatever it was still in his hand. I didn't.'

Without a word, the young man pushed the packet across the table to him. It was a padded envelope, unsealed.

'Go on. Open it.'

Inside the envelope was a video with a handwritten label on it saying: Walt Disney's *Snow White*.

'We were told to throw everything away. There was nothing of interest. No useful fingerprints, no trace of gun grease.'

'And you kept this?'

'I kept all of them, the whole bagful.' He was looking at the Marshal as though expecting him to throw a life belt. I've got two kids. It seemed a shame. Then, last night, they were being a bit of a pain and the wife's got flu – I thought of these films, keep them quiet for an hour. Thank God I stayed in the room. The eldest can work the video machine himself so I could easily have let him . . . as it was I threw myself in front of the screen and switched off. The youngest, my little girl Giulia, was already asking, "What's that man doing?"'

'Did you check the rest of them?'

'Of course, once they'd gone to bed.'

'And they're all pornographic videos?'

'Home made. And the worst of it is, you don't see much of their faces, as you can imagine, but I'm pretty sure it's the girl.'

'His daughter.'

'Yes. You don't look surprised.'

'How many are there?'

'Only three. A dozen copies of each. He must have been selling them. That broken video camera must have been his, too, but we can't get that back now. If only I'd put one on that first night I took them home I could have had them here the next morning and got a pat on the head for it. But after all this delay, what's he going to say?'

'Nothing,' the Marshal said, his face quite expressionless. 'He won't say anything. Send the lot to his office with a note. Then forget it.' He pushed the envelope back across the table and then met Ferrini's gaze.

The latter gave a long low whistle. 'Fancy that,' he said, 'just when I was thinking of taking up chicken farming.'

Florence was dark, silent and cold when the Marshal took to the road next morning at six-twenty, wearing civilian clothes and driving his own car. He was relying on his childhood memories of having served Mass at six-thirty. At eight he had to be present at the next interrogation and he was hoping that no one would ever find out where he'd been. His face was as dark and expressionless as it had been the day before when he'd looked at the package containing the 'Walt Disney' film. That evening he had telephoned Bacci at home.

'But . . . You haven't heard? Surely something's been said. I've been taken off the case.'

'Why?'

'Because of this Shawcross business. You must have heard about it.'

'This what businesss . . . ?'

'Shawcross. The man who disappeared. It's been in all the papers.'

'I haven't been reading the papers.' He had, but only to follow the case he was on.

'He was on holiday here and vanished. His wife, back in England, is making a terrible fuss and the consulate's been in touch with us. The thing is, everybody thought he'd just left her. There's nothing you can do in a case like that. But now it seems he's been spotted out in the hills living wild. The monks have been leaving food out for him but he won't come close enough for them to speak to him. They say he's stark naked.'

'Hmph.'

'They needed someone fluent in English.'

'I suppose so.'

'You don't think . . .'

'Think what?'

'Well, I didn't deal well with that business –'

'I – No,' the Marshal interrupted him quickly, still paranoid.

'Am I being paranoid?'

'I don't know. You think you're genuinely needed on this new case?'

'Yes, I'm pretty sure about that – and there isn't anyone else available, not anyone really fluent, that I know of.'

What was the point of encouraging him to worry, after all? It sounded, anyway, like the right sort of case for Bacci. In a situation like that, with the consulate involved, the Marshal would have chosen him himself. He'd never make much of an investigator but he was ideal for public relations. He was good-looking, courteous, practically bilingual . . . Of course, when you came down to it, that was what Simonetti had intended to exploit, using young Bacci on camera for the bullet business.

'Damn!' The expletive was only partly in response to the red light that would lose him time, though there wasn't a soul on the road, it was because he'd just remembered: he'd meant to ask Bacci about that red comment in the margin of the book last night. It would hardly be fair to ask him to waste his time writing out the list for him, now he was no longer on the case, but he was curious to know about that 'Is this us?' Too late now. Might as well turn his mind to the business in hand.

The village of Pontino at this hour was still pretty much asleep, but there was some subdued activity. The Bar Italia was open and lit up and an encouraging aroma of fresh coffee floated around on that side of the square. A number of workmen were having breakfast there, and at the bus stop outside the first big country buses of the day were pulling up with squealing brakes and musical horns, summoning schoolteachers and civil servants for the hour-long, winding journey down to the city. The rest of the square showed closed shutters, except for the baker's and the florist.

The Marshal would have given anything for a coffee in the bar, not to mention a nice oven-hot brioche with melting jam in it, but he didn't want to be seen here. The Suspect himself might be about. So he drove around the dark square and parked beyond the glow of a streetlamp near the church on the other side. He saw three old women come out of the church door and go their separate ways. Then, as he was locking his car, a small boy shot out of the presbytery door clutching a brioche wrapped in a paper napkin. His timing had been right.

A tiny nervous spinster opened the door to him.

'Father Damiani's having his breakfast. I never disturb Father when he's having his breakfast. If you could come back in half an hour or so.'

'Perhaps you'd ask him. I've come up from Florence and it's rather an urgent matter . . .'

'Well . . .' But she was sufficiently intimidated by the Marshal's bulk and authority as to scuttle away and then return to show him into a small overfurnished dining room. The priest was seated at the table, a large white napkin tucked into his dog collar. Jugs of coffee and hot milk were set beside his large cup and in a basket two hot, sweet-smelling brioches were peeping out of a fresh white cloth. The priest was biting into a third, showering soft flakes down his front as he observed the Marshal's entrance and nodded towards a chair.

'I suppose there's little point in offering you breakfast if you were up so early as to get here from Florence at such an hour.' His eyes slid to the remaining brioches and away again.

The scents of fresh coffee, vanilla and hot jam floated towards the Marshal. He made the required negative noises faintly.

'Marshal of the police or carabinieri?'

'Carabinieri.'

'I don't understand. I was told I wouldn't have to testify. It's not just a question of the secrets of the confessional, you know, it's the embarrassment it could cause for me here in the village.'

'Oh, I'm sure if that's what you were told then it's certainly the case.' How was he to find out what this man clearly thought he already knew? He looked like somebody and the Marshal couldn't get a hold on who it was. Somebody unpleasant, he was sure of that.

'It's all been very difficult for me. These things are not

as unusual as we might wish but, even so, this was a particularly bad case because of the girl's being so subnormal. She talked, you see, she talked a great deal around the village. It's a scandal that people in that condition should be at large, but since they closed the lunatic asylums it's left to people like me to try and deal with problems well beyond the real scope of my duties as a priest.'

'It must be very difficult . . .'

'Father Damiani for one. He's had it up to here.'

Had the barman said anything more explicit? Not that the Marshal could remember.

'I understand,' he began carefully, 'that she was taken in for psychiatric treatment at some point – I've not been on this case right from the beginning, but I did hear that.'

'Oh, yes, indeed. I did everything I could to see that she was taken away before things got any worse. She was never away from my door! As you've seen, her flat is practically on my doorstep – and, believe me, her advances were anything but subtle. Pardon me if I don't go into detail, suffice it to say that her manner of offering herself was terrifying, and deeply distressing. Deeply distressing.'

The deeply distressed man sucked in the last piece of the third brioche and refilled his coffee cup.

'What's more, I understand that she told quite a number of people that her "love" for me, as she termed it, was reciprocated. It's my belief that the child was possessed by the devil. I wrote to the bishop about it.'

'Very wise. You don't think it might have been her father rather than the devil?'

'Her father,' returned the priest firmly, 'is an agent of the devil.' A sudden thought struck him. 'She won't be allowed to testify at her father's trial?'

'I think she will testify, yes.'

'But that shouldn't be! The girl is not fit to testify.'

'I'm afraid she will, though. The purpose of my visit, in fact' – no one in their senses would believe it, but he was on safe ground since the priest wanted nothing more than to hear his next words – 'is to reassure you that she will be asked no questions by the prosecution which could in any way involve you.'

'And the defence?'

'It wouldn't be in their interest to dwell any more than is absolutely necessary on the sexual activities of their client and his family.'

'I suppose not. Well, it was thoughtful of you to keep me informed. I must confess that if I had seen in the paper that she was to testify I'd have been very worried indeed. There are a great many communists in this village, priest haters who'd do their best to make something out of nothing.'

'I suppose so.'

'It was a black day for all of us when that family came to live here. They're all tarred with the same brush, Marshal, believe me. There's little point in being senti-mental about it. God must be their judge, but however much they fight between themselves and condemn each other, they always close ranks in the end. You'll never separate the guilty from the innocent in that family. We are all sinners and we are all responsible for our own souls, no matter what modern psychiatry tries to tell us to the contrary.'

The Marshal was of the same opinion but he didn't say so. He didn't care much for the man, on top of which he'd just realized who it was he looked like. Younger, of course. His wavy hair was still black. But the build was the same, thickset and short limbed. The hooked nose and bull neck too, though not yet so coarsened. The object of the abused girl's sick passion was just a physically younger version of her father.

Thirteen

'Do you want to deal with your post?' Lorenzini waylaid the Marshal the moment he walked in.

'Not now. I'm late. Is there anything urgent?'

'No, just something odd.'

'Show me.'

Lorenzini handed him a small off-white envelope.

'Oh, no . . .' The address was made up of letters cut from a magazine. 'I'd better take it with me. It can only be —' But he was opening it as he spoke and the name FRANCHI caught his eye at once.

> Lot no. 79 was not painted
> by Antonio Franchi

He went into his office and called the Captain's number.

'Maestrangelo.'

'Guarnaccia, here. I've had an anonymous communication that I'm sending over to you. I'll have Lorenzini write a report –'

'Not something concerning a painting, by any chance?'

'I . . . yes. Yes, it is.'

'A painting by, let me see . . .'

'Antonio Franchi, sir – yes. You know about it?'

'I've got the same thing on my desk and a gentleman from the auctioneer's has just left. "Lot no. 79 is not by Antonio Franchi." '

'Yes, that's the same message. Letters are from some sort of glossy magazine.'

'And do you know something about it? I take it we're talking about somebody in your quarter, or at any rate, somebody who knows you. Otherwise –'

'It might be. The thing is, I know the – the young man who's selling.' He had almost said 'boy'.

'And is there some doubt about its authenticity?'

'He seems to think it's genuine. I wouldn't know. I'd have thought that was the responsibility of the auctioneer.'

'Yes, well . . . I got the impression they're not in the least worried on that score.'

'But they came to you?'

'They came to me because they're afraid somebody "probably unbalanced", and I quote, might create a scene

327

during the auction. That would be bad for their image, bad for business. What they would like would be to have somebody present – in plain clothes, of course, in case of a disturbance.'

'I see.'

The Captain wasn't one to expose himself by expressing any annoyance openly, but his tone was sufficient. The Marshal took it as read, replying to the unspoken.

'Well, they must surely have realized themselves that you can't employ your men on their private business. There's no crime involved.'

'No. But they have some big names on their board of directors.'

And they both knew what that meant. Somebody would know a magistrate who would bring pressure to bear. They would get their way and the Captain would suffer for his correctness. He would suffer because as well as being very correct he was also very ambitious. This was just the sort of episode which must damage him whatever course he took.

'I'm sorry.' The Marshal couldn't explain just how sorry he really was. In part, at least, he felt responsible because he had no doubt at all about where the letters came from.

'I suppose I could send this thing to the lab, go through the motions of trying to find the author of it. That might help if I start getting flack. I'll wait for yours to arrive here, of course. And if you know anything useful put it in your report.'

'I think I'd better come and see you. It won't be today – you know how I'm fixed with this other business. I'm late now.'

'Of course. I can hardly tell you it's urgent. Come over when you can.'

When he'd hung up, the Marshal wondered whether he shouldn't have told him not to bother sending the letters to the lab. Not, he supposed, since it was only the gesture that counted. He stared down at the letter. Anonymous my foot. What was he trying to do? Manipulate the Marshal? The carabinieri in general? Drum up a worthy audience and really make a scene at the auction? Whatever the motive for the letters, whatever the game, anonymity wasn't at the centre of it. The paper, for a start, was thick and fluffy edged. Hand made, you didn't need an expert to see that. As traceable as paper could be. Not that the paper was what the Marshal had noticed first. He'd known the minute he'd opened it and that whiff of unmistakable perfume reached his nose.

The Marshal waited patiently outside Pizzeria Dante but there was no sign of Ferrini. The pizzeria was on the corner near the bridge, halfway between their respective barracks, on the Marshal's side of the river. It was cold standing outside in the night wind but the Marshal didn't fancy going in alone so he stood there just the same, peering across the lamplit bridge, watching for Ferrini's unmistakable bouncing step. Nothing.

'Guarnaccia! Oh!'

'Good Lord. What have you brought your car for? We're not going anywhere, are we?'

'Your place after. All right for you, but I can't be bothered walking home. If I know anything it'll be three in the morning.'

'But you'll never find anywhere to park.'

'I will. Go in and get a table.'

The Marshal did as he was told.

'For two? Is this all right?'

'I expect so.'

It wasn't, of course. Ferrini arrived, grinning, the only person, surely, who could find a parking space in Florence at this time of night.

'Dante!' he roared immediately, and the owner of the place, a man in his fifties, appeared from nowhere. His paunch was encompassed by ostentatiously labelled designer leatherwear, his thick fingers heavy with rings.

'Well, look who's here!' He slapped Ferrini on the back. 'No, no, they're not sitting there. Put them at my table.'

'We have to talk,' Ferrini warned.

'So you'll talk. I never eat before ten. I'll join you for a glass of something good before you leave. Sandro! Look after them – and serve them fast, they've got work to do.' There followed an urgent sotto voce conversation with the waiter and then Dante waved a hand at them and disappeared. Sandro came with a bottle and corkscrew. The bottle was dusty and he set it down carefully and polished it. The Marshal raised a questioning eyebrow but Ferrini frowned and waved his hand.

'We'll work just as well on good wine as on poor. Besides –' – as Sandro went off for a menu – 'can't offend a friend. Now, let's concentrate on eating, then we can get on.'

The Marshal resigned himself. They'd had a number of these get-togethers over the case and somehow or other they all seemed to him to consist of ninety per cent eating and stories of Ferrini's past cases. They never got down to work before eleven, and often it was midnight. This time, the Marshal had only himself to blame. He'd refused an invitation to eat at Ferrini's house with the family since the entire evening would have slid happily by in chatter, only to remember that Teresa was coming home tomorrow and he couldn't possibly clean the kitchen again. He had suggested a quick bowl of pasta somewhere near, but needless to say, Ferrini knew a chap . . .

'Good, eh?'

'It's very good – listen, this is a quiet corner. . .' His big eyes scanned the room. There was nobody near enough to listen in. 'We could make a start while we're waiting, try not to be up till three.'

'If you say so.' He didn't look enthusiastic. Ferrini liked to concentrate on his food.

The Marshal persisted. 'It's just . . . this '68 murder. I'm not used to tackling a case second hand. It's one thing to read the transcript of what so-and-so said but if you're

331

there, if you're looking a man in the eyes, it might mean something different . . .'

'Well, I know what you mean, but even so, with or without proof I think Romola cleared that one up. Fabio Muscas must have been in on it or he'd have talked – if not at the time then when he was arrested as the Monster. The only reason not to defend yourself from a charge like that is that if you tell what you know, you're in for another charge. At his age one life sentence or sixteen, it's all the same. No, he wanted Belinda out of the way because of the family money she was going through. He was after that insurance money. He had no gun, though. The Muscas family were respectable in their way. Workers. No car, either. What about Silvano?'

The Marshal thought for a bit, wishing, as Ferrini lit up, that he'd at least wait until after their meal. He didn't say so. 'Silvano standing in the reeds . . . I think that's true. I'm sure he was the one who shot them – it's more complicated, though. That's why you need to see the man. Good heavens . . . What's this?'

'This' was a thick Florentine beefsteak, already carved into chunks off the bone and carried on a platter by Sandro.

'We can't . . .'

'Boss's orders,' Sandro said, putting down the platter. 'There's a green salad on its way and a few chips. Do you like baby onions, sweet and sour?'

They looked at each other. Ferrini chuckled. 'We might as well give in with good grace. You don't know

Dante – I remember the first time I ate here. I was on a case . . .'

'Silvano,' interrupted the Marshal, stabbing firmly at a great chunk of meat, 'if you ask me, had it in for Belinda for dumping their *ménage à trois* in favour of a normal man. But I bet he never said so. It's a feeling I have about him. I think he was pretty clever at manipulating other people and I'm willing to bet he offered to do the job as a favour to the Muscas family.'

'I think you're right. Clever bugger and cool with it. His sexual habits are beyond me – ah, these look good, go on, serve yourself first. I was having a discreet talk to one of our chaps yesterday. You don't know him but he was on the case in '84 when Silvano was the chief suspect and he told me some of the things they found out when they were following him. Jesus, he used to pick up truck drivers at the motorway exit and take them on there and then in the parked trucks. Not that I don't know it happens, but with him it was that or something else every day. They never got to see his orgies, his other speciality, that usually happened at home. Foursomes.'

'But didn't he have a son?'

'I'm talking about the eighties. The kid left home at fourteen or fifteen, and no wonder. Not that it mattered to Silvano. It was going on when the kid was small, too. He told us about it when he was questioned. Besides, years before that when Silvano was still with Sergio he'd set up orgies down the park and take the lot of them with him. Not just Belinda who had to perform but Sergio and the kid, Nicolino, as well. Is that a bit of fillet there . . . ?'

'You take it. I can't manage any more.'

The restaurant was filling up but Sandro guided the customers away from their corner, glancing their way each time he passed in case they needed something.

Silvano . . . It was hard to get a grip on Silvano.

'He was a good shot. Seven bullets on target close together, then one shot to be fired by Sergio so he could get himself convicted, that would be the bullet that went into Belinda's arm from another direction. Did you ever think that Sergio liked being accused, I mean, after so many years of being laughed at for his wife's goings-on?'

'I'm sure he did. He never seriously tried to get out of it. The only thing he was hiding was his homosexuality. Of course, he knew nobody would believe he was up to it, not by himself. That's why he accused Flavio. Everybody would believe that. He had a record and everybody knew all about his affair with Belinda. Poor sod, when they were after him again in '83 he didn't get out of it easily, either. Even when that German couple got killed and he was inside. They reckoned his nephew had shot them just to get him out and that's why it wasn't a proper job. Are you giving up on that?'

The Marshal was indeed giving up his battle with the beefsteak. He felt quite exhausted with the effort.

'I don't think I can even manage the salad.'

'Do you think we should have a *digestivo*?'

'I do.'

They did, resisting at the same time all Sandro's efforts

to overwhelm them with puddings and cakes. With only another twenty minutes' delay, whilst Dante joined them with his glass and listened to one of Ferrini's juicier cases, they were on their way back to the Palazzo Pitti. The night was so cold that the Marshal was glad enough as they crossed the bridge and drove along the embankment to be snug in Ferrini's car, which was a good deal faster and more comfortable than his own. And if they did have to go all the way round the one-way system to come back over the river again and end up two minutes away from where they started, how could anyone complain when it was one of the most beautiful detours in the country? Especially in such cold clear weather when the reflections glittered in the water and the floodlit palaces looked too good to be real. That beefsteak had been a bit much, though. The Marshal eased himself further into the passenger seat as they joined the after-cinema queue near the Ponte Vecchio. Probably keep him awake half the night.

By the time they arrived, he and Ferrini had agreed that the only real mystery in '68 had been who accompanied Nicolino to that faraway house, and why.

The Marshal, fishing for his key as they climbed the stairs to his office, thought he might have the answer to that one.

'Salvatore Angius.'

'Who . . . ? Oh, the lad who was Silvano's alibi, playing billiards. That one?'

'Yes, that one.'

'Lord, Guarnaccia, it's freezing in here.'

'It's midnight. The heating's off. This Salvatore Angius wants a bit of looking into. He gave a false address; his official residence in theory – he's Sardinian, of course – was his brother's house, but he was really living in Via Torrente, right next door to the Rossini house where Nicolino was left.'

'And nobody noticed at the time?'

'Romola did, eventually. But not knowing yet that Silvano was homosexual he didn't realize what their relationship was. Where will you sit?'

'I'm all right here, chair of the accused. So, he could have taken the kid, left him to ring the bell and slipped in at his own door.'

'That's right. And he knew that lane, I'm sure. He was practically a vagrant when Silvano picked him up, out of work and penniless. Silvano gave him odd labouring jobs in Signa. That lane was a short cut from his house to Signa. He had no transport. And another thing, his was the house Sergio pointed out when they asked him to indicate the Rossini house. Nicolino said he thought somebody he didn't know had taken him there.'

'We ought to find him, then.'

'Yes. I've no idea where he is now.'

'I'll find out – he could have taken the gun, too, not just the kid. That way, if for any reason Silvano's car was seen or stopped, there was nothing to connect it with the murder. No gun, no kid. I'll find him. Leave it to me. Now' – he looked at Bacci's pile of translations of FBI reports – 'how did you get on with those?'

'Well, at least they're real. I mean, we're fumbling in the dark, they're telling us about people who've confessed and told their entire life stories. They're American, German, Swiss – some are Italian by blood though living in America – Canadian, French, English . . .'

'They're bound to be different, then, aren't they, after all . . .'

'To tell you the truth,' the Marshal said, 'I started out thinking that, too. Now, I'm not so sure. Now, what sticks in my mind is how they're all the same. We weren't shown the whole of the profile they did on our killer, that's the trouble. I suppose that's because it didn't fit the Suspect.

'And I think I can guess the most important aspect that doesn't fit. His age. Bacci wrote up the cases most similar to ours. The oldest started at twenty, the youngest at twelve. They start as soon as they're sexually mature, not when they're middle aged.'

'But . . .Where does that leave us with Silvano?'

The Marshal looked at his list. 'I don't know. I really don't know. He was born in 1935, so he was fortyish when the maniac killings started in '74, nearer fifty when they were at their height . . . I suppose he could be the only exception to the rule but it was the same with that girl . . .'

'What girl? What are you talking about now?'

'The Suspect's daughter. We were asked to believe that one fine morning, years after the fact, she got up and decided to go to Police Headquarters and report that her father used to rape her. Just like that. Even though we've

337

seen that she can barely get two words out about it now. Well, it could be true, but I reckon it would be the one and only case in the history of the world. And according to the statistics a serial killer who started work at fifty, as the Suspect would have had to do, would be another.'

'And Silvano?'

'Forty. Practically as bad, but there are other problems, aren't there? I mean – like the Suspect – Silvano's sex life, whatever your opinion of it in moral terms, was anything but impoverished. He was evidently a sexual acrobat, enjoyed women, men, groups – and he was always, *always,* in charge, directing operations.'

'I thought we were trying to accuse Silvano,' Ferrini protested, 'but you're defending him.'

'No, no . . .' the Marshal said. 'I'm just refusing to trim the facts to fit him. There's a difference. I suppose . . . I suppose what I'm trying to do is to go forward from where Romola had to leave off. This is where he was when they pushed him off the case. It doesn't mean he would have stopped here.'

'That's true. It was Silvano in '68, though. I reckon he'd never have budged from that.'

'No, and neither will I. A gun that's killed can't be sold, either. If it changed hands it had to be stolen. But it's not just the gun, is it? It's the other little details.'

'What details?'

'The bodies. The way they were separated after death. That's an odd and very particular thing to repeat from '68. Then the handbags, he fiddled in their handbags, tipped stuff out – but without taking money from them. In '68 the bit of money in the woman's handbag wasn't taken, they were after something bigger. And then, the scene of the crime. It's always the same.'

'Then we're back to Silvano again! Guarnaccia, you're going round in circles.'

'Oh no.' The Marshal spoke quietly, as if to himself. 'That's why it can't be Silvano. It can only be someone who wants us to think so. Someone with a memory, perhaps a garbled memory of '68. Or even someone who got most of it from the newspapers and who didn't know, since the crime has never been properly solved until now, that it wasn't Silvano who did those things. It was probably Fabio who went through the handbag, as Nicolino said – and Silvano was already hidden in the reeds. It was Sergio who separated the bodies, or said he did, and the victims themselves chose the place where they parked and made love and where they were murdered. Serial killers, as far as I can gather, repeat themselves. They don't repeat three or four other people. This one seems to have reconstructed the '68 murder for our benefit because we let Silvano go unpunished. And when nobody noticed there was a letter to make us notice, telling us to look at the court proceedings of '68.'

'That's pretty impressive,' Ferrini admitted, 'but what about his little vice of mutilating the bodies?'

'It came later. Did you notice something? I was thinking about it this morning whilst Simonetti was going on at the Suspect . . . When the murderer started

339

cutting into the girls' pudenda he stopped bothering with their handbags from then on.'

'Oho, Guarnaccia! Very Freudian! And very unlike you, I'd have thought!'

'What d'you mean? I was thinking of my mother.'

'Even worse.'

'I don't follow you.'

'Sorry. I'm taking the mickey. So, where does your mother come into this?'

'She doesn't, not really. It's just that I remembered she slapped me once. She hardly ever did, so I never forgot the few occasions. It was for going through her handbag – I wasn't stealing anything, it was just curiosity. I was convinced she had fascinating secrets in there. You know how mothers are, my wife's the same: she'll say to one of the boys, "Bring me my handbag, it's on such and such a chair." But never, *never* are they allowed to go in the bag themselves and get the money.'

'It's true, that. But what –?'

'And even as an adult, you wouldn't dream of going through a woman's handbag any more than you'd touch her. The same would apply to going through her pockets . . . anyway, I suppose I'm not making much sense. It just seemed a natural development for someone with his own sex problems.'

But they were back where they started. You couldn't say that about Silvano. For half an hour they went round and round this circular path and found no exit. When at last they did find the exit it was when they'd stopped

340

looking for it. If they couldn't see Silvano as the Monster they had to give him up. If they gave up Silvano they had to give up the Beretta 22 he'd used in '68. That was why they turned to the ballistics and autopsy reports in the vain hope of finding some loophole, some element of doubt about the gun being the same. There was no loophole, but there, before them, was the exit from the vicious circle. There, where it had always been, staring them in the face. The truth was that it was only a matter of luck and because they were frustrated and tired, that they noticed it now. Each of the crimes, starting from '74, was listed in their files with its relevant ballistics and autopsy reports attached. But '68 the Marshal took from Romola's document while Ferrini extracted '74 from their suspect file. They both began hurriedly reading, half aloud, and suddenly they both stopped.

'Each victim was hit four times and the entry wounds are very close together with the exception of one shot fired into the woman's arm . . .'

'The girl had received three bullet wounds in the arm which had not killed her. She had been killed with a knife . . .'

Silvano, in '68, had been a good shot and done an efficient job, just as his decisive character would suggest. Four bullets for the man, three for the woman, entry wounds close together. On target, efficient, two victims dead without a chance to react, and a bullet left over to inculpate Sergio. The gun might have been the same in 1974 but the hand that held it was another's. A messy job, an inefficient job, begun too late when the couple had finished making love and separated themselves. Even then, when they were in a tiny, enclosed space and totally distracted, unsuspecting, he'd made a mess of it and had to stab the girl to death. This was somebody who had been in a position to borrow or steal Silvano's gun, somebody connected in some way with Silvano and the '68 murder. Here, whoever he might be, was the person who would fit the psychological profile of the Monster. Someone young, capable of getting hold of a gun but not yet capable of using it properly. Someone weak, damaged and resentful who had it in for loving couples, or for the world in general. Or for Silvano.

'It's hopeless. We're just guessing. There are three people young enough but we're not going to get any further than that without more information, more facts. Besides, I've run out of cigarettes and I'm frozen.'

But the Marshal was reluctant to let go. He was afraid that it would all slip away from him, that he was working against time, that once you grasped at the truth something would intervene, the way it had with Romola.

'Nobody will give us any information,' he said. 'We'll have to work with what we've got in this report and what we can find for ourselves.'

'Find for ourselves? You do realize that we can't find

anything for ourselves without it being known we're looking for it? Who can we trust? And if it's someone we can trust, how can we justify the risk of getting them into trouble? I'm pretty sure we've got all three of them on file but where do we put our hands on the files without involving anyone else?'

'We don't.'

'Eh? So how . . . ?'

'Those three files mustn't be moved. With the people who have them we'll have to play it by ear. If they're trustworthy we talk to them and go through the files on the spot. No official request, no taking the stuff away with us. After that, we've never been there.'

'But in the end, when we're sure . . .'

'What if we get it sorted out and worry about that later?'

Ferrini grinned. 'Well, we can't start looking for these files at this time of night, but I've thought of another source of info. Flavio.'

'Are you serious?'

'Dead serious. I never met Silvano but I did once, in the course of my duties, as they say, come across poor, wicked Flavio. Nothing at all to do with this case so don't get excited. It was something and nothing, the theft of a truck with a few sheep in 1980. Flavio had done a few jobs of the sort – you know the trail, the Apennine trail from above Bologna to down near Rome. All stolen sheep go that same route and are deposited with some shepherd at the farthest point from the original robbery. Flavio had the usual bit of

343

land and an abandoned cottage and sheepfold up on the hills, but it just so happened that this time he was innocent and I was the one saved his skin. Somebody was putting one over on him, using his place while he was away. We were poking about in the area at the time because of a kidnapping and I'd spotted the real culprits, even taken the licence plate of the van in case it turned out to be relevant to the job I was on. Well, it wasn't, but a mate of mine asked me about whether I'd spotted any movement around Flavio's place, knowing I was up there. Flavio had named some men he suspected of having it in for him. It was a godsend for him because he couldn't provide an alibi worthy of the name. He'd gone up to somewhere near Como to bring his nephew home. He'd got in some bother up there and been ordered to leave. You can imagine that a member of that family was no sort of alibi and nobody else had seen them.'

'He should be grateful to you, then. But what's he likely to tell us?'

'I can't be sure, but he's bound to be able to give us some personal stuff that will make things clearer. Stuff about his quarrel with Silvano. I mean, on what grounds did Silvano say he hated him because he'd corrupted his son? And wouldn't Flavio know whether Nicolino was really Silvano's son and if the kid knew it? And then there's our friend . . . what's his name again?'

'Salvatore Angius? That's true.'

'He wasn't just Silvano's boyfriend, he was a relation of some sort. I'm going to try. Can I use your phone?'

'What? At this hour?'

'I'm not calling Flavio. I don't know his number but I know who does. A certain Captain Frilli, man after my own heart. Promoted from Marshal and went through officer training with me. He's in the right area and he'll have a file on Flavio.'

'But it's still two in the morning!'

'He'll be watching telly. He sleeps about two or three hours a night, lies there with films running on the telly at the end of the bed with the sound low so his wife can read herself to sleep. Don't worry, they'll put me through to him.'

But the Captain wasn't in bed watching television and the carabiniere who answered the phone wasn't surprised by the call. It was for Ferrini to be surprised.

'I'm not with you . . . How could he . . . ? No, no. No. You must have got your lines crossed. Whoever he was expecting hours ago it wasn't me . . . Well, where is he now? Mm. Mm. No, no, I didn't. Tell me from the beginning . . .'

There was a long silence on Ferrini's part as he listened, his alarmed eyes fixed on the Marshal's, but unable to break off and give him a clue.

'What time was this? Mm . . . Mm . . . well then, does he know for sure who . . . ? I see. Right. Right. Listen, we'll leave right away and come straight to you. If he's back, well and good, if not we'll go out there.'

Ferrini hung up. 'We have to go out.'

'Out? Where?'

'Pisa. It's Flavio. You're not going to believe this but there's been a murder. Two bodies in a car –'

'No, no, you can't tell me after all this that we're back to Flavio again after eliminating him so certainly.'

'No, we're not back to Flavio again because some-body's eliminated him for good. He's one of the two bodies in the car.'

They couldn't see much. The night was black and the area too far from any source of light. The nearest village was some miles away. With torches they could only get a vague impression of steep wooded slopes, a pale stony road and a ravine dropping away to their right.

'If you'd turned up when the fire engines were still here they had good lights. You can't see a thing down there now.'

They peered down into the ravine but even with their headlights and those of the Captain's car they could make nothing out. The smell on the night air was overpowering as the wind wafted it up to them. The acrid stink of burnt green leaves, burnt rubber and plastic, and burnt flesh.

They spent an hour or so with the Captain back in his office. He was a good man, as Ferrini had said, and he knew his business. He'd been called out at three that afternoon, along with the fire brigade. A car was burning down in the ravine and it had set fire to the surrounding trees to the extent that the flames could be seen from a considerable distance. It had taken a little time to deal with the fire and as yet the car hadn't been retrieved.

They'd have to leave that until daylight tomorrow. It had been photographed *in situ,* as had the bodies which they found in the boot and which were later taken to the Medico-Legal Institute. They were burnt beyond recognition. Nevertheless, the Captain knew who they were, though it would have to be confirmed officially.

Flavio's car was easily recognizable and stuck out like a sore thumb in this sleepy rural area where people drove three-wheeled trucks and old utility cars. His was a massive estate car with a huge roof rack of his own invention. It had been seen parked outside the one bar in a nearby village where Flavio and his companion, a shepherd boy he'd taken into his employ and protection recently, had stopped for a coffee. The village was perched on a little hill and only two roads led out of it. One, the one they'd arrived on, curved up on to a higher hill, and the nearest town. The other was little more than a stony track leading down into a valley and to the next village. It was this lane they had taken, after having asked the barman directions to a farmhouse lying in the centre of the valley. The car had not arrived at the next village and could be assumed to have stopped at the farmhouse mentioned. At about the time they would have reached the farm a number of shots were heard by a hermit living in the woods nearby. Within an hour the fire was reported. There was a trail of blood from the farmhouse along the road to the ravine. An attempt made at disposing of the car and its contents by pushing the vehicle down the ravine had failed when it stuck between trees at a depth where it was still visible from the road. So it had been burned.

'I've got every possible proof I could need,' the Captain told them. 'His rifle was still hanging behind the kitchen door. He's a terrible character and I'm pretty sure that this isn't the first time he's thought fit to bump one of his enemies off.'

'And why was Flavio his enemy?' Ferrini asked, hoping against hope perhaps that there would be something in all this for them.

'Vargius? No, it was the other chap he was after, the shepherd boy. Vargius got shot because he happened to be with him. It's a running quarrel that's been going on for some time now between two rival clans. This kid worked for the farmer in the valley and never saw a penny for a year. He slept with the animals and was given bread, cheese and wine, barely enough to keep body and soul together. He ran away and started work for Vargius, who's friendly with the opposing clan. They went there that day to get the lad's wages. What they got instead was shot. No, when I called Florence it was just that I thought somebody ought to know Vargius was dead. He was a suspect in that Monster case, wasn't he? I'm not mistaken?'

'No, you're not mistaken,' Ferrini said, 'but who did you call? I knew nothing about this. I called you because I wanted to talk to you about Flavio but I had no idea he was dead.'

'I see. I understood you were on the case, on this

special squad. To tell you the truth, I wouldn't have been in such a hurry to be bothered calling if it hadn't been for you.'

'Thanks. I mean that. But whoever you did tell didn't think fit to communicate the news to the rest of the group.'

'I see. Well, I must confess this man Simonetti they put me through to was little short of rude. I got the impression he was anything but pleased.'

'Yes.' It was the Marshal who spoke, and the other two looked at him as though they'd quite forgotten he was there. He hadn't opened his mouth since they arrived. 'I think,' he said, addressing his own big hands that were planted squarely on his knees, 'that he doesn't want the name Vargius to be mentioned in connection with our investigation. And I think you shouldn't mention, if you can avoid it, that we ever came here at all. Ferrini, I think we should leave.'

Fourteen

Late the next morning the Marshal was feeling very queasy and so had more than his usual difficulty in concentrating on what was going on. Tiredness was at the root of the problem, and the fact that he'd had two coffees instead of the usual one that morning in the hope of waking himself up. He'd have done better to stay sleepy. The coffee had begun to irritate his stomach almost at once so that when the bad news started to arrive it was inevitable that it would, as it were, attack him in this already weakened spot.

He'd been consoling himself, as he shaved, with the thought that, tired or not, nauseous or not, the day would end better than it had begun because Teresa and the boys were already on the train on their way to

Florence. It was just a question of getting through to supper time. He had to sit through another wearisome session with the Suspect, whose act never varied and whose situation seemed to worsen daily. He intended to try and get a word with Ferrini over lunch and avoid working on their private investigation tonight so as to be with his family. In the afternoon they had to go out again to the scene of the last crime with the day's witness. Then, with any luck, they'd finish reasonably early and he could . . .

That was when it had started. The phone had rung and the day had begun to fall apart before it had even begun. There he'd stood, a picture of misery, his chin half shaved and half lathered, protesting. As if protesting would change anything.

'But . . .'

'It can't be helped, Salva.'

'But why couldn't you have booked earlier?'

'How could I book earlier? I didn't know when all the tests would be finished, and who was to say she was going to be all right? You don't expect us to travel without couchettes?'

'Of course not . . .'

'Needless to say, the boys are delighted because they'll miss a few days of school.'

So at least somebody was happy. He'd been so upset that he'd stumped back to the bathroom and irritably splashed his face and dried it before seeing his half-black chin in the mirror.

Then the post. Well, that had been a pinprick in comparison, but he was too tired to distinguish between pinpricks and brickbats and the business was still irritating him now as he sat in their usual overheated conference room listening to this man Nenci, a noisy and aggressive character, known to be a friend of the Suspect and here to give evidence against him.

He should have opened the post last night, but he hadn't. There hadn't been time before going out to meet Ferrini and his intention had been to look through it all before going to bed. Then there'd been the business of Pisa. Well it was too late to do anything now, but Marco's note had left him uneasy.

> 'The auction's tomorrow at eleven. I'm not asking you to be there – I know you'll be far too busy – but I want to phone you tonight. There's something I didn't tell you and it's bothering me.'

Well, he'd known that all along for what it was worth. He'd hardly forced the lad to tell him.

> 'The photograph is for Dr Biondini. I wish I'd let him see it before. Well, it's done now and I'll just have to trust the auctioneers. I think what's making me uneasy more than anything is Benozzetti. I've seen him again and he's behaving very strangely. He's excited about the auction the way children are excited about Christmas. At times he struck me as really

crazy, or hysterical. It could be I'm reading too much into everything here because such a lot depends on the outcome – about forty million lire to be precise. But then, why should Benozzetti care? He doesn't stand to gain or lose anything. In any case, I apologize in advance for disturbing your evening as I intend to, but only briefly.'

And, of course, he'd found nobody in. The Marshal glanced surreptitiously at his watch now. The auction was underway if not over. Had nobody told Marco about the anonymous letter? Had Benozzetti by now staged some sort of scene? He ought, if anything, to be trying to concentrate on what was going on in front of him since he couldn't do much now about Marco. Not that he could do anything about this lot, either. For what it was worth, he knew the man across from them was lying through his teeth, and there was bound to be a terrible scene any minute when the Suspect was brought in to be confronted with him.

Young Noferini was on his feet, distributing photocopied maps of the area concerned. The Marshal accepted his, keeping his eyes fixed on Nenci who, on the other side of the table, was trying to maintain an attitude of someone sitting in a bar, passing the time of day. He was a tall, well-built man, a bit pockmarked. He kept one foot crossed over his knee and the foot gave away his agitation since it never stopped wagging. He held an ankle with one hand but there was no keeping it still, even so.

He was pushing the back of his chair, tipping it as if to look absently at the ceiling. Once or twice the Marshal saw him purse his lips as if he were about to whistle a tune but remembered in time that this would be out of place, however helpful it might be in showing just how relaxed he was.

The Marshal wondered why this should be. Nenci's story was that, on Sunday evening, September 9th 1985, he had been returning by car from a weekend trip to the seaside with his family. He had described the route he'd taken home, which at one point joined a fork coming from his left, coming, to be precise, from the scene of the murder of the French couple. Travelling in his car along this road from the left had come the Suspect. They had reached the fork at almost the same moment and Nenci had seen his face quite clearly.

All of which might or might not be true. The Suspect had been asked for an alibi for that night and produced one, but it wasn't by any means watertight. But as far as the Marshal was concerned it was the all too familiar story. How come after five years someone appears who's quite sure he saw the Suspect near the scene of the crime that night? It wasn't credible.

The question had to be asked, of course. It would be asked in court.

'You waited a very long time to come forward.'

'Nobody asked me to. Besides, it was only when I found out you suspected him that I remembered.'

'If you didn't suspect him yourself, why remember?'

'Maybe I did suspect him. I mean, I heard about the murder next evening on the news and then I remembered seeing him. On that same road. So of course I remembered. He doesn't live round there. Why should he be there by himself? It just struck me, that's all. Stayed in my mind, you know? I should have come forward then, I realize that. Only, you don't, do you? Then I saw his picture in the paper and I started having a conscience about it.'

There'd been a moment's silence. Simonetti had sat back and looked at young Noferini, who was typing all this rapidly into his computer. Perhaps that moment's silence unnerved Nenci. At any rate, he was unable to tolerate it and, with that foot wagging faster than ever, he'd suddenly blurted out:

'All right?'

It had been a rehearsal, not an interrogation.

Now they were bringing the Suspect in. Beside him, his lawyer was fidgeting nervously. There must have been some preliminary discussion and he knew there was going to be trouble.

At this point the Marshal would have liked to look the two detectives, Di Maira and Esposito, in the face but they were seated on the other side of Simonetti who was to his right and he had no chance to even glimpse their expressions.

Ferrini, on his left, only looked bored. Still on his left, but separated from everyone else down at the end of the table, Noferini was perhaps the only one to look interested. Simonetti at least had the good sense to seat the lawyer between the Suspect and Nenci on the opposite side of the table. Both looked capable of coming to blows if an argument ensued.

An argument ensued. It took barely a minute before Nenci's claim to have seen the Suspect that night brought his red-faced adversary to his feet.

'You lying bag of shit! You –'

The lawyer grabbed at him, but it took the carabinieri of his escort to get him down into his seat again. The debacle that followed could hardly be called a confrontation in any real sense since Nenci never looked at or spoke directly to the Suspect, who did little except accuse him, in the foulest terms he could muster, of lying through his teeth. The Marshal had never seen him so enraged, even the day they'd 'found' the bullet. Since he was of the same opinion as the Suspect himself he didn't find it very surprising, but he didn't understand what the underlying quarrel was about.

These two had been friends; Nenci didn't try to deny that like so many others had.

'Of course I know him or I wouldn't be here, would I?'

'You went out together?'

'A time or two. When he wanted a woman I'd sometimes take him down to Florence. He didn't like spending too much so I took him to one or two I was friendly with. They gave him a good price.'

'Didn't like spending? *I* didn't like spending? *I* paid

356

for the fucking petrol every time we went out.'

'So what?'

'You great stinking bag of –'

'Sit down! And keep your voice down! Did you frequent these same prostitutes yourself, Signor Nenci?'

'Frequent them? What d'you mean by that?'

'Were you a client?'

'Well, why didn't you say so? Of course I was a client. What else do you go to a prostitute for except –'

'Thank you. Were you aware of your friend's activities as a Peeping Tom?'

'I know nothing about that.'

'Can we return to the night in question? Can you remember commenting to your wife, or even your children, on seeing the Suspect?'

'Not that I remember, no.'

The lawyer, keeping a restraining hand on his client's arm the while, asked permission to speak to the witness.

'You can ask what you want,' bellowed Nenci, as though he'd been threatened. 'I go where I want with whoever I want and I'm not ashamed of anything I do! You ask anything you feel like but don't imagine that I give a tuppenny shit for what he says or what you say!'

'Signor Nenci! It is for me to decide who may or may not speak here! Go ahead.'

'Thank you, Mr Prosecutor. Signor Nenci, would you mind telling me what you had for dinner that evening?'

'Eh? I don't know. We stopped at a pizzeria, I think, on the road. We always do that when we're coming back from the sea.'

'Thank you. What sort of pizza did you choose that evening?'

'You what? What sort of fucking stupid question is that?'

'Signor Nenci –'

'Is he off his bloody head? Is he half-witted, or what? What sort of pizza did I choose some night five years ago?'

'I was just wondering. How very fortunate then that for no apparent reason you remember seeing my client pass near you in his car. After five years.'

The lawyer looked Simonetti in the eye without further comment. Simonetti only shrugged and changed the subject. He had Noferini pass a copy of the map to the lawyer and began to explain the events as described by Nenci. But in seconds the Suspect threw off the lawyer's grip and stood up roaring.

'You creeping Jesus, you toad! You never used that road to come home from the sea! That's not your road home – that's not his road! Look at a real map, it's miles out of his way!'

Simonetti cued Nenci in with a faint nod of his head.

'It's not my usual road. I never said it was. I had to make a detour because my road was closed for repairs.'

At this point there was a slight disturbance at the end of the table. Noferini had stopped typing and stood up. Simonetti, without turning to him, sensed his movement and held up a warning hand. The boy came forward, even so, his face red, and a whispered conversation followed.

'I'm sorry . . . I left it on your desk . . . But surely they . . .'

The Marshal caught no more of it than that. Noferini was dismissed to his seat and returned there looking as mortified as a punished schoolboy.

'If we can continue: Signor Nenci, you are absolutely certain that it was the Suspect you saw that night?'

'I've said I saw him and I saw him – oh, there's nothing in this world that's a hundred per cent certain, is there? I am as certain as you can be about anything. Put it this way: if there's a doubt it's not more than say fifteen, twenty per cent. Let's say twenty per cent.'

'I'm not sure I take your meaning . . .'

Simonetti, for once, was a little nonplussed. The Suspect, on the other hand, took his meaning, whatever it was, and rose to his feet purple with rage.

'You cretinous clown! You filthy baboon! I'll twenty per cent you, you and your shitty poisonous lies! I'll twenty per cent you!'

This time nobody could stop him. He was hysterical with rage and in the end he had to be dragged forcibly from the room, still screaming. The witness was dismissed. There was no point trying to interrogate the Suspect any more. They broke for an early lunch. And it was decided that he should remain under escort and be fed in a nearby room in the hope that he would calm down sufficiently to be further questioned on the details of his alibi for that Sunday night.

'I want one of you with him, in case he should let anything slip while he's in that state. Ferrini.'

So there went their lunch-time chat, thought the Marshal wearily. Then he remembered how little it mattered, since Teresa and the boys weren't coming after all, and his heart sank.

They passed a cold and wearisome afternoon going over the witness's story on the spot, taking measurements, judging distances and, when it went dark, visibility. Only once were they sufficiently out of earshot for the Marshal to say to Ferrini: 'What do you make of this twenty per cent story? I'd say there was something behind it. Those two were as thick as thieves but there's been a falling out. It sounded like blackmail, but twenty per cent of what?'

Ferrini only shrugged. 'God knows.'

When at last the day's work was over and they took their separate ways he said, 'I was hoping Teresa and the boys would be home but they haven't set off. If you want to have a bite with me we might as well eat up the stuff I bought for them. We can talk as we eat and finish a bit earlier.'

'No, I'll get home. There'll be something ready. I'll give you a call later, maybe.'

No hope of an early night, then. Ferrini seemed out of sorts but he must be tired and it had been an unsatisfactory day, even for Simonetti who must surely be wondering to what extent he'd be able to control his witness in court.

To compensate for the emptiness of the flat, the Marshal left the little television in the kitchen on after putting some water to boil for pasta, and went to have a shower. He watched what was left of the news as he ate, anxious now that there might be a rail strike or some other calamity that would prevent Teresa coming home. There was no rail strike. He switched off the television and washed up meticulously before going to his office and bringing his notes and files back to the kitchen so they could talk there. That way Lorenzini wouldn't find a smoked-out office in the morning. The kitchen had an extractor. Ferrini still hadn't rung. It was getting late by this time and the later it got the more irritable the Marshal became. He couldn't do with being up half the night again. If it got past a certain hour he was going to bed. Even if Ferrini rang now he still had to get over here, and after that they wouldn't get down to business until an hour of anecdotes and a pack of cigarettes later.

'Ouffa!' His patience exhausted he rang Ferrini himself.

'I had a few things to do, you know how it is. We'll have a chat some other time.'

'Is something wrong?'

'No, there's nothing wrong.' His tone said clearly that something was very wrong indeed.

The Marshal thought of Di Maira's watchful eyes and then said, 'Has somebody said something to you?'

'We'll talk about it another time.'

'Not over the phone . . .'

'No, no, no! I don't give a toss if my phone's tapped. It wouldn't be the first time. I'm just sick of wasting my time, that's all. There's never going to be a proper outcome – I'm talking about a judicial outcome, am I making myself clear? With Flavio dead we'll get nowhere unless it's to work the thing out for our own satisfaction. And I'll tell you straight, I've no interest in that. I've better ways in life of finding satisfaction, you know what I mean? I'd rather spend time with my family. I'm not like you, Guarnaccia. When you get your teeth into something you can't let go but I've been thinking it over . . . Anyway, we'll talk about it sometime . . .'

'Well, if you feel like that . . .'

'I do feel like that. This job's hard enough to do at the best of times. Not a day goes by without asking myself why I don't pack it in. I mean, why bother? And on top of that to be looking for trouble . . .'

'Something has happened. If you want to tell me about it tomorrow that's all right.'

'No, no, no! It's nothing like that. You're being paranoid again. If you really want to know, I'll tell you. I was left alone with him at lunch time, that's what happened.'

'The Suspect?'

'It wasn't for more than a few minutes. We weren't even alone, strictly speaking. The two carabinieri were just at the door having a fag. Anyway, it just came into my head to ask him something, so I did. I said to him, listen, I said, strictly between you and me? I'm offering you a word of advice. You've done time for murder once, I said, but this is altogether different. If you play your cards right this could be all over in less time than you'd get for stealing a car. What you ought to do is confess the lot and plead insanity. With any luck you'll avoid even going to trial – they can find you unfit to plead – you'll go to some psychiatric ward somewhere for a bit with every journalist and trick cyclist in Europe coming to hear your story. Then, when the fuss has blown over, you'll be sent quietly home because of your age and your heart condition. You want to think about it seriously because if you go to trial and defend yourself you're a goner.'

'And did he give you an answer?'

'Not right away. He sat there looking at me sideways, dead still, like he does sometimes with that little watery eye of his. He was thinking about it, you see. He was actually *thinking* about it as a way out!'

'But . . . you can't be sure what he was thinking. Didn't he say anything?'

'Oh, he said something all right. After a long time staring at me, all of a sudden he said, "And what do I tell their parents?" Well, I don't know what that means to you?'

'What he said? Or that he gave the idea some thought?'

'It's the same thing, isn't it? We've never given him any serious consideration, but what if it really was him?'

'But apart from anything else, his age . . .'

'His age, his age! There'll be some explanation for that. All this stuff in Bacci's books . . . books are all very well but that's all foreign stuff, anyway. At the end of the day you can only rely on your own experience.'

'Yes . . .' the Marshal agreed slowly, 'but we don't have any.'

'Come on, a murderer's a murderer – and this chap is a murderer, we know that. Oh, I'm not saying I'm completely convinced, I'm just saying there might be something in it, after all. I mean, however many tricks they've pulled on him – we've all pulled a few in our time – that doesn't mean he's innocent. Anyway, now you know. They might be right, Romola might have been right, you might be right. It's just not our responsibility, so why bother? Our only hope was to find Flavio and he's dead. That's it.'

There was nothing the Marshal could say. After he'd hung up he stood where he was, wondering what to do. Then he went back into the kitchen and sat down at the table. He was carried forward by inertia as much as anything, and perhaps by there being nothing to stop or distract him. If Teresa had arrived as she should have done then everything might have gone differently. If the official enquiry had been more convincing . . .

He sat for some time without touching the papers in front of him, thinking about what Ferrini had said about his conversation with the Suspect. He could imagine that rheumy sideways stare, weighing up Ferrini, weighing up the proposition.

'*And what do I tell their parents?*'

He could think of one girl's father, in particular, who wouldn't accept such an outcome and who might well think he had nothing to lose by punishing the Suspect himself with a hunting rifle. But did his awareness of that danger mean the man was guilty? He must know by now, given the tricks that had been pulled on him, that Simonetti would stop at nothing to get a conviction and that against a false accusation there can be no true defence. The man wasn't stupid. He knew what he was up against. He had an animal sense of danger and a peasant's faith in lies. The path mapped out for him by Ferrini would be no less attractive because it was dishonest. Defending himself by lying, denying he was a Peeping Tom, denying, the Marshal recalled on one occasion, even the murder he'd done time for, came naturally to him. If he thought a string of lies would get him off the hook, he wouldn't hesitate to tell them, even to his lawyer, or perhaps especially to his lawyer. Those were the rules he played by, that was the world he lived in. Lie and lie and lie, lie to your lawyer, first of all, so you'll have someone respectable to tell your lies to the judge. But in this case there were fourteen sets of parents with ruined lives behind them and his trial before them. It was a very big risk to take. Besides which, it was his proper business to lie, but he couldn't get his mind round the idea of Simonetti's lying, even though the fact was staring him in the face. His rage and frustration were owed to a childlike belief that authority was there to be lied to and made a fool of but that authority must be just. However much he smelled danger and saw treachery, he was having difficulty relinquishing his traditional beliefs. Unless he did so, and adjusted his defence accordingly, he was done for. In the Marshal's opinion, he knew that and must have seen the sense of Ferrini's proposal. But then, Ferrini's proposal might be a trick . . .

'*And what do I tell their parents?*'

'No, no . . .' The Marshal spoke aloud to the table. Whatever the Suspect's reason for not rejecting the insanity plea faster, he couldn't see its being guilt. What might be the problem was his having something else he needed to hide. At his age there's a limit to how many years you can serve in prison and a sentence for something rather less drastic than fourteen murders would be enough to ensure he'd never see daylight again. That something, whatever it might be, was probably the reason for his denying being a Peeping Tom. That was not a sensible or useful lie. Being a Peeping Tom would have been an acceptable reason, a credible reason, for his presence in lonely country spots at night, even in the face of a more suitable witness than Nenci. There were hundreds of these men out there on any Saturday night and the ones like the Suspect went about their business in groups. Admitting to his vice and calling the rest of his band as witnesses could be what would save him. But he denied it; Nenci denied it. Whatever was being hidden here it seemed the Suspect thought it worth the risk of being tried as the Monster. He wasn't the Monster and so should be acquitted since there could be no proof. The alternative, the true story that would release him from the false accusation, must be serious enough . . .

'Those videos . . .' The answer, the Marshal felt instinctively, lay in that direction but he couldn't grasp it. 'Twenty per cent of what?'

'Boh . . .' He slapped a big hand on the table. No use breaking his head over that. Something might well come out as they went along. He opened the '68 file and tried to concentrate his mind on his own line of enquiry. It took him half an hour to recognize the fact that it was impossible. He'd worked on his own before and, however much he'd bumbled about, written useless lists, grumbled, and lost faith in himself, it hadn't been like this. Thinking about it now he couldn't remember how all this had come about. In some way or other it seemed to have started and gained impetus of itself. There'd certainly never been any conscious decision on his part to start looking for the truth in this case. But however it happened, for whatever reason, Ferrini was inextricably bound up in it. Losing Bacci had been a blow because he was useful. The information, books and notes he'd provided were useful. He'd really needed the list of symptoms he'd promised to provide and still didn't know how he'd manage without it. But Ferrini was different. It was because Ferrini wasn't sitting in the chair opposite, lighting up his tenth cigarette and launching into one of his stories to prevent the Marshal from getting on, that he wasn't getting on. The sheets of paper before him remained just sheets of paper, the notes just notes, the lists meaningless. The same ingredients were there but nothing was happening. The Marshal tried to remember just how they had made such progress as they had made, but he couldn't. He remembered their meals, the stories, the clouds of smoke, Ferrini laughing at him, provoking him with cynical comments. Ferrini the devil's advocate, forcing him to defend his position.

Well, now there was no Ferrini and he might as well pack it in and go to bed. He might not feel so wretched if he got a decent night's sleep.

He slept, but it was a disturbed and unhappy sleep. He seemed to spend the whole night exhausting himself with the effort of trying to convince Ferrini of something or other. The few times he came to the surface and got up to wander half awake to the bathroom or to the kitchen for a drink, he couldn't for the life of him remember what his insistent arguments had been about. Nevertheless, the minute he closed his eyes he was off again, trying and trying, but always failing, to convince Ferrini of something, whatever it was.

The worst thing was that he realized even as he dreamed that he no longer knew what he was talking about himself. The alarm went off at a quarter to seven and he opened his eyes with relief. After relief came a sinking feeling in his stomach that everything was wrong. Teresa hadn't come home, that was the first thing that registered. Ferrini had abandoned him, that was the next. What else . . . Marco, he hadn't phoned him to hear how things went. Too taken up with his own problems and perhaps reluctant to hear any more bad news . . . It could be a good sign, though, that Marco hadn't phoned himself. It might mean everything was all right. There was something else, something he had to do. With a sigh, he recalled that though he had the morning to himself to go through the business of his own station with Lorenzini, he had been given the task of visiting the mother of one of the murdered girls to whom the trinkets recovered from the Suspect's house were thought to belong. Having assembled all his troubles he got up and looked at himself in the bathroom mirror, adding to the list of temporary problems the permanent one of which he always felt more conscious when things were going badly: he was overweight.

An hour or so later he was feeling a little better because of the effect of sitting a while in his own chair, in his own office, talking to Lorenzini about familiar problems. He found himself thinking wistfully of some calamitous crime occurring on his doorstep so that he could be released from the special squad to deal with it. As it was, he didn't think two snatched handbags, a fight in a bar and a missing dog offered him much hope of escape.

'Anything in the post?'

'Nothing you need bother with. How's your business going?'

'Oh, you know . . .' The Marshal shrugged. It would have been comforting to confide in Lorenzini, to have someone to talk to about all the things that were disturbing him, not to feel so alone. But it wouldn't be fair. He said nothing. Lorenzini waited a moment and then said, 'I'll get back next door.'

'No, no . . . Stay. I think . . . I'm going over to Borgo Ognissanti . . .' He got up from his desk and went to reach for his greatcoat. 'Give them a ring, will you? Check that the Captain's in.'

He buttoned his coat slowly, thinking of the first day when Captain Maestrangelo had sent for him. He'd been embarrassed and must have known all along that things were not as they should be. It was time they put their cards on the table; he couldn't go on like this, not alone.

'He's with the Colonel,' Lorenzini said, hanging up. 'The usual morning meeting. It'll be over by the time you get there. They'll tell him you're on your way.'

'Thanks. And while I'm thinking about it, that big envelope there . . .'

'This?'

'That's it. Send it round to Dr Biondini's office, will you? It's a photograph he wants to look at and I don't want to go there myself just now.'

On any other day he'd have been pleased to, but today he felt too put out to make conversation or to discuss anything other than what was weighing on his mind.

'Do you want Di Nuccio to drive you?' Lorenzini called after him as he started down the stairs.

'I'll walk.'

The weather had changed, that was the first thing he noticed as he came out under the archway into Piazza Pitti. The mountain wind had dropped and the temperature had risen enough for a few clouds to gather. The fog that always hung over the river in the mornings hadn't risen and the buildings were damp, their colours muted. It seemed an age since the Marshal had found time to walk anywhere, sniffing the morning smell of coffee, exhaust fumes and fresh woodsmoke. He was tempted to stop for a coffee but he didn't want to risk the Captain's having been called away when he got there so instead he quickened his pace. He crossed Ponte alla Carraia, glancing down at the sludge-green water that smelled strongly on the damp and stagnant air of mud and rotting vegetation carried down from the country, and more faintly of the sea air from Pisa.

He would talk to the Captain, tell him straight what was going on and get his advice. And whatever that advice was, whether he agreed or not, he would follow it, and let that be an end of the story.

It was as he walked in at the entrance to the cloister, nodding to the carabiniere on guard duty, that he remembered something he should have told Lorenzini, or rather asked him. He put his head in round the guard-room door and asked them to get his number.

'Lorenzini? Listen, I meant to ask you. If you open the top drawer of my desk, right there by the phone . . . there's a book.'

'Wait a minute . . . An English book?'

'That's it. There's a slip of paper marking a page. Have you found it? And a note at the top right-hand margin in red biro.'

'Mm. Right . . . it says, *"Is this us?"* Is that it?'

'That's it. I think it's a translation of the phrase near it that's been underlined, something about special investigations. You know a bit of English; can you translate those few lines?'

'I think so. I'll have a go, anyway.'

'Thanks. I'll not be long.'

As he made his way along the cloister a large car drove out towards him. The driver was a policeman and in the back were Simonetti and his registrar. They seemed to be sharing a joke and the Marshal saw a flash of Simonetti's brilliant smile as the car slowed to wait for the automatic gate. He himself was in shadow and stayed very still, but he felt that, as the car moved on, Simonetti's glance caught his, quick as a snake's and away again before he could be sure it had happened.

Well, there was nothing to be done about it. There was no reason, he thought, as he climbed the stone staircase to his right, why he wouldn't have legitimate business here with his commandant. He reached the upper corridor and then paused by a large rubber plant as he saw the officers from the various departments coming out of the Colonel's room. Their footsteps echoed loudly on the highly polished red tiles. He didn't see Captain Maestrangelo among them and, thinking he'd already gone back to his own office, he walked on a few steps. Then he stopped dead, hearing the Colonel's voice raised in anger.

'No, no, no, Maestrangelo, it's out of the question. We can't spare him! He's the best investigator we've got and

372

I'm not taking him off that money-laundering business until he's cleared it up – and not even then am I sending him over there! Find him another Bacci, somebody polite who'll give him no bother and looks good on television. Find him another Guarnaccia from some other superfluous little station, but I want my investigators working here for me! If they're running an idiot investigation they're only getting idiot men!'

He didn't stop there. The Marshal could still hear him shouting as he turned at the end of the corridor and started back down the stairs to go home.

He went back across the river. He was walking quite slowly but his heart was beating fast, and despite the cool damp air his face felt hot.

He should have known. He should have been able to put two and two together. The Captain's discomfort when he'd asked, 'Why me?' Then there'd been that funny remark of Esposito's the first week. He'd complimented him on having solved that transsexual murder.

'Under the circumstances I was a bit surprised to see you here. Just goes to show it doesn't pay to listen to gossip.'

Everybody knew. It was common gossip. Ferrini, of course, knew all along and then assumed that he did too. How could he not have cottoned on? Why was he so slow? Ferrini had gone on and on about the decent cases being given to youngsters with his same rank and no experience. To him it had been obvious that this was a police show and that they were only there because it would have looked bad if the carabinieri, known supporters of Romola, had been absent.

And when he thought of poor Teresa trying to convince him against the evidence that he was considered a good investigator! If only she were home . . . But then, how could he tell her the truth?

'*If they're running an idiot investigation they're only getting idiot men!*'

The remark was burnt into his memory. They say, of course, that eavesdroppers . . . He hadn't overheard on purpose.

'Marshal? Good morning!'

He looked up, dazed, surprised to find he was back in front of the Palazzo Pitti. Dr Biondini was looking at him quizzically. 'You were miles away! I can see you're concentrating on catching your Monster. I just wanted to thank you for the photograph. One of your men brought it. I shall have a good look at it this evening. I'm sorry not to have seen you at the opening of my exhibition.'

'Yes . . .' The Marshal frowned. 'Later, I can't . . . Good morning.'

He turned away and went under the arch and up the stairs, feeling for his keys. Fortunately, Lorenzini was in the duty room discussing some problem with the two lads in there and the Marshal was able to go into his own office, shut the door behind him and sit quietly at his desk with his own thoughts. So lost in his ruminations was he that he'd been staring at the sheet of paper which

Lorenzini had left there for him for a long time before he thought to actually read it.

> *One of the obvious problems with special investigation squads was that the participating police departments did not give up their best detectives. They detailed some for whom they had little use otherwise.*

Beneath it in brackets Lorenzini had added Bacci's comment: 'Is this us?'

Fifteen

Behind his dark glasses, the Marshal had only the vaguest sense of buildings and people going by, sometimes swiftly, more often very slowly.

'One long traffic jam, this road . . .' commented the carabiniere driver beside him. 'I'd hate to live out this way and have to get to work in the morning.'

This was the fourth or fifth remark of the sort he had made since they set off out of town on the road north. He got no answer this time either. The Marshal was aware of being spoken to but it took him so long to come to the surface that the moment for the appropriate banal answer had always passed. He wouldn't want the lad to think he was angry or anything of that sort but he couldn't put together any kind of reassuring explanation for his profound silence. The truth would hardly do . . . I'm feeling out of sorts because the Colonel just pronounced that I was an idiot. The truth was that it was the Captain whose opinion he cared about. The Colonel was neither here nor there, since he'd only been in Florence since September and couldn't be expected . . . to what? Notice that the dull silent NCO commanding a superfluous little station was really a wonderful detective? That was what was so awful: the Colonel had simply confirmed his own opinion of himself. There was no defence against it. He couldn't even feel wronged. He *didn't* feel wronged. And yet the Captain . . . Captain Maestrangelo was a good man, a serious man and an honest one. They knew each other well and the Marshal had always felt there was, if nothing else, a sort of respect. He knew he had no brains and in cases where both brains and logic had been required he'd always been the first to acknowledge his need of the Captain's help and had sought it. And still, he thought he'd contributed something and that something, whatever it was, had in turn been acknowledged by the Captain.

Again and again, he went over the scene in Maestrangelo's office that first morning, in the light of what he knew now and had then failed to understand. It was always the same with him: images, movements, scenes, etched themselves on his brain, but he invariably failed to make them add up into sense.

He saw the Captain's smooth brown hands turning the pen on his desk over and over, and the grey eyes always avoiding the Marshal's questioning gaze.

'Why me?'

He'd been given no answer, he'd been told no lies. And he'd wondered, even then, he remembered, why Simonetti should have been willing to take on such a hopelessly difficult case.

'He didn't strike me as a man who'd care for such a public failure.'

'No. He wouldn't like that.'

And still he hadn't cottoned on. The Captain could hardly have said outright that the intention was to create a 'test-tube' Monster and rig the proof as a simpler alternative to finding the real man. Perhaps that hadn't been the intention right at the start when the case had been snatched out of Romola's hands, but it must have been the case by the time this latest squad was set up. By then there had been a long enough gap for it to seem improbable that the real killer would strike again and destroy their case as he so often had Romola's. The ground had also been prepared through the provocation of the incest trial. Only after that was it safe to bring on the innocents like himself, Bacci, that youngster Noferini with his computer and his enthusiasm and who in some way or other must have stumbled over the truth yesterday and had been reprimanded for it. As for Ferrini . . . The Marshal no longer knew what to think about Ferrini . . .

'Who made the choice of the three carabinieri?'

'It was made here. We made it.'

If he'd said the Colonel made it – but he didn't. He said We. He'd even emphasized the We, and at the time the

Marshal had found that reassuring because the Colonel didn't know him but the Captain did. A fine piece of irony that turned out to be since it was that We which was now the chief source of his hurt.

'I think this is where we turn, isn't it?'

If only Teresa were here. It was true that she'd been wrong, too, but then who would ever have imagined . . .

'The Captain thinks a lot of you.'

It wasn't like Teresa to be wrong about something like that. She noticed things that he missed, but even she couldn't explain away what he'd overheard this morning.

What did she think of Ferrini? She'd once said he'd spent too much of his life catching villains and that it had affected his personality, that instead of making conversation he had a tendency to interrogate. Sometimes, she said, he had a positively threatening air and she could imagine how it might feel to have him clap handcuffs on you and advise you to make a clean breast of it – 'I don't know if I'm making myself clear!' But she had been laughing aloud as she imitated him and then she'd said, 'Why don't we have them round for a meal? They always cheer me up.'

'Marshal?'

That was true. There was something about Ferrini, even at his most infuriating, that was in some way cheery.

His wife, who was plump and pretty and always laughing, would roar with mirth as he raged on. 'He was born that way, you know. Take no notice. Isn't he a scream?' And then he'd start laughing too. They adored each other.

If only Ferrini were here now. What he wouldn't say – he'd rain curses on the lot of them. Guarnaccia! What else can you do in this job? Cynical? We're just going through the motions, looking for a likely suspect who can be put behind bars and, unlike the previous ones, stay there.

Why hadn't the Marshal believed him in the first place, really believed him, instead of taking his remarks as the usual cynicism.

'If they're running an idiot enquiry . . .'

How could they class Ferrini that way when he'd solved so many cases? He'd even been given an officer's rank from being an NCO because he'd solved so many. The Marshal had never known the Captain to be unfair but there was no getting away from it this time and he felt resentful on Ferrini's behalf. For himself he only felt ashamed. Ashamed of his presumptuousness in thinking he could take on a problem that had defeated a man of Romola's calibre.

'We're wasting our time. Who needs it?'

'Marshal?'

'What's the matter? Did you say something?'

'Just that we're here. This is the address you gave me. We've been here for –'

'You should have said . . .' The Marshal got stiffly out of the car, hoping to leave his own problems behind him until he got back. It was wrong to be feeling sorry for himself in the face of the people he had to deal with now.

The Marshal had rung the bell and braced himself for the meeting with a bereaved mother, but it was the dead girl's father who opened the door of the first-floor flat.

'You'd better come in. The wife . . .'

There was no sign of her, and the father, thin and beaten looking, led him into a small sitting room.

'Will you take a chair? I'm sorry, she . . . It's Saturday night, you see . . . But I did tell her so she'll be back if you don't mind waiting. I did tell her.'

The Marshal sat down, looking about him without speaking. He didn't understand at all what the problem was or why the reference to Saturday night when it was a little after three-thirty in the afternoon, but he made no comment.

'Do you smoke?'

'No. No, thank you.'

'I smoke too much since . . .' As if to demonstrate this he was taken by a long and painful fit of coughing, after which he lit up. 'I haven't seen you before.'

'No, I've not been on the case long.'

'They've come and gone . . . So many of them. I remember them all, every one. They all promised . . . They meant it, too – oh, it won't bring her back . . .' He smoked in silence, gazing at the enlarged photograph of his daughter on the sideboard. The Marshal was convinced that he had been a robust, well-built man at one time but that grief had caused him to collapse inward on himself. What bit of flesh was left on him hung loose on his big bones. What did you say to a man in these circumstances?

He certainly wasn't going to make the promises all the previous investigators had evidently made. It wasn't the sort of thing he did, anyway, and after all these years it would sound pretty hollow, even ludicrous. He, too, looked over at the photograph. It was the girl with the long dark curls whose pre-autopsy picture had so upset Bacci. He hoped to God they hadn't let the mother see the body. The father, he knew, had been the one to find her.

'Our lovely Sara. She was a beautiful child. We used to wonder how we came to have her because there's no good looks to speak of in this family. The wife was well enough before she put weight on but nothing out of the ordinary, and I'd win no beauty competitions. But Sara! Those big eyes and the shiny black curls . . . her mother would never cut her hair when she was little. I used to worry about her in the summer, all that weight, you know, in the heat . . . The things you worry about. Like, I was against her having a moped. I worried myself sick for years, I hadn't a minute's peace. But what can you do when they've all got one and besides, she needed it to get to school. Worried myself sick . . . I worked as a hospital porter so you can imagine. I'd seen that many youngsters brought in – I suppose in your job it's the same . . .'

'Yes,' admitted the Marshal, his stomach tightening at the thought that the moped problem was going to have to be dealt with in the near future.

'Have you children?'

'Two boys. I feel the same way about mopeds, I must say.'

'Yes. That's it, you see. You worry about so many things, try to protect them. You imagine you've thought of everything. I was relieved when she took up with Silvio and they bought their little car . . .

'My mother, God rest her soul, used to look at Sara and say where did we get her? Where did we get this little angel? She'd go on like that, saying she was an angel who'd been lent to us. Her last words to us when she went were, "Look after that child, she's marked to die young." The wife was blazing mad. She hates superstitious stuff and doesn't believe in it, but it gave her a fright and she got so she was worse than me about being overprotective. That night, they weren't more than half an hour later than they'd said. I don't want to give you the impression I played the heavy father, I never did that. I just liked them to say when they'd be back and ring up if they were going to be late. I think that's only sensible. You'd do the same, am I right?'

'Of course . . . It saves worry.'

'Less than half an hour . . . only, she was a good girl to us and she knew . . . She always phoned, or Silvio would. Less than half an hour late, and then they were only down the road having a pizza, but the wife . . .

'She said, "Something's happened. I know something's happened. We're going to look for them." I said, "Come on now, give over, they said about half past eleven. They'll arrive any minute and if they've changed their plans they'll phone." She said, "Something's happened to her." She went into the bathroom and she was sick. That's when I got the car keys. I thought to myself there could be no harm in running down to the pizzeria . . .

'They say women have a sixth sense about their children, don't they? I said to her, "Stay here. They'll come home. Stay here." She stayed but she didn't believe me. Outside the pizzeria I saw some friends of theirs who were just leaving. The place was closing and a waiter was stacking chairs on the tables. That's when I felt sick, like my wife. I didn't know what to do. It was their friends who said, "We'll find them. Don't worry, we know where to look." I knew what that meant, and it was only a few months after . . . after what happened at Scandicci. You know . . .'

'Yes.'

They weren't parked at the first lane we went down. The kids told me not to worry, they'd probably already set off for home but that there was another place we could try. We got back in the car and – I don't know how to explain this, but I was thinking that I'd give them what for when we got home for giving us all this worry and yet, at the same time, I knew I had to find them tonight because otherwise maybe strangers would find them tomorrow. I even decided I'd better call the wife's sister and wait till she got here before I broke the bad news. I had this terrible feeling that I've never forgiven myself for, of wanting it to be over. It's not natural, that. There must be something wrong with me.'

'No, no . . . That's not true. You knew exactly what you were afraid of. It's a natural reaction.'

'D'you think so?'

'I know it is. I once had a phone call that made me think my son had been kidnapped. I was completely wrong, but in the first few seconds I'd gone over the whole procedure, from roadblocks to ransom. If you think back, you'll find it probably happened the same when she was out on her moped. Didn't you imagine dealing with a road accident?'

The father fixed his lightless eyes on the Marshal in the hope of some relief from his misery, however small.

'You're right . . . I used to imagine her on the stretcher in place of some poor youngster I was wheeling into the hospital. And you think that's normal?'

'It's perfectly normal. When you love people you're always frightened, for them and for yourself having to cope with losing them. We all have those imaginings and then when things turn out right we forget. Only, they so often don't turn out all right, as I know because of my job and you know because of yours. That's what makes us more likely than most people to imagine the worst. We see it too often.'

The father sat silent for a moment, gazing at the photograph, the ash on his cigarette falling unnoticed to the floor. Then his taut shoulders relaxed just a little.

'Thank you. I can't tell you how much it's bothered me all these years.'

'You've enough grief to cope with without inventing problems for yourself. All parents are much the same. Any of your friends could have reassured you.'

'Maybe they could, only I never told anybody. I felt a bit ashamed. I don't know why I told you.'

'Sometimes it's easier when it's a stranger.' The Marshal ventured to take a small package from his greatcoat pocket. 'I wonder if it might be best if you looked at these things. If you happen to recognize them it might save your wife the upset.'

He accepted the package. 'The things they told me about over the phone?' He gazed at the contents of the polythene bag, shaking his head. 'I don't know . . . She always wore the gold necklace we bought her for her first Communion. She did have some coloured bangles and bits she wore in summer but . . . No, you'll have to ask the wife. I'm sorry about this. I did tell her but she doesn't remember things like she used to and with its being Saturday . . . She goes down there, you see, with a few flowers. I wish she wouldn't because it only seems to upset her, but there it is. I draw the line at her being down there in the dark, so at this time I usually walk down and bring her home. I did tell her you were coming –'

'Don't worry. If you walk there it can't be far?'

'Five minutes.'

'Then I'll walk with you. It's only a question of my showing her these things.' He took back the little package and slipped it into his pocket. 'I won't keep her more than a minute. I wouldn't want to upset her.'

'I don't think you will. She doesn't take a lot of notice these days. I'll get my coat.'

The grey winter afternoon was fading into evening and

metal shutters were rolling up one after the other as the shopkeepers opened up and turned on their lights. As they came out of the street door a greengrocer carried out a crate of oranges with shiny leaves and set it on his stand outside the shop window. When he saw his neighbour, together with the Marshal, he paused to ask, 'Is it true, then? Have they really caught the right man this time?'

The Marshal didn't answer and the man beside him only shrugged. He hadn't even bothered to ask about that himself. After so many years and so many failures he must have given up hope.

The Marshal's driver started up his engine as he saw them approach.

'No, no . . . We're not leaving yet. I'll be half an hour, or so.'

'It's this way . . .'

They left the village by a sloping tarmac road which petered out after fifty yards and became a country lane with a stream running along one side. Within a very few minutes they were looking down to their right where a marble cross marked the scene of the murder and where the Marshal had stood not so long ago in the pouring rain looking up at the bleak, bandit-ridden mountain that was now at their backs.

He didn't see the mother at once because she was standing so still in the gloom. Then he realized she was standing behind the cross with her head bent, perhaps even with her forehead resting on it.

'You'd better go down there by yourself,' her husband

suggested. 'If I'm there she'll just look to me to answer anything you ask her. If you look up when you're finished I'll come for her.'

The Marshal started down the slope between the rows of dead vines. She must have thought he was her husband and without looking up, she asked, 'Is it time?'

'Signora?'

She raised her head slowly and looked at him. 'Oh.' She made no other comment on his presence. She clearly only registered him by his uniform as one more person who would ask her a lot of questions to which there were no answers. Her gaze wandered beyond him.

'Your husband will be here in just a moment. I'm sorry to disturb you like this but –'

'Do you know why I'm here?'

'I . . . Your husband said you liked to bring a few flowers.'

'Did he? Is that what he tells people?'

There were no flowers.

'He worries . . . But we all have to cope as best we can. I have to come here. He doesn't understand that. He thinks I should go to the cemetery. Flowers!' She pulled her wool coat tighter over her chest. 'It's cold . . .

'He was here, you know, my husband, that night. He could have done something. They wouldn't let me near. I made him bring me as far as where he's standing now. Then they stopped me. They kept hold of me. Why did they do that? Why? Why didn't anybody understand and give her back to me, my little girl? For hours they left her lying in the dirt, taking photographs, measuring -- and even then, after all that, they wouldn't let me near her.' She came at the Marshal with a sudden burst of energy and clutched his arm. 'Nobody should be allowed to do that to anyone, do you understand? Nobody! Men are so stupid . . . They hid her from me, hid her wounds as if that way I wouldn't suffer. Where do they get these ideas about women? We're the ones who bring you into the world, nurse you in your sicknesses and lay out the dead. That's the way it's always been and that's the way it should be. How dare they steal my child from me! It was for me to lift her head from the dirt and hold her. I needed to comb her beautiful hair and clean her poor little body. Why can't you understand what you did to me, you people?'

She pulled at his arm, her devastated face staring up at his, and he felt foolish and ashamed of thinking, as he had, that he hoped she hadn't seen her child's body. Because she was right, though he could offer her no solution to the problem.

'That evil creature ripped her apart and then she was dragged about and manhandled by other men, strangers . . . I saw them . . . I saw them from up there, I saw them turn her over . . . Oh, God help me, I knew I'd lost her. I promise you, I accepted that. If she had been taken from us, I accepted it, only I begged them please, please, let me hold her! Let me wash and comfort her poor young limbs, let me say goodbye. Let her mother's hands be the last to touch her as they were the first, but they took her away from me. They took her away and left her in a fridge. It's not natural and it's not right – and what good did it do? They never found him. He went on killing and I'm condemned to come here every Saturday night for the rest of my life. I can't mourn for her because I was never allowed to do what had to be done. I can't let go because she still needs me, her poor abused body needs me. I want to hold her! I want to hold her just once and heal all that hurt!'

Her grip on the Marshal's arm loosened and she turned back to touch the little porcelain photograph of her daughter attached to the marble cross beside that of her lover. It was the picture the Marshal had seen in the sitting room.

'He'd prefer me to go to the cemetery with bunches of chrysanthemums, or go to church and pray, but I won't go near, I'll never set foot in there again. The last time was the funeral and I knelt there looking at the statue of the Virgin with the dead Christ and I couldn't stand it. Whatever she went through they gave him back to her and she could hold him. She wasn't condemned to climb Calvary over and over because she hadn't done a mother's duty. I don't believe there's a man on this earth who's capable of understanding that. Look at him up there. He doesn't understand, he thinks I'm losing my mind. Well, we've neither of us long to live because we've nothing left to live for. We'll soon be gone and there'll be an end of it.'

'It's getting dark,' the Marshal reminded her gently. 'I think you should come home.'

Only then did she notice that he had come down for her instead of her husband. 'Why are you here?'

'I need to show you some bits of jewellery we found, in case you think they might have come from your – from Sara's handbag.'

'Show me, then. You needn't worry. I won't get hysterical or anything of that sort.'

'No, no . . . It's just that you can't see so well here by now. Perhaps back at the house . . .'

But out from the big pocket of her coat she pulled a torch. She must have had her way about staying down here in the dark more than once, then. She shone it on the package of coloured bracelets.

'Those are not my Sara's. Is there anything else?'

'No, nothing else.'

In that case, will you give me your arm up to the road? My legs seem to swell up a lot these days and I've trouble getting my breath.'

He gave her his arm and when they reached the top of the slope her husband supported her on the other side until they reached home.

'I won't come in,' the Marshal said. 'There's no need to disturb you any further.'

The mother went in without a word when her husband opened up for her. Holding the banister with both hands, she began to climb the stairs slowly, towards the empty flat.

The father watched her go and then turned. 'I'd best follow her. She has trouble with the stairs. I thought we'd be a comfort to one another, but . . . I miss her . . .'

'Yes.' The Marshal understood that he wasn't referring to his dead daughter. The door closed and he turned away.

'*We're wasting our time. What's the point? Who needs it?*'

Well, now he had his answer. It might help them. It might not. It was all he had to offer.

In silence he got back in his car. In silence they took the road back to Florence. They were almost there when the Marshal was roused from his private thoughts by the driver.

'Shall I go straight there?'

'What? Where?'

'You didn't hear?'

'No . . .' He had been aware of the radio communication without paying attention to what was said. I'm sorry, I was miles away. What is it?'

'Captain Maestrangelo wants to see you. I was saying do you want me to drive straight there or do you want to go to Pitti first?'

'Pitti.' Not that putting it off for half an hour would help. 'Did he say it was urgent – ? Oh, yes . . .' It had slipped his mind. He'd said he'd go and explain about the anonymous letter. Well, that wasn't so much urgent as too late, and he'd had enough for today. In that case putting it off would help. You can have enough upset wished on you for one day without going looking for more. He felt a real need to be by himself, though goodness knows, he thought ruefully, I haven't much choice there. He'd go over to see the Captain tomorrow. 'Sufficient unto the day is the evil . . .'

But the day wasn't over, not by a long chalk. As they drove in under the archway, his driver peered forward and said, 'That's a police car. What's it doing here?'

The Marshal's stomach lurched as a bulky figure got out of the strange car and came forward. They pulled up and the young driver leaped from his seat and went round to let the Marshal out. He was too late. The waiting figure had moved heavily forward and opened the car door. Even in the darkness the Marshal had recognized his stance. It was Di Maira.

'Guarnaccia? Can I have a word?'

They faced each other across the desk in the little office, but the Marshal, avoiding the other man's gaze, stared at the map of his quarter on the opposite wall, waiting for whatever was going to befall him next. Whatever it might be he knew in advance that he was too tired and overwrought to deal with it. Whatever wave hit him now would carry him away without so much as a word of protest. Presumably the worst thing that could happen would be a transfer to some godforsaken place and he'd just have to put up with it. Nobody, after all, had obliged him to make the enquiries he had made. Ferrini had had the good sense to pack it in before it was too late, and he hadn't. Of course, it would be Teresa and, even more, the boys who would suffer: changing schools, losing their friends, another upheaval when they'd just settled down. How could he have let himself in for this? How could he have barged ahead so selfishly, never thinking of his family? It was unforgivable.

'I'd rather spend time with my family . . .'

Ferrini was right. Anybody in their right mind would feel the same.

'I'm not like you. When you get your teeth into something . . .'

Why didn't the blasted man speak? Let's get it over with. I've made a fool of myself and I'll take what's coming to me. Just get on with it.

But Di Maira didn't get on with it. He looked far from happy, when the Marshal finally dragged his gaze from the map to meet the other's. The steely eyes glanced off those of the Marshal uncertainly. It was incredible. The man was waiting for help. Well, by this time, what did it matter? The Marshal made his last effort of the day.

'I'm not surprised to see you,' he offered. 'I noticed right from the start that you were watching me.'

'You did?' The big man leant forward, elbows on his knees, hands dangling, and scanned the Marshal's face doubtfully. 'Well, I wasn't sure if I was right. If I wasn't, just say so and send me packing. There's no excuse for getting you into trouble unnecessarily. It's the sort of thing . . . Well, it happened to me once and it's not the sort of thing I'd wish on anybody. I suppose what started the confusion was that rumour going round at the beginning that the carabinieri put on this case were going to be spare wheels that nobody needed elsewhere. But then Esposito remembered that transsexual case and we began to have doubts right away about you and Ferrini. Then, just the other day, Simonetti recalled some case you were on. It seems you messed things up for him. He doesn't much care for that sort of initiative.'

'I suppose not. Well, even so, the rumour you heard was true.'

'The spare-part story? That's not the way it's being told now. Anyway, if I haven't spoken to you before, it was because nobody was too sure where you stood.'

'And now you are. So what are you going to do next?'

'I'll tell you straight. Publicly, I can't do anything.'

Did that mean he wouldn't be transferred? Was that what he would consider public? Could it be he'd get away with a reprimand and being taken off the case? If that were all there was nothing he would like better.

'I got into bad trouble once. You know the sort of thing – I won't go into details. Stuck my neck out, the way you do when you're young and don't think. Anyway, some very important people in this town were after my hide and they'd have got it. He stood by me, saved my skin. So you see, I can't work against him. All I can do is offer you anything you might need. I worked on this case in the days when it was a serious investigation. Anything you need to find out you can find out from me. That's as much as I can do. He made a point of having me on the squad. You can imagine how it would have looked if nobody at all from the Romola days was with him. I couldn't say no, but I've no liking for what's going on. No liking at all. Anyway, there you are. My cards are on the table.'

The Marshal, too stunned to speak, stared at him with bulging eyes. Yet even in his astonishment one thing rang false. 'He stood by you . . . ? Simonetti?'

'Good God, no. The Chief Proc. Simonetti . . .' The way he spoke the name left no room for further comment. 'You people don't like the Chief, I know, and it's pretty much reciprocal. Even so, however difficult a character he may be, however much of a steamroller in his tactics, in my case he showed generosity and courage without gaining anything in return.'

The Marshal didn't answer. Having got over his first shock he was able to register both that the Chief was being paid back with interest now by at least appearing to have this much-respected investigator on his side, and also that he would be foolish to say so.

'How far have you got?' Di Maira asked.

'I've read Romola's acquittal.'

'Then you know it's Vargius, Silvano.'

'I . . . It was certainly him in '68. I haven't got a lot further than that . . .'

'It's him, it's him.'

Again, the Marshal kept his counsel. The last thing he should do now was alienate this man who, whatever his opinions, must have so much information that he needed.

'What a brute. I've come across some characters in my time, but Silvano, my God . . . We followed him, you know. Followed him for months in '85 but he was as cunning as a fox. He knew, of course, that was the thing.

His favourite trick was to slow to almost a stop approaching traffic lights on green, getting everybody in a rage behind him. Then the minute they turned red he'd shoot across the junction and we'd lost him. Same with his phone. We had a tap on it for weeks before he found out and if you heard the conversations. Sex, never anything but sex, and always men – though for some reason he insisted on having women performing on the side for him. I don't profess to understand that. Anyway, once he'd cottoned on that we were listening in he'd play every trick in the book on us, especially dialling some non-answering number to set our machine going and then leaving his phone off the hook till our bobbin ran out. We tore his house apart, too, after two of the murders, but we never found anything except that rag and that was whipped away from Romola pretty smartly. I tell you, in all my career I've never known a villain who had Silvano's luck.'

'From what you say it wasn't entirely luck.'

'No, he was a clever bastard, too, but he had luck all right. Getting away with the murder of his first wife, for a start, not only once but twice. I've brought you what I could on that.' He pulled a batch of papers from his raincoat pocket. They were rolled up and secured with a rubber band.

'The full report's in the archives but . . .'

'No, I don't want to involve anyone. I'll be glad to see anything you've got.'

'I didn't bring the search reports since we found

nothing useful – though I can tell you there was a moment – it was the gun we were after, of course, but the morning after a murder you can imagine that we might have found the bits he took away, you know what I mean. We were searching his workshop opposite the house and one of your men noticed an old fridge in the corner, not plugged in, just being used as a store cupboard. He opened it and, Jesus, a damn great cloud of iridescent flies flew out at him. We thought this is it. It wasn't, though. They were feeding on meat all right, but it was animal meat. Then we found a plastic bag full of their larvae. He was breeding them for fishing. I don't know whether we were more disappointed or relieved. We should have known better than to have any hopes of finding anything. He was always one step ahead of us.'

'Except with the rag. Funny . . .'

'I know. Still, water under the bridge. We'll never find out the truth about that. I ought to be off – unless there's anything else I can tell you.'

'There is. This Suspect. Oh, I suppose it's irrelevant now but I'd just like to understand. Why him?' Hadn't they both been in the same boat, the Suspect and the Marshal?

'I'm not the one you want! Why me?'

Di Maira shrugged. 'I'm not privy to all their little secrets. Esposito was in on it, but he'll say nothing. I only know they needed somebody with a previous conviction for murder, or GBH at least and he had to be a Peeping Tom. Once they'd discounted the real culprit, who'd left

398

the country, anyway, there wouldn't have been much of a choice. I'm only guessing here but you can be sure they'd pick somebody poor and helpless who couldn't afford a fleet of fancy lawyers. The real piece of luck, though, was the daughter. Everybody in the village knew he was having it off with her and that she wasn't right in the head. All they had to do was convince her to sign a report and they were ready to announce him as the Monster. Joe Public won't make the connection, if you ask me. Incest's too tricky a subject.'

'It can't have been easy, though.'

'I don't see why. It was probably the first thing that came to light when they started checking him.'

'No, no . . . I mean getting her to sign. Convincing her to go into court. She seemed so terrified, so ashamed.'

'She was. Terrified and ashamed. It was a dirty trick – even Esposito, who wrote the report they made her sign, thought it was a bit much. They hauled the girl into Police Headquarters, asked her if it was true what they'd heard about her father touching her and so on and then said sign here. If she'd refused they could have accused her of calumny. So whether she wanted to or not . . .'

'That's what I thought.' The Marshal thought this over, remembered the videos and added, 'She didn't object to her father's buying her a flat.'

'No. Even so, it's about the only intelligent move Simonetti's made, because nobody, not even his lawyer, will dare touch the subject, and you mark my words, he'll be done for the Monster's crimes because of it. Everybody and his dog will know Simonetti's case against him doesn't hold water but nobody will defend him because of this incest business. That's what settled their choice and he'll be tried for that again because it's all they've really got. Oh, by the way, if you do want those search reports I mentioned you can have them, you know. I'm not keeping anything back. I just thought –'

'No, no . . . If you found nothing, there's no need. But maybe . . . I was wondering if these three . . .' How to put it? 'If these three had anything to contribute, or even if you thought they might be in any way involved . . .'

Di Maira frowned at the three names on the paper the Marshal pushed across the desk.

'Ha, yes, well, they've all given us a hand in one way or another, but I imagine anything they've told us will be in Romola's acquittal.'

'You haven't read it yourself?'

'No, of course not. I was part of it, if you like. Who reads those things? Last year's weather forecast, a bureaucratic formality.'

'I know . . . normally. Well, all three are mentioned here and there but I'm not too clear . . . This Salvatore Angius, for instance?'

'One of Silvano's boyfriends, passed him on later to Flavio but stayed in contact with him. He was generally regarded as an adopted son of Silvano's, and they were related – he came here from Sardinia when he was orphaned as a kid. Worked a bit as a shepherd boy and I reckon was pretty well starving as well as homeless when

Silvano picked him up – he was his alibi in '68, that must have been in the report.'

'Yes, it was. There was also a mention of his living near the Rossini house and I did wonder whether he might actually have been at the scene of the crime.'

'If he was, we'll never prove it now. He has a record, though, so if you want to know more you can check him out. He was presumably disillusioned with Silvano in the end because he withdrew his alibi when we went over it all in the eighties.'

'He collaborated against Silvano?'

'Up to a point. Then he stuck. If I remember rightly we did him for reticence somewhere along the way. Searched his house, too, just in case he'd got hold of the famous pistol but we didn't find it. If you're thinking of any of these as a suspect I might as well tell you we've checked them all.'

'I'm sure you would have. No, I just like to know all about the people involved . . . For instance, are they reliable as far as their evidence goes – I mean, what sort of life do they lead – drugs, prostitutes?'

'Drugs all three, of course – not addicts, though, the type that takes anything that's available to get high, you know the sort of thing. Prostitutes – same thing, they all pick up what's available – Angius, though, I'm not sure about. Couldn't make out whether he really was homosexual or just dragged into it by Silvano. If he really was, well – you know the way it goes with that sort. They manage to be more or less kept until a certain age and then they wake up one morning and zak! It's over, and they're having to pay for it. Nicolino, now, he really was Silvano's son, as far as can be made out. You knew that?'

'Yes. But did they keep in touch?'

'Couldn't say. I can't imagine the kid would want much to do with his mother's murderer, would you? Mind you, with that band you never know. I had the feeling he was frightened of Silvano, myself, as well he might be. A castrator of sons, if there ever was one.'

'That's something . . .' The Marshal paused, turning this idea over.

'What?'

'It's just that . . . it's something they tend to say about mothers.'

'You're right. It is. But apart from the fact that the poor sod didn't have a mother for long enough, Silvano wanted all the sex that was going for himself, men and women. He didn't want any competition. Nicolino never mentions him any more and I'm convinced it's fear. He saw Silvano that night, or sensed him, standing in the reeds.'

'Yes, I remember that.'

'You do? Well, *he* doesn't, not any more, or so he says. We took him back there, you know, in the eighties. I suppose he'd have been about twenty. It was a warm day and we were standing right there where it happened, waiting to hear what he'd have to say, dying to give him a prod but not daring to.

'He stood there a long time, then he shook his head.

'"I don't know . . . it's all gone . . ."'

'He was staring straight ahead in the direction of the Pistoia road. We'd no way of knowing whether he really didn't remember or whether he'd decided not to talk. He's pretty backward, you know, and they're the hardest type to judge. Just then, a bit of a breeze got up and the reeds moved. They were dry and they made a rustling noise.

'"I touched her hand."'

'It was as if he'd been switched on. I thought right away it was the reeds and I was right. He said as much afterwards.

'"I touched her hand and it fell down in between the two seats. The back window was open and I climbed out and started running. I was screaming and screaming and then there was a voice in the reeds . . . Somebody . . . Then we were going away and they kept telling me: Remember to say your dad's ill in bed. Remember . . . I don't know where they left me. I only remember running across the main road because I was so glad to see the big light."*

'That's as much as he was able to tell us, but I think he was doing his best to help, and God knows he'd had enough of it when he was a kid. Nobody wanted him, you know, in the family, any more than they wanted Sergio when he was released from prison. I reckon what they really didn't want was any more trouble with Silvano. They knew the kid was his, and they didn't want the truth about the real relationship between Sergio and Silvano coming out. So Nicolino grew up a mess, unwanted, and Sergio died in the ex-prisoners' home.'

'*He what?*'

'Oh yes, he's dead. You'll hear nothing about it until our case is further along. Nobody wants the Vargius story resurrecting just now. What do you expect? Who's this third one, then? Ah, Amelio. He was more of a help, but then he knew more. And he told us about the orgies going on in that flat when he was a kid – the ex-wife confirms it all, too. She'd wake up in the night and find two men in bed with her, Silvano plus his latest boyfriend. Then it got to Silvano plus boyfriend plus boyfriend's wife, and if she protested he'd beat the living daylights out of her. The kid tried to defend her a time or two but all that meant was that he got the same treatment.'

'Why didn't she leave him?' The Marshal was always a bit dubious about this sort of story from women who'd tolerated the same treatment for years.

'She tried. Went back to Sardinia to her parents in '74, but there was nothing but poverty and unemployment and they packed her back off to her husband. You made your bed, you lie on it, style of thing. She did leave him for good in the end in 1980, though she moved back into the flat when he was arrested for his first wife's murder. Our theory is that it was being abandoned by her that set him off in '74 and then again in the eighties. Not to mention the son leaving him, too, in '75. He went to live with Flavio and that didn't go down well at all. The brothers fought like cat and dog about that, and I suppose that's why the kid got away altogether then and went up north to his own mother's sister for a few years. A shame, really, since his stepmother had tried to be a mother to him, but life with Silvano must have been an inferno.' Di Maira pushed the sheet of paper back across the desk. 'By God, I wish I could have done him for it. We didn't even manage to send him down for doing in his first wife. Not that there wasn't evidence, witnesses too, even after twenty-seven years. The trouble was there'd been no autopsy. No photographs, either. It had been set up to look like suicide and nobody, *nobody* lifted a finger to show that it wasn't.'

'You mean people knew?'

'Everybody knew. We're sure, for a start, that the village Marshal knew. He was long dead when we started investigating the matter but the station records show that he had Silvano in and measured his thumbprint against the bruise on his wife's neck. He knew, all right, but he didn't stick to it and we don't know why.'

'Could he have been afraid?'

Di Maira shrugged. 'I suppose he might have been. The Vargius family was big and they were a vicious crew. Then, that village, it's the arsehole end of the world. A Marshal in a place like that would be very much on his own. A man could meet with a nasty accident in a place like that long before any help could arrive. Anyway, we'll never know now. There was one of his carabinieri, too, he's still alive, or so he was when we went there in the eighties. He was the only one who actually worked on the case, if you can call it a case when nothing much was done, with the Marshal. Blasted man actually found the body and couldn't tell us a thing. Turned tail and ran for the Marshal – not that he wasn't right to do that, but he didn't look at anything so that with the Marshal dead – there's an HSA report, of course, as there has to be in any case of sudden death, but the local doctor took one look at the gas canister standing by the bed with the tube leading to the young woman's mouth and signed a death certificate without a murmur, which meant the Marshal could only report suicide.'

'Yet people were sure it wasn't?'

'That gas canister was empty. Not one of the people who entered the room – and the neighbours were in there within minutes – the young carabiniere, the Marshal, the young woman's family, had any problem with gas or even remembered a smell of gas or thought to open a window. What's more, the baby was standing up in its cot screaming the place down. It would have been dead long before the mother if the canister had been full. And if that weren't enough, the mother had knocked at the house next door twice that evening to ask them to warm the baby's milk because she'd run out of gas, once at about six-thirty and again at ten. She was found dead at eleven-thirty.'

'By this young carabiniere, you say.'

'By Silvano, *he* says. The neighbours heard him hammering at his own door and screaming. Then he hammered at their door and when they opened up he said his wife had a man in the house and wouldn't let him in. He made a great show of breaking the door down in their presence.'

'Had he an alibi for the time immediately before?'

'The usual Silvano-style alibi. He'd been seen in the bar and the billiard hall, and every other place in the village he frequented regularly, in the company of his brother-in-law, Giuseppe. The truth is that nobody actually saw the pair of them after about ten-thirty so they had all the time in the world to do the job, but with the brother-in-law backing him up and saying they stayed out together until two minutes before Silvano started hammering at his own door . . . Well, you know enough about Silvano, if you've read the Romola report, to realize that the wife and kid were for show and the real relationship was between Silvano and the brother, Giuseppe. *That* never got out in the village so his alibi, fishy though it was, was never broken.'

'But . . . the dead woman's family?'

'Yes. The family. She was only nineteen, you know. Margherita, her name was. I'm sure her mother knew exactly what had happened but she never said a word. I suppose, from her point of view, she'd lost her daughter and nothing could bring her back. If the truth had come out she'd have lost her son, too. Plus, like everyone else, she was scared of Silvano. Then, the shame if the homosexual story came out. They'd have had to move away and they had land there. No, no, nothing would have induced her to talk then and nothing would induce her to talk even in the eighties when the famous pistol – which, incidentally, belonged to her brother and disappeared when Silvano left the village – had killed so

407

many people. We tapped her phone since she wouldn't open her mouth much to us. She was on the phone every day to her surviving daughter who lived up near Como – the one the kid Amelio went to when he ran away from Silvano. You've got the transcripts there. I made them myself by hand and kept my copy after I'd typed them up. I hope you can read my writing . . .'

The Marshal unrolled the sheets of paper. The writing in ballpoint had faded a little to a brownish blue.

'I think so.' But he didn't try for a moment. 'Why? If he needed the wife and child for show, why kill her? Was there another man?'

'There was, but that wasn't the reason – interestingly enough, the other man's name was Amelio. I wonder Silvano let that pass because this Amelio was her intended before she was forced into marrying Silvano. You'll find that little story amongst the stuff I've given you. Even so, although she did start seeing him again before her death he wasn't the reason. What precipitated things was that she was leaving him, not for the other man, though. She must have been sick to death of the life she was leading, half-starved and regularly beaten by that monster of a so-called husband. She'd made her decision and applied for a job as a resident maid-of-all-work in an orphanage where they would let her take her kid. She'd bought a long-distance bus ticket. She was leaving him the next day.

'Of course, now there's nobody who can tell us about it but there's every reason to think he'd been forcing her to join in his sexual acrobatics with her brother and when she wanted out he bumped her off. We get the same set-up in '68 when Belinda Muscas wanted out of the Belinda-Sergio-Silvano triangle and got the same punishment. He probably even bragged about it when he was setting up the '68 job. It was Sergio, after all, who told us: "He murdered his wife in Sardinia and the kid was saved that time, too." Who else would have told him except Silvano himself? Then in '74 his new wife tries to leave him and he turns murderous again. In '80 she really does leave him and all hell's let loose. See what I mean, now?'

The Marshal couldn't help wondering why, if he'd had no scruples about killing both the first wife and Belinda for daring to leave him, he didn't do the same to his second wife rather than going out to kill fourteen strangers with a pistol that was bound to leave a trail back to him. He was wise enough not to say so but he must have looked unconvinced.

'You don't follow?'

'Oh yes . . . I – perhaps I'm just amazed at how simply he got away with it all. To be that simple, you've got to be clever, I think.'

'Well, remember, he was always hiding one thing: his homosexuality. Without knowing that you'd never suspect him.'

'That's true . . .'

'You'll find a name and address and phone number amongst my notes. Margherita's younger sister, the one who lives near Como now. Talk to her. She'll tell you what Silvano is. She was only twelve when Margherita was murdered but if you aren't convinced that Silvano's the Monster after you've talked to her . . .' He got up and the Marshal rose to follow him.

'There's another thing.' Di Maira stopped on the threshold and turned. 'There was a rumour going about – and the papers, of course, made the most of it – that the real Monster would never be revealed because he was some Florentine bigwig. I don't know if you remember that?'

The Marshal thought for a bit. 'Was that about the time they were saying he might be an eminent surgeon and so on?'

'That's it. Two separate rumours rolled into one. They came from two separate sources, one of which matters, the other doesn't. The surgeon thing came out of an autopsy report saying the excisions were so precise, etc., but so is a butcher precise when he joints chicken – all rubbish, in my opinion. I saw the bodies and I can tell you that any Sardinian who'd ever skinned a dead lamb . . . You know what I mean?'

'Yes, yes, I do . . .'

'Well, be that as it may, the other story, the Florentine VIP one, does matter so don't get your fingers burnt.'

'But if you think it's Silvano?'

'It is Silvano. That rumour – and I don't know how it got into circulation – was distorted. We were checking out the Peeping Tom brigade at the time and, I can tell you, we were all taken aback by what we found out. In the first place because it wasn't a hobby we were dealing with but a business. Control of each section of countryside around Florence was divided between the various bands. Permission to watch had to be asked for and paid for. On top of that there were audio and video tapes made of unsuspecting couples. Now, a business has clients. Do you follow me? That's where your Florentine VIPs came into the story and, as you might expect, that information was classified. Something leaked, as something always does, and that's what started the rumour of the Monster being some big shot whose name would never be revealed, especially when Sassetti was arrested and wouldn't talk. The Scandicci car was under his control and he must have accompanied a client there that night. It's rubbish as far as it goes, but even so, keep well away from that area of enquiry. You would fall foul of some very powerful people, all of them masons, you know what I mean? And it's not worth it. Silvano was a loner and nothing to do with those gangs.'

'Yes . . . unless they came across each other . . .'

'How d'you mean?'

'The gangs were well organized and covered every country area outside Florence, you said?'

Di Maira's face changed. 'How do you mean? We checked them all, you know. If they had come across him we'd have got wind of it.'

'Unless they had a good reason for keeping the news to themselves.'

'Like what?'

'Like profit. They were, as you said, in business.'

'Ah, you mean blackmail. There was a lot of that going on, but no. Silvano hadn't money, not their sort of money.'

'No. But those VIP clients had. Didn't they buy films, tapes and so on?'

'Christ Almighty! You're not serious? You are. You could be right, at that! They were after him to film him. Do you know what a piece of film like that would fetch in certain circles?'

'I hate to think.'

'Well, the price of your snuff films going round this city now would be nothing compared to it!'

'Well, well . . . we might as well forget it. In fact, from what you say, we'd *better* forget it. But was that what Nenci wanted twenty per cent of? Had he been left out of some deal?'

'You're right. It's a separate issue and you'd need a lot of power and protection behind you to tackle it. You stick to Silvano. Just get that bastard for me, will you? You'll be doing us all a favour.'

Sixteen

TO THE TRIBUNAL OF FLORENCE
-Instructing Judge ROMOLA-

TO THE PUBLIC PROSECUTOR OF FLORENCE
-Dr SIMONETTI-

<u>Report on the death, filed as suicide, of Margherita VARGIUS, née MELIS in 1960 in the province of Sardinia presently being investigated in connection with the double homicides committed in the province of Florence between 1968 and 1985.</u>

1. The marriage between MARGHERITA MELIS and SILVANO VARGIUS took place in 1958. The marriage was arranged on behalf of Silvano by

GIUSEPPE MELIS, Margherita's brother, when she was eighteen and Silvano was twenty-three years old. A homosexual relationship had already existed for a number of years between Silvano and Giuseppe. Margherita at this time had a fiancé, Amelio Cangio, whom she intended to marry. Cangio was threatened and separated from his sister by Giuseppe whilst Silvano was allowed by him to frequent the house in the absence of his parents and to constrain Margherita to enter into sexual relations with him until such time as she became pregnant and was obliged to marry him. The resulting child was born in February 1959 and named Amelio.

2. During the following year Amelio Cangio returned to the village and resumed his relationship with Margherita Vargius, who described to him the severe physical ill-treatment she was suffering at the hands of Silvano and declared her intention of leaving him as soon as she could find a means of survival.

3. After requesting help from her obstetrician, Margherita found a residential job as a cleaner in an orphanage. A letter was found in her possession confirming she was expected, with her child, at the orphanage the day following her death.

4. Silvano, aware of his wife's relationship with Cangio, went to considerable lengths to inform the entire

village of Margherita's betrayal, including reporting her immoral behaviour to the local Marshal of the carabinieri.

5. On the evening of her death Silvano and Giuseppe went out –

Lorenzini buzzed the Marshal on the internal phone.

'That call you asked for: I have Ida Melis on the line.'

'Put her through.'

He put the papers to one side and picked up the other receiver.

'Signora.'

'Has something else happened? He hasn't – ?'

'No, no, signora. Nothing's happened. I just wanted a word with you. It was Sergeant Di Maira who gave me your name. Perhaps you remember him?'

'Yes, I do.' She sounded relieved. 'It's about Silvano, then.'

'Yes, signora. He suggested I talk to you about the death of your sister Margherita. I hope it's not too upsetting for you to talk about.'

'Upsetting? I haven't had a day's peace of mind or an uninterrupted night's sleep since then. I left Sardinia as soon as I was able to and I've never set foot there since, except for the trial in '88, but even so . . . That man –'

She had a great deal to say about 'that man'. As she talked, the Marshal tried to imagine what she looked like. Twelve, she'd been in 1960 when Margherita was murdered, so she'd be forty or so. She sounded older. Perhaps because she sounded bitter.

'It wouldn't be until eleven, eleven-fifteen.'

'I'm sorry . . . ?' He'd been doing his usual trick of listening to her voice instead of what she was saying. 'Can you hold on and I'll get my diary? Yes, so what date?'

'The day after tomorrow. I don't know the date without getting out the letter from the clinic. The migraine clinic, do you know it?'

'No, I don't think I do.'

'Well, it's in Careggi, near all the other hospitals, so I can easily come in to Florence on the bus afterwards. I go there once a month and I've Silvano to thank for that, too. I'd never had a problem before that night but I've had it ever since. Do you want me to come to your office?'

'No, I – no. I'll find the clinic. I'll be there before eleven. You'll see a car waiting for you when you come out.'

'A police car? Or are you with the carabinieri?'

'Carabinieri. But I'll come in my own car. If you'll just stand still a moment as you come out I'll find you. Thank you for talking to me.' He hung up.

6. The body of Margherita Vargius was found in the bedroom. The kitchen gas canister, with its tube still attached and the tap open, was standing by the bed. The tube had been placed on the pillow. Witnesses disagree as to whether the body was on the bed or on

the floor beside it. The body was naked except for a pair of knickers. There was a patch of whitish liquid on the stomach, blood between the legs, a bruise in the shape of a thumbprint on the left side of the throat and numerous scratches on the face. The baby was standing in its cot, screaming.

Silvano. The Marshal pondered the problem of Silvano for some time, sitting alone in his office, staring, as always, at the map on the opposite wall without seeing it.

Di Maira was a good investigator, a much-respected one, and rightly so. Not only that but he had seen all these people face to face, talked to them.

'It's him. It's him.'

He was a murderer, he had sexual perversions – a photographic file at the back of the report he'd been reading showed a hair-raising collection of sex aids and pornographic comics. A note signed by Di Maira himself stated that the subject was totally deaf in his right ear and should always be interrogated from the left and that his deafness was a result of his being viciously beaten around the head by his father at the age of ten.

Silvano . . .

There was a photocopy amongst Di Maira's papers of a clinical report dated April 1981, made out in the psychiatric ward of a Florence hospital.

Patient is deeply anxious and suffering from acute depression. In answer to questions he states that he

417

has no particular financial or work problems at present and that, though recently separated from his wife, he doesn't consider this the cause of his problem. He is not abulic – on the contrary, he claims to be always full of plans and ideas for the small firm he runs. Asked if he has other causes for worry he says: 'The real problem is the boy.' He is unwilling to enlarge on that remark. Not, in general, very communicative, though here by his own request.

Patient left the hospital after 10 days.

There was a doctor's signature and the date. Nothing more.

According to the books sitting there on his desk, Silvano was too old, too dominant, too successful at getting what he wanted. But what did the Marshal know that he could seriously pit generalized information from these foreign books against the first-hand experience of a man like Di Maira?

What, if it came to that, did any of them know about this type of crime, including Di Maira? The day's papers were on his desk, too, with all the latest news about the Suspect. Wasn't it just the same story? A murderer, a pervert . . . It's him, it's him!

Why shouldn't Silvano just have murdered his second wife the way he did his first and then Belinda? He was getting older, that was why. His reactions became less, not more, violent . . .

If only Ferrini . . .

The phone rang.

'Salvatore, old thing! All right, are you?'

'Ferrini!'

'Were you expecting somebody else?'

'I – no. No!'

'Listen, I've got hold of a little bit of treasure. I can't get away tonight, we've got people to supper – come along if you want, but we won't be able to talk, you know what I mean.'

'Yes, but in any case I'm a bit tired . . .'

'Tomorrow I can't . . . the night after, then. I'll bring you this stuff over – I tried to find you yesterday but your man there said you were over here with the Captain and when I went to look you'd vanished.'

'Yes . . . I didn't wait to see him in the end . . .'

'You sound peculiar. What's up?'

'Nothing, I just – well, I thought from what you said the other day that you didn't want to be bothered with this business any more, that's all.'

'Come on, Guarnaccia, I was just pissed off. Doesn't that ever happen to you?'

'I suppose so . . .'

'You do take things tragically.'

'That's what Teresa's always saying.'

'Well, if she'd been here she'd have said it this time, too. Is she not back yet?'

'No, not yet.'

'That's what's wrong with you, then. Get a decent meal

down you and cheer yourself up! I'll tell you what, when we get together I'll take you to this place of a friend of mine – it's a bit far out in the country but it's worth it and we needn't linger . . .'

Ferrini chatted on for a good quarter of an hour and the Marshal intoned the responses contentedly. Afterwards, he felt so much better that he decided to get through at least some of the paperwork Lorenzini had left for his signature and to look through the post and the newspapers. Lorenzini himself put his head round the door at eight o'clock.

'I'm off. Shall I switch the phone through or will you do it?'

Calls coming through after the station closed were automatically transferred to the emergency number at Headquarters.

'Do it now – I'm practically finished here . . .'

There was a handwritten letter from Marco which he didn't open but propped against the phone to remind himself to call him sometime tomorrow. The next letter he picked up was a long envelope with a number of typewritten sheets in it and a hurried note attached by a paper clip.

Sorry to be so long about it – desperately busy on this case (and not sorry to be off the other). This comes from a research centre and has more to do with prevention than detection but might help. You really need the whole FBI profile on your man but

420

no hope of that, I suppose. Good luck. (Keep the books for now.)

It was from Bacci. He hadn't forgotten, then. The Marshal unfolded the typewritten sheets.

SYMPTOMS OF SUBJECTS WHO SHOULD BE CONSIDERED HIGH-RISK POSSIBLE PERPETRATORS IN THE EPISODIC AGGRESSION CATEGORY.

The first contact may come either through an attempted or successful arrest, whether for a major or minor offence or through the subject's seeking psychiatric help. In both cases he may attempt to warn the authorities overtly of an urge to kill. Such warnings should always be taken seriously and the subject examined with reference to the following:

1. Has the person already committed two or more crimes of violence, particularly rapes or assault?

2. Does the person drink to excess? Is he a drug abuser? Chronic substance abuse can trigger innate violence and may also cause mental blackouts which cause the person to forget having committed acts of violence.

3. Manic depressive symptoms. Does the subject suffer from violent swings of mood which cannot be accounted for by outside provocation?

4. Insatiable sex drive. There is nothing abnormal or

unhealthy about a large sexual appetite. What is dangerous is an insatiable appetite which cannot be satisfied with sex alone but requires violence, even torture, to stimulate orgasm.

5. An excessive interest in blood, horror and death, often fed by films and magazines, together with other symptoms, can be a sign of impending danger.

6. Is the person cold and indifferent to the suffering of others? Such indifference caused by a lack of affectionate contact during infancy, is very dangerous.

7. Has the person been convicted of arson or been known to have amused himself by setting fire to things as a child?

8. Is the person gathering an arsenal of weapons? This may be an unconscious preparation for the turning of fantasy into fact.

The Marshal sighed and gave it up. Bacci was right. It was far too general. One minute he thought he was reading about Silvano, the next it was a portrait of the Suspect. And as far as the three younger men he suspected were concerned, what was the use when he had never seen them or talked to them? The information just wasn't available. What was he supposed to do? Track down Salvatore Angius and ring him up to ask him what films he enjoyed?

In any case, this was all psychiatrists' stuff, it wasn't police work. Disheartened, he decided to call it a day and take Ferrini's advice. He was tired and hungry. He gathered up the newspapers, thinking he could glance through them after a cheering bowl of pasta, switched off the office light and locked up.

'Blast!' he muttered as he felt for the key of his own door. He could hear the television going so he must have left it on at lunch time, which showed how tired . . .

But the lights were on and the supper was cooking and the boys were skidding towards him helter-skelter through the tiled hall, shouting. 'Dad! Da-a-a-ad! We're home!'

They had passed an evening that was as noisy as it was happy. The washing machine went on, then the television, then Toto's tape player that he'd got for Christmas. Teresa bustled from room to room, cooking, unpacking, reorganizing, whilst the boys dashed about creating chaos out of her order. The Marshal wandered around happy and aimless, not wanting to let any of them out of his sight for a second. He realized he had forgotten it was the Epiphany today, only remembering when Giovanni got in a row with his mother for starting to eat a huge lump of sugar coal from his stocking before supper. The Marshal was told to remove it from him and he stared at his plump son with his huge eyes which he thought were threatening.

'Do you want a bit?' Giovanni had whispered, misinterpreting the pop-eyed stare. And he'd eaten some.

It was after eleven when it quietened down. The house was warm and tidy and the lingering good smells of supper were gradually being overpowered by an open bag full of pungent oranges and lemons picked the day before down home.

'I forgot to tell you,' Teresa said, giving him a cup of camomile tea and sitting down beside him with a happy sigh. That nice boy Marco called just before you came in.'

'Why didn't he call me at the office?'

'He did but he said he got put through to the emergency service.'

'Ah. Never mind, I was going to call him tomorrow anyway.' He slid an arm around her. 'Shall we go to bed?'

'You said you had to read the papers in case there was anything about your case.'

But he didn't answer.

'Signora?' He had recognized her the minute she came out of the door, even before she paused to look around for him. She was a slight woman who looked older than his calculation of her real age. She was well wrapped up in a tweed overcoat and a brown woollen scarf.

'Marshal?' They shook hands and he opened the car door for her.

'The less you stand about in this cold wind, the better.'

'Oh, I don't mind it. The cold up north is damp . . .'

Inside the car it was really very warm, sheltered from the wind and with the strong sun beating on the glass. Despite his dark glasses, the Marshal was obliged to fish out a big white handkerchief and dry his eyes.

'Is something wrong?'

'No, no . . . it's an allergy I have. The sunlight hurts my eyes.' He was also playing for time. It occurred to him, now that she was actually here in his car, that he really didn't know where to take her. It was more than probable that Simonetti and the rest had never seen this woman. Nevertheless, his feeling of being under observation hadn't passed, even now that Di Maira had revealed himself.

He frowned as he turned the ignition, trying to think of a solution. She must have sensed his tension.

'You did say nothing had happened? You weren't deceiving me?'

'No, signora, no. I was just wondering . . . perhaps you'd like a coffee, something of that sort . . .' He signalled and pulled out.

'Well, that's very kind of you. It has been a long morning. I had a little operation, you see, six months ago. It wasn't what could seriously be called a cure, but they remove a little piece of bone behind your nose. It sometimes helps but it hasn't helped me. I had to tell them today. There's no difference that I can detect. People have no idea what a curse migraine is when it's really bad. I lose my sight, you see, even before the headache starts. It happens so suddenly I've never had the courage to drive a car. And, of course, it's difficult to keep a job.'

'Yes, it must be.'

'They're very understanding where I am now. I work in a bar very near home so I can get back quickly when it comes on and give myself an injection – even then, you see, the injections, they cost more than a hundred thousand lire each. It's no joke.' She took off her sheepskin mittens and placed them neatly on the handbag on her knee. He glanced at her thin, shiny hands, the nails cut short and straight.

'Is your husband a help to you in all this?'

'I never married.'

'I see. Then it must be even more difficult. Coping alone.'

'After what happened to my sister I decided I would never, ever, put myself at risk. It wasn't just her death, you see, it was how he treated her when she was alive. She was only nineteen when it happened. Did you know that?'

'Yes. Yes, she was very young. A tragic business.'

'Nineteen. Of course, at the time I thought of her as a grown-up, a woman. I was only twelve. But when I think of her now, whenever I see the girls of eighteen, nineteen or so, who come into the bar . . . She was practically still a child.'

'That's true.'

She fell silent for a while as they drove towards the centre and slowed down behind a queue of cars. Her coat smelled of mothballs and there was a faint whiff of mint on her breath each time she turned to talk to him. He noticed that she didn't say, 'I've already told the others everything I know,' the way most people did in these circumstances. He took the tree-lined avenue up to

Piazzale Michelangelo. There were always tourists up there whatever the season. They could mingle with them and have coffee in one of the bars.'

'Oh . . . !'

What was the matter with her? He parked near the balustrade and then turned to look at her.

'You've never been up here before?'

'No! It's so beautiful! The river's quite green, isn't it, and all the red tiles and the marble . . . You'd never imagine! I just have to catch my train, you see, when I leave the hospital clinic so I've never – Well!'

'Shall we go and have that coffee?'

'Oh, I'd really prefer to just sit here, I think. Do you mind? I spend my days stuck in a bar.'

'Of course, I hadn't thought.'

'It's so nice and warm in here with the sunshine. Look, that's the cathedral – and what's that great place over there on the right?'

'That will be Santa Croce. Perhaps, on your next visit to the clinic, you should think of staying on for a day.'

He was pretty sure that this woman had never done anything purely for pleasure in her life. She'd been dragging her anxiety and grief around with her ever since that night. It seemed like an act of cruelty to remind her of it now and he waited a moment or so as she gazed down at the city, hoping as he did so that she wouldn't ask him to name some building that he didn't know or didn't recognize from up here.

In the end, she was the one who came back to the business in hand.

'I'm so sorry, you didn't come to meet me so as to look at the view. I don't know what you must think of me.'

'No, no, signora. Don't worry.'

'But my train's at one. You'd better start asking your questions.'

He couldn't explain that it wasn't that simple. He didn't especially want to ask questions, since the facts were all in the report he'd read. What he wanted was contact. He hadn't been at the scene of the crime, that was the trouble. That was the one moment when you understood everything. You could smell the people who'd been there, follow their movements by everything they'd touched, feel the atmosphere they'd left behind. There was nothing of that in the report, and the only contact with it was this woman who'd dragged the weight of it through her life.

'You still hate him, I imagine.'

'Silvano? Yes, I still hate him. It's a hatred that gets deeper and blacker with every day that passes. If they'd convicted him in '88, I'd have felt better. They dug up Margherita's body, you know that, I suppose. But still it did no good. It had been almost thirty years.'

'It must have been upsetting for you, the exhumation.'

'It was upsetting for me that he got off. I'd have seen her dug up a dozen times if it had done any good. He's an evil man, and as clever as the devil himself. Those eyes . . . I mean it. Marshal, he is diabolical. But I gave evidence against him and I'd do it again tomorrow, even at the risk of his murdering me. My mother was against it and she did everything she could to stop me. I'll never understand it! Margherita was her daughter, for heaven's sake. Of course, she was terrified of him.'

'That's understandable.'

This woman didn't know about Silvano and her brother, that much had already become clear from Di Maira's transcript of her telephone call to her mother when Silvano was arrested in '86.

'You keep out of it, I'm telling you.'

'I will not keep out of it. I'd testify against that devil with my last breath.'

'Keep out of it! It won't bring Margherita back and what about your brother? What about Giuseppe? They'll arrest him, too, and then how am I to manage now your father's dead?'

'What's Giuseppe got to do with it?'

She didn't know.

'She was so frightened of him she wouldn't take the baby afterwards. She said if she took him then Silvano would have an excuse to be coming to the house all the time and she didn't want that. She said she didn't want him laying hands on me.'

'That's understandable, too, though that poor child —'

'Well, he left almost immediately, in any case, taking with him a pistol that he stole from my uncle and that he used to kill that couple. Those people need never have died if someone had cared then about what he did to Margherita.'

It was clear from her pinched look and the bitter downward turn of her mouth that the beautiful scene spread below them was no longer visible to her. She was back inside her dark memories.

'You never believed in the suicide story, then, even as a child?'

'Suicide? Nobody believed that, but she'd been seen with another man, you see, and that put her beyond the pale with everybody in the village. I didn't know that then but I did know I'd spent the day of her death helping her to get what few clothes she and the baby had together, ready to leave. She didn't dare put them in bags or anything because he'd have seen. We just made a little stack in the drawer. There was a letter, though, I saw it. A letter from the orphanage saying they were expecting her, and she had her ticket. I was the only person who'd seen those things. She hadn't even told my mother she was going. They'd have stopped her, my parents. It was an unthinkable disgrace to leave your husband, no matter what he did to you . . .

'I was there with her until about six o'clock. Then she said:

'*"Warm Amelio's bottle for me, then you'd better go."*

'I put some water on to boil so I could stand the bottle in it. Up to then I'd just felt excited, because she was doing something daring and new. I suppose I caught the excitement from her, but we were frightened, as well. Frightened that any minute he could come in and suspect something.

'We kept our voices very low, as if he might be listening. But then I went in the bedroom to get the baby. He was jumping up and down in his cot and he was starting to cry a bit. Then, when he saw me, he stopped and smiled and pointed at me. I said to him, "Say Ida." I'd been trying for ages to make him say my name.

'"*Dee-da!*" It was the first time. Then I realized they were going and that I didn't know if I'd ever see him again. Margherita had been more of a mother to me than a sister, being so much older. Then I heard her burst into tears in the kitchen and I ran back. She was sitting at the kitchen table with her head down on her arm. All her tension was gone, she'd just collapsed. I went closer and touched her hair.

'"*What's happened?*"

'"*The gas has run out, I can't do the bottle, and these are the only stockings I've got for tomorrow and they're laddered.*"

'"*I can ask Mum for some stockings for you.*"

'"*You can't, she'll know there's something going on.*"

'"*I can run to Marcello's then, and tell him to bring a canister of gas.*"

'"*He won't come. I haven't paid for the last one and I've no money. Just go home.*"

'"*I could stay for my supper.*"

'I often did because *he* almost always ate at his

mother's and then went out. I was scared of staying, really, that night, because I was sure he'd know something was up and start hitting her, but I was scared of leaving her like that, as well. The baby started crying for his milk. I suppose he could hear her.

'"*We've got to warm his bottle. Shall I ask next door?*"

'We were always having to do that.

'"*I'll go myself, you go home.*"

'"*I could stay for –*"

'"*No!*"

'It was because she had no food. She didn't want me to know because she was ashamed. I think she felt more shame about that than about the black eyes and things. I found out the next day when it was all over. The woman from the flat next to Margherita's came round to see my mother after the carabinieri had been there. I saw her coming from the window and made myself scarce. Then I crept to the kitchen door and listened in. I couldn't hear much of it, but though the scraps I did hear were incomprehensible I sensed what it all meant.

'"*I told the Marshal . . . my husband the same . . . then again at about ten-ish. Now, if there was no gas . . .*"

'"*Doctor didn't know his business . . .*"

'"*Make a complaint . . .*"

'"*Scratches all over her face . . . and another thing, if she'd intended to do away with herself she wouldn't have wanted to be found in that state. Her knickers soaked in blood. And she'd never in this world . . . It stands to reason, she'd have seen to herself . . .*"

'"My husband said he must have . . . you know . . . all over her stomach. I hadn't the courage to go in. How you could have . . ."

'"Dirty pig and in front of the child . . ."

'"Do you think it's true she was intending . . ."

'"No, no, no, I'm not having that. No daughter of mine would leave her husband."

'"He did used to paste her, though, after all."

'"She made her bed and she had to lie in it."

'"Oh . . . you're a hard woman . . ."

'"It's a hard world . . . We've had enough shame brought on us without looking for more. What's done is done."

'"I can't help thinking . . . She was so hungry she was in tears. That second time she knocked I gave her a big bowl of bean and pasta soup I'd made for today . . ."

'I ran away then and broke my heart. I don't know why but I thought of that bowl of soup . . . She must have been hungry most of the time and she had always sent me home when there was no food so I wouldn't realize . . .'

She fumbled in her handbag, but the Marshal, always well supplied with clean handkerchiefs for his eyes, was quicker.

'Thank you. I'm sorry.' She stared unseeing at the brilliant scene beyond the windscreen, then turned a little away from him and blew her nose.

'I'm sorry,' she repeated. 'It's the stupidest little things that bring it all back. The bean and pasta soup, the ladder in her stocking. I shouldn't have left her, should I? If I'd stayed he couldn't have done it and the next day she'd have been safe from him.'

'You were only a child.'

'What did that matter! He couldn't have murdered her in front of me. Amelio couldn't talk but I could. I'll never forgive myself as long as I live.'

Was that what the headaches she talked of were about? Punishing herself? You heard a lot of talk about that sort of thing. It wasn't something the Marshal knew much about so he took a different line.

'No wonder you hate Silvano.'

'I detest him. I'd kill him with my bare hands if I'd the strength.'

'He destroyed your sister's life and it sounds as though you've let him destroy yours, too.'

'He's destroyed more lives than mine and Margherita's. What about that couple he shot? And the child who was in the car? What sort of life can he have had after that? What about his own child? I thought when the boy ran away from him and came up north to me it was some sort of sign. I'm not religious, Marshal, I confess I'm too bitter for that. Even so, I thought that was my chance to make up for abandoning my poor sister that night, to give him a home, as my mother didn't want him either. The poor thing attached himself to Flavio who must have been about sixteen and who, in any case, was no better than his brother. Then when *he* married again, Flavio brought the boy to Florence. You can imagine the life . . . the things he told me.'

'I suppose it was difficult, a stepmother, and so on.'

'Stepmother? He was glad enough to get anything in the way of a mother but it didn't last. *He* drove her out with his violence and the boy ran away and came to me. He tried running to Flavio Vargius first but there was no escape from his father there. Well, my mother said I'd rue the day and, of course, I did.'

'He didn't stay?'

'Oh, he stayed. At least, he was officially living with me until he was twenty-one. But a lot of that time he was in prison. I realized even before that that something was going on when he came home in a fancy red car when he was out of work. There's never been anything of that sort in our family and I couldn't cope. When the police ordered him out of the region it was a relief, I confess. You can imagine my mother, at that point:

'"*Don't say I didn't warn you. He's his father's son as well as Margherita's.*"

'Anyway, suffice it to say the whole thing was a failure.'

'You did your best.'

'I keep on doing my best, Marshal, but it's never good enough, is it? My sister, then this . . .'

'I understand how you feel, signora, but I wish you'd consider whether you're going to allow Silvano to ruin your whole life. Blame him, not yourself. He killed your sister, not you.'

'But nothing I told you people last time helped to convict him, did it? So why do you want to hear it all again? Are you looking for him?'

'Not exactly . . .'

'You still don't know where he is?'

'Are you afraid of him?'

'I don't know.' She considered this a moment, folding and unfolding the handkerchief between her fingers. 'I haven't spoken to him since I was twelve, since the days immediately after Margherita's funeral. He left then and I left Sardinia the minute I was old enough to get out. The next time I saw him was in court in '88. That's the only time I've ever set foot in Sardinia again. As to being frightened, I don't really know. The truth is, I wouldn't have recognized him if he hadn't been in the dock. His hair had turned grey, as mine has. Anyway, for what it's worth, I do know where he is. He's in Uruguay.'

'He's . . . ? How did you find that out?'

'From my nephew. I never see him now and I don't want to. And he never contacts me unless there's some news of his father. You'll think we're obsessed by him . . .'

'No, no.'

'Well, there's a third person who probably hates him as we do, or nearly. The second wife. I've never met her but I gather she, at any rate, still sees Amelio. The reason we know where Silvano is now is that she gave him a divorce which he asked for through his lawyer in Sardinia because, if you'll believe me, he wanted to marry again and did so. In Uruguay. That's the only new thing I can tell you, for what it's worth.'

'I'm glad to know about it, whatever it turns out to be worth. And now I'd better drive you to the station or you'll miss your train.'

When she left him he watched her walk into the station, her shoulders a little hunched, her bag clasped tightly, her face anxious and defensive. So many ruined lives. He could hear Di Maira's voice: *'Get that bastard . . . It's him, it's him.'*

Di Maira, too, had talked to this woman but, obsessed as he was with Silvano's guilt, he didn't seem to have listened too carefully to what she had to say.

Seventeen

'Marco? I know and I'm sorry, but I didn't open the papers yesterday. If you've had your lunch come round here.' He hung up, and went back to reading intently.

FULL CONFESSION!
'But I'll never go to prison.'

'Oh, Lord . . .' There was no mistaking the man's face with its manic expression, nor the enlarged detail of the picture behind him, the long white neck and the lock of dark hair curling over the shoulder. The Marshal searched the colour supplement for the article. Had he committed suicide? Was that what he meant by saying he'd never go to prison? There it was . . . He scanned it rapidly but there was no mention of any suicide. More photographs . . . paintings, drawings . . . and then the studio with a corner of one of the great safes just visible. Next to that, Benozzetti himself dressed in a shiny smock. On the easel beside him the portrait of Anna Caterina Luisa dei Gherardini.

I am not a forger. I am not a criminal. I am a painter. I have dedicated my entire life to the art of painting and never been appreciated. I have never put a false signature on a painting or suggested any false attribution or false provenance. The dealers and gallery owners paid what I asked, which was never more than I would have asked for a painting recognizably mine. They made no comment, asked no questions. They sold my pictures for vast sums, sometimes a thousand per cent of what they gave me. Not one of them ever accepted a picture signed by me. Almost every expert in Europe and America has attributed at least one of my paintings, or drawings, to Corot, to Rembrandt, to Dürer, to Augustus John. I have played them off one against the other. I have put in deliberate mistakes of style which they failed to notice. I have sat in the greatest auction rooms in the world and watched pompous, ignorant men make fools of themselves for my amusement. I have seen clients pay over enormous cheques for works they don't understand and which they would never have bought had the true artist's signature, mine, been on them.

I have the original receipts for all the paintings and drawings shown or listed in this article, beginning with a tiny 'Corot' drawing of forty years ago and ending with the 'Antonio Franchi' portrait sold this week at auction in Florence. I received nothing for that painting. I gave it to an expert, Landini, who got rich in his lifetime through my talents, like many others. He died without understanding the truth, but had he been alive to read this he would have denied it as all the others will deny it. I was set to copy the Antonio Franchi portrait by Landini in 1974. Unknown to him I made two copies. I then amused myself by letting him distinguish between 'the copy and the original' whilst the third picture was concealed in my safe where it remains to this day. I watched his perplexity as he struggled to understand. I made no comment and in the end he removed the two pictures without declaring himself. An intelligent enough line to take, after all, pretending it was so obvious which was the copy that there was no need to say it.

He sold what he must have decided was the copy to an American museum for a vast sum and kept the other. He stole from that museum just as he stole the original painting which, in truth, belonged to his wife.

Am I, then, a criminal? I have suffered the indignity of being despised or ignored by the so-called art world but I have had my revenge on the fraudulent, the ignorant, the arrogant, the thieves and speculators who govern that world. I chose my victims carefully: the genuine, studious lover of art was never among them.

I shall paint no more pictures because no true artist can survive in that world and I am a true artist, not a forger.

'There is no such thing as a forgery, there are only false attributions.'

'He's right, isn't he?' Marco said as soon as he sat down in front of the Marshal and saw the article on his desk. 'What he says is true.'

'No,' the Marshal said, 'he's lying.'

'But my father –'

'I'm not excusing your father, I'm talking about Benozzetti.'

Wasn't this what he had been battling against for so long in the case against the Suspect, though without managing to put the problem into words? 'Every fact he states is true but he's lying. He's always lying, even to himself. I don't know whether your father stole that painting from your mother. But if that's the original in Benozzetti's safe, which it could well be, then *he* stole it, from her and from you.'

'I suppose he did – if it is the original –'

'And he says your father never realized the truth. I'd say he suspected it. I'm sorry to say it, but if he'd been sure of the value of that picture I think it would have gone to his second wife like everything else.'

'He was amusing himself by leaving the problem to me?'

'I don't know. You knew him better than I did. Now, would you like to tell me what it is you've been hiding all this time? I take it you knew about the sale to America?'

'I'm sorry . . .' Marco's face was dark red. He pushed at the hair falling into his eyes and then felt around in his pockets, only to think better of it. 'Sorry –'

'Smoke if it helps.' After all this time with Ferrini what was one more cigarette?

'Thanks. My father did steal it from my mother in a way, though he'd have said she gave it to him. It used to hang in my mother's bedroom. My father persuaded her to sell it. I must have been about thirteen, I suppose. I didn't understand what was at stake but I remember a lot of quarrelling. That's probably a muddled memory since they were on the verge of separation anyway, but I connected the fighting with the picture. My father already had a Chair at the University and he was becoming known as a critic but there wasn't much money. I suppose he persuaded her to sell. I didn't see the painting go but I remember her shut in the bedroom, crying. Again I connected that with the picture but there could have been any number of other reasons. I suppose the painting was sold after it had been illegally exported. I don't know much about it, but I do know that my father used the money to set up house with another woman and that after the divorce he married her. My mother did tell me, years later, that she never saw a penny of that money.'

'And she did nothing about it?'

'It had been illegally exported.'

'Not by her.'

'She couldn't prove that, though, could she? It was hers. She has a horror of scandal, whereas my father . . . Well, you know something of what he was like. The risks he must have taken if what Benozzetti claims is true . . . If I didn't tell you all of this before it was because of her, I promise you . . .'

'Don't worry about it. It wouldn't have changed anything anyway if you had told me.'

'Do you really think so? In any case, after this' – he looked at the offending magazine – 'she won't go out of the house.'

'She'll get over it. After all, Benozzetti says quite clearly here your father stole it from her so no one can suspect her of anything.'

'I know that.' Marco was shocked at the idea. 'But he was still her husband. She's still ashamed and embarrassed at everyone knowing he robbed her to set up with the other woman.'

'And you?'

Marco stubbed out his cigarette and looked down at his hands, thinking. 'In a funny way . . . I don't know how to explain it, but I feel better. He always overshadowed me, always made me feel – I suppose a bit of a wet, incapable. I mean, he was so brilliant. Now, well, if he was just cheating to get where he was going I suppose I don't mind so much. I feel surer of myself. Does that make any sense?'

'I think so. Now' – the Marshal leaned forward a little and fixed Marco with his huge eyes – 'before you do anything, or say anything in response to this article, remember he's a liar. If I've understood his character, I don't think he'd have been able to resist showing your father a copy next to the original. That's where all his satisfaction lay. Whether he did or didn't take the money for the job doesn't matter, though I'd be willing to bet he was lying there, too. He has to eat, the same as the rest of us. You can be sure, then, that your father took the original and one of the copies away with him and he wouldn't have gone to all that trouble if his only intention had been to sell the original. He didn't give the copy to your mother, or offer it to her at any time?'

'No. I talked to her about it last night. She heard nothing about the picture from the time he removed it from the house to the time when she read in the paper that it had been bought by an American museum – that was almost a year later.'

'In that case you have every reason to believe that yours was the original.'

'That's what I told her. It brought nearly fifty million and I wanted her to take half. She said no. She said she'd gladly have taken the painting back and kept it in the family where it belongs. I suppose she resents my not telling her. It was hers, after all.'

'You were trying to protect her from a scandal. The scandal's broken and she is protected. Marco, just take the money and get on with your life.'

Marco looked at him gratefully. 'I suppose that's why I came to see you in the first place. I needed you to say that. You're the only person I believe.'

He stood up. 'Thanks for everything.'

The Marshal walked with him to the outer door and watched him start down the stairs. Then he went back to his office and put on his greatcoat. Hat in hand, he called, 'Lorenzini! I'm going out. Di Nuccio can drive me.'

He wasn't kept waiting this time and he was almost sure that Benozzetti was more than eager to see him. Just as well, too. It had been so muggy that first November evening, but now the mountain wind was fierce and, despite the bright sunshine which made his eyes water even behind dark glasses, he was very glad of his thick black greatcoat and warm leather gloves. The door clicked open and the Marshal pushed it. Benozzetti was waiting behind the inner door and the brief glimpse of his face he obtained before he withdrew was enough for the Marshal to see how agitated he was.

'I was expecting you. I knew you'd come.' He almost pushed the Marshal inside so as to shut the door quickly. 'If you hadn't come today I would have telephoned you.'

'Or written to me,' the Marshal said without a trace of irony.

'Perhaps.'

445

What did he want? An audience? After that splash in the colour supplement he must have had all the audience he required.

'You want to see the painting, of course.'

The Marshal had no interest in seeing the painting at all but what he did want was going to be tricky to obtain and the last thing he needed was to put the man on his guard.

'I'd be glad to see it. Thank you.'

'This way.'

The Marshal was carrying his hat, and the cold in the studio made his head ring. No windows, no ray of winter sun cheered its great length. The picture was on the easel where the veiled 'Titian' had stood last time, which was a pity. That was one of the things he intended to find out the truth about and he'd have liked to see it again.

'There! Fault that if you can.'

'I . . . no, it's faultless.' He'd been about to say automatically that he didn't know enough about the matter to comment, but he swallowed his words. It was quite by accident that this man who despised everybody in the art world had decided that the Marshal was fit to judge his pictures. He might as well see what could be gained by such an unexpected turn of events. At any rate, it made a nice change from being thought to be asleep on his feet by almost everyone he met. Benozzetti was mad, of course, but you have to find consolation where you can in this life and if it turned out to be a useful misunderstanding, all the better.

'I can't fault it,' he repeated.

'Ha!' Benozzetti was breathing down his neck and the Marshal turned his head to one side, trying to escape from his perfume. 'I knew you wouldn't be able to! A perfect Antonio Franchi.'

'Oh, no,' the Marshal corrected him quietly. 'It's perfect because you painted it.'

He waited for the reaction but it didn't come. His remark had been ambiguous enough to make Benozzetti hesitate. He didn't know how to react to the idea of a perfect painting done by himself. The Marshal turned and faced him. The snake's eyes slid away from him uncertainly. He pursued the same line. 'It's not Antonio Franchi I'm interested in, you see. It's you.' Wasn't that what he'd always wanted and never had the self-esteem to demand after his first negative experiences? 'You have all this talent, you don't need to hide behind an Antonio Franchi.'

'Hide? *Hide?* I can paint like Franchi and better than Franchi. I can paint as well as Corot, as Rembrandt, as –'

'You can paint,' the Marshal said. 'That's all, though, of course, you don't have to believe me.'

Benozzetti met his gaze now, though the manic glitter in his eyes had blanked out on impact with reality.

'On the contrary, Marshal, you are a man whom one has to believe. Though where you obtained your knowledge of art is beyond me.'

'Well, well, being at Palazzo Pitti, you know . . .'

It wouldn't do to have him think too long on that. It

hadn't crossed his mind that what the Marshal had was a knowledge of people, because that was one thing he had no experience of himself.

'Nevertheless, it's a fascinating business and I don't understand in the least, in spite of your great talent, how you can make a painting look old. After all, these days, there must be so many possibilities of checking, scientific tests and so on . . .'

'Scientific tests! God help us all! What do you think these people know that I don't know – quite apart from the fact that your so-called scientific tests are long and expensive and nobody asks for them when all they really need, all they really *want* is the expert. The expert and his attribution which will enable them to sell. To *sell*, Marshal, that's what it's all about, not art. And what sort of figure does your expert cut if he can't judge with his own eyes. I've always been able to count on the arrogance of my experts.'

'I can imagine . . . Even so, I mean, just making a picture look old. The years of dust they must pick up –'

'Dust? Not dust, Marshal, but fifteenth-century dust, sixteenth-century dust, seventeenth-century dust! Why do you think I learned to restore? I don't restore great paintings because I don't want to be known or seen. That's where Landini was useful. He brought me worthless or relatively worthless paintings from his acquaintances to be restored at low cost. The paintings were worthless but the dirt I washed from them was worth its weight in gold. The dirty water they left would give one, when it evaporated, dirt from the right century which I then applied to my pictures.'

'And these cracks . . .' The Marshal peered at the 'Franchi' portrait.

'Cookery, Marshal, cookery. I bake them in my oven at a low temperature, then apply my dust.'

'Who taught you?'

'The artisan who taught me to restore. An ill-tempered man who made money out of me like the rest of them. People with valueless paintings they're fond of want the damaged parts restored and "aged". From that to producing a whole aged painting is a short step.'

'I see. Yes.' But what he was trying to edge near to was not the how but the why. He was no longer aware of the ice-cold room.

'Even so' – he stepped carefully – 'it's hard to understand why someone like you should spend his time on something he got no credit for. You don't seem to me a person whose interest is just financial gain. I suppose it's a living, but not much of a one, I can see . . .' He looked around him at the comfortless space, letting his gaze rest pointedly on the screen half hiding the bed.

'A living!' Benozzetti moved quickly to block the Marshal's view of that little personal corner, his face red with anger. 'You may know something about painting, my dear Marshal, but you evidently know nothing of its commercial side. If a court portrait like Franchi's brought fifty million yesterday, what do you imagine I earned for a Rembrandt?'

'Ah, well, yes . . . I see . . .'

'You don't imagine I'm interested in bourgeois acquisitions in property, in furniture and all the rest of the trappings? Paintings, that's what I bought, good paintings, great paintings, because I do know a good painting when I see one!'

'Oh yes, I'm sure that's true.' He lied, then, in his 'confession'. Probably made a fortune. That was one thing out of the way. 'It's not really money I'm talking about, though. Still, I can see why you got disheartened if you felt no one appreciated your work. I imagine that professor you were telling me about had a lot to answer for.' As he went doggedly on, his face became more and more expressionless until he might almost not have been present. Benozzetti, having been 'switched on' now seemed to forget him and to be ranting to himself.

'They laughed at me, those worthless half-baked students, good for nothing more than to teach schoolchildren to daub. Laughed at me because of him. The professor, the man who should have taught and helped me. The man who, had he understood my talent, would have thrown down his brush like Verrocchio, never to paint again. But I made them pay, I made them all pay, pay with their cheque books, pay by making fools of themselves, pay by giving me a lifetime of laughter at their expense – pay –'

'When did your father die?'

'What . . . ?' Benozzetti halted, breathing heavily, aware all of a sudden of the Marshal's presence.

The Marshal wandered away from him, looking carefully along the workbenches and shelves at the brushes, bottles, pestles and strange tools he couldn't recognize. He looked at everything but touched nothing, his big hands still grasping his hat.

'Oh, you know how it is. A person as interesting and talented as you are . . . it makes you wonder where it all came from. Was your father a painter, too, for instance – this stuff here, what is it?'

'Ashes. For making ink.'

'Ah.' The Marshal wandered on, still looking at everything except Benozzetti, who followed him uncertainly, asking questions without waiting for an answer. He knew that when he hit the right question there would be no wait for an answer. Benozzetti would react like a wounded animal. The Marshal's heart was beating fast, he could hear it in the long, silent room, as though he were afraid the reaction might be a physical attack rather than a verbal one. It even occurred to him to wonder whether the man might have a pistol by his bedside in case of burglars, but it was too far to wander casually over there. Besides, there was the screen. He wasn't armed himself.

'Mind you, I don't know why I should think of your father – unless I had young Marco Landini in mind. He's artistic like his father, isn't he? Not like you, of course, not to the same level. But perhaps you inherited some of your talent from your mother.'

'No! Don't!'

The Marshal jumped as if the other man really had fired a shot. He wanted to look at him now but didn't.

'I'm sorry. Should I not be looking at these jars? I haven't touched anything –'

'No. No, it's all right.'

Even without looking, the man's painful breathing told him he was close to the mark. Should he go on or wait. Wait. His back was prickling as though he were expecting claws to be dug into it. Dangerous. He'd known from the start that the man was dangerous and yet he'd come here unarmed. The voice behind him spoke again, but it wasn't Benozzetti's voice. A smaller, weaker sound.

'I don't care. I don't need –' It tailed away.

He'd lied about that too, then, to Marco. She was dead now but if she'd died when he was small, he wouldn't even remember, let alone say, 'I don't care.' He wished fervently that he hadn't got himself into this situation, trapped in this great big tomb full of treasures with its mad occupant. But he was here, now, and it was too late. The tension of the man behind him was so great as to be unbearable. Distract him. Distract –

'Ah.' He gave a deep sigh and silently begged his dead parents' forgiveness for what he was about to say. 'I suppose you must have gone through something on the lines of what I had to go through. My mother left when I was small. The usual story, another man. Of course, these days, a mother would never abandon her child, but then no woman who could be called immoral could ever claim custody. And we victims have to try and understand their

452

dilemma, especially. . .' The scar, the scar on his ear . . . 'Especially when there's cruelty involved. How is a woman to defend herself?'

'And how is a child to defend himself?' It wasn't that other, childish voice now but Benozzetti's own. The Marshal turned and looked at him. His face was quite changed. The mask through which his snake's eyes had looked at him was gone, dissolved. The tight muscles were flaccid. He was looking at an ordinary man now, or what was left of him. Benozzetti pointed slowly at his own ear. 'It wasn't just this, this sort of thing wasn't the worst of it, Marshal. The hatred was the worst of it because, you see, I looked like her, and as you very cleverly guessed, I inherited her talent. His second wife hated me, if anything more than he did.'

'So you were taken away from them?'

'Nothing so vulgar, Marshal. My father was a wealthy man and a man of some importance in the pharma-ceutical industry. Nevertheless, when this injury which has left me deaf in one ear brought me near to death, something had to be done. My father agreed to send me away to an expensive college where the monks kept me, even during the holidays, and there was no prosecution.'

'I see. You must have suffered a great deal. I'm sorry if I've upset you by mentioning it. It's just that, as I told you the first time we met, I rarely get to meet anyone as fascinating and as talented as you. You've never told anyone all this before? I mean, you didn't mention it in your piece for the paper, although you gave the impression you wanted people to understand you. Shouldn't you tell – well, someone competent, of course, not the general public?'

His face was hardening again and he now regarded the Marshal with smiling disdain. 'You're surely not talking about a psychoanalyst? I'd thought better of you. Those people are as foolish and arrogant as the art experts.'

'Oh, I'm sure you're right. But it might come in useful to you, just the same, without your taking it too seriously yourself. After all, this confession you've published –'

'That wasn't a confession! Did I call it a confession? Am I responsible for the idiocies of the newspaper world?'

'No, no.' He was back to normal again, then. 'I hadn't thought. It was just a headline, of course. But even so, there'll be a reaction and if you should be prosecuted –'

Benozzetti laughed bitterly. 'How little you understand these things, Marshal. Who do you imagine will throw the first stone? The auction house? You think they'll admit they've let a forgery through their hands? No one would buy there again. The buyer, then, you expect him to admit he's spent fifty million on a fake. I know who that buyer is, though he wasn't present at the auction himself, and I can promise you that he will *never* admit that he's been made a fool of!'

The Marshal had no answer to that. He still felt sure the painting had been genuine, but what difference, after all, did that make? If it were, then the one sold years ago to the American museum would be a fake and the same arguments remained. Besides, wasn't he, like everyone

454

else, wanting to believe the painting was real for Marco's sake? They were all in the same boat, weren't they?

'Well, Marshal?'

'I understand what you're saying.'

'I'm glad of it, because your young friend Marco isn't going to throw the first stone, either, is he?'

'No, I suppose not. What about that American museum, though? Won't they want to check up on their picture now?'

'Ha! When I was preparing my little denouncement I wrote to them, warning them that another version was about to go to auction in Florence and sending them the photo of me with the third one that you saw in the papers. What do you think they replied?'

'I don't know . . . They asked for further proof?'

'Further proof! Further proof is just what they don't want. Further proof of their stupidity, their ignorance, their wasted dollars? They didn't reply, Marshal. They will never reply to anyone on the subject. They will lie low, keep quiet until it's all blown over and their "Antonio Franchi" will remain just that. You'll see that every picture I ever painted will remain somewhere in its museum or private collection.'

'In that case –' He mustn't make a mistake now. 'In that case, why did you stop? You did this because you're giving up, didn't you? But why? What will you do?'

'Do? I'll do whatever I feel like doing! I don't need all this! He waved an agitated hand around him. 'I don't *need* anything. Or anyone.'

'You needed Landini.' That was it. That was what explained it.

'Landini! A critic! Another fool! He used me to further his career!'

'Yes, I believe you.'

'Let me tell you, that man –'

'He understood you, didn't he?'

'Nobody is capable of understanding me or my work.'

'All right. But as far as it was possible he did understand you. He told you what to paint, didn't he?'

'Nobody tells me what to paint.'

'He suggested, then.'

'If you mean he knew the market, then yes, he suggested.'

Yes, thought the Marshal, and I can't say it, I can't say he knew the clients and you didn't. I can't say you've fallen flat on your face because he wasn't there to stop you.

'And now he's dead. Well, no doubt you've worked hard all your life and have as much right to retire as the rest of us.'

'Quite.'

What would he do? Go on living with his failure in this vault? The Marshal shivered. He put on his hat to go, then paused. Without looking at Benozzetti he asked, 'The painting you showed me the last time I was here. You wouldn't let me look at it again, would you?'

'So you can say it's not by Titian?'

'No, no . . .'

'So you can say it's *faultless*? It isn't. I've destroyed it.'

'Ah . . .' As he left, he avoided looking Benozzetti in the face, not wanting to see what was there. He only touched him briefly on the arm as he went out.

The afternoon was fading to darkness, but only the freezing wind made the outside world colder than the studio. Benozzetti wouldn't kill himself, he felt sure of that. If he were the sort to blame himself for his failures, he'd have done it as a young man, the young man who failed as a painter. What would happen to him? Perhaps it was only to cheer himself up that the Marshal muttered as he opened the car door to the welcome blast of the heater, 'Perhaps he'll try and paint.'

'What?' Di Nuccio asked.

'Nothing, nothing.'

'I kept the engine going – it's so cold.'

'You did right.' At any rate, he'd found out all he needed to know. As to why he needed to know, he was quite unconscious of the reason and he wasn't one to ask questions of himself.

Eighteen

'And what I'm wondering is . . .' It was always difficult explaining things to Ferrini. Explaining wasn't the Marshal's strong point, and then you never knew what mood he would be in. 'I mean, it's difficult enough being an adolescent . . . I don't know if you remember.'

'Oh yes. I thought about sex all the time, day and night.'

The Marshal, full to bursting from dinner out in the country where they had 'not lingered' until after eleven, seemed to remember thinking more about eating. He'd spent half his adolescent life in search of food and the other half worrying about being fat. He decided against admitting to this.

'Well then, how would you have felt if you'd known – known, not suspected, that your father was homosexual?'

'I'd have been terrified.'

'Exactly.' They looked at the three photographs in the open files on the Marshal's desk between them.

'They used to take Nicolino with them down to the Cascine for their orgies,' the Marshal said. 'He'll have known, or realized later when he grew up. Amelio, from all accounts, saw it going on in the house.'

'And Salvatore Angius? We know less about him, but we do know Silvano picked him up from the gutter and "adopted him". It's a different situation, but who's to say he really was homosexual? That might have been the price of Silvano's help.'

'That's what Di Maira wondered. And a good reason to detest him, too. Well, these three lads start out even, then:

'Previous convictions for Amelio and Salvatore. Theft mostly, possessing flick knifes, both, illegal detention of arms . . . and . . . this!'

Ferrini pulled out a photocopy of a newspaper article recounting the arrest of Salvatore Angius for armed robbery together with two other men.

'No,' he said, seeing the Marshal scan the small column once and then twice. 'It doesn't specify the type of gun and I thought I'd be sticking my neck out if I asked for the file.'

'You were right . . .'

'But look at the date.'

'Only three months after the '68 murder.'

'You still think he was there?'

'I can't prove it. But if he took the child away to protect Silvano, he may have taken the gun, too.'

'He'd have been pretty stupid to use it in a robbery when it had been used to kill,' Ferrini pointed out.

'He may not have fired it, or even intended to fire it. Besides, he doesn't look or sound too bright to me. He got caught.'

'Yes, he did. *And* he got put away. *And* he tipped up in the next cell to Sergio Muscas who was waiting trial for the '68 murder. Now, listen to this: his lawyer contacted Muscas's lawyer to tell him his client had made a statement of sorts about Muscas. He said, "That poor goop didn't do it. I know who did. It was Flavio Vargius." Here we go round in circles again.'

'Not really.' The Marshal was unperturbed. 'Not now that we understand the relationship between these men. All that means is that he was still dependent on Silvano and putting his oar in to protect him when he saw the chance.'

'Even so, you have to admit that Silvano had a lot of the right symptoms. I mean what you've been telling me about how he murdered his first wife when she tried to leave him, and this business Di Maira was telling you about. His second wife taking off in '74 and then in 1980 . . .'

'So why didn't he kill her?'

'How d'you mean?'

'He started off on the same track, going to the carabinieri and reporting her for desertion. He killed his first wife when she betrayed him. He killed Belinda Muscas when she betrayed him. So why didn't he kill his second wife if he was feeling murderous? You honestly believe that, at his age, he suddenly changed character and, instead of attacking the person who'd offended him, he went out and murdered a bunch of total strangers? And he *didn't* change. You can see the pattern. His first wife and her brother, Belinda and her husband. The second wife and the men he brought home. To the last, before he was arrested, he had a live-in woman and a regular man friend, apart from his usual extra orgies and pick-ups. He never changed. Besides, he was too clever to use that Beretta 22 again and risk incriminating himself for the '68 job. Nobody would do that unless they wanted to get caught.'

'But they do, don't they?' Ferrini insisted. 'We've learned that much from Bacci's stuff. A lot of them do want to get caught.'

'Some of them. But Silvano didn't confess when Romola accused him of being the Monster and tore his house apart looking for proof. Far from confessing, he left the country.'

'All right. I was just provoking you. Here.' Ferrini grinned and handed over whatever remained in the large envelope.

The Marshal slid the contents out, wondering as he did so how it could be that he had spent the last two or three days in a state of total deflation, suspecting Silvano, but that the minute Ferrini put that suspicion into words . . .

'What's this?' He stared at the sheaf of papers, then at Ferrini.

'Just a few notes of mine. I thought I'd surprise you. Well, go on. Read.'

'But –'

'Read.'

The Marshal read the first few lines but his glance at the first line had been enough, though there was nothing to indicate the source.

'Ferrini, how in God's name did you – ?'

'A few notes of mine, as I said. By the way, our little chirruping friend Noferini was feeling a bit down last time I saw him. It seems that, in his enthusiasm, he took it upon himself to get in touch with the council for confirmation of the roadworks that caused one of our prize witnesses to take a certain detour one Sunday night and see the Suspect near the scene of the crime.'

'And I suppose there weren't any roadworks?'

'How did you guess? He made out a report for Simonetti and got a rocket in return.'

'I thought as much. But it's ridiculous,' the Marshal pointed out. 'The defence will check.'

Ferrini shrugged. 'That's what Noferini tried to say and all he got for that was, "The council is no doubt mistaken." Anyway, we should worry. It was pretty convenient for us that he was feeling disillusioned – oh, he still thinks the Suspect's guilty, he just doesn't think the end justifies the means. I promised I'd look into it and into one or two other things. Relieved his conscience for him. That' – he indicated the notes – 'was the price. He doesn't know what he's given me. It was in English. He

462

typed it on to the computer without understanding more than two words. I got on to Bacci, who read it to me, translating as he went and I wrote my notes. Now' – he sat back and lit a fresh cigarette – 'read them.'

The Marshal read.

FBI BEHAVIOURAL SCIENCE UNIT
NCAVC, QUANTICO Va.

Profile based on information received related to 16 murders committed between 1968 and 1985 in Florence, Italy.

Scene of Crime

The scene of all these murders, an isolated country lane among vines and olives, could be said in all cases to have been 'chosen' by the victims who parked there. Nevertheless, it tells us a lot about the offender. It suggests previous activity as a Peeping Tom, as does the fact that most of the victims had just finished sexual intercourse when attacked. Couples who habitually have sexual intercourse in parked cars tend to frequent the same place regularly. The offender probably stalked couples on a Saturday night until he found one parking habitually in a spot which suited his purpose – this meant having somewhere discreet to leave his own vehicle for fast removal from the scene, a sheltered spot where he could operate on the female without his activities being visible to a passing car, and perhaps water available if he needed to wash himself.

The point of his departure for this stalking phase could well be a disco or other locale where young couples collect. To frequent such a place without attracting undue notice the offender would necessarily be of a similar age to his victims. This preparatory period of stalking, choosing and watching the couple until the darkest night of the month made an attack viable, would be an important part of the gratification of killing which would be further prolonged by the enjoyment of the body parts taken away with him and the resulting newspaper articles, TV coverage and investigation.

Modus operandi – The offender brings his weapons to the scene of the crime and removes them afterwards (see note 1). It is probable, though not provable, that he shoots the male first and the female second. The female victim is removed a little way from the car and mutilated. The male is also attacked with the knife and piercing instrument.

The '68 murder shows no hallmarks of a serial killer type crime and it may be that its relation to the murders which followed is that of a catalyst or model for someone connected with this group of people.

The '74 murder bears the hallmarks of a teenage – or at least beginner – lust murder of the organized type. The site has been chosen and the weapons brought, but the offender has failed to shoot to kill. His intention, based on long-nursed fantasy, might have been to rape the female victim whether before or after the stabbing but, finding himself impotent, he was obliged to use a vine branch on her instead. The offender is likely to have worked himself up to this realization of his fantasies by the use of drugs. A person in a normal state would be unlikely, however frenzied, to have inflicted as many as 96 stab wounds. The attack made on the dead man with the knife and puncturing instrument suggests his anger is directed equally against the male, but the blows being confined to the trunk and neck suggests a fear of contact with the male sexual zones (see note 2).

The murders from '81 onwards suggest a more clearly established rite. The problem of impotence on the scene of the crime is resolved by the removal of body parts which can be 'enjoyed' in safety and leisure. The cooling-off period between '74 and '81 could be caused by fear, especially if the offender is very young or has been approached by the police for some reason. However, this is mere hypothesis since the offender may have been absent or confined for other reasons or have temporarily fled the area for fear of arrest.

The sending of a cube of flesh to one of the investigators after the last crime could be due to the fact that the victims were foreign holidaymakers camping in a secluded spot and might not be missed. It could also be that he hid the bodies to give himself time to announce his crime in this sensational way. In either case, the time of death should be double-checked in view of the condition of the female victim's body. It appears that the German victims of '83 were murdered at the exact same period of the year in the same area and left in the enclosed metal container of their camper without any such deterioration in the cadavers.

Absence of clues at the scene of the crimes indicates that the offender worked with care and forethought and was not courting arrest. On two occasions, '82 and '83 when the plan went awry, the killer abandoned the scene without mutilation of the bodies. It was essential for him to be in total control of the situation and he could not deal with any reaction ('82) on the part of his victims, who must be defenceless and die without being aware of the attack. The reaction of the '82 victim caused him to flee without checking that the man was dead. In fact, had he been found sooner he might well have been able to identify his attacker. The offender had, by then, consumed the bullets loaded into the pistol but could quickly have dispatched his victim with the knife. He was clearly panicked by loss of control and by human contact, probably eye and voice, with the victim. This would have destroyed his fantasy image of himself as all-powerful, his victims succumbing in silence.

The attempted flight of his last victim does not appear to have had this effect. It is probable that there was no eye or voice contact and a fleeing, naked, wounded victim fitted in well enough with the fantasy not to destroy it.

Although his last crime was followed up by direct contact with the investigators (other communications received cannot be proved genuine), the addressing of the package to an investigator by name – the only woman to have worked on the case – indicates that the killer took an active interest in the investigation and is highly likely to have made personal contact with the police and/or returned to the scene of the crime on occasions to observe police activity. This behaviour is so common with this sub-group of serial killers as to render the strategic placing of telecameras at the scene during investigation routine.

Diagnosis – Non-social organized lust murderer.
Background – Economically and culturally poor, probably rural – the excision of the body parts shows signs of the flesh being lifted from the body before cutting, in the way that animals are skinned. Background of domestic violence and of excessive physical punishment in infancy and childhood.

Probable childhood offences: stealing, truancy, cruelty to babies or infants, torture of animals, persistent lying. Lack of mother or mother substitute to establish affectionate behaviour patterns. Negative rapport with father or father figure.

Adult profile – Extremely low self-esteem. Deep-rooted feelings of impotence caused by ill-treatment in childhood and adolescence. Lying and conciliatory behaviour in the face of stronger characters or authority caused by fear of aggression. Accumulated anger and resentment well masked by superficial friendliness. He will have to develop a keen sense of what anyone stronger than himself and/or in authority requires of him and to appear to provide it, through lying if necessary.

Enjoys appearing innocuous whilst nursing his hidden fantasy made real in which he is all-powerful. His lust killings are about power rather than sex. His own sex life need not be particularly abnormal, but long-lasting affectionate relationships are difficult for him. He will prefer sex with prostitutes whom he can consider his inferiors because they are social outcasts and in his pay. He appears to have a fear and hatred of homosexual tendencies in himself which may or may not have a basis in reality. He is likely to seek companionship among people even weaker and less successful than himself, such as drug addicts, prostitutes, vagrants, who will alleviate his sufferings caused by low self-esteem. Normal intelligence but underachiever. Constant use of awl or screwdriver as a weapon indicates that he is almost certainly an unskilled manual worker. He will be inconstant in work and often unemployed. He probably has a criminal record and will have spent brief periods in prison for theft, arson, drugs, detention of arms, even armed robbery – probably unsuccessful. He will be interested in his physical appearance, in clothes and cars in an effort to boost his self-image.

The offender will undoubtedly have followed the enquiry closely through the newspapers and television and may have tried to insert himself into the investigation as a witness or informer. The preparatory stalking and the following of the investigation prolong the gratification of his desire for power and revenge which inspires the crimes.

Whilst the serious trauma causing the original damage to the offender is most likely to have occurred in infancy and may be buried too deep for conscious memory, it is likely that it was reawakened or reinforced at some point during adolescence. There will probably have been some negative exposure to sex at an early age, causing anger and resentment.

The lack of connection between killer and victim makes proof in these cases hard to find and is limited to the physical. However, when a killer of this type is pinpointed, the invasion of the real world into his fantasy world is likely to break down his defence system and a confession usually results. It should also be noted that, despite the time lapse, physical proof in the form of body parts should still be sought. They are taken so as to help the killer relive his crime and are often photographed. Cf John Christie in whose home four sets of pubic hair, neatly waxed, were found stored in a tobacco tin. They did not match the bodies of any of his known victims. These proofs are more likely to be found than the gun because the offender will like to keep them near him. However, if he does not live alone he must necessarily have access to some private location where he can store and enjoy his trophies. In this case the gun will probably be stored in the same place.

1. The use of the firearm in this type of murder is highly unusual. However, Ed Kemper did use a gun since he

always attacked two girls at a time; he then removed their bodies for mutilation.

2. The targeting of the couple is unique. This and the weapon suggest a re-enactment of the '68 precipitating crime. Otherwise the subject should be checked for possession of pornographic material which might have inspired this anomalous choice.

'Digested all that, have you?' Ferrini asked.

'Yes . . . But then, all three of them . . .'

'I know. All three of them hated their father or father figure, all three of them lost their mother, all three of them did some thieving and were inconstant at work. What's more, they all at some point collaborated with the investigators. And the only thing we can do now is to start all over again reading Romola's report and pick out every single reference to each one of them until one of them emerges clearly and the others fade out because something doesn't add up – and added to this description are some plain facts which are more up our street. We have to show that he could have got hold of Silvano's gun, we have to explain the gaps between '68 and '74 and between '74 and '81 and, what's even more difficult, understand why he stopped – I remember a case I was on once . . .'

The Marshal didn't try to interrupt him. He didn't get annoyed at his smoke-filled office. Now that Ferrini was back he could function again. He felt calm and sure. As

Ferrini chattered on he divided up the Romola report between them and prepared three sheets of paper each with a name at the top. He wasn't consciously thinking about it but somewhere inside himself he knew they were going to find the answer, however long it took.

They talked a lot as they worked that first evening, exchanging questions mostly.

'Why do you think Silvano suddenly lost his grip and put himself in a psychiatric ward?'

'Had the killer told him he'd used the '68 gun to murder?'

'Could he just have been terrified of exposure as a homosexual, an exposure he'd gone to enormous lengths to avoid?'

'Did he screw up on the German murder just to get Flavio out of prison?'

By the second evening they were exchanging answers.

'There, look! He botched the shooting in '74 but then he worked on it – and he was smart enough not to practise with the famous Beretta or we'd have had him years ago.'

'No, we wouldn't. Things would have gone just the way they did.'

'I suppose you're right.'

'There could have been more episodes of arson; we only know about the one that was reported.'

'And there you have his obsession. How we missed that the first time round I don't know.'

'I do. I'm no hand at jigsaws and in this one you have to work out whether the piece belongs at all before you start looking for where.'

'Every case is like that.'

'I suppose you're right.'

'There are gaps, though,' Ferrini pointed out. 'Things we don't know.'

'But nothing that we do know that eliminates him. We'll fill in the gaps . . . if we're allowed to.'

'The thing that convinces me most,' the Marshal said, 'is perhaps the only thing we can't prove. That it was his car on the scene that night. Nobody will ever be able to prove it but I know it. The car of his fantasy world. By day he was an out-of-work labourer chugging around in a little utility car like the rest of us. But by night . . .'

'Clever these FBI birds. They don't explain the famous bloodstained rag, though.'

'I don't think,' the Marshal said, 'that anybody ever told them about it. Silvano was off the scene by then. In any case, we do know the most baffling thing: why Silvano didn't turn a hair when they found it and why he said, "There might be bloodstains but there can't be gunpowder." Do you remember how that left Romola perplexed? The gun had been stolen years before and that bag presumably wasn't where he kept it when he still had it. The killer must have hidden it there after the '74 job and then taken it away with him. The bag obviously carried no message to Silvano in '85. We'll never get further with it than that.'

'Will we get further than that with any of it? I mean, have you thought what in God's name we're supposed to do next?'

The task they had just completed was the easy part. What they should do next was much more difficult to decide.

'Maestrangelo's our best bet,' Ferrini said.

How could the Marshal tell him what he had overheard? He couldn't. And because of that he lied.

'You may be right. As a matter of fact, he wants me to go over and see him this week. I'll go tomorrow, drop a hint, see how he reacts.'

He had no intention of dropping any hints but he was playing for time. He'd think of some other way.

Ferrini yawned and looked at his watch. 'Twenty to three . . . The things you get me into! My wife'll divorce me . . .'

When he'd gone the Marshal gathered up the papers on his desk and locked them into a drawer. After that, he sat still a moment staring at the map, wondering at the strangeness of things.

Their checking of the document had been scrupulous, slow and precise. On the point that 'If you check, you check everything' the Marshal was immovable. But somehow or other he must have registered all those tiny things the first time round because, however dark and tortuous the road, he'd known where it was going to come out.

'Guarnaccia! Come in, come in, take a seat.'

The Marshal, hat in hand, sat down. It wasn't his way to let his feelings show on his face, but the Captain at once looked at him hard and asked, 'Are you all right?'

'Oh, yes. Yes, thank you. Perhaps a little bit tired.'

'I was told you came to see me the other day –'

'Yes. Yes. You were busy with someone and I had to leave . . . Simonetti and so on . . . I'm sorry. I imagine you were wanting some information on that letter about the painting?'

'No.' The Captain seemed more embarrassed than annoyed. 'It wasn't that. I was just wondering . . . I heard you found some evidence yesterday . . . ?'

'So it seems.'

The Captain's eyes were more than usually watchful. 'Another anonymous letter, I gather.'

'Another one, yes.'

It wasn't the Marshal but the Captain who seemed to want to test which way the wind was blowing, but what did he want? Was he trying to find out where the Marshal stood, what he believed? Was the expected reprimand to come from him, not Di Maira?

'Ferrini and I were both at the scene of the crime in Galluzzo,' the Captain said, the grey eyes still watchful.

So was he afraid the Marshal would blow the whistle? How could it be that this man he'd trusted for so many years could suddenly be so . . . dishonourable. Because that was the only word for it. And hadn't he said himself yesterday that people don't change to that extent, not at his age?

'I shouldn't have got you into this.' The Captain got up abruptly and went to stand at the window. With his back to the Marshal, he repeated, 'Both Ferrini and I . . . Didn't he say anything to you about it?'

Ferrini had said plenty, that very morning when it was announced that both the soapdish, whose contents had proved so useless, and the sketch book, whose notes had led nowhere, were in fact vital clues. According to an anonymous communication just received, these two objects had been stolen from the camper of the two young German victims at Galluzzo.

'He never set foot in the blasted camper!' raged Ferrini. 'Never set foot! Simonetti'll never get away with this – there are photographs! That van was only an improvised camper. When they had the bed down every piece of junk they had in there was under it. If he'd wanted to get at any of it he'd have had to climb over the bodies, *move them* and lift the blasted bed up. For a soapdish! Like as if – and if he'd wanted a silly souvenir there was a suitcase full. The suitcase they'd propped the door open with to get some fresh air while they slept. It was on the ground where it fell when the killer opened the door to shoot. Not even open – and another thing: there's the search report; I wrote it. They didn't have so much as a pencil, a rubber, a crayon, inks, colours, sketches, nothing! So why should they have had, Jesus Christ, a sketch book? He's got a nerve!'

'Yes,' murmured the Marshal now, 'he did seem to think it a bit unlikely.'

'I'd hoped . . . I'd hoped that you and he might have – Listen, Guarnaccia, I shouldn't say this but I'm going to . . .'

Which remark coming from the man known to all journalists as 'the Tomb' was pretty startling.

'When we had to make a choice of men for this job, the Colonel had no intention of giving up his best investigators, given what I imagine you by now have understood to be the circumstances. He was right, of course, but still, I didn't like it. I still don't like it. We'll be tarred with the same brush, you know, if all this blows up in their faces.'

'Yes.'

'So I came up with what you might well think was a foolish idea. The Colonel hadn't been here long, you see.'

'No.'

'He knew all our important investigators but there was a lot he didn't know, people he didn't know or even notice. People who had a certain experience but whose careers didn't really indicate it. You and Ferrini, you see, appeared to fit the Colonel's requirements. Ferrini was pushing paper about in an office. You were over at Pitti. I'd no business to do it, of course.'

'Perhaps you should have told us.'

'No, that was out of the question. That would have meant involving you in a move that wasn't strictly correct. I thought that, if you came round to my way of thinking on your own account, you'd have come here to see me. I hoped, when I heard you were on your way over the other day . . . Well, it was an unreasonable expectation. It's just that, somehow or other, I felt sure that you were the one person who had the tenacity to get to the bottom of all this, to cut through all the hysteria and exaggerated fantasy that had built up around the case. And with Ferrini to help you and the literature I lent Bacci . . .'

'You did?'

'It's all in English. I found it hard going when I was struggling with it myself in '83 but Bacci's English is excellent. Well, I was asking too much, I suppose.'

'No, no . . .' The Marshal stood up. 'No, that's not the problem. With your permission, I'd like to go back to my office.'

'Of course.' The Captain turned and faced him, his voice cold. 'You must have a great deal to do.'

'I'll be back, if you have time for me, in about half an hour or so. You see, we've found out who killed these youngsters but now we don't know what to do, so, if you could decide . . . With your permission . . .'

He left quietly, leaving the Captain staring after him.

He was as good as his word and returned within the half-hour to deposit with relief his burden of papers and worries on the Captain's desk. Then he sat in silence, gaze fixed on his big hands planted squarely on his knees, until Maestrangelo had finished reading.

'You did all this, you three?'

'No, sir. Judge Romola had already done all the work but he never had the chance or the peace to understand all its implications.'

'Even so, I don't begin to understand how you found the time.'

'No.' And yet, thinking back on it, he could only remember Ferrini's dinners and stories . . . that and all the tiring reading in the night . . . 'Anyway, we don't know what to do now.'

'I'll tell you. What we shall do immediately is to send a report to the Chief Public Prosecutor with a copy to Simonetti and the Preliminary Enquiry Judge. I hope that for the moment they'll simply ignore it as they have all other information that's come in. I think the very connection with the Vargius family should ensure that. Then we'll have to sit on it until your Suspect goes to trial and hope he gets off. Even so, there's an element of risk. So, who will sign it? Do you want to?'

'I'll do whatever you think is right.'

'You'll be safe from risk if I sign it, but on the other hand, if we could ever get it into court . . .'

'Glory's not really in my line, Captain.'

'No, I know it's not. Still, there's Ferrini to consider – and Bacci. I think you should talk it over and then come back to me. And whatever you decide, Guarnaccia, my compliments. I'm glad to know my trust in you was warranted.'

'Yes . . . So am I.' The Marshal took up his hat, correcting himself, 'I mean, thank you, sir.'

'Well done. Marshal! You succeeded where I failed. Couldn't get anywhere near.'

'I'm not surprised,' the Marshal said, offering Dr Biondini his hand, 'but I didn't even try.' He indicated the glass of red wine he was holding. 'Somebody going round with a tray gave it to me. I'm not much good in crowds.'

'And there's certainly a crowd this evening. I'm delighted you managed to get here this time. Have you had a look at the paintings?'

'No, no . . . Perhaps another day my wife and I will walk up again. I was just admiring the view.'

'Isn't it wonderful? And such a perfect evening.'

It was September and the evening sun was dissolving over the city into a lake of pink and green and misty purple.

The stone parapets of the star-shaped fort were still warm to the touch and people were pouring out across the lawns from the exhibition to sit there and marvel at the magical beauty of the city they spent most of their days complaining about. The Marshal, after losing Teresa in the crush, had been standing there for some time, listening to snatches of their gossip: the notorious stinginess of a certain marquis, the scandalous behaviour of a countess, the failure of the municipal authorities, the inaccuracy of that article in the paper . . .

'They say it was the daughter, ingenuous soul, who called the carabinieri, thinking the mother had been kidnapped, so what could *he* do when he got there but play the part. Imagine his embarrassment when she swanned in at dawn in her evening gown, rather smudged, to find them all sitting round the telephone waiting for the ransom demand. My dear, I ask you!'

'So she's trying to sell the villa before he's actually declared bankrupt . . .'

'No, no, the marriage is to be annulled. It's a tedious business but his uncle's a member of the Holy Roman Rota so it won't take as long as some . . .'

But in the end they all fell silent before the daily miracle of the sunset over red tiles and white marble below.

'We don't come up here nearly as often as we should,' the Marshal said, 'and each time we do I ask myself why not.'

'The answer's all too simple, my dear Marshal,' said Biondini with a rueful smile, 'we don't get the time. But you really must come up and have a look at the exhibition on a quiet day. I'll send you round some free tickets.'

'No, no . . . There's no call . . . we'll come anyway.'

'I insist. There's a painting by a friend of yours, you know.'

'A friend . . . ?'

'Antonio Franchi! A portrait of Ferdinando de' Medici, from the Uffizi. Genuine, I believe.'

'Ah, I should like to see that.' It occurred to him that Biondini was one of the people Benozzetti referred to as genuine studious lovers of art. 'What did you think? You saw the two photographs.'

'I couldn't fault them. Of course we never got a chance to see the third.'

The story of the third version in an American museum

had come out in the papers without mention of its provenance. The museum still refused to comment, much less produce a photograph for comparison.

'You don't think,' suggested the Marshal, 'that when the fuss has died down they will try and check whether it's genuine?' He explained, as best he could, Benozzetti's version of how things would go.

'He's quite right,' Biondini laughed. 'Think of the money they spent on it. They'll never get it back. Not to mention how ridiculous they'd look. They'd lose their reputation entirely. No, once a painting's that far along the line it has to remain genuine. The world's galleries are full of Corots and De Chiricos, like the churches are full of pieces of the true cross, a veritable forest full! Your friend Benozzetti was cleverer than most. He took on much more difficult artists and with a lot more success.'

'What about Titian?'

'That would be much more difficult indeed – at least, his later work. The photographic style is easier, that or the very modern. Titian's late work would be impossible to imitate, I think.'

'That's why he retired, then,' the Marshal said. 'That's what he was trying to do when I met him and he failed. Landini's presence was essential to him. Well, I'm glad I can't afford to buy paintings, I'd be sure to be made a fool of by someone as clever as that.'

'No, you wouldn't. You'd buy something you enjoyed looking at and if someone came along and said it was painted by artist B instead of artist A you'd still go on enjoying it. It's people who buy paintings as investments who are in danger. I don't think you or I need worry. At any rate, you can be sure that you'll not hear another word against the three Antonio Franchi portraits of Anna Caterina Luisa dei Gherardini. Think of the auctioneers, the museum's buyer of whoever made the attribution. No one will react because there's too much at stake.'

The Marshal sipped his wine for a moment, frowning, then his face cleared. 'At least, it's the best thing for young Marco, who was used as an unknowing accomplice.'

'You see? Nobody wants to hear the truth, so Benozzetti might as well have kept it to himself. He had his brief moment of glory and his private satisfaction, but there's no possibility of his being acknowledged. Anyway, I promise you the Franchi portrait in my exhibition is impeccable, so come up again. I take it your life has quietened down now you've found your famous Monster?'

'Yes, except that I can't . . . Ah, you mean the arrest of the Suspect . . .'

'Didn't I see it on the news?'

'Yes, yes, of course . . . I'm sorry, I wasn't thinking.'

'You're not going to tell me that, after all the fuss and publicity, he's a forgery, too?'

'There's no such thing as a forgery. Isn't that what you told me? Though I didn't understand it at the time. Benozzetti said the same.'

'You give me too much credit, as usual, Marshal! "There is no such thing as a forgery. There are only false attributions." It was said – or rather written – by a very great art historian.'

'Ah. Well, like the painting, it went too far for anyone to retract, and since he's such a dreadful character anyway . . .'

'I see. Depressing for you. I mean you worked so hard for such an unsatisfying conclusion. What a world! I'd better get back inside, I suppose. I'll send you those tickets.'

Most of the brilliant colour had drained from the sky by now, leaving only a silvery yellow light, reflecting from the smooth chilly water of the river. The surrounding hills topped with pines and cypresses had merged into one black silhouette.

He had his private satisfaction but there's no possibility . . .

Did he, too, stop because his whole plan failed? Silvano had come near to being arrested as the Monster but, then, as always he slid away. On the other hand, perhaps he felt he'd succeeded. As long as he had that pistol he had power. He'd rid himself of Silvano's presence and should he ever dare to set foot in Italy again he'd shoot somebody with it. In the meantime, in Silvano's absence, he would never again strike at a courting couple, of course. On the other hand, he might not have lost his acquired taste for killing and mutilating. If he hadn't, and he killed again, he might well be caught and then confess the lot the way they all did . . .

What was he thinking of? He could hardly wish death on some other innocent soul just for the satisfaction . . .

He had to let go. Like Romola. He felt sure that, in the

long run, he would only remember that dead girl's parents waiting in their separate loneliness for the final release from pain. And a woman living out her joyless life, the loneliness only punctuated by devastating headaches. And Romola who had cared, and fought, and lost. And yet he had been right. He had been on the right road and he had uncovered everything. But to see your way clearly you had to walk the road the other way like the road Nicolino had taken, running at the last, towards the big light.

Silvano as the protagonist. And Silvano as the victim, hunted and destroyed without ever really understanding why and by someone so innocuous – not only – but who ought, if anything, to be grateful to him. It was outside the range of his comprehension that he had destroyed someone's world not once but twice. Silvano was guilty of murder and he couldn't point the finger at the one who had brought down this terrible punishment on him without admitting his own guilt. The seventeen innocent people who had died at their hands were forgotten by both of them, a matter of indifference, battle casualties. And the battle was presumably over. Unless Silvano came back.

The huge autumnal sun dropped out of sight behind the dark silhouette of hills, and lights sparkled softly all over the city.

'It's so beautiful.' Teresa came and slid her arm through his, looking down with him at the floodlit marble towers and the sparkling reflections in the dusky river.

'We should come up here more often.'

'Yes. I was saying the same. But it's going dark . . .' For some reason the falling darkness made him feel an ache of sadness and anxiety. He realized why when she answered him.

'We should be thinking of going home. The boys will be waiting.'

He thought to himself, 'We're so lucky. Please God let it stay that way.' But aloud he only said, 'They'll be hungry. Let's go now,' and he held her arm close to him as they steered their way through the crowd.

Property of Blood

Magdalen Nabb

The American-born former-model Countess Olivia Brunamonti, now a Florentine fashion designer, has been kidnapped. Her daughter Caterina, who may have been the intended victim, reports the disappearance to Marshal Guarnaccia. Kidnapping is almost a second business for the Sardinians nominally engaged in raising sheep in the Tuscan hills. The government's official policy is not to permit the payment of ransom. But if the money isn't paid, the kidnappers cannot let their victim go free. It would set a bad example . . .

Magdalen Nabb's latest Marshal Guarnaccia mystery is her most powerful yet, bringing her inimitable detective and her usual pitch-perfect sense of place together with a stunningly observed sense of the experience of kidnapping and the unique psychological impact of this most Italian of crimes.

'Fascinating . . . Nabb's elegant writing style and her ability to perfectly frame a novel enrich this compelling psychological portrait of a kidnapping . . . *Property of Blood* draws the reader deeply into other worlds; every word should be savored.'
Washington Post

'Credible, classy and compelling, this is crime fiction at its best' *Sunday Times*

'Marshal Salva Guarnaccia . . . is one of the most endearing and believable creations in modern crime fiction . . . An eerily haunting thriller whose low-key telling makes its Jacobean plot all the more disturbing.' *Glasgow Herald*

a r r o w b o o k s

ALSO AVAILABLE IN ARROW

Some Bitter Taste

Magdalen Nabb

When it comes to motives for crime, the past can never be forgotten.

Sara Hirsch is a nervous elderly spinster who still lives in the flat above the long-standing Florentine antiquities shop in which she was raised. Frightened, she calls Marshal Guarnaccia for help, sure that strangers have been in her apartment. The Marshal knows she is a lonely old woman but he is preoccupied with an investigation into an Albanian prostitution ring. Before he can respond to her latest alarm, she is found dead.

The Marshal's search for the villains who caused her death brings him into confrontation with the past, with Jewish refugees from fascism, and with English expatriates, including the ailing heir to the elegant Villa L'Uliveto, Sir Christopher Wrothesly . . .

'Pleasure from beginning to end' *TLS*

A perfect example of crime-and-pleasure . . . so cunningly plotted that it is only at the end that you realise that not one strand of the intricate tapestry has been superfluous . . . [*Some Bitter Taste*] will at one and the same time surprise, amuse and finally sadden.' Antonia Fraser, *Spectator*

'A wonderfully satisfying read.' *Daily Mail*

arrow books

The Marshal Makes His Report

Magdalen Nabb

When the body of Buongianni Corsi is found lying face down in the courtyard of the Palazzo Ulderighi there seems no doubt in the minds of his family that his death was an accident. The Marchesa, wife of the dead man, will entertain no other possibility and her power and status in the city means that Marshal Guarnaccia questions at his peril. But question he does.

The death could have been suicide, or even murder. Guarnaccia knows something is not quite right, and resents being expected to go along with any possible cover up. The Palazzo is a maze of passageways, darkened corridors, locked rooms and something else, a family secret. Can he ignore his instincts and his integrity? Should he press on with the case, risk his job, and maybe more? As he paces the courtyard of the Palazzo, he is haunted by the strange piano and flute music that filters down from above, as well as by the irresistible conviction that something truly sinister has happened there. . .

'Magdalen Nabb's books are set in Florence so vividly brought to life that I long to go back there after reading each one.'
Susanna Yager, in the *Sunday Telegraph*

'He shares with Maigret a rounded solidness; strong reactions to weather, a sense of small community relationships and a readiness to relieve the plod of routine by intuitive flashes.'
Sunday Times

arrow books

ALSO AVAILABLE IN ARROW

Doctored Evidence

Donna Leon

When the body of a wealthy woman is found brutally murdered, the prime suspect is her Romanian maid, who has fled Venice. As she attempts to leave the country, the maid runs into the path of an oncoming train and is killed, carrying a considerable sum of money and forged papers. Case closed.

But when the old woman's neighbour returns from abroad, it becomes clear that the maid could not have been the killer and that the money on her was not stolen. Commissario Brunetti decides – unofficially – to take the case on himself.

As Brunetti investigates, it becomes clear that the motive for the murder was probably not Greed, rather that it had its roots in the temptations of Lust. But perhaps Brunetti is thinking of the Deadly Sin altogether . . .

'Leon's talent for sketching Venice with equal measures of affection and exasperation is undimmed, and Brunetti and his serious, thoughtful wife Paola remain subtle and pleasing creations.'
Sunday Times

'[An] enjoyable addition to a fine series.' Susanne Yager in the
Sunday Telegraph

arrow books